Quests

of

Mirstone

EDITED BY RICHARD FIERCE

Quests of Mirstone © 2023 by Richard Fierce

This is a collected work of fiction. All events portrayed in this book are fictitious, and any resemblance to real people or events is purely coincidental. All rights reserved, including the right to reproduce this book or portions thereof in any form without the express permission of the publisher.

Cover design by Keith Robinson
Anthology Editor: Richard Fierce

Dragonfire Press

Print ISBN: 978-1-958354-43-8

E-Book ISBN: 978-1-958354-42-1

First Edition: 2023

CONTENTS

INTRODUCTION

Welcome to the third anthology set in the world of Mirstone!

In the first one, we did lots of world building, and with the second one, we explored magic and magical items. For this one, we're doing quests! Whether it's a journey to be rid of demons, or a flight on an airship to retrieve a friend, this anthology has quests of all kinds!

Happy reading!

-Richard

The Hunt for the Wandering Mystic
A.R. Cook

The Feywilds was an enchanted place of beauty and mystery, the arboreal realm where it was believed that the Fae lured unsuspecting mortals with promises of adventure, wonder and wealth—except for the dwarf and the mousefolk who were currently running for their lives away from the horde of screeching ooze mephits on their tails. It had been, overall, not as fun an experience as either of them had hoped.

"I thought you said elementals were helpful!" Aruyin shouted, pumping her short legs as hard as she could. Sweat drenched her normally fox-red hair, turning it copper, and the freckles on her face were practically hidden by the red flush of exertion.

Brax Tenderfoot eeked with each terrified breath, his round ears plastered back against his furry head. "I said, they c-c-c-could be helpful, or they c-c-c-could also k-k-kill us!"

I seemed to have missed that second part, Aruyin thought. Although after one look at the onslaught of slimy, putrid, pickle-hued imps flapping their mucus-coated wings and baring their rows of tiny piranha teeth, anyone with sense might have concluded they were not the cuddly sort. Like most dwarves, running was not Aruyin's favorite activity. Even being pursued by ooze mephits, which were arguably slow given they were more at home in water than on land, was wearing her out more rapidly than she would have liked. "How about you whip up a spell, Loremaster?"

Brax shot a wide-eyed look of terror at her, which was magnified by his large round spectacles on his pink nose. "What, against a hundred of th-th-them? I don't even have f-f-fireball down pat!"

"Yeesh, don't they teach you anything at that Mouse Magic School of yours?"

"Well, I don't see you tr-tr-trying anything, and you've got the c-c-curse and all!"

Aruyin grimaced—she did not want to resort to that, but he did have a point. She had never summoned enough of her "demons" to combat this many opponents, but maybe her pack could buy them enough time to escape. She tried to concentrate, which was no easy to do while on the run, imagining the dark, quiet place in her mind where the Shadowy Shapes would come from.

Picture the tree, blackened and bare,

Hear the deep growl, rumbling there,

Watch for the eyes, burning blue,

Out of the dark, they come for you…

A chorus of squeals erupted behind her, and when she turned to look, a pack of twenty wolves—not quite wolves, as their wispy, wraith-like forms shifted about like dye poured into water—had materialized before the oncoming horde. Snapping jaws of black teeth, burning blue orbs for eyes, and howls like the raging wind sent terror through the 2ephitis, as several wolves tore through their wings and chomped down on their squishy bellies. The 2ephitis attempted to bite and claw back, but their teeth and nails simply pass through the wolves with no more effect than if they were fighting smoke.

In the face of what they assumed was dark magic, and feared more dark creatures were to come, the oozy elementals shrieked and retreated into the depths of the forest from whence they came.

"Wow, b-brilliant!" Brax squeaked triumphantly, once he and Aruyin knew the 2ephitis were all gone and they could stop to catch their breath. "Sh-shame we had to lose all our supplies, b-b-but b-better to have kept our skins."

Aruyin sat down on the thick roots of an oak tree, grousing. "I was so sure the answer would be here. I figured, if anyone would know how to rid me of this curse, the Fae would know. Instead, I get attacked by slime goblins."

"Mephits aren't g-g-goblins, not even related. Both unp-ppleasant, I'll give you that." Brax patted his cloak and robe pockets to make sure he had not lost anything else in the chase. "But you're sure you want to get r-r-rid of your shadow summons? Seemed p-p-pretty handy to me, just now."

Aruyin frowned at him, dusting off her cloak. "My demons are not 'handy,' Brax. They cooperated this time, but they're getting more and more unpredictable. They've been showing up more and more, without my calling them. Look, they're still here! They should have evaporated by now."

As she said, the wolf pack hovered nearby, their flaming eyes fixed on her and Brax. Brax scooted away from them, scuttling behind Aruyin. "Wh-wh-when will they leave?"

"When they feel like it. But that's the problem. If they keep doing whatever they feel like, if I can't control them…" She sighed, removing a small, worn compass from a pocket in her cloak and orienting herself before she began walking again. "I don't worry about what'll happen to me, but you, and Da—I mean, Boggs. These things, these demons, can really hurt someone. They've killed before."

Brax twitched his whiskers and adjusted his spectacles. "That wasn't your f-f-fault."

Aruyin sighed. "So Boggs says. But neither of you were there."

"You were a child. They attacked your f-f-family. You were defending yourself. I mean, that's why I want to be a loremaster, so I can p-p-protect the people I care about."

"I thought it was so you could read books all day."

"Which I'd much rather be d-d-doing right now than getting lost in this forest." Brax looked behind him and let out a sigh of relief to see the shadow wolves had vanished. "Any idea how c-close the nearest town is?"

Aruyin grinned. "I thought a loremaster is supposed to know everything. But you're a lucky mouse, Brax. Next stop: El Tal."

"And you th-th-think you'll find someone who knows how to lift your curse in El Tal?"

The dwarf shrugged. "Who knows? They've got a famous sorcerers' guild there. If anyone would know a spell for banishing demons, someone there must."

*

"I d-d-don't know about this, Yin. You can't trust th-th-these…*creatures.*"

The creature that Brax referred to was sitting upon a collection of lush feather cushions underneath a red-and-gold merchant's tent, helping itself to an array of wine bottles and jugs that surrounded him. The vendor had set up his little display outside an inn that was a few days' trek from El Tal – presumably he set up shop here because he could not get past the city guards. Since the Jackal and Badger Inn was located on a main road, it hosted a good number of travelers, so the Marid had attracted a suitable crowd who looked upon him with morbid curiosity.

"Yes, come one, come all, and the great Malvolio the Marid will grant you a wish—for a small fee. The more generous you are, the more generous your wish will be!" The Marid, a portly, robust—man?—had a booming voice that came from his wide mouth that spread from ear to ear. His skin was green, with webbing between his sausage-thick fingers, but his fine silk clothing contradicted his amphibious appearance. At his feet was a large basket full of coins, and no one was even allowed to step into his tent without tossing a coin or two in first.

"So, explain to me how a Marid is just sitting here, in the open?" Aruyin whispered to Brax, as they watched from the back of the crowd. "I thought these guys lived in caves, or lamps. You know, like djinn."

Brax shrugged. "Normally, they do. I-I-I can only guess s-someone used a wish to set him free."

"That was awfully nice of someone."

"N-n-not necessarily. Marid are clever tr-tricksters. Besides, if he's a free Marid, then he c-could return to the Plane of Water where the Marid come from. Wh-why sit around in some tent in a field, s-selling so-called 'wishes'?"

"Dunno, but if this Marid is really granting wishes…"

Brax fiddled with his fingers. "I d-d-don't like it, Yin. Let's find that sorcerers' guild you were t-t-talking about."

"Come on, Brax. It wouldn't hurt to ask. What's the worst that could happen?"

"Marids can be very d-d-dangerous, and a free one even more so."

Aruyin placed her hands on her hips. "Come on, are you a man or a—"

"D-d-don't say it." He crossed his arms, clicking his large incisors. The old phrase *Are you a man or a mouse* did not sit well with mousefolk.

Aruyin grinned. She knew she should not tease Brax, but he was so darn adorable when he was irritated. She knew he had been reluctant to come on this journey with her; he would certainly have preferred to stay with his books at that Magic Mouse School, or whatever it was called. But her mentor was too old and tired for "these damn fool quests" anymore, and Brax was the only loremaster apprentice that she knew. Mousefolk were good at sniffing out things, and loremasters contained all knowledge of legends, real or rumor, in Mirstone. A mousefolk loremaster, she figured, would be perfect to sniff out all the leads she had about curse-lifting objects, spellcasters, or magical types. He had successfully helped her find all her leads to this point, even if every lead had been a dead end.

"Bah, a brass farthing? What do you take me for, some cut-rate wizard?" boomed the Marid at his current customer. "Either cough up a silver, or be gone with you! You do NOT want to incur the wrath of the Marid! Why, I could summon a terrible storm that could swallow your whole measly city!"

Aruyin grinned, her eyes growing wide in interest. "Do it!"

The crowd turned at looked at her, aghast. The Marid pushed himself up on his cushions to try and get a better look through the crowd. "Who said that? Does someone doubt the power of the magnificent and majestic Malvolio?"

"No, I just want to see you do it," Aruyin called again. "My old mentor used to summon storms too. It's fun!"

The crowd shuffled into a wide circle, whether to get farther away from Aruyin or to avoid the Marid's wrath, maybe both. The Marid stared down the dwarf as she casually strolled up to the tent. "Your old mentor, eh? Some half-wit wizard, I suppose. Any magic you've ever witnessed is nothing compared to the might of a Marid, child."

"First, I'm not a child. I'm a dwarf, and I'm eighteen. Second, my mentor was Darquethorne Boggs of the Stormguard," Aruyin replied with a smirk. "The best wizard in the world. Anyone in the mountains would tell you so. But Malvolio the Marid…I haven't even heard of you."

Brax clenched his hands into fists and pressed them against his face, his eyes dilated in fear. "Y-Y-Y-Yin, don't make him mad!"

Malvolio snickered and clapped his hands together. A small, whirling cloud slowly formed above his head, and it crackled with tiny bursts of green lightning, rumbling like a lion. "You have not heard of me, because I was contained within a prison for thousands of years! But now that I am free, I have returned to my former glory. There is no magic beyond my abilities, no wish too grand for me to grant. Your Stormguard wizard may think he can do anything, but the Marid can do *everything*, infinitely greater."

"Okay then." Aruyin turned to Brax. "Brax, hand me a silver."

Brax placed his hand on the coin purse hanging from his belt. "But Yin, I carefully b-budgeted—"

"Brax, silver."

The mousefolk grimaced, digging into his coin purse and slapping a silver coin into Aruyin's outstretched hand. "There goes a hotel room for the n-night," he sighed.

Aruyin tossed the coin into Malvolio's basket. "Now, what can you do about *them*?"

In a blink, she was flanked by her shadow wolves, all staring with hellish hate at the Marid. The crowd, at first amused by the banter between the Marid and dwarf, now fled in a torrent of screams and shouts of alarm. The Marid shifted his gaze around at the various flaming demon eyes, little beads of sweat popping up on his forehead.

"You just drove away all my customers," he eventually said, wiping his sweat away with a sleeve. He managed a jittery laugh. "Some silly prank of yours. You know basic illusionary spellwork. You can't fool a true master of magic."

"Oh, they're not an illusion. They're very real. Just ask all the little mephit blighters I drove away a few days ago in the Feywilds."

Malvolio pursed his lips tightly, his brow furrowed. "And what do you expect me to do?"

Aruyin crossed her arm, narrowing her eyes on the Marid. "I want them gone. They're part of a curse I was born with. I'm starting to lose control of them. I just want to be…you know, I want to sleep at night without worrying they'll materialize on their own and hurt people."

Brax thought, for a moment, he could see the eyes of the shadow wolves dim a little. Were they sad that Arutyin wanted them gone? No, they were incorporeal summons, and summons did not have feelings, right?

"I…see." Malvolio rubbed his chin in thought. "Well, that looks like a pretty powerful curse, milady. Which will require a pretty powerful wish, one that would certainly need to be more generous than a mere silver—"

"Then grant a not-so-powerful wish worth a silver that'll cure as much of it as possible."

"Ah, an economical wish. You won't get the best, but Malvolio the Marid never does shoddy wish-granting." He plucked a few bottles from around him, and poured their various contents into the air before him, where they swirled around like serpents into a tightly wound sphere. He then spoke a few words in a strange language, waving his hands about with presentational flair. Dancing lights leapt from his fingertips, twirling around him like rainbow-kissed fireflies, until the lights seeped into the floating sphere he created.

"Now a dash of god-spun lightning, a hint of a dreamer's deepest desire, and a splash of…uh, peppermint." Malvolio moved his hands around the sphere until a glassy sheen washed over the surface, rendering it a shiny, purple-and-crimson marbled orb. "Now, just take this home and put it under your pillow for three nights while wearing a chicken's foot around your neck. On the dawn after the third night, crack this open over a bowl carved from willow wood while saying the words, 'Apage, lapsus, shoo! Spirits of shadow, away with you!' Then drink the contents, spin around three times while throwing salt over your left…no, right shoulder, and your curse shall be lifted."

Aruyin cocked her head at the orb. "Huh, who knew all I had to do was act like an idiot while drinking a nasty cocktail, and my curse would be gone? I feel like that's something Boggs could've whipped up."

"Do you doubt my powers?"

Aruyin shrugged. "I thought wishes were instant."

"You wanted the economical wish. Those take longer. Now, if you want a premium wish—"

"You want me to hike all the way back home, wait three days to find out this is rubbish, then hike all the way back here, which would altogether take a few weeks…plenty of time for you to have moved on someplace else to con a new sucker."

The wolves' eyes flared bright, and they growled in unison.

The Marid scooted backwards on his cushions, trying to smile but failing. "Now now, wishes only work if you have faith—"

Aruyin's face scrunched in irritation. "Faith? I've been to clerics, and they were about as useful as you are. If you're capable of real magic, then you better stop holding out!" She dropped the orb and it shattered on the ground, the faintly peppermint-scented contents seeping into the cracks of the cobblestone road.

Brax scuttled over and gently put his hand on Aruyin's shoulder. "Yin, we should j-j-just go—"

But the shadows would not have it. The wolves melded together, twisting and writhing, growing taller and taller as a malleable blob, until it solidified into the shape of a black three-headed, purple-eyed chimera. The shadow beast pounced, and with one of its three heads, it clamped down on the tent, ripped it clean from the earth, and incinerated it in a burst of violet flame.

The Marid scrambled clumsily to his feet, as he struggled to get up from his nest of cushions. "You've made your point! Get your demon away from me!"

Aruyin stared, perplexed, at the shadow chimera towering over them. "I…I didn't want it to do that. I'm not doing that!"

"Yin…" Brax cowered behind her, shaking from whisker to tail. "Please, take a d-d-deep breath…I think your d-d-demon's angry because you're angry."

She spun sharply at him. "And I'm not allowed to be angry? That this con artist is trying to dupe me? That I have been lied to, again and again, people assuring me they'd help me, and all I get are a bunch of empty promises?" Aruyin's hands clenched hard into fists, her voice pouring with venom. "Why shouldn't I be angry??"

By now, the shadow beast had snatched Malvolio by the back of his shirt, and was dangling him off the ground like a puppy. The giant opened all three of its mouths, as tendrils of smoke and purple flame belched from them. The Marid flailed, little sparks of lightning popping from his fingertips in panic, although it did nothing to deter the monster. He cried, his once grand voice now reduced to a snively whine. "Okay, fine! I'm a fraud! When I was released from my prison, my magical powers were infinitely diminished. All I can do is for show! My charms are worthless! But I know someone who could help you. If you'll let me go, I'll tell you who!"

Aruyin slowly unclenched her fists. She sighed. "Another lie, I suppose."

"No, not a lie! I speak of the Wandering Mystic! They could remove this curse!"

The dwarf raised an eyebrow, and then looked at Brax. "Who's he talking about?"

Brax scratched his chin. "Well, there have been r-rumors that have reached the Academy Rodentia Rituale. They say p-people have reported about a mysterious traveler who heals, as if by m-m-magic, but casts no spells or uses material components. They claim the healing is d-d-divine, beyond that of even the most skilled clerics."

"And you didn't tell me about this, because…?"

The mousefolk pointed a little pink finger at her. "I-I-I've been guiding you t-t-to where *you* want to go. I've been following *your* leads. B-b-besides, it's all rumor. I d-d-didn't think you'd take stock in rumors."

Aruyin thought on this, and then turned to the dangling Marid. "Where is this Wandering Mystic?"

The Marid blanched, holding his hands up in an unsure gesture. "Well, no one could say…you know, a *wandering* mystic. Doesn't stay put. BUT-but-but-but, I heard they were last seen near the Floating Isles, just north of here."

The Floating Isles…that was a long, long way north, past the dangerous Ash Mountains. Aruyin figured Malvolio was just giving her a location that would take her as far away from him as possible. She held her hands up towards the chimera. "He's not worth burning. His carcass would probably stink up the whole area for miles. Let him go."

The chimera hesitated for a moment, but then gave Aruyin a low rumble of agreement. The shadow dissipated, and the Marid dropped heavily to the ground. Without a further word, he hastily grabbed his basket of coins and ran, sending a few coins spilling onto the road as he waddled away, blubbering.

Aruyin picked up a few silver coins from the dirt and handed them to Brax. "Look, a refund."

Brax finally let out an exhale, having been holding his breath for the last minute. "I'm sorry that was fruitless. I-I-I guess he's fooled a lot of people with all that g-g-glitz and glamour."

"Well, you know what they say," Aruyin said as she started down the road. "Polish a toad, it's still a toad."

"I think you mean…n-n-never mind."

*

The room at the inn was not an extravagant one, but it was a more than welcomed comfort to Brax, after all the nights of camping outside on the cold ground. He also calculated, with the few extra coins they had picked up from the Marid's hasty retreat, they could resupply with enough food and water before heading out in the morning, and then get more supplies once they reached El Tal. Yes, El Tal was south, but there would be so few towns from here to the north, El Tal was their best hope to get decent supplies before heading to the Floating Isles. Plus, it would not hurt to confirm with the sorcerer's guild if they had any information on this Wandering Mystic.

While Brax was squeak-snoring almost the moment he hit the hay-stuffed mattress, Aruyin lied awake in her bed, unable to sleep. It was pure luck that the innkeeper had permitted them to stay, after he had heard from several of his guests about "the dark dwarf mage and her evil spirits." However, it was not the first time a sorcerer had stayed at his inn, and he would overlook it as long as there was no funny business—and as long as Aruyin's money was good, which it was. But it was another reminder that nothing for Aruyin would ever be easy – wherever she went, her curse would precede her, and next time it could lead to trouble.

She reached under the neckline of her tunic and pulled out a golden music box, no bigger than a thumb, that hung on a chain around her neck. It had been a gift, something to remind her of her family, and that she was never alone. Even now, holding it in her palm, it made her think of the only family she had left…

*

"Start with a visual. A place in your mind where these manifestations of yours can live, can be contained until you summon them." Boggs's gristly voice complimented his rough appearance, a stocky dwarf with straw-pale hair and a gray-streaked beard. His eyes were hard, centuries worth of wrinkles entrenched in his face, but there was patience in his tone. Aruyin often thought of him like a boulder, constant and strong—a very short, grouchy boulder.

Aruyin was only ten years old back then. She had been living with Boggs since she was about six, but he said she would not be ready to train how to control her abilities until age ten. Those years before he could start training her must have been hell, caring for a child who every time she threw a tantrum, she unwittingly summoned a barrage of various shadow animals who would magnify her tantrum tenfold.

Aruyin sat cross-legged on a rug in Boggs' front room, the place they had started her training sessions. She took a deep breath and closed her eyes. "Like, what? A cave or something?"

Boggs stroked his beard. "Caves are hollow and dark. We should pick something that will symbolize the strength you seek. Something steadfast, something that will protect, something that will help you grow."

"Help me grow? Hmmm…strong, protective…like a tree?"

Boggs smiled. "A tree will do. And you must remember to water it, give it sun, give it space to grow."

Aruyin opened her eyes and tilted her head in confusion. "But…it's in my mind. How would I do that?"

"We can all water, feed, and grow our minds. Many forget to do so as they grow older. Now, visualize the tree. Invite your manifestations into it. Let them know they are safe there, as you are safe here."

The young dwarf closed her eyes again, breathing deeply and slowly. A tree…a tree…like the one on her family's old farm. She would play in that tree for hours, while her mother and father worked the land…until the land stopped providing. Until they had to travel to the Verge to find food, until…

Aruyin slammed her fists on the floor. "No place is safe! Safe isn't real!"

Boggs sighed, his gaze steady and even. "Hot-headed girl. Yin, you need to trust yourself—"

"I *do* trust myself! It's everyone else I can't trust."

Boggs pulled up his chair closer to her. "You haven't spoken much about what happened to you, before you came to me. It is important, for the sake of controlling your anger, and by extension, your demons—"

"I told you, I don't want to talk about it!" Aruyin felt her face growing hot, but she swallowed her rage, because she knew it might bring her shadows. She crossed her arms. "The world is full of evil people. Heck, the word *elves* almost has all the same letters as *evil*."

"Yes, elves did unspeakable evil to your family. But an elf also saved your life. An elf brought you to me. We must not judge people by their heritage, or where they come from. We must judge people by their actions. And we cannot let the evil that others do to us consume us. We cannot let it change who we are. There is so much good in you, Yin. Goodness must be your tree. That is what you must water and allow to thrive. That is what will make you strong."

Aruyin bit her lip. "And then, the shadows will…leave me alone?"

Boggs shook his head. "No, but you will no longer need to fight them. You will understand them."

*

El Tal was truly an architectural marvel, a grand cityscape of crimson pagodas with onyx-tiled roofs trimmed in golden details, streets of colorful tiles arranged in ornate designs, and painted lanterns strewn among the flowering trees lining every street. A long, tiled stairway led up to the city gates, where two guards stood in constant watch. As Aruyin and Brax climbed the steps and approached the entrance of the city, one guard—a tall, brawny woman built like a warrior—brought her spear around to block their way.

"Identify yourself," the guard commanded, looking squarely at Brax.

The mousefolk shivered, his eyes focused on the shiny spear tip a few inches from his face. "I-I-I'm an apprentice from the Ac-c-cademy Rodentia Rituale, W-w-we c-come to ask—"

"No. Identify your SELF," the guard reiterated. "Are you female or male?"

Brax's eyes widened in mortification—he had heard of El Tal being a matriarchal city, and the woman residents were treated with far more respect than the men, but they had not figured out a way to tell which mousefolk were male and female? Granted, his clothing provided no clues; he wore the loose, knee-length green robe of an amateur mage under his basic traveler's cloak, and no shoes or hat. Still, it felt a bit insulting.

Aruyin put an arm around her friend, smiling at the guard. "Oh, don't mind Braxeen here. It's her first time. She's not used to the rules. We were hoping we could speak to someone at the sorcerers' guild."

The guard grimaced, but then pulled back her spear. "Take the road to the left, pass the Bazaar, and around the garden plaza. You'll see a stained-glass tower. It's inside there."

Brax, deciding it was best to not say anything else, followed Aruyin through the gates. Once they were out of earshot of the guards, the mouseling huffed. "Really? Must I p-p-pretend to be a girl?"

"Sorry. It's either that, or I'd have to tell them you're my man—er, mouse-servant. You know how they treat men here. This way you'll be treated well and have an easier time getting around." Aruyin gave Brax a sympathetic look. "It's just for a little bit."

"B-b-but I don't know how to a-a-act like a girl."

"It's not that different from a boy. Just don't burp, don't fart, and cross your legs when you sit. Oh, and when you're meeting someone, say something nice about what they're wearing, like, 'I love your shoes!' It's easy."

"Hmm…" Brax pitched up his voice a little, although it was hardly necessary, given his natural squeakiness. "I love your shoes. I *looooove* your shoes. I love *your* shoes…."

El Tal's Bazaar was a pandemonium of activity, sound, and smells, with stalls of every shape and size selling anything imaginable. Aruyin marveled at all the bangles and baubles, the trinkets and trifles, the bric-a-bracs and knickknacks, the fabrics and…Mmmmm, food. So, so much food! She noticed Brax was staring glassy eyed at a vendor's stand selling all varieties of gourmet chocolate, and she had to whisper to him that, "Ladies also don't drool."

She was so taken with the sights and sounds, Aruyin almost missed a voice calling above the cacophony: "Yin? Is that Yin Boggs? Yoo hoo, over here! Sweetheart!"

Aruyin turned to see a dwarf pushing through the crowd towards her. She was a robust woman with curly auburn hair, wearing a light blue tunic and leather breeches, with apple-blush cheeks and a sparkling smile. "My stars, you've grown! You were just a wee bairn when I saw you last. How's old Boggs? Still as ornery as ever, I'm sure!"

It took Aruyin a second, but then the woman's dazzling eyes triggered her memory. "You're the lady that runs Boggs's favorite tavern. Merry Brews!"

"That's right! Millie Merrybrew, of Merry Brews. We make the brew that's just for you!" She giggled, and gave Aruyin a bear hug. "What a small world this is, finding you here. But you're like me, you never liked being cooped up in Venzor. The best education in the world is to travel. Oh! You must meet my daughter. Now, where did she get to? Flora? Flora, dear!"

Out from the crowd appeared a girl, and Aruyin could tell immediately she was not dwarven—she must have been about eight years old, and already stood a good foot taller than Millie. The girl wore a woolen poncho that covered her from her shoulders to her shins, and a matching woolen cap with ear flaps that covered her hair. Her skin was tanned a deep bronze, and the irises of her eyes were gray as storm clouds. She came to Millie's side and looked upon Aruyin and Brax with silent curiosity. It was no surprise to Aruyin that Millie would take in a foundling, even a human one, and it must have been a recent adoption since word of a human living in Venzor would have spread like wildfire.

"Flora, this is Yin. She and her fath…her *guardian* used to visit Momma's family tavern. And this is…I'm sorry, I didn't get your name," Millie gently said to Brax.

Brax, who had been mentally preparing for this moment, took a deep breath and curtsied. "My name is Braxeen Tenderfoot, and I love your…" He looked down, only to discover Flora's feet were bare, and in a moment of panic, he blurted, "…f-f-feet! No, wait, I thought you'd have shoes…I mean, your feet are n-n-nice and all, I have no p-p-problem with them. But it's not like I *love* feet, I-I-I don't collect them or anything…" He quickly snapped his mouth shut, his pink nose reddening in embarrassment.

Millie and Flora glanced at each other, and then Millie gave him a gentle, concerned smile. "That's nice, dear."

Aruyin put a hand on Brax's shoulder. "Anyway, it was lovely seeing you again, Millie, and meeting you, Flora, but Brax and I were on our way to the sorcerers' guild, so we better get going."

"Ooooh, were you? Flora and I were so hoping to get a tour of that guild! She's been interested to learn how they teach magic here, haven't you, dear?" Millie took Flora's hand in hers, patting it. "Let's all go together, and then we can have a nice lunch in the gardens. Doesn't that sound lovely?"

Aruyin was a bit irritated at Millie inviting herself and her daughter along, but it would only be for a short while, and then she and Brax would be on their way in a few hours. "That would be nice," she confirmed, forcing a smile. "Come on, Braxeen."

*

"Out! OOOOOUUUUUUT!"

Aruyin, Brax, Millie and Flora all scrambled out the front door of the Sorcerer's Guild Tower, as a tall, spindly woman with long black hair chased them out. There were two guards at the entrance of the tower who were caught off guard by the commotion, and watched in confusion as the woman stormed past them.

"Never in my life have I witnessed such blatant mockery!" the woman shouted, her eyes afire with rage. "If you even set foot within twenty paces of this guild again, I will have the guards throw you in the dungeon!" She whipped around and went back inside, giving the guards a pointed look as she went. After she was inside, the guards stood directly before the doors, giving the four visitors the evil eye.

Aruyin adjusted her cloak and sighed. "Geez, you try to make one suggestion about how to cast a spell, and they get all haughty on you."

"I think they were angry because you called their Arch-Mage a…poofy…" Millie tried to remember, but had to stifle her giggling.

"A p-p-pompous, pretentious, puff-brained p-p-poof who wouldn't know how to summon a dust bunny, let alone a real rabbit, from a h-h-hat or any other apparel," Brax recited, cleaning off his spectacles. "Y-y-you do have a way of making an impression, don't you, Yin?"

Aruyin raspberried towards the guards. "Eh, bunch of half-penny frauds, I say. Waste of our time. Probably don't know anything about the Wandering Mystic anyway."

"The what now?" Millie was dusting off Flora, readjusting her hat on her head.

"The Wandering Mystic. Some kind of divine healer. I was hoping…eh, he probably doesn't really exist." Aruyin started down the road. "Back to square one, I guess."

Millie and Flora followed after her, Brax in tow. "Well, I don't know much about divine powers," Millie said, "But I know the gods and goddesses exist. What would you be needing healing for?

Oh, is it Boggs? Is he sick?"

"No, it's for…"Aruyin stopped and turned around to face her. "Look, you don't want to spend time with me. Bad things happen to people who hang around me."

"She's not k-kidding," Brax concurred.

Aruyin gave him the side-eye before looking back at Millie. "And what I'm looking for is kind of important. Like, change my life important. *Save* my life important. And I've got a long way to go, so no offense, but I don't need you two slowing me down."

Millie thought on this for a second. "You know, I've been traveling around a lot lately, seen a lot of things. And I've learned when you're trying so hard to find that change-your-life treasure, you're missing out on all the beautiful little things. Why don't you take a break from your quest, and spend a lovely week at Roselake with Flora and me? We're going to go meet up with our friend, Jimmy. Some rest and rejuvenation may help clear your mind. How about it?"

Aruyin wanted to tell her no, but she was exhausted. Even thinking of hiking all the way to the Floating Isles for something that probably was not there anyway made her bones and muscles ache. Brax looked at her with big, pleading eyes.

"A-a-a vacation sounds n-nice," he said softly.

Aruyin rolled her eyes and made a light snort. "I guess that would be fine. But just for a few days. And I don't cook. Boggs wouldn't let me near a stove again after the last time I made porridge and nearly burned down the house."

Millie beamed a big smile. "Wonderful! Then let me get our cart and horse from the stables, there's plenty of room for you to sit in the back. We'll get some dinner for tonight from the market before we leave. This will be so lovely!"

As they walked down the road towards the communal city stables, Flora made a series of hand gestures at Millie. Aruyin had seen sign language before, and it only dawned on her now that Flora must be mute. She had assumed her silence had been due to shyness.

Millie shrugged to Flora's hand gestures. "No, I have no idea how you burn down a house with porridge…"

*

The cart hobbled along the road, pulled by a dappled Clydesdale. Millie and Brax sat in the box seat while Aruyin and Flora sat in the back with the provisions. Flora dangled her bare feet off the edge of the cart bed, looking up at the clear sky in a wistful sort of way. Millie and Brax had discovered a mutual fondness for pub songs, and they warbled an off-key duet of "There's a Toad in My Ale" while the teenage dwarf contemplated throwing herself from the cart.

"So, you been to Venzor yet?" Aruyin said to Flora, more to distract herself from the singing than anything.

Flora shook her head.

"Consider yourself lucky. Full of stuffy old gits." Aruyin laid down on the bed of the cart. "Millie's one of the good ones, though. She'll be a good mom to you. I was adopted too, kind of. I don't think my old man really wanted me, but he knew I'd cause trouble if he didn't."

Flora tilted her head curiously at her.

"That's what I do. Cause trouble—or, a part of me does. But I'll change that, once I find this Wandering Mystic, if he's even real. You ever hear of a Wandering Mystic?"

Flora shook her head.

"Of course not. Although, I wonder if he could, you know, help you talk. He's supposed to be a healer of some kind. He could probably fix you, too."

Flora frowned, her eyebrows pinching inwards.

Aruyin rolled her eyes. "Don't get offended. I'm just saying, wouldn't you rather be able to talk than not? Talk to your mom? Sing awful songs with her?"

Flora softened her expression, looking away to the sky again.

Aruyin groaned, placing her hands over her ears as Millie and Brax hit a glass-cracking high note. "Although maybe it's better if you don't."

Flora turned back to Aruyin and signed something with her hands.

"Sorry, I don't know what any of that means."

Flora stopped signing and stared intently at Aruyin for a long, still moment, like an owl focused on a mouse.

The dwarf gradually grew uncomfortable. "What? What're you looking at?"

Flora's shoulders slumped a little. She cupped a hand around her ear, giving Aruyin a questioning glance.

Aruyin was confused by the gesture, but then she chuckled. "Pfft, yeah, I wish I couldn't hear that caterwauling either. Maybe when we stop, we can gather some tree sap to stick in our ears."

Flora grinned weakly, but there was disappointment in her eyes.

The ride to Roselake was a few hours from El Tal, and was a mostly isolated journey on a dirt road that cut through fields of long, waving grass. By evening, the waters of Roselake glistened in the distance, a golden glimmer underneath the setting sun. The cart rolled up to a small camp, a bonfire burning in a firepit, and a white, dome-shaped yurt erected nearby. A clothesline with a row of drying laundry next to the yurt revealed a dwarven dress, a child's tunic, and a human-sized cloak.

As the cart came to a stop, a man pulled back the entry flap of the yurt and stepped out. He was lanky and tall, youthful but weathered, his wheat-blonde hair pulled back into a top-knot and a thick, curly beard puffed out from his face. He wore a flowing robe, navy blue with silver embroidery, overlayed with an orange, sleeveless coat vest and matching hand wraps. A small indigo diamond was painted on his forehead, a perfect color match for his eyes.

"Jimmy!" Millie leapt from the cart to go give her friend a hug.

"I hope your day wasn't too boring. I just know you would have had no fun at all in El Tal."

The man spoke with a tone as cool and calm as a spring breeze. "I had plenty of time to meditate and delve into the deepest recesses of the eternal ether. And again, it's Voyantico the Cosmic Eye, not Jimmy. I see you brought guests. Lost ones?"

"Not really, although they've been on the road for a while," Millie replied. She waved Aruyin and Brax over. "How about you help me and Jim—I mean the Cosmic Eye, prepare dinner, Yin? Brax, why don't you and Flora wash up and fold the laundry? Oh, it's so nice to have company."

Aruyin scrutinized Jimmy, or Voyantico, whoever he was, before asking, "What's with the outfit?"

The man folded his arms into his robe sleeves. "These robes are symbolic of my spiritual journey. I used to lead a frivolous life in the pursuit of great power, trapped within the dark, soulless armor I had created."

"You mean, your father created," Millie said. "I thought he built that suit of armor—"

"Speaking metaphorically, Millie," Jimmy said with a slight sigh. "But yes, I wore the literal armor of a conqueror as well. But now that I cast that aside, I see the true power lies in the cosmos, in the life essences that surround us. Only through tapping into the powers of the universe can we grow, and ascend, and heal."

"Is that a ch-ch-chakra?" Brax said, pointing to Jimmy's forehead. "I've studied them at the academy. That's the third eye. It helps y-y-you with intuition and seeing beyond sight."

Jimmy paused before hesitantly nodding. "Y…es. Very observant of you."

Millie grinned. "I thought you said you painted that because it made you look 'mysterious'—"

"Thank you, Mill. How about dinner? The soul may feed on the universe, but the body…needs grub." He went to the cart and began to unload the provisions, while Millie went about unhitching the pony and bringing it over to a drinking tub.

Aruyin pulled Brax aside while the others tended to their chores. "Are you thinking what I'm thinking?"

Brax took off his spectacles, squinting. "I-I-I think so, Yin, but if I p-p-painted a third eye on *my* head, would I have to g-g-get another pair of glasses for it? Maybe a monocle?"

"What? No! That guy! A cosmic diviner who lives in a yurt, which means he *wanders* from place to place. Talks about *mystical* stuff. Ring any bells?"

The mousefolk put his glasses back on, and he lightly gasped. "Ooooooh, d-d-do you think he's…I-I-I don't know, s-s-seems implausible that at the same time we even hear about this W-w-wandering Mystic, we happen to run into an old friend of y-yours who not only knows him but brings us right to him."

Aruyin shrugged. "Fate? The universe aligning?"

"Y-y-you believe in that now?"

"When it's convenient."

Brax glanced over at Jimmy. "I-I-I suppose there's no harm in asking. Just try n-n-not to insult anyone. I could use a good meal." He then strolled over to where Flora was, scrubbing up at a wash basin beside the yurt.

Aruyin walked over to Jimmy, who was finishing unloading the last bag from the cart. "You said something about tapping into the universe can heal people. Can it also heal people from, let's say, curses?"

Jimmy, perhaps seeing an opportunity to share his profound wisdom, straightened up and folded his arms again. "I suppose one wouldn't be 'healed' from a curse so much as 'liberated.' Curses, after all, get as much power from the one inflicted by it as the one who cast the curse in the first place. We can choose not to be imprisoned, although it is difficult to change our mindset, if we have convinced ourselves that we *must* be cursed."

"Oh yeah? So, a curse would be all in my head, is what you're saying?"

"Essentially. A simple case of mind over matter."

Aruyin frowned. "How about a curse like this?"

Brax overheard her, and snapped his head in her direction. "Oh gods, not again…"

Aruyin closed her eyes, and when she reopened them, she was surrounded by—well, she decided perhaps something less daunting than wolves was called for—a herd of black rabbits, rows of flaming blue eyes all fixed on Jimmy.

Jimmy's jaw dropped open and a strange, wheezing sound escaped his throat. "Little…bunny…demons…" he managed to say as he backed up a step or two.

Millie, on the other hand, was ecstatic at seeing the infernal fluffle. "My gods, Yin! You're a summoner too! Just like me! Although your summons are a lot cuter than mine. No offense to my swarm elemental, but he's not exactly huggable. And he buzzes a lot."

"These aren't summons," Aruyin said. "Summons come from other planes of existence parallel to ours. These come from inside me. And I can make them look however I want. Bunnies, wolves, monsters. But I can't always control them. My command on them is slipping. I'm worried I'll hurt someone with this. I want this curse lifted. Can Jimmy, or Volcano the Cosmic Pupil or whatever, remove it? I can pay you, if that's how this works."

Jimmy seemed hypnotized by the demons, and did not even notice right away that one was already chewing on his sandal. He gingerly lifted his foot away, and gritted his teeth into a crooked smile. "Right. Hmmm, magic curses, that's a whole other ball of wax. But, through the universe, all things are possible…I just need to consult with my acolyte first."

Millie looked around, befuddled. "Your who? Is someone else…" When Jimmy took hold of her by the elbow and led her into the yurt, she said, "Oooh, me? I'm an acolyte now? How exciting!"

Aruyin sighed. "Another fraud. Great. Well, at least we'll get a free meal from this one."

She felt a small tug on her cloak. She turned around to see Flora, looking at her with worried eyes. The girl picked up one of the shadow bunnies, which, oddly enough, seemed to melt into Flora's arms, completely at ease.

The dwarf smirked. Usually her demons did not like anyone else. "Trust me, they may look cute, but they're not pets. I was a little younger than you when they started manifesting for me."

Flora set the rabbit down. She pointed to Aruyin, pointed to the rabbits, and then made a sharp, swiping motion with her hand, like severing a cord.

Aruyin thought she understood what she meant. "Yeah, I don't want to be connected to them anymore. I want to be…liberated."

Flora nodded. She took Aruyin by the hand and led her over to a spot by the firepit. She then disappeared into the yurt for a second—when the flap opened, Aruyin could hear Jimmy and Millie talking, "This is crazy!" and "Oh, it's not like it's her fault"—and when she returned, she had a spouted bowl and an empty glass bottle. She came back to Aruyin, gestured for her to sit, and set the bowl and glass on the ground. Flora, sitting cross-legged across from Aruyin, closed her eyes for a quiet minute.

Aruyin knew this kid was weird, but she could not figure out what was going on. "Are we playing a game, or something? I don't know human games—"

Suddenly, Flora's eyes shot wide open, and Aruyin thought she saw stars, pure brilliant stars, swirling in her eyes. The dwarf did not get a good enough look because Flora slapped one of her dainty hands over Aruyin's mouth, and a warm, fuzzy sensation rippled through Aruyin's head, her throat, her belly, down to her toes. Everything grew blurry, full of soft color and light, until all that fuzziness centered on her stomach. As soon as Flora withdrew her hand, Aruyin wretched. Oily, dark ooze belched forth from her mouth, which Flora was ready to catch in the bowl. Every obsidian drop left Aruyin's mouth into the bowl, after which Flora poured the contents of the bowl into the bottle. She stopped the bottle with a cork, and held it out to Aruyin.

Everything had happened so quickly, in the space of a few seconds, Aruyin was disoriented. Gradually, her wits returned. "Wha…what the heck was that? What did you do??"

Flora kept holding out the bottle to her. Aruyin looked around. All her demons were gone. Something felt different. Almost like, she had been living with the feeling of a heavy, pressing weight on her chest, and now…she could breathe.

"Is that…my curse?" she asked, pointing at the bottle. "Did you…my gods, are *you* the Wandering Mystic?"

Flora smiled, continuing to hold the bottle out. Aruyin slowly took it, turning it in her hand to observe the contents inside. Within that abysmal ooze, she could see flecks of flame, and could feel vibrations, as if it were still alive, still moving…still growling.

A small squeak came from nearby. Aruyin turned to see Brax, who was staring at them with abject amazement. He was speechless, until he softly uttered, "That's no mystic." He then picked up the load of laundry and scampered quickly into the yurt.

*

That night, as they all slept inside the yurt, Aruyin was awakened by the smell of smoke. She snapped fully awake when she heard Millie scream, "Fire! The yurt's on fire!"

Smoke rapidly filled the yurt as the fabric walls were devoured by flame. Everyone scrambled to their feet, running for the exit, when Aruyin realized Brax, who had been sleeping beside her, was not there. "Brax? Where's Brax?"

When they made it outside, they realized they weren't alone. A band of dark-cloaked figures—it was hard to tell what they were from the hoods covering their faces—stood right before them. Each of them held a weapon: crossbows, axes, cudgels, torches, and swords.

"Bandits," Jimmy said, a snarl in his lip.

One of the figures, tall and deep-voiced, stepped forward. "Which one of you is Galvanius of the Violet Flame?" He pointed

25

to Jimmy. "You, I presume? Although you don't look much like a dark lord to me."

Jimmy crossed his arms. "You know, you try getting your name out there for over ten years, and only *after* you stop using it do people suddenly remember it." He pulled the ribbon off his top knot, and let his shoulder-length hair flow loosely. "I used to be Galvanius, but I have since been reborn. Who wants to know? And why did you set my yurt on fire?"

"We know you found something in the Ash Mountains," the stranger continued. "Something priceless. Something ancient. And we want it."

Millie hugged Flora tightly. "Now who told you a fool lie like that? We're just nomads, trying to carve out a simple life."

The bandits cocked their crossbows and firearms at them.

"Don't play dumb with us," the leader thundered. "We went digging around those mountains, and the local goblin freaks were very helpful after some forceful persuasion. Said a dark lord and his band of mercenaries has stolen the god machine from the old treasure vault. Something like that must be worth all the fortunes of all the kings in Mirstone. Hand it over."

Jimmy and Millie glanced at each other. "First of all, we're not mercenaries. We're treasure hunters," Millie corrected. "Second, we did find it, but the thing sort of came to life and flew away. Haven't seen hide nor hair of it since."

"Besides, do we look like we found treasure? Yeah, I just choose to live in a yurt rather than a castle," Jimmy huffed. "Speaking of which, you all are going to pay for that yurt—"

"I'm giving you to the count of ten," the bandit leader seethed, pointing his broadsword at them, "and if you don't give us what we want, we kill your furry friend here."

One of the bandits stepped up, holding a shaking, terrified Brax by his arm.

"I'm s-s-sorry!" Brax cried. "I-I-I just came outside to use the little mouse's room, and they c-c-caught me…"

Aruyin felt a burning storm of panic and fury in her gut. "Let him go, or you'll be sorry!" she called, malice in her tone.

The leader spat a thick, wicked laugh. "Are we supposed to be scared of two dwarves, a mouse, a child, and a…what, a circus freak?"

Millie reached into her pocket and took out a silver whistle. "Now that, I don't know. But what you should be scared of are two summoners, a wizard, and a dark lord." She blew the whistle, but rather than a clear tone, the sound that came out of it was a horrible, teeth-gritting buzz.

Before any of the bandits could reply, a sudden cloud materialized out of the air and engulfed them. They realized quickly that it was not a cloud, but a buzzing, biting, stinging storm of insects. They screamed and swatted, dropping their weapons as the bugs got into their eyes and under their clothes. The bandit holding Brax released him, and the mousefolk scurried as fast as he could over to Aruyin.

So that's what a swarm elemental looks like, Aruyin thought.

"You sic' em, Swarmy!" Millie called.

The bandit leader snarled, lunging forward at Jimmy and the others. He swung his sword, missing Jimmy by mere inches as the former dark lord jumped out of the way. Jimmy side-stepped another swing and kicked the bandit in the stomach. He brought his fist around in a hook, but the bandit blocked it. It was clear that Jimmy remembered his battling days, but he would not last long without a weapon of his own.

Brax raised his hands, which were shaking. "F-f-fireball, what're the words f-f-for…*scintilla, ignire, ustilo, c-c-comb-b-us*…shoot, *scintilla, ignire, u-u-u-stil*…darn it, *s-s-s-scintilla*…"

Aruyin took a breath, and tried to concentrate on the tree in her mind…but she could not visualize anything. She glanced down at the bottle hanging from her belt. She no longer had the curse. *I can't summon the demons!*

The bandit leader lunged at Jimmy again, but this time Millie tackled him around the legs and sent him sprawling off balance.

One of the other bandits freed herself from the swarm, rushed over and grabbed the unguarded Flora. "Call off the bugs, or I cut her throat!" she threatened, pulling a knife from her belt.

"No!" Millie, prone on the ground, held up her hands. "Please, you don't know what you're doing!"

Aruyin panicked. That's all there really was to it, all it took for her to rip the bottle off her belt and fling it as hard as she could at the female bandit. The bottle shattered on the ground at the bandit's feet.

Time froze. The buzzing, the crackling fire, the skirmish, all dropped to dead silence. Aruyin thought, for a second, she heard a faint, high-pitched cry, a child's wail, before the bottle suddenly exploded into darkness. Out from the bottle came living pitch in the shapes of skeletal hands, tendrils, fangs, talons, and spidery legs. One would have seen the monstrous appendages for only a glimpse, because then the sludge ballooned, and ballooned, and kept ballooning, taking in everything around it. No one had a chance to run, or even scream. Inky, suffocating blackness took them all in one heartbeat, and then…

*

Oh gods, not this dream again.

Aruyin knew this nightmare all too well. She trudged alone through a sun-starved rotting landscape that echoed the Verge, but while the Verge was dry and barren, this place was damp, musty, and brimming with oily muck up to her knees. The trees were little more than black lines, as if painted with a thick brush, and overhead, moss hung from branches like curtains of night. The silence was deafening.

Pumpkin-sized bubbles formed at the surface of the muck, and floated up into the air around Aruyin, hovering around her like dozens of watching eyes. She always tried to avoid the bubbles in this dream, because they always screamed when they popped, screamed in voices she only barely remembered. One of the bubbles blocked her way, and she heard something different coming from within this time. A soft, whimpering voice was trapped in the bubble. "I'm n-n-not good enough, they're g-g-going to expel me…"

Aruyin strained to listen, and realized the voice was coming from another bubble, and another, and another. She followed the trail of bubbles, each containing hushed weeping, until she came to the wagon. It was the same wagon she had been discovered in, all alone, after her family died. What was left of it was just the frame, the cover torn to shreds and the wheels broken. Sitting inside was Brax, and every time he opened his mouth, a muddy bubble floated out from it, stealing his voice.

"Brax! Hold on, I'm coming." Aruyin waded over to him, and lifted herself up into the wagon to sit beside him. "Brax, can you hear me?"

The mousefolk hesitated, as if half asleep, and then turned to her. Sorrow etched deep lines around his eyes. "Oh, Yin. I-I-I can't do it. I'll never be a loremaster. Th-they're going to expel me from the ac-c-cademy."

"Huh? Where did that come from?" She looked around at the wasteland, knitting her brow. "Oh, the demon sludge. It made this place look like my childhood nightmare. I guess it's making us think negative thoughts. Brax, that's just the demons talking. They're trying to confuse you—"

"No, no! I can't sp-speak the spells right. Incantations have to be p-precise, or they won't work. I c-c-can't even do the most basic sp-spells. I-I-I've been buying time at the academy with all my research, b-b-but I'll never p-pass if I can't do the spells. They'll fail me. I'm useless."

"Is it because of your stutter? That's why the spells don't work?"

Brax squeezed his eyes shut, tears running down his cheeks.

Aruyin rested her arms on her knees. "Hey, it's okay. I mean, if they thought you couldn't pass, you wouldn't even have been accepted, right? They don't just kick out students because of a stutter." She put an arm around Brax, thinking. "Look, Boggs always told me it's not so much about the words when it comes to magic, but how you feel. Maybe trying to say all the words perfectly makes you too nervous. If the words are getting in the way, try something else. Something that makes you feel good. What makes you feel good, Brax?"

Brax sniffled, and was quiet in thought. Eventually, he started to croon a tune:

I went to the pub down the lane

To meet my lady so fair,

I ordered for us a mug of ale

That my love and I could share,

But alas, our mug held such a sight,

It made my lady turn pale,

For bobbin' in our frothy brew

There was a toad in me ale.

A toad in me ale! A toad in me ale!

I cried, why's there a toad in me ale?

And the toad said to me, I'll tell you, Pops,

Only the best of ales in Mirstone have hops!

Aruyin chuckled, and was relieved to see Brax was laughing too. Then she realized something. "Brax, you got through that whole song without stuttering."

The mousefolk scratched his chin. "Well, yes, songs I-I-I remember really well, so I always know what comes next. I-I-I don't have t-t-to think about what I'm g-going to say."

"Then why don't you just invent songs to go with your incantations? That might help you remember them so you don't stutter. Or just say the words to a melody you know."

Brax twitched his whiskers in thought. Tentatively, he held up a hand, and softly sang to the same melody:

Scintilla, ignire, ustilo, combustum,

Fire, spark and ignite!

Show me the way, show me the light...

Within his palm, a small spark blazed into existence, and settled into a steady ball of flame, illuminating the area around them. Brax stared at his little fireball, stunned, and then let out a squeal of joy. "Yin, look! Look look look, I made a f-fireball!"

Aruyin hugged Brax, her smile almost as beaming and bright as the fireball. "You did it! See, we're stronger than this place. Now let's go find the others."

The two jumped down from the cart and trekked through the muck, with Brax's fireball lighting the way. For some time, it all looked the same, the same black streaks for trees, the same silence, the same endless darkness. Then a faint sound wafted their way; a muck bubble floated their way, with the weak voice inside. The voice sounded male.

Another trail of bubble led them to a clearing, empty except for one lone tree in the center. Millie and Jimmy were waist deep in the sludge—which, given that Aruyin and Brax were only ankle-deep, this was quite troubling. They seemed unable to register Aruyin or Brax's presence, with Jimmy muttering, "I'll never be good enough, even when I'm someone else I'm not good enough..." Millie, looking distraught and defeated, kept crying, "I'm a terrible mother...I left my daughter exposed...I'm a terrible mother..." No matter what Aruyin and Brax tried, nothing seemed to shake them from their horror.

"Yin, look," Brax whispered, pointing at the tree.

Flora stood at the base of the tree, her feet on top of the muck's surface. She was looking up at the brittle, gnarled truck, and as Aruyin approached her, she realized this was the same tree she had always visualized when calling on her demons. "Flora? Are you okay?"

All will be well, Aruyin.

The dwarf blinked, not sure if she had heard what she thought she had. "You can talk here?"

Flora removed the hat from her head, allowing her long, sea-form colored hair to cascade down to her ankles. While her lips did not move, her voice was gentle and kind. *This place is tied to your mind, and I can speak to others in their minds if they are open to it. I have been trying to touch your mind since we met, but you were unable to hear me before. My natural voice cannot be heard by mortal creatures, only the gods. I fear my true voice would, literally, blow your mind away.*

"Just what the heck are you?" Aruyin asked.

"She's n-not human," Brax said. "She's a goddess. S-s-she can perform magic without inc-c-cantations or materials, without being physically or mentally t-taxed. Only gods can do that."

Aruyin's jaw dropped. "Huh, what? How's that possible? You're a kid!"

Flora smiled. *That's true, I am young. The ancient treasure that Jimmy and Millie found in the Ash Mountains is what brought me into existence. It was a god creator. I am even younger than I look, and I am still learning about you mortals and your ways. But there are still things within my divine power I can do, as you know.*

"Then, can you get us all out of here?"

No. You must do that.

"I can't! You lifted the curse from me. I can't control the demons anymore."

This is true, and also not true. Flora placed a hand on the tree. *Jimmy was partially correct, although I doubt he knows why. What we believe are curses can be changed, can become blessings if we want them to be. You wanted the curse removed, but you had the ability to do that the whole time. I have simply provided you the opportunity to understand that.*

Aruyin looked up at the tree. "You're doing kind of a crappy job, because I don't understand."

Why did you want your power taken from you?

"Shouldn't a goddess know everything?"

I do. I'm asking because I don't believe you know the answer.

Aruyin clenched her teeth, her hands balling into fists again. "Are you kidding? If I'm stuck with those demons for the rest of my life, I'm going to be alone! No one will risk being near me! Brax will leave me! Boggs will leave me! I'll have no one, again! I'll die alone…" She paused, looking around. "Although…I guess dying like this isn't much better."

You cannot fight this alone. But you're not alone, Aruyin. You are surrounded by love. You are love. Look at your tree. Because you believe you don't deserve love, you have not been taking care of it. Help your tree grow.

Aruyin was going to snap back that it was the same spiel that Boggs had given her, that it made no sense since the tree was not real, but instead, she inhaled deeply, and released her breath slowly. "How?"

Compassion is your rain. Kindness is your soil. Love is your sunlight. You possess all these things. Help your tree grow. Then invite your magic in. Let it know it is safe in your care. Your powers are not your demons. Yes, your demons come from within you, but they do not have control of your magic. You do. Invite your magic home.

Aruyin sighed, placing her hands on the tree. Flora gently set her hand over Aruyin's left hand. Brax came over, standing beside her.

"Brax, I…don't know what I'm doing," Aruyin confessed. "I need…your help."

The mousefolk nodded, then he reached for the chain around Aruyin's neck. He pulled out the tiny music box and wound it. He then placed his little pink paw over Aruyin's right hand. "Maybe…a song?"

Aruyin had not sung that song in a long time. She barely remembered the words, barely remembered when her mother would sing it to her. But, as she calmed herself and closed her eyes, as she heard the music box's chimes, the words drifted back to her…

Across the land to the cyan sea,

Over mountains we will glide,

Follow this song, and you'll find me,

And we'll always walk side by side.

Ah toora loora lay,

Ah toora loora lay.

Remember, child, where'er you be,

Even if you and I grow apart,

I'll be with you, and you with me,

'Cause I carry you in my heart.

Ah toora loora lay,

Ah toora loora lay.

The muck melted at their feet and receded into the soil, and there was cool, refreshing rain on their faces, and there was sun. The beautiful, blessed sun…

And the magic came home.

*

The cart rumbled along the road in the early morning light. Millie drove the cart while Jimmy slept in the back, exhausted from last night—actually, what had happened last night, he could not quite recall. All he knew was he had had a terrible dream about bandits, and a shadow that ate everyone, and feeling very terrified and alone. He was relieved it was all over, but the nightmare had left him drained.

Aruyin sat in the box seat besides Millie, while Brax and Flora sat on the back end of the cart, swinging their legs in unison as the road glided under them. Brax sang short little tunes, and periodically a tiny fireball would shoot up and fizzle out in the air. Flora would clap every time a successful fireball arched into the sky.

"What do you think happened to the bandits?" Aruyin asked Millie.

Millie grinned. "Oh, I'm sure they'll be fine, once the shock wears off. The way they all high-tailed it out of there once we were all free of that nightmare swamp, I imagine they won't be coming after Jimmy anymore. They might even reconsider their choice of profession. But what about you? How are you feeling?"

Aruyin looked up at the clear sky, not a cloud in sight. "Still trying to process it all. But I'll be okay."

"I know Boggs will be so happy to see you. He'll be so jealous he missed out on all the excitement. I hope your journey has given you the answers you were looking for."

"Not all the answers," Aruyin said, as a small rabbit, its fur a wash of twilight hues and patterned with shimmering stars, materialized in her lap. She stroked its head gently. "But I'm learning more every day. I know there's a future for me, and for the first time, I'm not afraid."

THE END

Anathema
Richard Fierce

1

Evard scrunched his face as the aged hinges of the old wooden door creaked. He held his breath and looked over his shoulder, expecting to see his father rushing into the room, sword in hand.

Tilting his head, he listened intently. It was faint, but he could hear his father snoring. Exhaling in relief, Evard stepped out into the chill evening air and slowly closed the door behind him. Oddly, the hinges didn't protest this time.

The moon shone brightly overhead, illuminating the shacks that were scattered about this part of town. Evard hated living in the Low District, but he hadn't chosen his lot in life. That didn't mean he couldn't change it, however.

He pulled his cloak tight against the cold and swept his gaze around again, making sure no one was out. Discretion was his ally this night, as it was most nights. Evard often snuck out at night to the nearby forest where he studied ancient manuscripts he'd found buried in the back of a cave.

The small treasure was mostly animal skin scrolls, but there were a few leather-bound books with black and silver runes engraved on the covers. He'd "borrowed" a book on foreign languages from a local trader and spent weeks learning to decipher the words written on the scrolls.

Once he was able to read the magical language, the spells came as naturally as breathing. Evard treasured knowledge above all else, and his passion was magic. His father, on the other hand, was not the academic type, and he didn't approve of his son's scholarly pursuits.

Evard made his way cautiously into the forest. Though he knew the path to the cave as well as he knew the way around his own home, he'd accidentally stumbled upon a wild animal once.

Were it not for his sword and minor skill with it, he would surely have been injured that night, possibly even killed. A smile pulled at his lips as he remembered having to explain to his father how his shirt had been torn to shreds in the middle of the night.

His father wasn't the brightest man, and Evard often used that to his advantage. He respected his father, but he knew that sheer strength and skill with a blade didn't—and couldn't—solve everything. Sometimes things needed to be handled with diplomacy. He almost laughed aloud at the thought. Were he so strong in his convictions, he would have already explained to his father that he didn't want to be a soldier.

His father was employed in the nearby lord's army, and though he was at the bottom ranks, he thought highly of the position he held. This time, Evard did laugh. He didn't want to be a mere extension of someone's fist.

As he reached the boundary of the forest, he glanced over his shoulder to make sure no one was following him. Satisfied that he was traveling alone, he stepped into the tree line and began walking toward the hidden cave. His awareness was not from being timid, but from prudence. As he began to more fully understand the spells he was reading, he knew the consequences if he were caught would be great. The practice of magic by anyone who had no formal training was prohibited by the local constabulary, and the practice of the dark arts was *expressly* forbidden. They didn't even teach that form of magic at the academy anymore. Not since …

Evard shivered from the cold and tried to pull the cloak tighter only to hear the sound of fabric ripping. He released his hold and shook his head in disappointment. He hated living in destitution. Pausing outside the cave entrance, he looked up at the night sky and stared at the moon for a long moment.

I will be a great mage one day, he promised himself.

Stepping into the cave, he immediately realized that something was amiss. He stood still in the darkness, waiting for his eyes to adjust to the deep gloom of the cave. He was not alone, but he wasn't sure if the presence was a threat or not.

"You are young indeed to be studying dark magic."

The voice sounded loud in the cave. And the words cut through Evard's heart. Fear welled within him. Was this one of the school's enforcers? Had they discovered what he'd been doing? He was tempted to run, but the shadows gave him confidence. He cleared his throat.

"Who are you?" he asked.

He heard a shuffling sound and took a step back, but whoever was there did not approach him.

"That is not important. You should be asking *why* I am here."

Orange light flared to life, illuminating the cave. Evard staggered back, shielding his face from the brightness with his right hand. The light had come from a fire, a fire fueled by his scrolls and books. Evard stared in horror.

"No!"

He flung himself forward, dropping to his knees before the flames and tried to grab dirt from the cave's floor, but the manuscripts were old and dry, and they burned too quickly for him to save them from the blaze. He cast his gaze at the robed figure behind the fire, anger pushing his fear aside.

"Do not be upset." The figure waved a hand at the dimming fire. "These are petty compared to the books in my collection. There were probably placed here by an amateur wizard in fear of being caught."

The stranger pulled his hood back to reveal a gaunt and unnaturally pale face. His head was bald, and his eyes were sunken deep into his face. A scraggly goatee hung down from his chin. He was a figure of gothic power, ready for the grave.

Evard couldn't hide his look of disgust. The man's appearance was appalling, yet there was something about him that drew his interest … a sinister power of great proportions. He could feel it in the air, radiating from the pale man.

"This is my true form, though I do not walk the world with this look."

Covering his face with his hands, the man whispered words of magic. When he removed his hands, his beauty was staggering. Golden-brown hair cascaded down around his shoulders, his flesh a healthy tanned hue. The figure's eyes, however, remained devoid of any light. Even the dying light of the fire seemed to be sucked into their depthless void. Evard's skin tingled, and he wondered if it was because of the sight he beheld, or if it was from the magic.

"Power has a price, a costly one. The dark arts will drain your health, but it will give you such unlimited possibilities. Though the magic within those petty books was weak, it called to my spirit. I have sought you out as a wolf seeks out its prey. How did you learn these spells?"

"I taught myself," Evard replied.

The man smiled.

"A natural wizard. Intriguing. I can give you knowledge unrestrained, but you must weigh the cost. Is it worth the sacrifice for you?"

Evard slowly rose from his knees. He kept his gaze on the man, stared through him, turning his sight both inward and outward. He searched his soul yet looked out toward the vast world around him. Magic might have a price, but Evard was convinced he could avoid its effects. He met the man's eyes, the fury of his desire reflecting back at him.

"I am Evard, and the world will tremble before me."

*

Evard stood with his arms folded across his chest, staring out the window of his chamber at the city outside. His room was small, roughly eight feet by ten. The academy put one student to a room, and Evard was no different. The only furnishings consisted of a bed and small side table, atop which a single candle burned. The walls were smooth and nondescript, the color of fresh snow. Made of magic, one could find no flaw in the construction that one might with buildings made by the hands of men.

The window was made of crystal, and it was as clear as plain glass. Many of the students didn't know that, but Evard did. He knew almost everything there was to know about the academy. His master held nightly sessions with him, tutoring him in the ways of the dark arts and about the history of their order. During the day, he was a simple student learning the basics. From the hierarchy of the Order to its humble beginnings—and, of course, about magic.

To the right, in his periphery, he could see the sun setting on the horizon. The sky boasted colors of reds and pinks all swirled together. Evard envied the display. How he desired to be immortalized by something he created.

Like the gods, he mused.

As the cloak of night descended upon the surrounding landscape, the lights of the city began to twinkle into existence. The sight reminded him of home, in a way. The town he grew up in was far smaller than this city. Zelphor was one of the major cities of the human kingdom, home to thousands of every people and culture. It was the epitome of diversity.

Evard's thoughts went from his home town to his father. He wondered what his father might be doing, but even as the thought entered his mind, he answered his own question.

He's probably still just a soldier.

He frowned as he considered how he left home with his mentor. The night he met him in the cave and accepted the cost of discipleship, he had left. He didn't even tell his father goodbye. He paused mid-thought to conjure up an image of his father in his mind. It had been two months since he had left his old life behind. Two long, grueling months of study and discipline, but he knew the reward far outweighed the sacrifice. He pushed the thoughts from his mind and turned his attention to the descending sun.

"Daydreaming?"

Evard didn't bother turning around. There was only one person could penetrate the magical defenses he placed on his room: his master. He inhaled deeply and composed himself, knowing that his mentor would frown disapprovingly at any display of weakness.

"Hardly," Evard replied as he turned to greet the man. "Reminiscing, perhaps. Never daydreaming." He bowed low to his master before meeting his gaze.

Etrix, his master, stared at him intensely.

"Do you know what I see?"

Evard shook his head, confused by the question.

"I see a youthful boy. One whose passion for the craft is unrivaled by any except the masters of the order." Etrix smiled, but it was hidden within the depths of his hood.

"I am glad you see how much I value knowledge. What will we be studying tonight, master?"

"Nothing."

Evard scowled in disappointment. He thought his mentor had mentioned the practice of shadow casting at their next session. His facial expression revealed his disappointment as well as his words would of.

"We will not be studying anything. Tonight, we shall *practice*."

Evard's heart leaped in his chest. His master was going to allow him to cast dark magic tonight? His joy burst forth in laughter and a smile that took up his entire face. His rebuking was swift.

"Do not get excited!" Etrix never raised his voice above a certain level, but he did put force behind his words. "You will need complete focus for this task. Bring your book and meet me in the auditorium."

Evard watched his master fade from sight. His exhilaration had him soaring.

*

Things had not gone well. At least, that was the thought that continued to run through Evard's mind. He wrung his hands together nervously as he quietly made his way back to his room.

Another—a student—had seen them casting magic. Etrix was a master of the academy, true, but they were not merely casting light globes and conjuring fire. They were summoning foul spirits of the netherworld. It didn't take an experienced student to know that kind of magic was proscribed. The ramifications swirled through his mind like a whirlwind. He bit his lip in an attempt to divert his mind elsewhere, but it was futile.

Evard paused as he reached his room. He put his left hand on the door to lean against it, forgetting the defense magic in his panicked state. A burst of electricity jolted through his body. He cried out in agony and shock and watched his arm fall lifelessly to his side. Pain slowly gave way to anger. How could he have let such a small matter affect his rationale? And worse, he hadn't been paying attention. He could likely have lost his life to the magic that guarded his door.

"Control," he reprimanded himself.

Calming his emotions and forcing them back to their silent corner, he dropped the magical shield and entered his room. Evard stood in darkness, having blown the candle on his table out before he left to meet his master. He closed his eyes and let the darkness envelope him completely, comforting him like nothing else could.

How long he stood with his eyes closed, he didn't know. It could have only been a few minutes, but Evard assumed it had been much longer than that. His legs had fallen asleep under his unmoving weight and they tingled numbly as he shifted them around. He opened his eyes and immediately noticed his master staring out the single window the room provided. Evard's face scrunched up as he attempted to take a step. The numbness in his legs had not diminished, and he tumbled to the floor. He had yet to master the elven technique of meditation.

"It seems that a student will be missing in the morning," Etrix whispered softly.

Evard didn't move his legs in the hope that the tingling would subside.

"What do you mean missing? He went back to his room. I saw

him.”

Evard looked to where his master was standing and noticed it was still dark outside. The sun had yet to rise.

“He will tell the Council. You are not safe so long as he is here. I’ve left a gift on your table. Use it before daylight.”

And then his master was gone.

It felt as though hundreds of needles were trying to escape his legs. He lay very still, waiting for his circulation to restore itself and looked at the table to glimpse what gift his master had given him. As if on cue with his thoughts, a shaft of moonlight spilled through his window to reveal a small dagger with runes etched along the blade. The runes glimmered with a faint bluish radiance.

Use it before daylight.

The words burned in his mind. The tingling in his legs finally subsided and he got back onto his feet. He made a mental note to look back through his book on *torpor*, the elven art of resting without being fully asleep. Evard picked the blade up off the table and examined it. He couldn’t decipher the meaning of the runes, but they did remind him of a book he had seen once when his master had taken him to a secret chamber underneath the academy.

He would never forget that book. It emanated magical power so strong that it made his skin crawl just being in the same room with it. When his master had opened it, dazzling white and turquoise light burst forth from the pages. He decided then that one day he would subdue the power of that book. He forced his thoughts back to the present. The student who had seen them lived down the hall. Evard couldn’t be seen outside his room, couldn’t risk being associated with what he was about to do.

He pulled a small wooden chest from under his bed. It was adorned with a tiny, nondescript imprint of a dragon. Inside was a small crystal with a dim red hue, a book of spells his master had given him, and a silver brooch that matched the dragon on the chest. He paid a small fortune for the chest from a Choshech’alfar trader. The elf swore superior quality on his goods, but Evard had yet to test any of the items. He pinned it to his robes, which were the customary dull brown of a novice, and watched as his hands slowly became opaque, then completely invisible. A smirk spread across his face as a wave of adrenaline rushed over him.

"Such *power!*" he whispered aloud.

Being hidden from sight, able to walk the halls of the academy in secrecy, without anyone knowing he was near … it made him feel dangerous. Invincible.

He had little trouble getting the door to his fellow student's room open. It swung inward soundlessly. Evard paused in the doorway hesitantly, the risk of what he was about to do sobering him from his power-hungry stupor. Peering into the darkness, he could vaguely make out the silhouette of the bed. He glanced around the hallway to make sure none of the council guards were nearby, and certain that all was acceptable, he stepped into the room.

It was essentially the same as his own abode, but while his room had a window, this room did not. Evard crept up beside the bed and quietly slid the dagger his master had given him from his boot. The runes glowed faintly and added to the eeriness of his task.

His peer sat up in his bed. "Who's there?" he asked.

Without another thought, Evard plunged the blade into the man's throat, twisted it, then pulled it free. Blood spurt from the gaping wound and a gargling sound filled the silence of the room. He watched the dreadful scene with an impassive face. The body slumped back down onto the bed, and Evard slipped out of the room back into the hallway. It was still devoid of anyone's presence, and he swiftly made his way back to his own chamber.

When he was younger, his father often told him stories of newer soldiers who had to take the life of another for the first time. In each story, the reaction was always the same: it made them feel ill. Evard attributed that to the guilt of killing another person. He wasn't sure what he should be feeling, but he didn't feel guilty for killing the other student. In fact, he was unemotional about it. He did what needed to be done. What his master wanted him to do.

The following morning when he "awoke" from *torpor*, he found his master standing by the window.

"What have you done?" Etrix hissed, turning from the window to face him. Evard was confused. "I did what you instructed—"

"I did not instruct you to kill him," his master interrupted. "The dagger was to be used as a gift to bribe his silence and make him withdraw from the academy. Where is the blade?"

Evard shrugged. "I threw it away," he lied.

"Lucky for you the guards have not found it then. The runes on the blade were telepathic magic. If you would have been intelligent enough to bribe him with it, the runes would have helped to convince him to keep his mouth shut about what he saw and make him leave the academy altogether. But now …"

Etrix shook his head. "Now the council is on alert. They fear someone within the school committed the murder. If they discover it was you, you are on your own. My hands are tied in this matter."

"You could simply use your power to convince them to forget the matter," Evard replied.

"I am outnumbered and overpowered. Though my knowledge of the dark arts is extensive, I could not hope to overpower the others. Do nothing to bring attention upon yourself. Nothing!"

And then his master was gone.

As the days passed, Evard took his master's advice and laid low. From what he could gather of all the rumors being whispered, the Council had launched an investigation into the murder, even going so far as to bring in a psionicist. Often referred to as "mind mages," they drew their powers from their own consciousness using methods that usually needed to be replenished by resting. His own master had developed similar skills.

Evard wasn't concerned. There was no evidence that pointed to him. His thoughts had been on the dagger that his master had given him. The runes had stopped glowing the faint blue since the night he used it to kill the other student. Now they glowed with a dull murky color. It wasn't the color that had him intrigued, however. It was the runes themselves. Evard had gone through almost every book on runes in the library, but he could not find anything similar to what was etched on the blade.

The harder he tried to decipher them, the more frustrated he got. Until it hit him. Etrix's book had runes on it as well. Ones different from anything he had seen before. He could sneak to the underground room where his master kept the book, but it would not be easy. He wouldn't need long, just a few minutes … he pinned the brooch on and headed to the secret door.

Etrix had taken him there on multiple occasions, but he could count the number of times he had seen the book on one hand. His master claimed that the book was invaluable, filled with incomparable knowledge and power. Evard believed it, too. He knew that his master was a powerful wizard, not only from the respect he had among the other council members, but because as he studied the histories of not only the academy, but the art and Order itself, he saw that the most powerful wizards in times past were those who followed the darker side of the art; the shadow mages.

Ages ago, when magic had first been discovered to exist, the wisest of those possessing the power divided into factions. Some thought it should be used for the betterment of humanity, while others thought that those who had the gifts should be elevated as lords and rulers of the people. And another group felt that the power was for neither good nor evil but used according to the wishes of the caster.

Thus the Order of the Sun was born. The factions of shadow, upright, and neutral held their own views on the use of magic and never agreed on much. As time passed, the upright gained in strength and number, and eventually—under the reign of King Cen Tra—banned the study and practice of the dark arts. Despite the ban and subsequent persecution that followed, some still risked their lives to practice the forbidden powers.

Evard had learned from his master that these people usually stayed out of the public eye for fear that the academy's council would track them down and kill them. His master was a rarity, however. He lived a dangerous double life to keep the shadow mages alive inside the academy. As far as he knew, he was Etrix's only apprentice. He paused as he came to the end of the hallway, a wall seeming to lead to a dead end. He traced his finger along lines he had memorized on the smooth stone.

The wall shuddered slightly, then slid to the side to reveal a carved passageway. He attempted to step through, but some invisible force was holding him back. He didn't remember his master putting any fields of magic on this door in the past, but he could feel the power of the unseen force and decided to break through it. He would replace the spell when he left. Easily blasting through the defense, he stepped into the passage. Evard knew the way to the hidden room he was looking for, and soon he would know what those runes meant.

*

Etrix entered the assembly chamber to meet with Shalareven, the head of the council. He had been abruptly summoned, which was not in the leader's character. Assuming it had something to do with the murder, he answered hastily. Shalareven was there waiting on him.

"Welcome Etrix. I appreciate your urgency. This matter is of the highest priority."

"Has the psion found anything?"

Shalareven shook his head. "Not definitively, though what I am about to show you may give us a clue."

The center of the room was occupied by a large rectangular table. Towards the middle of it, the surface was indented. Picking up a silver carafe, Shalareven poured water onto the table. It collected in the depression and formed a small pool. Whispering an incantation, an image formed onto the watery surface.

Etrix recognized it immediately as his hidden room, but his face did not betray his thoughts. "What are we looking at?" he questioned.

Shalareven seemed taken aback. "You don't remember this room? It was where the shadow mages used to gather."

Feigning remembrance, Etrix nodded. "Ah yes, I remember now. It's been so long, I'd forgotten about those chambers. Why are we looking at this one?"

"The student you brought here is inside."

Etrix laughed. "Impossible. I sealed the entrance myself years ago as you instructed. No one but a member of the council could undo the enchantment on that door. And I do not see anyone in the image."

"Focus your attention at the desk. He is not visible with the fleshly eye, but with the magical one. He has some sort of book."

A burst of blinding bluish white light lit up the image. Etrix looked closer and concentrated his power to reveal the unseen. Then he saw Evard, looking through *his* book … and he had the dagger! Anger washed over him, and he slammed his fist onto the table, causing the image on the water to ripple. He realized that Shalareven was staring at him intently.

"How could he betray us in this manner? Betray me of all people … I brought him here, taught him the craft."

The head of the council frowned.

"Perhaps our judgment about him was misguided. This is not the only disturbing news I have. The psionicist has found a chest enchanted with dark magic in his room. There are guards waiting for him there, and I have sent the psionicist for him. I thought that book was destroyed?"

"As did I," he lied.

"You know what the law demands."

"All too well," Etrix replied as he watched his apprentice hide the book within the folds of his robes.

*

He was out of his mind.

At least, that's how Evard felt. The power of the book had coursed through the air so strongly that he knew he needed to take it. His master's power seemed weak and inconsequential in comparison. It had to be his. Logically, he knew his master would notice the book missing, but he didn't care. He would deal with the consequences when they came.

As he made his way back to his chambers, he felt a soft droning sound in his ears. He ignored the noise and halted outside his door, ensuring no one was around when he pulled the brooch off and became visible again. The power to be undetected was an addicting thing. Evard had to remind himself of his self-control. He pushed the door open and saw two guards and his master standing within.

The guards rushed forward. One grabbed him and pulled him in the room while the other quickly shut the door. Releasing his grip, the guard struck Evard on the back of his head and knocked him to the floor.

The room started to spin, or perhaps it was just his imagination. He heard his master berate the guard, but he couldn't make out the words. They sounded distant and muddled. He forced his eyes shut and tried to get his bearings back. When he opened them, the guards were gone.

"You *fool*!" his master whispered harshly at him. "Did I not command you to keep unnoticed? The council knows you are involved in the dark arts."

Evard began to feel his grip on control fraying within his hands. How could he have been caught? He used the brooch; it wasn't possible anyone had seen him.

"Clever toy you found yourself," his master remarked, nudging the item with his boot. "But it will not save you. I told you I would not be able to aid you if you were caught. They are going to execute you. That is the repercussion of betraying the Order. That is not my problem, but you have put me in a serious dilemma. I saw you take the book, as did Shalareven. He will destroy it ... you know I cannot allow that. Give it to me."

Many thoughts rushed through Evard's mind with that last statement. He couldn't possibly give the book up, not now that he felt its power in his hands. He would not allow himself to die here, which left only one option: he had to fight. He would die for the power of the book. It was a last, desperate move. He wasn't even certain it would work. And he almost regretted it.

Almost.

Evard stood up slowly and reached into his robes. Pulling out the dagger, he lunged at his master and attempted to stab him in the chest.

Etrix grabbed Evard;s's wrist with his right hand, and using his left, he slammed his palm into his apprentice's elbow. A loud *crack* echoed off the walls and Evard dropped to his knees, but to Etrix' surprise, he did not cry out.

"Your treachery knows no bounds!" Etrix snarled. "You could have been one of the strongest. Such a waste ..."

Evard glared up at his master. His arm was throbbing with excruciating pain, but he would not allow the agony to show on his face. Whispering a few words, he aimed his good arm toward Etrix and unleashed a fist-sized ball of red flames. His master deflected it into the wall with a deft wave of his hand. Clenching his teeth against the pain, Evard got to his feet, sliced the wrist of his injured arm, and hurled the dagger into the air.

As soon as the blade left his hand, he covered two of his fingers in the blood coming from his wrist and ran his thumb over them. Too slick, it took two more tries before he produced a *snap*. The blood stretched, elongated, hardened, and turned a deep onyx color, forming a crude blade.

The dagger he'd thrown missed its mark, flying past Etrix's head, but his master's attention was off of him, which is exactly what Evard wanted. He flung himself at his master and drove the blood-formed blade into the left side of Etrix's head, right below the temple. The magical weapon shattered as it entered his flesh, and Etrix produced an unholy shriek.

Evard scrabbled across the floor and snatched his chest from under the bed. He lifted the lid and pulled the spell book and crystal out just as his door flung open and snapped off the hinges. A figure covered from head to toe in dark gray stormed into the room, the two guards that Etrix sent outside close behind.

"You are a crafty one," the psionicist said. "There are very few who can hide their thoughts from me. Drop what is in your hands and surrender yourself."

Evard lifted the red crystal and held it into the light. He could see some sort of creature suspended at an awkward angle inside it. Crafted by the only malevolent race to survive the Eradication, demon stones were semi-precious minerals enchanted with the darkest of magic to hold a lesser fiend in confinement. Once freed, it was supposed obey a single command to earn its freedom.

"I said drop what you are holding."

Evard hoped everything the merchant said about the items he bought was true. He tossed the crystal into the air and watched it shatter as it struck the floor. The room was bathed in a blinding red light. Evard stumbled backward, shielding his eyes against the brightness. It slowly faded, revealing a grotesque creature with red and black marbled skin. A demon.

"Kill them!" shouted Evard.

The demon killed the two guards, and Evard bolted out the door with the books and dagger. He could hear the beast battling the psionicist behind him. While he wanted to see the demon's rampage, he knew it was too risky to wait around. Etrix had told him the council knew, so it was only a matter of moments before the entire academy was in pursuit.

He pinned the brooch on and hastened down the hall toward the main courtyard of the academy. Where could he flee to? He wouldn't be safe in any of the neighboring cities. Not only was he in trouble for practicing forbidden magic, he was now responsible for the deaths of five people, one of them a master of the council. And he certainly couldn't go home. Not only would they be sure to look for him there, he never saw eye to eye with his father anyway.

Evard had no friends, and little money to speak of. As he stepped through the main gatehouse, he noticed the guards were absent from their posts. He smirked to himself as he considered how the council would react knowing he had walked out of the front entry.

With nowhere else to go, he set his mind on the only place he knew would be safe for him: the Ruins. He was taking the first steps on the path that had only just begun.

*

Shalareven looked upon the gruesome scene and could not hide his revulsion. Four bodies littered the room and blood was splattered from the floor to the ceiling. He stepped out of the room into the hallway as the rest of the council members arrived. The group of men looked over the room, then turned their attention to the council leader.

"How did an apprentice …" one of them spoke up, but his words trailed off as he seemed to be at a loss.

"Do this?" Shalareven finished. "Any number of ways, to be sure. I am inclined to believe he had some sort of device or artifact easy to activate. Evard was a promising student, but I am doubtful he can cast magic of any real power. He was not here long enough to learn anything reserved for those higher in rank."

A small contingent of guards entered the hall and approached the council members. "There is no sign of him on the grounds. Your orders?"

Shalareven glanced into the room. "Clean this up. And forget the traitor. He is of no consequence. To us, or anyone else for that matter."

He prayed he was right.

THE END

Go for the Gold
Jeremy Hicks

The man squinted against the morning sun, not knowing if it would be his last time to take its familiar cycle for granted. He would appreciate it more had it been shining over his shoulders rather than in his aging, sleep-deprived eyes. He could stomach it better if *his* familiar cycle hadn't been disturbed. The combination of camp food and slow, sickening days of rattletrap travel on the war wagon left him in need of a good shit.

He felt bloated in the chainmail hauberk, the only armor in his limited inventory that would accommodate his growing gut. His fondness for beer and sweet foods proved an obstinate enemy during his extended span of inaction. This season proved to be his first campaign in almost two years, the result of an injury that had ended his storied days as a scout and field archer.

Now, he was back to the front despite a ruined back, a bum knee, and limbs that betrayed him more than any friend or cohort. Ignoring the parade of officers before their staggered line of battle, he focused on relieving the tingling and numbness radiating down his shield arm. The man rolled his shoulders, relishing the bits of relief that radiated out from them into his neck and arms. He imagined the *pops* audible to those around him, but no one seemed to notice over the talkative young bloods and the various reactions of veterans like him.

Survivors really, he reminded himself. *And richer for it*.

Countless fresh fish flooded into the weir of perpetual warfare, steered by the stream of generational poverty. It wasn't as though most veterans were blind to it anymore. It was that they didn't have a choice. Years of battle, bloodshed, and sometimes downright butchery took its toll on a mind, body, and soul. Yet those were mere moments in a sea of time.

The vast majority of his service involved backbreaking labor, from setting up and striking camps to digging entrenchments and latrines with the same pickaxe intended to double as a sidearm.

How long could one zone out staring at the blood-stained wood handle of a tool that excelled as a skull-crusher? *Not long*, he thought, recalling the sting of the whip on his back the last time he made that mistake in the presence of a Sergeant. *Not often, either. Pain is the constant reminder. Constant companion. I don't even need to see the scars to know that they're still there.*

"Gonna to go blind staring off into the sun like that."

"Huh?" The man turned in the direction of the commenter.

Blinking twice, he recognized the bent shape of an even older veteran than himself. He knew the face, but the name eluded him. Instead, he remembered the time they survived a cavalry charge together, armed with only bows and pickaxes. The man could have sworn the other archer had died under a warhorse's hooves, but it seemed his memory was going faster than his knees.

"I said, you're going tah—"

"I heard you. Wasn't thinking 'bout the sun. More like *my* son. If I survive, I get to go home to him. For a bit. Then it's hop another war wagon for another pointless war."

"Could always beat your spear into a plow as they say."

The man laughed at the bent veteran's suggestion.

"Soil back home won't grow anything but hay and winter wheat. Reaping and selling that to a mill will keep food on the table. Won't clothe a growing boy, though. Much less provide him any sort of future. Least if I die here, my kid gets a payout that will change his life forever. For the better."

Mercenary life hadn't always offered that kind of guarantee. Generations of warfare had left little more than widows, orphans, and mad, mangled veterans. Peasant levees had taken their toll, leaving entire counties subject to labor shortages that left crops to rot on their stalks. Finally, the solution arose out of necessity. Lords with more gold than manpower laid out formal laws for the creation of professional military companies. If a life of sellswording didn't hack it for the families of mercs, their handsome life insurance policies of gold sovereigns would ensure they didn't succumb to starvation, homelessness, and more loss.

"Just the one kid, eh?" The old man cackled, his throat dry enough to cause him to cough. "Me 'n the missus had seven." He bent farther, coughed up something chunky, bloody, and then inspected it.

"Had?"

The white-haired vet spat another gory glob onto the ground before he said, "Plague got two. Food poisoning another. One was a damn fool and followed me to the front once. Once."

A sigh of lament and downcast gaze completed his thought.

"Why I want better for mine. Why I'm here to fight." The man said, before echoing the other veteran's sigh. "Once more."

A third veteran approached the bent man, handed him a potion vial, and fell into line between them. His beard was streaked with gray but still the color of smoky flames. His eyes proved intense, the color of the sky itself.

"Going for the gold, eh? That's a damned man's approach."

The man squinted again and shifted his gaze back to the old timer. "Who's your friend with the bat ears?"

"Bad ears? No, Yorin here hears better than a hound. Bays twice as loud when I bed him, too. Just don't tell the missus."

"Hush," Yorin said, blushing a shade of crimson. "You'll have to pardon this rascal. Baylor is terrible at introductions. Terrible liar, too. The missus knows all about me and is happy to have help with the kids. Not like grandpa here can do much without his Go-Juice. Other than make more kids for us to raise."

"Now you hush it," Baylor said, dropping the empty vail into the grass. He straightened himself and stopped leaning on his spear. "You want me to be able to make it across the field, right? At least let me die out there than in the bed at home."

"Would that really be so bad?"

"Yorin, we've discussed this. I ain't got time to learn a trade.

Nor the energy. Nor the inclination. I'm a fighter. I fight."

"Going for the gold, too, then, old friend?" The man asked.

"Aye, but this damn fool won't let me go alone."

"That's smitten fool to you. One who intends on seeing you home, be it alongside you in the war wagon or on your shield. The family deserves to be able to say good-bye properly."

"Lucky," the man said, and he meant it. "Besides my son, I've got no one left at home waiting on me. My parents joined The Lumen and disowned me because of my mercenary lifestyle. So, you won't see me engaging in sunworship anytime soon."

"Son's mother dead?" Yorin asked.

"No, she took the boy and went home to her parents when she thought me dead. Couldn't blame her. I was in a prisoner camp for months and then it took me damn near another year to get home."

"Didn't you ask her to come home?" The old man asked, peering around his lover.

"Asked? Ida told that bitch tah come home!" A freshie remarked from the front row of their lines. Both young and old laughed and added their own vulgar assertions about how they'd handle the man's situation.

"Hey!" The man said, tapping his spear on the back of the other soldier's helmet. "Hey, loudmouth!"

"You talkin' to me, brother." The younger man turned to the veteran. He smirked when he looked down at what appeared to him to be a sagging, out-of-shape old man in a sea of fresh-faced recruits. "Or should I say granddad."

The man sighed. "Yeah, I was. Thought you could use some advice on how to carry your shield properly."

"What? Whaddu mean?"

"Well, lowering it when you turn like that is the real bitch." The man struck hard, fast, and only once. His shield slammed against the younger man's. The loudmouth stumbled backwards and landed in a pile of horse dung left behind by the Tribute

Wagon on its way to the rear guard.

The disarray of their lines went from raucous to near riot in an instant. The shit-smeared loudmouth stood but tripped over his own spear. Another peel of laughter rolled through the ranks. The veteran realized he had carried things too far when their horseplay drew the attention of a cluster of their officers.

The man winced at the blow of the brass whistle. The piercing sound penetrated his brain, eradicated any rational thoughts, and sent his body rigid. He snapped to attention out of habit as much as anything, muscle memory triggered by nigh on a lifetime of conditioning.

Whistles, horns, and drums played a pivotal role in training his body to operate in environments where his mind feared to tread. The experience started with the pre-dawn reveille horns of a mercenary camp, first heard when he was considered old enough to shovel manure, dig latrines, and cook breakfast (all with the same unclean hands) for two copper pieces a day. Later on, drums taught him to march as well as draw and loose in unison. Finally, whistles became both savior and boogeyman for him. The right bird call to the camouflaged crossbowman watching your back could save your life, whereas the tinny sound of an officer's whistle could make you want to shove it down their throat or up their arse.

"What's that mean, eh? Go for the Gold?" The spearman to his left asked. Instead of listening to the shushing around him, he repeated his query.

"It's merc terminology. You are a merc, right, kid?"

"C'mon, man. Don't freeze me out like that. I'm not like that rude little prick up front there. Isn't my first time, either."

"No?"

"Nope. This will make my second charge across an open field in less than a year. All for that silver. But now I'm hearing there's gold involved. Sign me up! I'm not looking to do this forever."

"Don't worry about it. You won't."

"Grim much. Fine. Don't tell."

The man surveyed the approaching officers, but they didn't seem to be in any particular hurry now that the men had fallen into line. Mostly. *Woe be unto those still out of formation when they arrived,* he thought.

The knights scrving as their officers looked like ornately armored assholes, but they weren't just *any* ornately armored assholes. With few exceptions in his experience, field officers were cruel but cowardly minor nobles relying on the protection of their family's crest and an array of sellswords. Some behaved as if they could get away with anything when it came to disciplining a commoner, even a mercenary. They could afford to pay the blood money to any surviving family time and time again.

"If you're still talking when the brass arrive, you may get to Go for the Gold without ever making another charge."

"What do you mean?"

"I mean, the gold we're talking about is the twenty sovereigns paid upon the final termination of a mercenary contract. If you Go for the Gold, it means you're ready to cash out."

"So final means 'deceased,' got it?" Yorin added, chiming into the conversation once more.

"Bruv, I know what termination means. I'm rural, not dumb."

"Pardon me, Mr. Hayseed-Knows-Things. Does that mean you know we could've been talking about robbing the Tribute Wagon? It's the pipedream of every merc and foiled retirement plan of more than one fool who tried it."

"Rob the Tribute Wagon?" The spearman laughed so hard that he snorted. "You'd be cutdown before you escaped with a single chest."

"Unless you steal the whole wagon. Not so smart, are we?"

"Why don't the both of you shut it, before—"

The whistle kept the man from finishing his thought, much less his sentence. As he snapped to attention, the pain in his left knee flared. He gritted his teeth and pivoted back and forth between the soldiers on either side of him. He planted his spear and leaned to his right, hoping to alleviate some of the fresh agony without drawing any further ire from his superiors.

The last thing he needed today was some privileged jackass in his face. Among his peers, he could take as much shit as they could shovel and fling it right back. It felt different raining down on him from above. It irked him. It irked him like little else.

The man felt that if he was willing to fight and die for someone they could at least shut up and either lead, follow, or get out of the way. That attitude had not made him popular, but it had earned him respect…and whip marks, lots of whip marks. Knowing when to draw the line had kept him alive and fighting for going on two decades now.

Today, however, was different. Fatalism hung like a fog. Something about the past few years at home, something about having succeeded in ensuring his own family's lineage survived, and something about having hundreds of cutthroat sellswords at his back emboldened him. At that moment, nothing about him felt common. Certainly not his suffering.

Despite the debilitating pain in every joint, his instincts and training told him to straighten his back and stand at attention. The approaching officers would want to see perfection.

Instead, he took a knee. He winced and sat back, leaning against the shield of the soldier behind him. He sighed and straightened the offending limb. The knee popped, sending fresh agony radiating into his hip and ankle.

"What in the Nine Hells are you doing?"

The man looked up into the youthful face of the speaker. The kid's wide, innocent eyes filled with terror at the blatant breach in battle protocol. No one sat without orders. No one rested without permission. No one died (officially) without orders. The freshie knew enough to know that the man's move meant trouble.

"Taking a break, kiddo. Knee needs a minute."

"Are you insane? You're going to get us both flogged."

"Maybe. But not today."

The whistle blew again. Close at hand this time. The man turned his head, glancing over his shoulder. He shut his eyes against the morning rays once more and cursed. He reminded himself that his so-called superiors had been the ones to position their army to charge into the rising sun.

"Goddamn idiots." He cursed under his breath. The man stood because he chose to this time, not because of the whistle. He paid more attention to the popping and cracking of his knees and ankles. Focused on the pain, he ignored the instrument.

"Do we have a problem in the ranks? Do we have to postpone the entire battle to beat some discipline into you fools? All you have to do it point a stick and run across a field! Is that too much to ask of you simple-minded spear jockeys?"

The officer who addressed them looked resplendent in his gilded breastplate and gem-studded helmet. The noble man was the embodiment of entitlement, privilege, and casual cruelty. The finery worn beneath his arms and armor were worth more than the man would make in a season of campaigning. To the man, he was the model of every problem with their society.

The man staggered past the rank in front of him, eliciting a fresh outburst from the officer and the squire at his side. He forced himself forward, but no one opposed him. In fact, the freshie who smelled of dung moved like a door on a spring hinge. A quick glance behind him ensured the man that the young blood had fallen back into line. Last thing he needed was a literal knife in the back. Mercenaries were not known for their loyalty.

"Halt right there, dog!" The squire stepped between the man and his knight. "How dare you—"

Dropping his spear, the man punched the mouthy little brat. The squire's overbite proved a bloody liability to both, cutting noble gums and common knuckles. The silenced noble spat teeth and gore rather than swallow them. The veteran let the fresh hell shooting through his arms sharpen his senses and tighten his muscles. Between the increased pain level and the vocal reaction of the troops, the man hadn't felt so alive in years.

During his recuperation, he had grown wooden and allowed himself to be shaped by external factors, like the toys he whittled for his son. That ended here and now. He would no longer be someone's toy soldier to be used until broken and then cast aside.

"Have you lost what little mind you had left, insolent peasant! I will have you flogged until there's no skin on your torso for striking my squire. An offense to one noble is an offense to all. Now, bow to your superior and prepare for your punishment!"

"His blood might make him a noble. His position might allow him to issue orders to me, but I say this loud enough for all to hear: Every man on the line is *his* superior. We're the ones who pay the price for his honor, his house, and yours!"

Each step brought the man closer to the befuddled knight. Fear, confusion, and anger collided in the nobleman's brain. The man saw reflections of his own fear and anger there, only there was no confusion. Not anymore. Even with the whistle blowing in his ear, he advanced on the real enemy.

"Yet to you we are dogs! To be whistled at, beaten, abused, and forced to fight our neighbors. For risking *our* lives to secure *your* fortunes, we are tossed a handful of silver, like scraps from master's table. No, sir! I will not stand for that. Not anymore. If we are dogs, I say we are dogs-of-war. And we dogs will have our day!"

The piercing shriek of the whistle stopped once the man's bloodied knuckles made contact with the officer's throat. His steel gorget was designed to protect him from the slash of a sword or an archer's arrow, but it made the perfect strike plate for the enraged veteran's hammerlike blow. A final discordant note escaped the instrument as the knight struggled to breathe.

He struggled harder to unsheathe his sword, but the man slammed his shield into the noble's upturned nose. The blade tip slipped the scabbard, but skipped along the vet's sturdy links of chain. The man caught hold of the narrow wrist of the frailer built officer and stared into his widening eyes. Confusion gave way to comprehension once the vet returned the knight's sword to its new sheath.

"Ah, yes, I see it in your eyes. You understand now, but I've been there. Steel in the gut is no way for anyone to go. Too bad we both learned too late in life to right our course. Tell our creators I'll see them soon. They have much to answer for."

A slight twist and gentle push ruined the knight's liver. The broad blade tip exited his back below his breastplate. His life fled faster than his blood spilled onto the field. The noble shared the one thing all men rich and poor enjoyed, a final breath before death. For once, the man relished it.

If he did not act, and act soon, it would all be for naught, though. The time had come. *Time to Go-for-the-Gold in the most improbable of ways. One suicidal charge is as good as another.*

He eyed the badges of office required to make his dream work, sword and whistle. Both were symbols of everything he had come to hate. Today, they would be the keys to his destiny, either a prosperous household—the kingdom all men sought—or Kingdom Come, the destruction most found while pursuing it.

Tossing the shield aside, he checked the line of battle once more. No one intervened, even if they thought it to be the right course of action. Without orders and leaders, his unit remained cohesive and static, but for how long?

Like a drawn bow, all it had to do was be aimed and loosed, but before the shot was lost. The true test of an archer was to know when to take his shot. The man had lost an eye, along with his position as a bowman, but he had not lost his instincts.

He crouched as low as he could, cursing his barking knees and aching back in the process. Though he loathed touching it, he plucked the whistle from the ground. Rising with a groan, he ignored the painful protests from his body. Instead, he focused on the sword stuck through the knight's gut.

Despite having used many different swords in fierce melees where one snatched whatever weapon was available, its wire-wrapped handle felt uncomfortable, even alien in his hands.

Unable to afford proper gauntlets, or chain gloves for that matter, the silver wire irritated his calluses and reminded him this single weapon cost more than his entire arsenal. Still, it had a power about it, being a symbol of knighthood, nobility, and leadership.

The man hoped he could channel this power long enough to affect the desired result, the dream of many a mercenary who'd traversed the war wagon trails that crisscrossed their fractured continent. The Tribute Wagon held their prize, enough gold to buy off a foreign army if its forces proved superior. With that amount, anyone fortunate enough to escape with it could write the destiny for them and their next several generations. One chest might be enough. That's why so many mercenaries had spent time on the trail hatching half-baked schemes to rob it. The Tribute Wagon's contingent of guards and masterwork lock had thwarted many would-be thieves over the years.

No one had tried to take the wagon itself, despite many old-timers suggesting it. He knew of no one foolish enough to propose using the entire mercenary unit to accomplish it. That sort of solidarity among the sellswords would be laughable without the right tools to compel them to follow the man in front of them, objective be damned.

Now, the man held them aloft for all to see.

"Whaddaya intend on doin' with those, sonny?"

The grin on the old man's face told him he already knew.

"We're going for the gold! All of us!"

Without giving anyone a chance to shout down his madcap plan, the man pursed his lips around the whistle and blew a series of commands. These commands passed to the horn players who relayed it to the drummers. The cadence of a quick march set the pace for their unit. Officers from other units, far down the line of battle, hastened to echo a call of battle they'd missed.

He went from spearman, to officer, and finally to marshal. The confusion triggered a battle still in the process of negotiation. Infantry units hastened to follow the pace set by his unit. Across the field, the enemy responded with their own musical commands.

Archers from both sides milled about confused, awaiting their own orders.

His unit's position on the right flank provided the position necessary to make a run at the Tribute Wagon possible. The noise and chaos of the men-at-arms on their left allowed him to issue a set of signals specific to his unit. A series of oblique movements masked their shift in objective. Their original target lay far across a field of sweetgrass, while the new one was close at hand.

His pain level built with every bone-jarring step, he gritted his teeth and whistled for a faster double march. Waving the sword overhead, his gaze shifted between his men and the Tribute Wagon. If any of those on his side had reservations about their new leader, they dared not slow down long enough to object. The mass of men and steel behind them ensured it.

Friendly banners and the ruse of a flanking maneuver obfuscated their mutinous intent. His unit maneuvered within twenty paces of the Tribute Wagon before any of the guards showed signs of worry. Of course, by that time it was too late.

A trill from the whistle pierced the air, followed by dozens of thrown spears. A few soldiers hesitated and threw late, but conditioning overcame any sense of confusion. Their spears fell among the wounded and dying one after another.

He was pleased. So far, anyway.

The men left on their feet would fight to the death. After all, they had nowhere to go. The Reaper awaited them one way or another. Any guard's failure to secure the Tribute Wagon was tantamount to stealing from it oneself.

He crashed into the first guard to cross his path. Spots passed across his vision as fresh sensations of agony exploded all along his left side. His opponent fell backward over a downed comrade, leaving himself exposed. The man ended him with a single stab.

The next guard proved more of a challenge, but the man dispatched him with little more than a cut across his forearm for his efforts. The muscle reflex of blocking without a shield proved fruitless and sanguine against a swordsman. Thankfully, the enemy's blade was duller than a butter knife. If he lived to see the next sunrise, he imagined the bruise would be worse than the cut.

The mattock swing to his blind side caught him unawares. The leather shoulder guard absorbed some of the impact, but the force of the blow drove him to a knee. Something popped. He roared. Screaming away the pain didn't help him to stand, so he drove the sword's tip into the foot of an enemy whose face he had yet to see.

He blocked a second swing with his bleeding arm. It provided more protection against hammer than blade, but only because his hand caught the mattock's handle. His enemy drew back, providing the leverage necessary for the man to regain his feet. At this point, he realized he was fighting two guards and not one.

The first guard to strike him with a hammer worked to remove the sword blade from his mangled foot. His mattock lay too far away to be of any use to either of them. The man dropped the whistle and reached for his sidearm.

Before he could draw the pickaxe, the second guard staggered forward to strike. Yorin and his lover struck him first. They hacked at him with the axe heads of their sidearms. A half-assed hammer blow from the dying guard rang against Yorin's shield. To the man, its gong sounded a signal for The Reaper. Another warrior was ready to depart the field. More would join him soon.

The unit fell over them like a murder of crows descending on a nest of coveted hawk eggs. They enveloped the Tribute Wagon and its surviving guards and panicked teamsters. Only the well-secured horses stayed in place amidst the skirmish. The post anchoring them in place, however, jerked with each buck and kick by the powerful animals.

The man seized the closest teamster by the collar and tossed him toward the wagon board. Not chancing an argument with a murderous merc, the wagon handler climbed into the seat and grabbed the reigns. The man clambered after him, slow but steady. Neither bum knee nor shooting pain kept him from reaching his objective, but he fought every instinct to pass out when his aching ass met a hardwood seat with all the padding of a church pew. *A real dagger in the back hurts less*, he recalled.

They achieved the easier objective by securing the wagon. Now, they had to escape with it and survive in the process. His forecast for their success shifted faster than the horses accelerated. Their fortunes darkened deeper than the shade that fell across them. Hazarding a glance, he saw that the weather was no issue. No cloud dotted the sky, much less obscured the sun.

Instead, it was arrows. Hundreds, maybe thousands of them.

With the whistle gone, there was no way to signal the unit. Few of them noticed the deadly missiles in enough time to cover themselves. Arrows thudded around them, felling most of the surviving mercenaries.

With no other shield at hand, the man improvised. He seized the wagon driver and drew him across his body. Arrows that would have slain him killed the teamster instead. The broadheads from close calls nicked his exposed arms and legs, and the fresh wounds brought fresh pain.

He hugged the arrow-riddled corpse and screamed into its shoulder guard. His breathing grew shallow and ragged. His pulse quickened as his heart imitated a hummingbird's wings. He gasped like the last fish in a drought-stricken lakebed before pursing his lips and blowing. He imagined the whistle was still there, imagined its commands fueling his actions once more.

The man groaned, cast aside the ruined meat shield, and grabbed the reigns. A sharp *snap* set the barded horses into motion. Hooves the size of dinner plates dug into the field, jarring the Tribute Wagon into motion. He guided the team in as tight a turn as they could make and headed for the bridge at the rear of their perimeter. Picket men would guard the span, but he doubted they would be able to stop six barded warhorses and an armored wagon at a full gallop.

Nothing can stop us now. Us, he lamented, casting his eyes behind him. A hundred men charged the Tribute Wagon. Less than a third their number followed it toward the bridge. They kept a tight formation, shields over their heads, but arrows stole more men's lives with each passing minute.

Yorin lay on his back, eyes wide at the sky. The man wondered if he saw The Reaper there beyond the clear blue. Arrows pierced his ruined form. The old man held his beloved comrade, weeping for him as if he'd lost a bride.

They locked eyes across the chaos caused by the wagon's flight through the camp and rear guard. The old man smiled a mostly toothless grin. He raised one clenched fist. The veteran returned the salute and watched as another rain of arrows carried the old man to be with his lover.

Blinking back tears, the man focused on the bridge, the final obstacle to an escape from their perimeter and a chance at making off with the entire hoard contained inside the wagon. They had to make it far enough, fast enough to be able to find a way inside and divvy up the treasure.

In less than the span of time it took to cross the bridge, fate—and the four pikemen arrayed at the bridge's far end—found a way. The man planted his feet at the base of the wagon board and jerked the reins. His muscles screamed as the leather snapped tight, but the horses had too much momentum and nowhere to go.

Pikemen and barded draft horses collided in a gory scene of steel, blood, and viscera. The man saw no more than the initial clash. Once wagon met horse flesh, he leapt from his seat. The force carried him over the side of the bridge and into the water.

He disappeared under the surface. The light faded. The man fought numbness and cold, along with the current, but the chainmail shirt threatened to drown him. He struggled until his boots met river bottom.

Standing in the mud and blinded by the silt, he slipped the armor over his head. Invigorated by the cold plunge, the man blew out the last of his air and kicked off the bottom. One boot slid free, a small sacrifice to break the surface.

The man gasped for air. Then he gasped with surprise once he realized his newest peril. Debris rained from above. Parts of the ruined guardrail struck the river around him, but it was the Tribute Wagon that had his undivided attention. From here, he thought the top-heavy conveyance was resting at a crazy angle.

No, not resting. It's pitching? Nope. Shit! It's falling.

The man knew rational thought had fled when he worried about the word choice of his inner monologue. Retreating inside his own head would result in a watery demise, so he retreated into the river's cold embrace. He forced his numb, pain-filled limbs to work with the current and fought to hold his breath while his teeth chattered against his lips.

The Tribute Wagon hit with the water with the force of a mangonel stone. Blind, half-drowned, and thankful to be alive, the man broke the surface again. He shook water from his eyes in time to see a four-legged figure strike the river in front of him. Followed by another. Then another.

His screams mixed with terrified neighs and whinnies. Hooves of helpless horses, some wounded by pikes, churned the water and threatened to smash his skull. He raised a leaden limb to respond, but the hoof of a doomed horse caught him with a glancing blow. The man reached for a floating piece of guard rail.

Blackness claimed him, along with the river.

When the man awoke upon a shining shoal, he mistook it for the Elysian Fields or some other such incarnation of a golden afterlife. He felt out of place, having been a killer longer than he'd been an adult. Perhaps the old tales of meads halls and golden fields awaiting warriors were indeed true.

Gold!

Coins, ingots, rings, necklaces, and myriad more golden treasures sparkled in the midday sun. Broken strongboxes littered the far side of the shoal, closest to the whitewater. The man observed a single intact chest. They had been designed to float despite the weight of their contents, but not to withstand the force of the rapids and rocks. Their dragon horde's worth of gold had washed ashore on the shallow bend of the river.

The whiny of a dying, half-drowned horse broke his reverie. From his position, he could see that at least one animal managed to escape the carnage at the bridge. Impaled on a tree fallen across the upriver end of the shoal, the animal's lifeblood mingled with the water and the source of the shine. The man rose to his feet, fighting the streak of blinding pain that ran from the nape of his neck to the tip of his left foot. Like the horse, the man wondered if their watery escape had only prolonged his agony.

Cries and clangs in the distance, far beyond the dense treeline at the river's edge, told the man two things. First, the battle had yet to be decided. Second, he had to behave as if headhunters were in pursuit.

Regular deserters were treated harshly enough, but he had committed a litany of capital offenses. If he survived long enough to meet the death penalty, it would be public and slow, grisly and gruesome. As grim as the prospect seemed, the man preferred it to time, entropy, and fate doing the Reaper's job.

He vowed they would have to catch him unawares to take him alive, because he wouldn't let them use him as an example. The man was done being a pawn. Surrounded by what he needed to buy happiness, to purchase security for his family, to live above anyone's law, he lumbered toward the chest.

He rolled his shoulders, relishing each pop in his neck and upper back. He cracked his knuckles and then did a quick inventory. His weapon belt and its pouches remained, but his sidearm was gone. The dagger worn at his back held fast, a plate of metallic ore ensuring it didn't slip from its sheath. The weapon, a product of dwarf forges deep in the mountains, had been worth the money. It had saved him, fed him, and even cleaned his toenails on occasion.

Now, it would make him rich. Its tip made quick work of the chest's ruined lock without suffering the slightest burr. He kissed its silvery blade and returned it to its home. The merchant had told him it was a custom among the stout folk. He had kept the tradition even after finding out it was a marriage tradition for exchanging knives from one clan to another. Either way, he felt it honored the smith, the laborer who made such a tool possible.

Setting eyes upon leather bags within the chest, he vowed then and there to kiss the smith, too, should he ever be fortunate enough to meet them. Their labor, his risk, and the sacrifices of countless comrades led him to this moment. Arthritic fingers and shaking hands fumbled to untie the first sack.

Seeing nothing at first, he sidled around the chest. The man cursed when he banged his sore knee on the sharp corner of its open lid. He cursed again once the sun struck the Sovereigns filling the bag. The same foul word was born of polar opposite emotions. Pain and frustration gave way to hope and joy, of possibilities beyond a different day and a different battlefield.

To hell with rich, the man thought, *I'm wealthy!*

Then he sighed, realizing the effort of lifting and carrying one bag would be difficult enough. He might make it with a second bag, if he tied the tops of two bags together, but the risk of injury and capture would be great, especially in his haggard state. There was no way he could transport all three, not with one dying horse and part of a fallen tree. Even a healthy horse and sharp axe, he had no time to make a travois.

If other mercs had made it this far with him, how much could he trust them to not want more than their fair share? Without the labor of others to exploit, the man settled for a chance at rich.

Even as he left the river with a single bag, he acknowledged that his chance would be slim. Securing the gold now did not equate to keeping the gold. Escaping today did not mean escaping the reach of aggrieved noble families and their bands of roving headhunters.

He vowed to flee fast, far, and with his family. In a new land, with a new name, they would find a fresh start for a more prosperous life. He fixated on those thoughts—rather than his sore shoulder and the burden it carried—and gathered his remaining strength. He found his center and then his bearings.

The man headed into the wilderness for the slow trek home.

THE END

Servant of Blood | Servant of Fire
David Jones

"How many times have you made the Loop?" asked Kelysen.

"More'n I could count. Been trading from Cross Over back here to Brandy Pine for close on ten years now."

They sat in the common room of a slant-house inn situated above the Balanth's Blade river. Dusk had passed away into a clear and bitter-cold nightfall that drove the townsfolk to their homes and cast the room in dancing pallid shadows.

Shadows the vampire Kelysen used to his advantage.

Brandy Pine, like many villages this far west, was small and peopled with farming families, river fishers, and lone trapmen who harvested the thick surrounding forests for skins. Few people traveled the north roads leading to Cross Over, Bluff, and Fair Bluff during winter, which accounted for the few guests at the town's only inn. Besides Kelysen and the merchant, there was one other couple, a man and his lady wife seated at a table in the far corner.

She smelled of a spiced perfume rich with lilac, he of a peach powder so popular among lesser lords these days. They chatted in low voices about their only son who had wed the Duke of Vanceth's third niece several nights ago. Kelysen might have taken more interest in them had it not been for the fat merchant he'd found just after dusk, breathing hard from climbing the inn's stairs, with food and ale on his little mind.

Kelysen lifted his wineglass to his mouth, let the noxious pink liquid brush his upper lip, then placed it back on the table. It was an insufferable charade, but kept the innkeeper quiet. Kel waved the young serving girl to their table.

"More ale for my friend," he said when the ashen-skinned girl came near.

"Very good," she said. "And will m'lord be having more

wine?"

"No. Only ale and anything my friend here might wish to eat."

The merchant smiled, revealing a mouthful of yellow and brown teeth. "Most kind of you sir. It isn't often you meet a person with charity in his heart on this road, 'specially this late in the winter." He turned to the serving girl. "A bowl of that stew I smell cooking and whatever bread you have that's not molded."

The girl nodded and looked to Kel who dropped four silver draggets on the table. Her eyes widened as she reached for the proffered money.

Kelysen's hand moved faster. He took her by the wrist and held her fast, staring into her eyes, holding her gaze as surely as he did her body. The girl blanched but couldn't look away.

"These should keep the ale flowing for the night I think," said Kel.

The girl watched Kelysen's pale gray eyes, her tongue working in her mouth though no sound came forth. After a moment he released her and she hurried off to the kitchens, tucking the coins into her apron pocket.

The fat merchant seemed not to notice the exchange. He slurped down the remainder of his ale from a heavy pewter tankard and slammed it down on the table, empty. It was his fifth so far since Kelysen invited him to the table.

"You were saying you've made the Loop many times," said Kel, "Aren't you afraid of the dragon?"

"Bah, her ladyship doesn't care a whit about merchants going by. The barons here and up at Cross Over have a long-standing pact with her. The red bitch loves horseflesh, you see, for gods know what reason, so every three months each town sends a boy to lead a nice stallion up to her lair. In return she don't bother people on the Loop. 'Course most people go the long way up past Fair Bluff, pact or no pact. It's the feeling you get up there on Mount Bryson, like something's looking down, waiting to make a meal of ya. But I don't mind it. Keeps my competition away."

"Then she doesn't hunt the mountain?"

"I've never seen her. A few of the old timers say they seen her once or twice, but them's mostly stories I says. I expect that old red hasn't stirred out of her gods bleeding hole in many a year, 'cept to eat horse meat that is."

"Two horses every three months? Seems a pitiful diet for a dragon," said Kelysen. "Especially one so large as the stories make Stynaserian."

The serving girl arrived with another tankard of ale, a bowl of steaming stew, and a plate of fresh bread covered in melted butter, all stacked on a tray. She placed them on the table and hurried away without a word or look for either man.

Once she was gone, the fat merchant took up his wooden spoon and set to shoveling stew, thick with animal fat, into his mouth. Much of the viscous fluid dribbled down his chin in brown rivulets, dropping onto his gray travel shirt. Kelysen did his level best not to sneer.

"It's said that dragons eat little, 'specially in their old age. Mostly they just sleep away their days, for months at a time, or so I've heard. And the Red Queen on Bryson is for certain old. Can't say as I know all that much about lifetimes 'o dragons, but she crushed ole King Bryson's castle, and his gods bleeding army, near eight hundred years ago. From what the bards sing she was the biggest red any man had ever seen even back then." The merchant swilled a long draught of ale and wiped his mouth on one corner of his cloak. "I expect eight hundred and more is old for any living thing."

Kel touched the wine to his pink lips then held his goblet before him so that the fire light passed through, changing it from pink to red. He swirled it and watched the wine ripple. Yes, eight hundred years was indeed old for any living thing.

"And the Red never harms the boys they send to deliver the horses?"

The merchant shrugged, "Not that I've heard tale of. I expect she's smart enough to know that would break the pact, or maybe she has no taste for man flesh."

Kelysen grinned, feigning embarrassment and said, "Sorry for all the questions. It's just that I've never been so close to a dragon. I know all the tales of Stynaserian. I could name each knight that sought to slay her over the last thousand years and how they died."

"They each died the same, lad, badly. And no bother for the questions. Seems every young man I meet on this road asks me about the red. I think all young men dream of seeing her in the flesh. But it's a fool's wish. Old men like me have the wisdom to leave her ladyship alone, else we wouldn't have lived to be old men." The fat merchant slapped his belly and chuckled.

Kel smiled and fingered his goblet. "Are you spending the night at the inn?"

The merchant dropped his wooden spoon on the table and took up the bowl in one meaty hand. "Aye," he said, before upending the bowl into his mouth, sucking the last bit of stew from it. When he had finished, he dropped it on the table and belched.

Kelysen placed his wine goblet on the table as well, forcing a deadpan expression. Wasn't he sometimes messy with his own meals? Perhaps he could extend a bit of professional courtesy to the repugnant merchant, at least for the nonce.

"How many horses did you say you had for the trip round the Loop to Cross Over?" he asked.

"Six. Four for the wagon and two for trade." The merchant picked at a swollen red sore on his fleshy jowl. "Were you interested in buying a mount?"

"Yes. Mine took lame several days ago and I've been stranded in this little river town ever since. I'm afraid I'm getting desperate to leave. I've seen enough slant-houses and waterwheels to last me a good long while." Kelysen watched the merchant's eyes.

The fat man chuckled, heavy snorts that issued from his ample belly. "I know that feeling. You seem a city-bred lord if I haven't lost my touch for marking young men. I should think these little hamlets a bore to you. But horseflesh isn't cheap this close to the dwarf mountains, what with winter coming on full now."

Kelysen nodded, an expression of regret on his pale face. "I thought to have an adventure, traveling along the Balanth's Blade from Lord Kellan's manor in Elmswood. But it's turned into a near calamity. I was forced to leave my favorite saddle in the woods some leagues away and kill my poor chestnut. Luckily, I was still following the river and it led me here."

"Lucky indeed," said the merchant, "There's many a wild animal in these mountain woods, not to mention wild men. A finely dressed lad such as yourself would be a plum target for the river brigands round this part of the Loop."

"I thank the gods small and great," said Kelysen, raising his goblet in toast.

"Indeed," said the merchant who raised his fresh tankard.

"Would you be willing to show me the mounts you have for sale?" asked Kelysen.

"Why certainly. Shall we meet at sunrise?"

"I would be most grateful if you would show me now. I have no wish to stay another night in this hovel. I'd prefer the open road."

"It's a might cold and dark for traveling don't you think m'lord? And besides, I haggle better by morning light."

Kelysen nodded to the now half-empty tankard, "The ale should keep you warm, to be certain. And the stew."

The fat merchant smiled, but there was no kindness in the expression.

"Charity and bribery walk a close path, my father used to say," he drained the last of the ale and rose. "My horses are next door in that stinking pit they call a stable. Shall we have a look, *my lord*?"

They descended a rickety stair to the banks of the river. The merchant picked his way slowly in the darkness, feeling for every step with the toe of his boot lest he slip upon the thin, white crust of ice coating each plank. Kelysen followed him in silence, sure-footed in the icy darkness.

Further inland from the tavern, whose back end rested upon thick poles set in the river, stood a long, low building made of thin boards which served as the town stables. The silver moon, called Brenner, after the goddess of love and family and healing, shone out of a clear sky, catching the clapboard stables in a cone of milky-white light, revealing to Kelysen its rickety walls and thatched roof.

The merchant was right, Kelysen could smell the musty scent of horse flesh and moldering horse manure from the inn's stairs. As they approached the little building it became almost overwhelming. The fat man drew a kerchief from his britches pocket. By the sight of the yellowed material, Kel wondered if it could smell any better than moldering horse shit.

The merchant entered a side door on the eastern face of the long building. He led Kelysen amongst the stalls of horses who whinnied and tossed their heads when they caught sight of the two men in the darkness.

"No guard?" asked Kelysen.

"Bah, in a little hamlet like this?" The fat man stopped in front of a stall and gestured towards a young gelding who tossed his head in greeting. "This is my best. Had 'em since he was a colt. Took a saddle the first day with nary a buck. His sire was owned by Prince Brallenor of Denholm who only allowed him to stud three times. You are looking at the third of the studs, and the strongest I'd say."

Kelysen regarded the horse for a moment. It was strong as the merchant said, but not worthy of a prince nor even a baron of low birth. It was full grown and not much taller than a pony.

"A fine bit of horseflesh," he said.

The fat man smiled in the dark. Kelysen could feel the heat from his body as the merchant began to warm to his trade. It floated in the steam coming from his mouth and coursed through the pulsating veins in the merchant's meaty neck and face.

"Here is another fine mount. Not so young and strong as the gelding there, but we can't all be royalty." He petted the speckled gray paint's nose. The mare moved forward, eager to be rubbed.

"What of your drafts?" Kelysen asked.

"The other four?" The merchant turned to face Kel, who was merely a deeper shadow against the back wall.

"Aye, and your wagon. Where is that?"

"Why would you want to know that?"

Kelysen stepped forward. His pale gray eyes flashing in the darkness. "I would know."

"My wagon is hitched in the back. The drafts are those we passed as we came in." The merchant stepped back from Kelysen as if he could hide behind the mare's head. As an afterthought he added, "I hired a man to sleep in it, under the tarp. Paid him well to guard."

"Did you? That was very smart. There are all kinds of thieves about."

The merchant swallowed and said, "If you want to buy one of these horses, I'd be glad to make a deal of it for ya, seeing as how you lost your mount and all." His skin was white in the darkness and his hand upon the mare's neck trembled.

Kelysen moved closer, stepping out of the semidarkness into a cone of silver moonlight passing through gaps in the ramshackle roof. The merchant could not look away from those pale gray eyes. They shone in the darkness like twin stars.

"Go, pay your man what you offered, then order him away. Hitch the wagon and make ready to depart."

The fat merchant's will folded like dough before Kelysen's demands. He hurried from the stables at a near run.

*

They drove north along a dual-tracked path mostly grown over with black briers and wild grass, the merchant's strong gelding and old paint hitched to the back of the wagon. No signs marked the way, and they passed no villages, nor homes of any kind. The Loop wended its way ever upward across Mount Bryson, hemmed in on all sides by dense forest. Miles passed with only the sound of the wagon, and the soft clop of hooves. The drafts pulled with their heads down, steam rising from their mouths. The merchant did little in the way of guiding them or urging them onward. He sat silent beside Kelysen, reins held firm in his large hands, swaying with the gentle movement of the cart, his eyes never leaving the road.

The silver moon passed overhead, clear and bright and small. As it disappeared behind the canopy of firs and stark gray oaks lining the road, it's larger twin, the red moon, Nyssor, mounted the heavens. Kelysen watched the dull orb rise above the canopy, a crimson circle hanging low over the world. Upon the center of its face, black and mottled, was the wound of a meteor strike. The scorched crater formed a perfect circle of burned rock that gave Nyssor the appearance of a huge red eye passing through the cloudless night.

It was named for the Night Lord, Nyssor, bringer of death, sickness, and rot. Nyssor, Kelysen's only master. The only god he had ever served in nearly nine centuries of life.

Yes my lord, watch me this night. The strength I gain shall be for your glory.

Hunger gnawed at Kelysen's mind. It wasn't the ancient hunger for food in his belly, which he had known as a young man so many years ago, but the relentless tug of a want so immediate he likened it to the undertow of the sea. He felt it all the more as Nyssor rose directly overhead. Its red glow lit the forest, tinting the darkness a pale crimson, as if every tree, every leaf, dripped warm, succulent blood. From the corner of his eye Kelysen watched the merchant and willed himself to sit still as stone. It wouldn't do to kill the man, not yet. If the Red Queen sensed anything, Kelysen hoped it would be the fat man, and horseflesh. And besides, Kel needed the hunger tonight. It was sharp as a razor's edge, and it made his senses just as sharp. He hadn't taken blood in three nights and the ache was palpable in his breast.

"Tell me when we are closest to Bryson's castle," said Kel.

The fat merchant nodded. "Not long now."

Another mile passed away and Kelysen noticed that the night sounds had ceased. He could sense no animals in this part of the wood where before the forest had been befouled with the stink of deer, wolf, lynx, and rabbit. But here there were no animal smells. The night air was quiet and black.

The fat merchant reined to a stop. His horses whinnied, stamping their hooves and tossing their heads as steam poured from their flared nostrils.

"We're 'bout level with the castle ruins now," said the fat man without looking at Kelysen "If'ing you should travel cross country through the wood, due west, you'll happen upon it."

Kel dropped from the wagon and untied the gelding. At first the young horse snorted, his ears flattened, and he made as if to bite, but Kelysen snatched up his halter and looked the animal in the eye. After a moment the gelding settled and followed Kel to the front of the wagon without further protest.

"How many miles west?" Kel asked, looking up to the fat merchant.

"Only about one or two I'd say, though I never ventured out there 'afore." He glanced at Kel but looked away quickly.

Kelysen placed a gloved hand on the merchant's arm. The shock of his touch locked their gazes and the merchant quaked in fear.

"Please let me go home to my wife."

Kel could see her in the merchant's mind. A fat and ugly woman who had filled the man's house with seven children. But though he considered her ugly, the merchant loved her with every fiber of his gravy filled heart, for she was kind and gentle and longsuffering.

"Remember nothing," Kelysen whispered, holding the man's gaze.

The merchant gave his horses rein and the wagon rolled away, creaking and groaning, the sound almost offensive to the night's silence.

Kelysen placed one cold hand on the gelding's forehead, touching its bestial mind, calming it. He led it into the forest, whispering a silent prayer to his god that the dragon would be sleeping when he arrived. If not, he must convince her that the gelding was her peace offering from one of the neighboring townships though the appointed date was still weeks away. With any luck her hunger would outweigh her doubt.

Thick undergrowth and layers of dead leaves grabbed at Kel's boots but could not slow his steady progress. Nyssor's great, red eye hung low over the forest, as if his dark majesty were intrigued with Kel's quest. Its red glow might have done little for a human in the depths of the forest, but it revealed much for Kelysen's preternatural eyes. He followed the star called Juda's Hammer, a blue-white speck in the sky, due west, weaving in and out of gnarled trees. After several minutes, he beheld a clearing ahead, bathed in Nyssor's light.

The gelding snorted and reared, kicking out his fore-hooves, his brown eyes rolling.

"Quiet beast," Kel whispered. He raised a gloved hand and the horse stilled, though he remained skittish. Kelysen lashed him to a nearby oak, making certain the knot was tight, and trudged ahead.

Across the clearing, which was long and wide as a wheat field, he could see the tumbled down remains of an ancient wall, with the rubble of other stone edifices beyond. Portions of the wall remained, several ancient parapets looming up in the moonlight, but most of it had fallen into ruin.

No trees grew near the wall. The earth was scorched for many yards in a long, sweeping arc. The ground was bare dirt and ash, with only a few fire-blackened trunks and scorched boulders dotting the expanse. Stynaserian might be old, but she was no fool when it came to guarding her lair.

Kelysen crossed the burnt land faster than the human eye could have seen, his leather boots barely touching ground, raising only small puffs of ash with each step. But there were no human eyes to see; no living thing save the trees and Kel's horse. He wondered if even ghosts remained in this cursed place.

Kelysen crouched in the shadow of an arched entrance, only half of which remained standing. Beyond lay stone rubble heaped against a bare face of mountain granite. In the center of that debris stood a cave entrance high enough to accommodate a mountain troll, and wide enough to swallow a pirate's galley.

Kelysen dashed to the entrance, making no more sound than a fox, and leaned against the granite lip of the cave mouth. Heat wafted from the opening, bearing with it the smell of sulfur. Underlying the sulfurous smell was another scent, something Kelysen had never experienced. It was a living smell, something akin to that of the great lizards he'd once seen on the Jevian Islands, beasts that tore men apart in packs like wolves. Yet this scent was keener, more compelling. It seemed to call to Kelysen, to the hunger that swelled in the center of his being.

The cave was pitch dark. Though Kelysen's inhuman sight was powerful, it could do little to cut through the inky blackness. Fortunately, Nyssor favored him this night, for the red moon's wan light stretched pink fingers into the cave. Weak as it was, it nevertheless picked out the cave's rough contours. It showed Kelysen that the tunnel didn't narrow. It progressed straight for hundreds of yards, dropping in a gradual slant. Quickly losing the light as he moved deeper into the cave, Kelysen slid his fingers along the wall to keep his bearings. Taking measured steps, his every sense keen for danger, he plunged into the darkness.

No sounds of bats flapping their wings or adjusting their perches came from overhead, nor the skittering noise of insects or vermin racing along the floor. But that didn't mean the cave was silent.

A deep, sibilant sound filled the darkness ahead. It rose and fell, rose and fell like the blowing of a house-sized bellows. Kelysen followed it, his leather boots silent on the cave floor, until he rounded a slight bend and saw a flame flicker for several seconds before winking out. A circular patch of the cave floor, directly below the flame, glowed orange. By its weak light Kelysen perceived a forelimb—a clawed reptilian hand large as a mountain pony bejeweled in crimson scales. He squinted into the darkness and could just discern the double arches of a snout, each nostril as big around as a pumpkin.

Nyssor was with him, the red beast slept!

For several moments Kelysen stood still in the blistering hot cave, watching the huge dragon slumber. She was larger than he had imagined—at least sixty feet measured from her snout to the tip of her tail. Membranous wings, colored black and gray, folded down from just above her forelimbs to wrap around her back, which was crowned with large, bony spikes. A horn, crimson to match her scales, protruded from the dragon's head like the ramming beak of a ship. With each exhalation, a gout of flame flickered from Stynaserian's nostrils, licking the stone beneath her head.

Slow as winter coming, Kelysen drew forward, step by step, following the contours of the cave wall as far from the dim, orange light as possible. His eyes traced the curves of her form, noting the way each scale fit into the next, like links in a fine chain. They were the red of fall leaves, shiny as if wet, shaped like thousands of plates stacked one atop the next. They appeared thinner than the steel plate men wore to battle, but Kelysen knew they were stronger.

At first, he thought his trip might have been wasted. Her armor was perfect, not a scratch, not a blemish shone on her crimson coat. But upon closer inspection, he noted irregularities in her scales. Some were smaller than others and not just on her limbs and near her eyes. Along her left flank, near the jut of her belly, were several scales shaped the same as the rest, but miniature in comparison. They left no gap, but Kelysen could see where the dragon had suffered a wound and the scales had grown back misshapen. He moved closer, feeling the heat off her flank, searching for more.

Kelysen found what he was searching for along Stenesarian's

neck. Two hand spans worth of scales had been ripped away as if by a claw, exposing a line of pink flesh. Dragons were known to be territorial, often staging titanic battles whenever a rival dared infringe upon their land. Kelysen hadn't heard of any such recent dispute, but then he had no idea how long it might take a dragon to regrow her scales. Considering their longevity, it might be decades before the red's injury would fully heal. Not that it mattered. Kel had found what he was searching for.

The blood thirst came on him then. Pain blossomed in his breast, in his throat, in his mouth. His fangs extruded in a frisson of ecstatic anticipation. The need for blood was almost as thrilling, as tantalizing as the taste. And Kelysen wanted this blood like nothing he had wanted in his entire dead existence.

Lips parted, fangs exposed, Kel crept from the shadows. The hunger screamed for him to act quickly, but he resisted its call. He hadn't come this far to end up burning like a living brazier. Tentative as a deer taking food from a hunter's hand, he laid his palm upon the sleeping dragon's neck. Heat radiated through his gloves, warming his ice-cold fingers. Slowly, Kel pressed his lips to the exposed flesh, which was soft as a maiden's breast. The dragon's skin was so hot he feared at first it might ignite his lips, but the hunger kept him in place. He pushed forward, lost in the heat. Blood scent tickled his nose until it became his entire awareness. With a soft pop only he could hear, Kelysen's fangs broke through the skin.

And then came the blood.

A torrent of liquid fire filled Kelysen's mouth like molten honey. It poured into him, through him, over him, the taste somewhat like human blood, except more metallic, heavy with iron, and saltier. As always when he drank, Kel's own dead heart sprang to life, beating a jubilant tattoo against his sternum, exultant in the wellspring of life it had found.

Kelysen was rarely sloppy when he drank, but he couldn't stop Stenesarian's blood from running down his chin, driven in powerful gushes by a heart many times larger than a man's. Its sound filled his ears like rolling thunder.

For the first several moments, Kelysen feared the dragon might wake, but then that fear passed away, replaced by blood and heat. They filled him like a pitcher, quenching the hunger as it had never been quenched. His heart fluttered in his chest, it too burning like cinders. Even his fingers and toes, ever cold as ice, tingled as the sweet warmth poured through him.

Once, as a child, before that whore who called herself his mother had left him, he'd been playing Sword and King with several other boys behind the brothel. An older boy, Thomar, had said he knew of some hot springs up the mountain path. Kelysen's mother was apt to stay the night in the brothel with little care for her son's whereabouts or safety, so he had agreed to the trip without hesitation.

The water bubbled up, yellow with sulfur, belching heat and a foul smell from several shallow wells. The boys stripped and eased themselves slowly into one of the larger pools. It was almost unbearable at first. Kel had grimaced, biting his lips to avoid yelping in pain. Once in, they lay very still in the bubbling water watching first the silver moon and then its red twin mount the starry heavens. Kel found that, so long as he remained perfectly still, the water didn't burn. He floated in it, lost to the sensation of pleasure bordering pain, thinking that if he could, he would stay there for eternity. The night's cold couldn't touch him, and for the first time in his life darkness held no fear. There were no forest sounds, no sound of the other boys chatting. There was only the blessed heat, and the sweet steam filling his lungs.

Kelysen, the boy, had awoken from pleasant dreams of warm, embracing darkness, and realized he was weak. The heat had made his limbs heavy and his head dim. He had pulled himself from the pool, his naked body steaming in the cold night air, and fell gasping in the dirt. He lay there half the night, the other boys long away to their homes in the little valley hamlet. When he opened his eyes to gray morning light, Kelysen had found himself naked and dirty. He had wanted very much to dip back into the pool, to let the heat wash him clean again, but something told him doing so would be the end of him. He left the steaming pools to wait by the brothel door, shivering in the mists until his mother would come out.

The dragon's blood was like that sulfur spring. It enveloped him, washing away the night, the cave, the long, lonely years of blood and the stench of death. He drank and drank, more blood than he had ever consumed even on his busiest nights in the back alleys of Selerous and Laewaes.

At last, he could take no more. He lifted his head from the bloody flesh and found himself dizzy, a feeling he hadn't experienced in hundreds of years. Kelysen stumbled backward against the granite wall and slid to the floor, steam rising from his skin. He watched it swirl up into the darkness, like wispy clouds on a windy night.

He tried to rise, but his arms were too heavy. Morning had come, he could feel it, though no sunlight penetrated Stynaserian's lair. He must rise, he must run, but he could not. Kelysen lay in the darkness, his eyes closed, listening to the Red Queen's steady breathing. Pleasant heat burned in Kel's chest, urging him to sleep, assuring him that all was well. He was safe, enfolded in the warm darkness. No harm would come to him.

Kelysen resisted for as long as he could, but in the end the darkness took him.

*

When he awoke nothing had changed. The dragon lay before him, sleeping in the same position as before. Kel sensed that the day had passed, and night returned, though he wasn't sure how many days might have come and gone.

He rose, silent as shadow, and drew a long, slow breath. A smile spread his lips as his mind came fully awake.

Vast rivers of new strength flowed through Kelysen's mind and body. He heard Stynaserian's slow breath as before, but now he could number her teeth by the sound of the air passing between them. He could hear her heart, and the sound of her blood gushing in a steady rhythm through her veins. Reaching out, he touched the fearful thoughts of the gelding still lashed to a tree outside the dragon's lair. The poor creature was hungry and thirsty. He wondered when the cold master would return and give him sup.

Focusing, Kelysen found he could reach far beyond the mountain fastness. He bent his mind across the leagues to a small village called Cross Over. The fat merchant whose name he'd never asked was there, drunk again, this time on strong summer wine. He didn't remember why he'd made the Loop during the night, but he must have had a good reason. Perhaps he was chasing after that missing gelding.

Kelysen allowed himself a smile, but didn't laugh audibly, remembering that her ladyship lay next to him. He had no hunger for blood, it seemed the red's fire had quenched that annoyance, but he wanted to test his new strengths one by one. Brandy Pine would be a fine place for some sport and it was near to the Red Queen's lair. The thirst might not be on him now, but when it came, Kelysen planned to feed it more molten honey.

He started for the cave mouth, picking his way carefully in the near pitch darkness, moving with newfound ease, his limbs exuding strength he would not have imagined possible before tasting the Red Queen's blood.

The dragon's breathing, which had become a background noise for Kelysen, stopped and the vampire froze in place, his black heart throbbing in his breast. Kelysen flattened himself against the cave wall and stood motionless, his pale eyes staring back at the Red Queen.

Stynaserian raised her head on her long reptilian neck, her eyes two golden orbs floating in the darkness.

"Blood thief." Her voice was not so harsh as Kelysen might have expected. It was huge, but feminine.

He stood silent.

"I see you, though your skin is much darker than last night when first you stole into my lair." Red and yellow flames issued from the dragon's snout as she spoke.

Seeing no alternative, Kelysen stepped away from the wall to face Stynaserian. Could she burn him faster than he could run? He didn't want to find out. Perhaps there was another way.

"You saw me last night?" he asked.

Her laughter shook dust from the cave's roof, though it was only a chuckle.

"Have you a name? Or shall I call you only my blood thief?"

"Kelysen."

The Red Queen hoisted herself up on mighty scaled legs thick as ancient oaks, and strode forward, her step light for such a massive beast. Kel remained still, watching the dragon's eyes for any hint of an attack.

"Kelysen...what a beautiful name for a night creature." She lowered herself back to the stone floor within striking distance of Kel. He didn't know if a dragon bite could kill him, but he felt certain being chopped in half would. One bite from her ladyship would accomplish that feat easily enough.

"Then you were awake when I—"

"Fed? Oh yes. It was. . . soothing in a way. Dragons often shed blood during certain, shall we say, social interactions. I was pleased with the amount you took. And quite surprised. Do most of your kind drink so much at once?"

"I wouldn't know." Kelysen felt his heart beating hard in his chest, still animated by the queen's blood. It was a teasing mortal fear that threatened to overcome him.

"Nonetheless, it was a good amount. Even more than I'd hoped."

"What do you mean? More than you'd hoped?" A new fear crowded its way into Kelysen's mind, one he dared not examine too closely.

Stynaserian's thick lips pulled back from her pointed teeth in a serrated grin. "How long do you suppose it takes for dragons to grow new scales, Kelysen?"

Heat welled in Kelysen's chest, spreading quickly to his head, feet and hands. Blood sweat broke out on his forehead, his upper lip, his palms. Oddly, the feeling was hot and pleasant, as if he were still lapping at the queen's neck.

"I don't know," he said.

"It is long, no doubt in that, but wounds heal, even for dragons." Stynaserian stretched her neck until red and yellow flames from her snout licked at Kel's tunic. He wanted to run, but stood still, quaking. "Let me ask you another question, perhaps easier for you. How long do you think it has been since last I met one of my own kind—battle or otherwise?"

Kelysen understood. Perhaps he had known since before he heard the great beast stir in the darkness, but he answered anyway. He had no choice.

"Since before the fall of King Bryson, when you slew his armies and his family and took this mountain for your own."

"Many, many years ago. Longer than you've lived perhaps?"

Kelysen shook his head, "No, but close."

Stynaserian turned her head, exposing the gash where he had fed on her exposed neck. Dried blood covered the wound, but he could smell the fresh, hot liquid just beneath the surface. His thirst returned then, mild, but insistent.

"It hurt to rip them away," said the Red Queen. "I'm afraid I may have scarred the surrounding scales a bit more than I intended, but it made the wound look convincing, didn't it?" She turned back to face him, her golden eyes finding his pale gray ones.

Kelysen swallowed, staring into those golden orbs, large as a grown man's head. His thoughts raced. He tried to flee, but his body wouldn't comply. All he knew was the hunger and those giant, golden eyes.

"Why—" His tongue stuck to the roof of his mouth and no more words would come.

"There are so many delightful spells that can be cast with dragon's blood," said the dragon, her long tail swishing behind her like that of a cat. "But one aspect they all share is...beguilement."

"What have you done?" he managed to whisper.

"I have chosen you, my blood thief."

Kel tried to speak further, but again his words caught in his mouth as if his tongue were shackled.

"Be a good pet and bring me that nice, young horse you have tied up outside," said the Red Queen. "After that, I'll let you hunt a bit before dawn, but then you must return to my little cave. I wouldn't want the sun to find you afield."

Kelysen turned on his heels and started for the cave mouth. Once outside he beheld the red eye of Nyssor cresting the canopy west of the clearing, watching him like a jaundiced eye. He tried to escape, to run away as fast as his unnatural strength could carry him, but it was no use. He crossed the burnt clearing with all haste, frightening the gelding when he approached. He calmed the beast, unhitched it and led it toward Stynaserian's lair.

The gelding tried to bolt when it caught the dragon's scent, but Kel pulled it down by the halter and cuffed it soundly on the side of the head. It fell to the stony ground, still breathing, but unconscious.

He lifted it in both arms, its weight like that of a small child to him, turned and found that the Red Queen was waiting at the cave mouth.

"You are strong from my blood, Kelysen," she said, her voice low.

He placed the gelding before her and backed away as she began to feed.

"Yes my Queen," he said, without intending to say that at all.

The red dragon swallowed an entire haunch of bloody horse flesh and regarded her new minion for a moment.

"Strength has its price, doesn't it blood thief?" she asked.

The vampire bowed his head, the red moon shining down upon him, and wept blood-stained tears.

THE END

The Greater Good
pdmac

Cormun peered intently at the four gnomes sitting in his dining room, sipping their ales and talking gravely of the challenge ahead. Each one, still in the flower of youth, was strong and full of magic. Suddenly, he felt very old, which made sense because he *was* old. Just a bit past 400 years old, old enough to remember even older folks when he was a youngster who claimed they had met Jebido Bolthead, the gnome responsible for connecting the floating islands.

But that was so long ago that no one remembered what it was like to live on isolated islands, unconnected by stout bridges. It wasn't until Ynys Denligh started to sink that folks suddenly remembered their history. Not that it would actually help, but it was a start to remembering that gnomes really *do* stick together. When life gets tough, so do gnomes.

At least that sounded good.

Unfortunately, remembering gnomes stick together didn't necessarily mean *all* gnomes stuck together. When the so-called 'scientists' decided that magairite was needed to stop the island from sinking, the search for volunteers was, um… embarrassing. It wasn't until Skeeter, that brave young gnome, stepped forward that another five volunteered, himself included. He resented the skeptical glances and outright jeers when he volunteered. Yes, he was an old gnome. But it didn't mean he couldn't be a valuable part of the team. He had the wisdom and patience of age. And he also had an airship, and it was his airship after all that got them to Ynys Malfor.

Cormun chuckled at the memory of them arriving at the island, supposedly a place of headhunters and evil creatures, only to discover the residents were halflings more afraid of them than they were of the halflings. But that was a secret better kept that way. After all, Skeeter's life depended on it.

Yet the jeers and mocking had bothered him that day until he reasoned that their taunts were rooted in their own insecurities and cowardice. After all, he was an old gnome who wasn't afraid of a little danger. Were he a young gnome, he'd be embarrassed too if some wizened old gnome stepped forward when others quavered in their boots.

"You awake there, Pops?" Nimble grinned. "You were fading there for a moment. Can't have that if we're gonna do what we gotta do."

"I was merely contemplating our situation," Cormun harrumphed. He was about to add, "And don't call me 'Pops,'" when he thought better of it, for he realized that he actually liked being called 'Pops,' but only by these four young gnomes, for it implied an intimate connection between them that no one else could ever share. And it also implied his position as leader of this group.

"So, what have you come up with?" Nimble yawned and scratched his head.

"How long has it been since we returned?"

"A couple of months," Jerbo answered, wanting to get back to Ynys Muhr with the other forest gnomes. Not that he didn't like it here, but he was getting bored coming over here and sitting around wondering what to do about Skeeter. And Ella Waywocket was on Ynys Muhr, and who knew what other young gnomes were vying for her attention while he was wasting time over here. Sure, she said she was his girlfriend, but she was starting to fuss at him for coming here, wanting to know what was so special that he had to come here. It was hard to explain that these were his friends, that they had been on an adventure together and there was a bond there, something she wouldn't understand.

And things were different now. When they first came back, there were the usual celebrations with speeches from the island burgomasters, followed by feasting. Gnomes love a good excuse to eat and drink. But the fact that they didn't need the magairite after all, along with Skeeter's absence put a damper on the festivities. Yes, they had more than their fair share of attention and invites to various social events to retell their adventures, but after a couple of weeks, the excitement faded, and it was business as usual. Except for Skeeter's folks who placed a tombstone in the cemetery in honor of their son.

Jerbo let out a frustrated sigh, wishing they knew the truth about Skeeter, about his bravery, how he sacrificed himself for the good of all the gnomes.

"I say we just sail back over there and bring him back," Torgil stated, giving voice to what the others thought. "It's no good seeing Skeeter's folks all sad and everything, knowing that he's still alive."

"We've been through all this before," Warvyn huffed, staring at the tall gnome, known to be both brave and reckless. "We gave our word. Besides, we'd still have to get the magairite to take back."

"We all know where it is, Warvyn," Nimble replied. "In storage with the rest of the minerals, in a warehouse right here in Neeth. How many times have we walked over to see if it was still there?"

"Too many," Warvyn sourly said, scooting away from the table to stretch his legs. "I mean, we've been over there so much that they see us coming and say, 'It's still here. Go away.' It's not like we can just waltz in there and say, 'Hey. We'd like our magairite back.' And if we steal it, we're gonna be in big trouble."

"Whatever happened to 'Us gnomes stick together'?" Nimble argued. "We've been moping around here ever since we got back. I say we go for it. It's time to rescue Skeeter."

"While I agree," Torgil said, "it's not like we can just sneak away. Someone is bound to notice."

"We'll have to leave at night," Cormun announced, "which means we need to get enough supplies for the trip there and back." He saw their wide-eyed looks of surprise. "If we really believe it when we say, 'Us gnomes stick together,' then we can't leave Skeeter there. We *have* to rescue him."

"About time," Nimble exclaimed with a fist pump. "So what's the plan?"

The four younger gnomes all looked at Cormun.

"Like I said, we need food for at least ten days. We'll need fuel for that long too."

"What about the magairite?" Warvyn said.

Cormun slowly nodded. "We have to steal it back."

"It really shouldn't be that hard," Nimble said. "It's not like there's roving guards on the warehouse."

"I got an idea," Torgil announced, causing the others to twist their heads to gaze expectantly at him. "What time does the warehouse close?"

"They close at six," Nimble answered, "so they all can get home for dinner."

Torgil nodded. "So, on the night we're going to leave, after we've collected and stowed all the supplies and stuff, all of us will go to the warehouse around five-forty-five. We're there because we want to learn if there are other minerals better than magairite or some other excuse like that. The key thing here is to get them distracted enough so that they don't see one of us hiding somewhere so that he'll be locked in there when they close the building for the night. All he has to do then is get the magairite then unlock a door or window and sneak out. Once we get the magairite, we beat feet back here, load up, release the mooring lines and sail away." He folded his arms across his chest, quite proud of his plan.

"And who's gonna be the crazy one to stay behind and steal the magairite," Jerbo half-grinned until the others turned their heads to stare intently at him. "Why me?" he whined.

"Because we just voted that you be the one to stay behind," Torgil replied.

"I didn't hear a vote," he complained.

"Should've paid attention," Torgil answered, settling the issue.

"Um," Nimble interrupted. "How are we going to fill the airship envelope with nobody noticing? It took us near a whole day the last time we filled her.”

“We fill her up starting tomorrow,” Cormun said. “Then we take her out a few times to get gnomes used to seeing it flying around or tethered in place.”

“What reason do we use?” Nimble asked.

While Cormun pondered likely excuses, Jerbo said, “Why don’t we just tell them that Cormun’s teaching us to fly.”

“And I’ll hint that I’m considering giving it to the best pilot,” Cormun added.

That seemed a good enough answer, causing Nimble to grin with excitement. “Boy, won’t Skeeter be surprised when he sees us. I’ll bet he’ll be back on board the ship before anyone even knows he’s gone.”

“And then we can hightail it back home,” Jerbo said.

“Uhhh,” Torgil slowly enunciated. “How do we explain to everyone when we get back that Skeeter wasn’t really dead. I think his folks are going to be pretty mad.”

“Not to mention the rest of them when they discover that we stole the magairite,” Warvyn added.

“We tell them the truth,” Cormun said. “Well… at least some of the truth. We had to steal the magairite to go back and rescue Skeeter.”

“Do we tell them about the halflings?” Nimble asked.

Cormun thought a moment then shook his head. “If I were them, I wouldn’t want anyone else knowing about us either. What we tell them is that we all felt guilty for leaving Skeeter behind, and though we believed he was captured by headhunters, we couldn’t be sure, and it was only fair that we went back to rescue him if he was still alive.”

“And we took the magairite thinking maybe we could trade, if he was still alive,” Torgil continued. “Anyway, we can make up a story on the way there. Let’s get this show on the road.”

*

Gnomes being a curious lot, Cormun had just started filling the envelope when the first visitors showed up. By the time it was halfway inflated, Cormun had grown somewhat irritable repeating the fabricated story. Mid-afternoon arrived and the envelope grew in size, as did the crowd of onlookers.

"You'd think they never saw an airship before," Torgil grumbled, looking at the gaggle of gnomes, mostly children with a scattering of adults.

"Watcha doin'?" one young lad asked.

"Making apple pie," Torgil responded as though the answer was obvious.

"Huh? No, you're not," the lad replied, not taken in by the absurd joke.

"But we are," Jerbo said with mock seriousness. "Y'see, once we get the ship ready, we load 'er up with apples." He pointed skyward. "Then we take 'er up a good thousand feet." Using his hands as he described the process, he thrust a finger at him. "Then we hover over the mash pit, right where you're standing."

The lad snapped his head down to look where he stood before taking a quick step backwards.

"We toss down one apple at a time until we know we're hitting the right spot. Then we unload all the apple crates as quickly as we can, and smash!" He smacked his hands together. "They all get mashed up really good, almost like applesauce. Of course we have to scrape out the worms and bugs and bits of dirt and pebbles… and the occasional flattened squirrel, but the result is perfect for apple pie. I think Cormun might even have one left over. You want to try a piece?"

The lad's eyes popped wide and he rapidly shook his head only to realize the surrounding laughter was at his expense. With his lower lip protruding, he spun around and marched off, determined to tell his Mom that they were making fun of him.

"See if you can do that with the rest of them," Nimble

whispered.

"We're not going anywhere today," Cormun groused once again at the crowd. "Go home."

It was dark when the last doubting stragglers finally accepted that nothing was going to happen and wandered on home.

"What happens tomorrow when they all show up again," Jerbo complained.

"Let them," Torgil replied. "Guarantee after a week or two of us just flying around, they'll all get bored and go home.

Two weeks later, he was almost right. There were a few diehard older fans of airships who were quite content to perch their chairs out of the way and watch the ship take off and land. Armed with snacks and drinks, they rarely left their chairs except to visit the bathroom or replenish their food and drink. Each evening, they'd merrily wave their thanks and head home. By the third day, they even left their chairs and small tables in place.

Provisioning the ship was not as easy as the first time when all of Gnomedom wanted to be seen as contributing to what was believed to be a suicide mission. Reminding them that this time was different, that they were sneaking away in the middle of the night because they had stolen the magairite to trade back for Skeeter, Cormun explained that it was better to buy just a little extra than a whole bunch at once so that folks wouldn't notice. Dried meats and fruits like apples, as well as potatoes and squash kept well as it would probably take them a few weeks to collect enough food and fuel that would last for the round trip.

Finally, after almost a month of collecting and positioning food and small kegs of ale and water down in the hold, Cormun announced they had enough to start the mission.

"We leaving tonight?" Nimble sputtered.

"Yes," Cormun replied. "You've already packed what clothes you need, and the food and drink are all on board."

"Fuel?" Warvyn asked, suddenly nervous.

"We got plenty of fuel," Torgil answered for Cormun. "It's time we get this show on the road. I, for one, am ready to get this done and over with, and the only way to do that is to go now, tonight."

Four of them turned their heads to stare at Jerbo.

"What?" he squeaked.

"You ready?" Torgil said.

Jerbo nervously cleared his throat. "Yeah. Sure."

*

A pleasantly plump middle-aged gnome looked up from his desk as the five adventurers walked in through the front doors of the Mineral Warehouse. His cheery face morphed to a frown as he shifted an annoyed glance at the time on the clock on the wall.

He leaned back in his chair and folded his arms across his ample stomach. "We're closing in fifteen minutes and it's still here. Go home."

"We know it's still here," Torgil replied with a polite smile. "Actually, we've come to ask a question and Nimble here," he hooked a thumb at his compatriot, "said if anyone knew, you'd be the one who would know."

"Oh?" His irritated frown vanished as he assumed the air of professional minerologist. "What's your question?"

"Yes," Torgil continued. "What is it about magairite and not some other mineral that causes the islands to float. And secondly, how is it that such a tiny amount of magairite has such a large impact?"

"Ah," the gnome nodded with a smile of satisfaction, for magairite was a particular interest of his. "Here then, come with me."

He pushed himself away from the desk in the middle of the large public display room at the front of the warehouse, tucked in his wheeled chair, and ambled over to one of the many display cases that filled the room. Tall windows, by gnome standards, filtered afternoon sunlight that slanted across the cases, floor, and walls. Opposite the front door, a set of double doors led to the main warehouse lined with rows upon rows of shelves filled with storage boxes of minerals, gems, crystals and other oddities, all labeled, categorized, and arranged alphabetically.

The gnome walked over to stand before a display case, the others surrounding him, pretending to be fascinated. Pointing to the sparkling onyx-colored gems, each the size of a thumbnail, he said, "That's magairite."

"We know," Nimble said. "We brought some back, remember?"

"Is that the ones we brought back," Nimble asked.

"Yes," the gnome replied, "some of them. The rest are in the back."

Nimble looked over at another display case and saw a beautiful green stone. "That's an emerald," he exclaimed, walking over to admire the gem. "What's to stop someone from coming in here and taking it?" Cocking an eyebrow, he glanced around the room. "There's just one of you here. You can't keep track of everything on your own. There has to be some kind of alarm that goes off if someone tries to open the case, right?"

"First," he officiously said. "Who would be so foolish to open a display case when there are so many eyes watching everyone here? You've been here before. You know there are more than just me working here. There's at least five of us during the day, but everyone goes home half-an-hour before closing as there's rarely anyone who comes in after five," he emphasized, looking directly at the four gnomes. "I stayed back to lock up. Secondly," he gravely added, "what gnome would dare come in here and steal from another gnome? Gnomes don't do that."

"Yet you still lock the doors," Nimble pointed out, noting he didn't say anything about alarms.

"Yes, well," he harrumphed. "Though gnomes might not steal doesn't mean they won't create mischief. Young gnomes can be quite mischievous when they have a mind to be.”

"You were telling us about magairite and how it works to keep our islands afloat," Torgil said, returning to the topic at hand.

The gnome glanced back at the clock. "I really don't have enough time to explain it all this evening. Why don't you come back in the morning when I have more time."

"Thank you," Cormun said. "We'll do that. Come lads. Let's let our fine host close-up shop so he can get home to dinner." He leaned in and slyly said, "Unless of course he's passing by a pub and happens to pop in for a quick ale on the way home. If he's doing that, we just might pop in with him."

The gnome's eyes brightened, and he grinned. Quickly glancing around, he saw all was in order. "Just let me get my keys."

The four gnomes cast furtive glances around the room, wondering where Jerbo had concealed himself. The warehouse gnome went to his desk, noticing his chair was slightly askew. Ignoring it for the moment, he slipped his hand over the back of the chair and reached down to pull the main drawer out in order to release a side drawer where is keys were. Retrieving the keys and closing the drawers, he repositioned the chair into the kneehole. Had he taken the time to investigate why the chair seemed awkward and heavy, he might have discovered a young gnome wedged in between the privacy panel of the desk and the base of the chair. Distracted by the waiting gnomes, he cheerily waved the keys and headed for the door.

Jerbo waited until he heard the lock in the door before counting to one hundred. Quietly pushing the chair out, he crawled out and slowly raised his head above the desktop until his eyes were able to get a clear view of the front door and the rest of the room. Judging that he was safe, he bounced up and raced to the door to ensure it was locked before hustling back to the magairite display case. His heart sank when he realized he had never noticed the locking mechanism that required a key, securely holding the lid in place.

His first thought was to find something to smash the glass, but that would cause too much damage. Besides, there had to be a display case key around somewhere.

Crossing over to the doors leading to the warehouse, he held his breath and prayed as he tried the door handle. To his surprise and relief, it twisted and he pushed the door open and stepped inside, immediately overwhelmed at the vastness of the warehouse. The only light in the windowless storage area was from the fading afternoon sunlight behind him, casting his shadow on the floor.

To his right on a low table were several oil lamps and a small shallow tray with small sticks of pinewood impregnated with sulfur. On the floor beside the table, the dull glow of coals emanated from a small brazier. With his foot propped against the door, he selected a lamp and raised the glass shade. Selecting a sulfur stick, he opened the brazier door and stuck the stick in, causing it to immediately burst into flame, at the same time emitting that unique sulfur smell.

Wrinkling his nose, he lit the lamp and pulled his foot from the door. Lifting the lamp, he stepped forward to survey the closest shelf, noting the alphabetical arrangement before heading down to the 'M' section.

Several minutes later, he stood before a section of shelving where the magairite, still in the small box of finely crafted silver they had brought back from Ynys Malfor. Quickly retrieving the box, he opened the lid to see the remainder of the onyx-colored gems.

Hurrying back to the front, he doused the lamp, placing it exactly where it was prior then slipped back into the display room and over to the magairite case. He stood rooted in indecision, one part feeling obligated to break the glass and get the last few gems, while the other said to leave it be so that no one would see it was missing. With a little luck, no one would know the rest was missing until they returned with Skeeter. His decision made, he crossed over to the window and waited for the daylight to vanish before crawling out and closing the window behind him, darting back and forth amongst the trees to Cormun's home.

The rest of the team, in good spirits, arrived an hour later.

Cormun saw the box and gave Jerbo a nod of respect.

"Well done, lad. It's all there?"

"Uh… almost."

"Almost?" Torgil demanded. "What do you mean 'almost?'"

"I left the ones in the display case."

"What?" Torgil fussed. "We need it all to get Skeeter back."

"The case had a lock on it, and I'd have to break the glass to get it," Jerbo explained with a bit of irritation. "This way they won't know the magairite's missing unless someone goes back to look for it."

Torgil was about to argue when Cormun stopped him. "He's right. Smart thinking, lad. They come in the next morning, and everything is like it was the night before. No one's the wiser. With a little luck we'll be back with Skeeter before they notice."

"My thoughts exactly," Jerbo said, giving Torgil an 'I-told-you-so' look.

"No more time to waste then," Cormun said. "Everyone take your place. Time to rescue our friend."

With the five gnomes positioned near the railing where the mooring lines were secured, Cormun said, "On the count of three. One… two… three."

Releasing the mooring lines in unison, the ship drifted higher into the night sky. Cormun waited until they were well above the island before telling Warvyn to go below and start the engine. A few minutes later, the engine coughed and sputtered before catching. With the engine running, Warvyn engaged the drive chains to the drive sprockets and soon the propellors whirled, pushing the little ship away from home.

Nimble turned to the others, his face flushed with excitement. "I can't wait to see the look on Skeeter's face when he sees that we came back for him."

*

For five days, the intrepid adventurers plotted and planned their rescue and explanations upon return. They finally decided that the truth was the best answer. And despite the promise to keep the halflings a secrct, they were gnomes and gnomes stuck together.

On the fifth day, with the morning sun filling the sky, Warvyn spotted Ynys Malfor in the distance. Excitement mounted as they impatiently willed the engines to make the propellors spin faster.

The vista looked the same as the last time they were here when Skeeter volunteered to stay behind in exchange for the magairite. Silence settled for a bit as they concentrated on the landscape, a thick forest of pines and hardwoods that came right up to the edge of the island.

"Let's head to the spot where we landed the last time," Cormun said to Torgil manning the helm.

Spinning the wheel, Torgil heeled the ship to starboard, causing the others to grab onto the railing.

"Hey!" Jerbo exclaimed. "You trying to kill us?"

"Sorry," Torgil sheepishly replied to the collective frowns.

Warvyn resumed his spotter's position and twenty minutes later shouted, "There it is."

A wide meadow opened up in the midst of the forest. Wildflowers in reds and blues and gold rippled in the wind. A low split-rail fence edged the side of the island as a reminder that it was a long way down to the ocean below.

As Torgil piloted the ship to hover in the middle of the meadow, the others tossed over mooring lines. Nimble and Jerbo scampered down the lines and secured them to anything immoveable, mostly stout trees. With the ship secured, the others tossed over a rope ladder and joined the two on the ground.

"Let's go find our lost companion," Warvyn exclaimed, hurrying towards the forest edge.

"Hold up," Torgil commanded, causing Warvyn to jitter to a

halt. "Something's not right."

"What do you mean?" Warvyn asked, glancing around.

"Where's the welcoming party? Remember the last time we were here? They knew we were here and made sure that we knew that they knew we were here."

"Huh?" Jerbo replied with a grin. "They knew that we knew that they knew we knew?"

"He's right," Cormun said, suddenly cautious. "There should be a welcoming group or another one of their fake monsters here. It's too quiet." Turning to Torgil, he said, "You take charge. I'll stay with the ship."

Torgil waited until Cormun had laboriously climbed back up the rope ladder. "Let's go. Single file. I'm in front, then Jerbo, Warvyn and Nimble. Keep a sharp eye out."

Torgil led the way across the meadow to the forest edge then worked his way along the edge until he came to a path leading through the trees. The gnomes continued in single-file, warily scanning the surroundings. It wasn't long before Torgil held up a hand and pointed. Through the gap between the trees, they saw several half-timbered two-story houses. Torgil pointed to his left and right, effectively telling the others to spread out far enough apart to provide early warning.

Waiting until the others were in position, Torgil then stepped out into the open and approached the houses, quickly discovering two things. First, these homes were part of a larger settlement of probably thirty to forty houses, all built the same, with flowered shrubs in front and second story window boxes. Second, the flowers in the window boxes had all withered and died, most likely from lack of water. The yards and shrubs were all overgrown and unkempt.

"There's no one here," Jerbo commented, walking up to stand beside Torgil. They were soon joined by Warvyn and Nimble.

"Where is everyone?" Nimble softly asked.

"Don't know," Torgil replied. "Let's find out. We pair up. Me and Nimble will head this way." He pointed to the street to his left. "You two go that way." He pointed to his right. "We'll meet at the other side of the village."

An hour later, the four gnomes stood at the edge of the village on the main road leading out of town, bisecting overgrown farm fields before disappearing in the forest in the distance.

"There's no one here," Nimble said, mystified. "The houses are all empty. There's no food or ale barrels or anything else. Even the furniture's gone. It's like they packed everything up and moved."

"Yeah," Jerbo agreed, "but where?"

"We need to tell Cormun," Torgil said. "Then we need to look some more. An entire village just can't simply disappear."

*

Cormun's lips tightened when told the news. "They must be hiding. Perhaps they saw our ship and hid themselves."

Torgil shook his head. "The town's been deserted far too long. The place is a ghost town."

"Even the furniture is gone," Nimble added.

"They can't have just disappeared," Cormun said, his frown deepening. "Pull up the mooring lines. We have to scour this entire island until we find them."

While Jerbo and Nimble climbed down the rope ladder to untie the mooring lines, Cormun lowered the ship to reduce the tension. Soon, all were aboard, the lines secured, and gnomes positioned to search for life. Cormun kept the ship a little above tree-level, hoping that no one would see them and give early warning.

For two days, they zigzagged across the island, praying for some sign of life. Numerous times they came upon villages, pausing long enough to determine no one lived there anymore. By the third day, their hope had just about vanished.

"We're going to run out of supplies for the return trip," Torgil warned. "Either we ration our food and water or head back now."

Cormun stood at the helm, guiding the airship over the treetops, his face flushed with frustration. They had one day at most before they would have to turn back. Even then, they were cutting it close. But this was crazy. How could an entire island population disappear? He could understand if a plague or something had wiped them out, but then there'd be evidence of that. As it was, it looked like they had pulled up stakes and moved somewhere. And that was what worried him. Ynys Malfor was the only island this far away from the gnome islands. After that, it was all ocean.

"I see smoke," Warvyn yelled, his finger pressed forward.

The other gnomes raced over to see where he pointed. Sure enough, in the distance, a thin trail of smoke curled above the trees to disappear in the wind. Torgil looked back over his shoulder at Cormun.

"Stop here!"

Cormun reversed the engines to slow the airship until it stopped and hovered in place, about twenty feet above the trees. Lowering the ladder and mooring lines, Torgil and the others descended to the ground while Cormun remained onboard. With the ship secured, Torgil led the way.

The four gnomes silently made their way single-file through the forest until Torgil held a hand up and motioned the others to come up. He pointed a finger ahead and they saw the gap in the forest where several houses nestled close to each other. Torgil dropped to his knees and brushed the leaves aside to clear a place in the dirt. Using a stick, he drew a circle.

"Here's us," he whispered, drawing an 'X' outside the circle. He stuck his stick in the dirt opposite the 'X' on the other side of the circle. "Warvyn is here." He then jabbed the stick on the left side of the circle. "Nimble is here. And Jerbo is here." He jabbed the sick on the right side. "I'll give you all to the count of one hundred before moving. Use magic if you have to, but let's find out if anyone is there first."

Nodding in understanding, Warvyn, Jerbo, and Nimble silently slipped away to get in position while Warvyn kept careful watch and counted to one hundred. It was while he was counting that he smelled it, the faint odor of farm animals, pigs most likely. He was at seventy-three when the door to the farthest house opened and an older halfling stepped out into the sunshine.

Unaware of the four gnomes, the halfling stretched and scratched his chin. He wore tan cotton breeches, dark leather boots, a white shirt with the cuffs rolled up, and a vest the color of his trousers. Though his sideburns were thick, the hair on top of his head was thin and white. Leaning back, he halfway turned around and opened the door to say something to someone inside.

Torgil made his move. Gnomes can be stealthy and quick when necessary and by the time the halfling turned around Torgil was twenty feet away. Seeing Torgil, the halfling let out a yelp and raced back into the house, slamming the door shut.

"We mean you no harm," Torgil called out. "We need your help. Please." He saw the window curtains flutter. "We're gnomes. Little people like yourselves. We need your help."

The door cracked open and a voice called out, "Who are you? Where'd you come from?"

"We were here before," Torgil explained. "We came here for some magairite and one of our friends stayed behind. His name is Skeeter."

The door opened and the halfling cautiously stepped out. "Any more of you?"

"Three more with me and one back at the airship."

The halfling frowned and shook his head. "They said you'd be back. We figured it too, but thought it'd be a while."

"Where is everyone?"

"Gone." He twisted his head to the left and right as the other gnomes joined Torgil.

"Gone where?"

"Away," he replied. "Why'd you come back?"

"We came back for our friend," Nimble answered. "We even brought back the magairite to give back."

"A noble gesture," he said with a nod of approval. "Story was that you needed the magairite to save your island. What happened?"

"Turned out it wasn't true," Torgil said, causing the halfling to chuckle.

"If everyone's gone," Jerbo said, "why are you still here?"

The halfling exhaled a deep sigh. "This is my home. Has always been my home. Didn't see the need to move someplace else just because gnomes wanted to live here."

"Who said gnomes wanted to live here?" Warvyn said. "Nobody knows about this island except us."

"And didn't you say you would never come back?" he countered.

"We came back because one of our own was here," Warvyn argued.

"The way I heard it, he volunteered," the halfling blandly stated.

"Where did they go?" Torgil demanded.

"Like I said, 'away.'"

"Where?"

"You all are wasting your time. Your friend made his decision to stay. Now it's best if you all go back home." He turned around to go inside.

"Wait," Nimble pleaded.

"We haven't told anyone about this island. All we want is to bring our friend back home to his parents. They think he's dead."

Surprised, the halfling turned back around. "Why do they think he's dead?"

"What else could we tell them?" Nimble said. "That he sacrificed his happiness for the safety of all gnomes, that he traded his life for magairite, that the only way we get it is if he stayed here because the halflings were more concerned with themselves than the happiness of a gnome?"

Jerbo added, "We promised to keep your presence here a secret. To do that, we had to lie. His parents are still mourning."

The halfling's face softened. "No mother should have to mourn the death of her child. No father either, for that matter." He leveled an intense stare at each of them. "You have the look of honest gnomes."

Nimble stuck his lower lip out and batted his eyelids, making his best pitiful look. The blatant attempt was so pathetic that the halfling laughed.

"You need to work on that," he grinned.

Nimble smiled in return. "It worked on my Mom when I was very young. Hadn't had a chance to improve it since then."

"Will you help us?" Torgil asked.

The halfling inhaled a deep breath. "I'm thinking about it."

The door creaked open then slowly widened before a head peered around the door jam, the cautious green eyes studying the four gnomes. Long silver-gray hair framed her face.

The halfling looked over his shoulder. "It's OK Corellia. They won't harm us." He turned back to the gnomes. "My wife, Corellia. My name is Jerimede."

"I am Torgil," Torgil answered then introduced the rest. "We have one more still on ship, an elder gnome named Cormun."

"Are there others like you," Jerbo asked, "those who didn't want to go?"

"More than you'd think," he huffed.

"Go ahead and tell them, Jerimede," his wife urged. When he hesitated, she said, "They're all taking a big chance. At least we know where we are."

Jerimede nodded and inhaled a deep breath. "They've left for another floating island."

Nimble frowned at him. "Uh, we sort of figured something like that when we noticed all the furniture was missing."

"How far away is it?" Torgil asked.

Jerimede shook his head. "You don't understand. When I say they all left for a floating island, what I mean is, it's a real floating island. It doesn't stay in one place."

The gnomes' mouths slowly slacked open as they stared at the halfling.

"How is that even possible?" Jerbo asked.

Jerimede shrugged. "Don't know. What we do know is that this island travels in a sort of circle. Every five years, it comes close to us. It gets to a certain point then moves away, kind of like two magnets repelling each other."

"How'd everyone get all their stuff across?" Warvyn asked.

"With great difficulty," Jerimede sniffed. "Lots of folks lost a lot of stuff down into the sea. Serves 'em right for wanting to leave."

"How long ago was the island here?" Torgil asked.

"A little over a month ago. The island only stays close for about a week, so it's probably three-to-four weeks away from here."

Nimble turned his head to look at Torgil. "What's that mean in airship time?"

"Don't know. Cormun would know."

"That's assuming we know which direction the island is floating," Jerbo pointed out.

"And how fast it's going," Nimble added.

"We barely have enough food and water to get back home," Warvyn reminded them.

"We can give you more than enough supplies," Jerimede quietly said. "Your problem is finding the island."

"So no one has ever lived on the island until now?" Torgil said with a frown.

"Oh sure," Jerimede said, "folks have lived there for quite a while. It's always a celebration when they come back. But five years is a long time and us halflings don't like being apart for that long, so there's fewer and fewer folks living there… until now."

"If there's been halflings living there," Torgil said, "then wouldn't they have exact locations of the island during the five years it was traveling?"

"Well sure they do," Jerimede said with a lopsided grin. "But all that stuff is on the island. Used to have it here but wasn't much interest in keeping it up since those on the island kept track. Took it with them when the decided to leave."

"What're we gonna do?" Warvyn moaned.

"We do what we set out to do," Torgil asserted. "Remember, us gnomes stick together."

*

Jerimede was good at his word and managed to convince other stay-behinds to provide more than enough provisions, especially water and coal for the airship's steam engines. Two days after they landed on Ynys Malfor, the gnomes were airborne and heading in a northwesterly direction. Cormun zigzagged the ship in a widening fan, hoping to cover more ground, or 'sea' in this case.

With each succeeding day of empty sky and sea, their doubts grew to hopelessness.

"We've been searching for five days now," Warvyn warned, already thinking of how they were going to explain why they had stolen the magairite when they returned home.

"We've come this far," Torgil stubbornly replied. "A few more days won't matter. Besides we have enough food and fuel."

"I bet we've gone farther than any gnome has ever traveled," Nimble encouraged.

"He's right," Cormun agreed. "We're truly adventure gnomes. And just think of what you can tell your grandchildren when we bring Skeeter back."

"*If* we bring Skeeter back," Warvyn mumbled, unconvinced. "Suppose we don't find this island. We can only search for so long before we *have* to go back home. How are we gonna explain why we stole the magairite and took off for so long?"

"We'll think of something," Cormun replied. "For now, let's concentrate of finding Skeeter."

"I see something!" Jerbo yelled.

Leaving Cormun to man the helm, Torgil, followed by Warvyn and Nimble, raced to the bow where Jerbo leaned forward over the deck railing, a spyglass at his left eye.

"Where?" Warvyn asked.

Jerbo pointed a little to his left. "There." He handed the spyglass to Torgil.

Torgil jammed the spyglass to his left eye and focused. "There is something there. Tell Cormun to increase the speed or we might never catch up."

*

It took another three days for the ship to gain enough distance on the island that the gnomes could begin to scan the shoreline for a landing spot, but much to their dismay, they had been spotted.

It began with high arcing balls of flames flung from shoreline ballistae. Thankfully, the gnomes were far enough away to watch the flaming balls fall from the sky and into the sea below where they sputtered and sizzled before sinking into the watery depths. Cormun immediately increased altitude until they were high enough that not only were the ballistae ineffective, by the time they hovered above the island, any other projectile weapons aimed straight up had the unfortunate effect of coming back down in the same spot.

With their gain in altitude, the island spread wide and long before them. It was much larger and more mountainous than they first suspected, covered with thick forests of oaks, elms, maples and pine.

"Wonder why they didn't want to live here before now?" Nimble said, admiring the vast forests and a lake larger than he had ever seen.

"Like Jerimede said," Jerbo replied. "Five years is a long time to be away from family." His thoughts drifted to Ella Waywocket, wondering if she missed him enough to wait for him.

"This island is huge," Warvyn commented, staring at the bald mountain tops. "We haven't even passed the peaks yet. Think they get snow when it's cold?"

Torgil looked back over his shoulder at Cormun. "Don't want to get too far away from the coast. We don't know how far away they are, and we don't want to be trekking across this island trying to find them."

"Think Skeeter's with them?" Jerbo said.

"He wasn't back on Ynys Malfor," Torgil replied, "so here's the only other place he could be."

Cormun steered the airship in a large circle, heading back the way they came, slowing the ship to allow them a better view below.

"There's a spot," Warvyn said, pointing to a small meadow next to a river.

Cormun slowly lowered the ship as the rest kept careful watch. They waited several minutes before Jerbo flipped the ladder over the side. Leaving Cormun on the ship, the other three descended and secured the mooring lines while Cormun hauled the ladder back up.

No sooner had Warvyn asked, "Which way do we go?" when the surrounding forest shook and halflings swarmed out, arrows notched, and spears pointed.

In unison, the gnomes raised their hands. Torgil was about to explain why they were here when a section of the surrounding halflings divided and two halflings regally strode through the opening. Torgil recognized Pemstoke and Kithzina. Though a smidgeon taller than Kithzina, Pemstoke was still shorter than the gnomes. He wore dark green tights tucked into leather boots. His dark brown leather vest covered a short-sleeved shirt, revealing tanned and sinewy arms. His long auburn hair was held back by a leather headband, revealing pointed ears.

Kithzina was dressed much like Pemstoke. Her long blond hair was held back with a braided leather band. Her emerald-green eyes, cold and imperial, glared at them. Lifting a hand, she flicked her fingers and another individual walked through the opening.

"Skeeter!" Nimble exclaimed, overjoyed to see his friend again. The other gnomes joined in the welcome until they noted his reserved demeanor. He was dressed like a halfling.

"What are you doing here?" Skeeter asked with a perplexed frown.

"Why do you think?" Torgil replied, irritated that Skeeter didn't appear to be all that excited to see them. "We're here to take you back home." He shifted his attention to Pemstoke and Kithzina. "We brought back the Magairite."

Skeeter's eyes blinked wide in fear. "What happened?"

"Nothing happened," Jerbo said. "Turns out they didn't need the magairite after all. Our whole trip was a waste of time."

"You promised to never come back," Pemstoke snarled.

"Yes," Torgil answered. "But that was based upon false information. You demanded that one of us stay behind in exchange for the magairite. We agreed, though it went against all we stood for, gnomes sticking together. We kept your secret safe, even telling his folks that he was dead, to protect you."

"They think I'm dead?" Skeeter sputtered.

"How else could we explain why you weren't with us?" Warvyn said.

"How did you know we were here?" Pemstoke demanded.

"Those still on Ynys Malfor told us where you went," Warvyn answered.

Pemstoke grimaced at Kithzina. "I told you we should've left no one behind."

"Who is 'they'?" Kithzina asked, ignoring Pemstoke.

Torgil shrugged. "You all look alike."

Pemstoke bowed up with indignation, while Kithzina smirked at the obvious jab.

"Just like all gnomes look the same to us," she said, "though I dare say Skeeter looks more halfling than gnome, even with the pointed ears. I suspect he has halfling blood in him." She slid an affectionate glance at him, which the gnomes couldn't help but notice was returned in kind.

"May I have a moment with my friends?" Skeeter politely asked Kithzina.

"Of course." She circled her finger in the air and the surrounding halflings retreated a respectful distance away. She placed a tender hand on Skeeter's arm. "Don't be too long. We have a festival to plan."

"I won't be long," he replied, squeezing her hand.

After Kithzina walked away, Pemstoke in tow, Torgil cocked an eyebrow at Skeeter while ticking his head at Kithzina.

"What's going on?"

"You shouldn't have come here," Skeeter chastised.

"What?" Warvyn sputtered. "We risk life and limb to come find you and this is the thanks we get?"

"You don't understand," Skeeter said. "I'm a respected person here. They admire me for sacrificing myself for the safety of gnomes. I get treated with deference and honor. They've even built me a fine house. I don't have to pay for anything. It's all provided. Besides, I *like* being here. You shouldn't have come."

Warvyn's mouth slacked open as he stared at his friend.

"So what you're saying…" Nimble quietly said.

"I'm not going back." Skeeter folded his arms across his chest. "And now that you're here, there's a good chance you won't be either."

"What?" Jerbo pursed his lips, his scowl deepening.

"The main reason we're here –"

"When you say *we*," Torgil interrupted, "it sounds like you're part of the halflings."

"I am. I make no apologies." Skeeter glanced at each of his friends. "When you all left, I believed this was my future, living among the halflings for the rest of my life. So I thought to myself, if I'm stuck here the rest of my days, I might as well fit in. And that's what I did. Much to my surprise, the halflings were more than impressed that I would sacrifice my own happiness for the safety and future of gnomes. They've gone out of their way to make me feel welcome."

"Yeah," Warvyn sneered, sliding a glance at Kithzina. "We noticed."

Ignoring him, Skeeter continued. "Like I was saying, the main reason we're here on this floating island is that the halflings refused to believe that gnomes wouldn't send someone to their island. In other words, they didn't believe you would keep your word." He exhaled a frustrated sigh. "And here you are."

"It's not the same," Jerbo argued. "We came here to rescue you. We never told anyone about the halflings. We even had to lie to your folks."

Skeeter turned solemn. ""I'm sorry you had to do that."

"What other option did we have?" Jerbo said. "We made a promise to the halflings to keep their island a secret, and we did. No one knows we're here."

"Yeah," Warvyn huffed. "We even snuck away in the middle of the night so no one would know we were gone until too late."

"It doesn't matter anymore," Skeeter replied. "I'm not going back and unless I can convince them otherwise, neither are you."

*

For three days, Cormun fretted, spending sleepless nights worrying what had happened to his young friends. Torn between leaving the ship to find out or staying put and protecting their only means of escape, he had just about decided to cut the mooring lines and head back when he heard a voice.

"You in the ship."

Rushing to the side, he looked down at a halfling staring back up at him. He looked vaguely familiar. "Yes?"

"Your friends are safe. You need to come down and join them."

"I don't think so. Why don't you just send them back and we'll be on our way home."

"Can't do that."

"Why not?" Cormun's fear mounted. Sure, he could pilot the ship himself. It might take a bit longer, but how would he explain what happened when he got back?

"Because they said they're happy and rather stay here."

Cormun snorted a derisive laugh. "Let them tell me that."

"I know there's only you left on board. Why not come down and join them? They've been dining rather well, a lot better than what I imagine you're eating."

"Again, let them tell me that. And by the way. You've got an hour before I cut the lines and sail away from here. Make no mistake. I know where this island is. I've kept careful records and have already plotted its course for the next several years. When I come back, I won't be alone."

The halfling bowed up to full height. "You threaten us?"

"Why not? You've captured and imprisoned my friends."

"No, we didn't," he shot back.

"They're being held here against their will. Same thing." He held up a sharp knife and started sawing away at a mooring line. "You now have less than an hour."

The halfling spun around and fled away. A half hour later the surrounding forest pulsed with the arrival of a halfling army, armed with spears, swords and crossbows. Anticipating the threat, Cormun had cut the mooring lines and now hovered high enough to be out of bowshot range. The last thing he needed was a crossbow bolt or a well-placed arrow penetrating the air envelope.

Realizing they had been temporarily thwarted, the halflings shook their spears and swords at him, crying out for him to come on down and fight. Suddenly, the shouting and clamor ceased as Kithzina regally parted the soldiers to stand in the open space below the ship. Four well-fed gnomes joined her. A moment later, Skeeter passed through the gap to stand next to Kithzina.

Cormun watched Kithzina slide a hand over to interlace her fingers with Skeeter's hand. He immediately knew that Skeeter was not coming back, that their mission to save him was a complete failure. Complicating that was how to rescue the other gnomes without placing the ship in peril?

Kithzina leaned over to say something to Skeeter who then cupped his hands over his mouth to shout for Cormun to come down, that the halflings weren't going to do anything to harm him or the ship.

Cormun studied Torgil and the other gnomes. They appeared relaxed. Despite his misgivings, he lowered the ship until it was low enough to toss the ladder over the side. As he lifted the end of the ladder to hoist over the deck, he heard that dreaded sound, the hissing of escaping air from the envelope. He jerked his head up in time to watch another arrow penetrate the envelope.

His anger erupting, he snapped his head to look down at the confused gnomes… all except Skeeter whose poise said he had known this treachery was to happen. Yet there was nothing Cormun could do. Unlike the newer airship envelopes with separate air compartments, this was a much older air envelope constructed as one large compartment. Any tear or hole compromised the whole thing, and from what he could tell, there were at least six arrows that had penetrated the shell.

As more air escaped, the ship started to dip lower. Deciding he didn't need to be on board when the ship hit the ground and heeled over on its side with the envelope deflated enough to drape over the ship, he tossed the ladder over and began the slow descent. Once on the ground, he stood back to stare up at his beautiful ship, angry that he had been duped by someone he had trusted. He heard Torgil and the others approach, but ignored them, preferring to watch the slow death of his ship.

"We didn't know," Torgil said, full of remorse.

"Not your fault," Cormun gruffly replied. He twisted his head to glare at Skeeter and Kithzina as they approached.

"It was the only way–" Skeeter began before Cormun snapped a hand up to stop him.

He turned to face them, the halfling soldiers slowly positioning themselves nearby. "You don't know what you have done," he grimaced, shaking his head before narrowing a hard stare at Kithzina. "You think that by keeping us here no one will know you are here? If they haven't already, they'll piece together the magairite missing and us gone. They'll know where we went. There's five gnomes here with families back home who will demand answers. They'll send a flotilla to Ynys Malfor first, armed to the teeth because they think there are monsters there. What do you think will happen when they learn it's not true? What do you think will happen when those left behind on Ynys Malfor tell them where we are?"

"That's if they can find us," she replied, not so sure anymore.

"We found you," he coldly stated, "and we're just one ship. Imagine the odds when there are hundreds of ships." It was an exaggeration of course, and he wondered why Skeeter didn't correct him.

Kithzina's eyes blinked wide at the thought of hundreds of gnome ships invading their island.

By now, with the keel firmly on the ground, the airship began to tilt to the side.

"You didn't even have the sense to arrange for blocks to keep the ship upright and off the ground," Cormun groused. "Not only did you lie to us and destroy my ship, we're now prisoners." He gave her a cold glare. "This will do much to enhance the reputation of halflings."

"You are not prisoners," she emphasized.

"What else do you call it when you're held against your will?" he shot back.

"You are guests."

"Bah," Cormun sniffed in disdain. "A guest can leave anytime he wants. At least you can use the right words. And you," he said, turning to Skeeter. "You call yourself a gnome? How much did she promise you to sell us out?"

"She didn't promise me anything," he meekly replied. "I like it here."

Cormun turned his back on him. "That's even worse."

Kithzina curled her hand at one of the halfling captains. "Take our guests–"

"She means *prisoners*," Cormun interrupted.

"Take our *guests*," she continued, ignoring him, "to the guest residence. Make sure they have everything they need."

*

For three days, the gnomes were housed in a well apportioned halfling house and feted with the finest food and ale, all served by the most fetching halfling young women. Even Torgil had to admit life was pretty good. Not only did they eat and drink to their hearts' content, they were free to wander where they wished. Halflings went out of their way to make them feel welcome, some even telling them they were glad they were here.

Life might have been grand had it not been for one gnome who refused to immerse himself into the day-to-day life of the halflings. Despite the pleadings of the other gnomes and even Skeeter, Cormun adamantly refused both food and drink, eating only bread and water.

"That's what you feed prisoners," he retorted.

"You can't live on bread and water," Torgil counseled.

"Exactly." Cormun leveled an intense stare at him and the other gnomes. "I'm an old gnome. Most likely I'll die here. You've got to promise me that if you ever get back to our own islands, you'll take my bones with you. Bury me in my own lands, not some foreign island filled with halfling traitors. Promise me."

Skeeter appeared in the doorway to the dining room. His heart sank at the wane old gnome who seemed to have shrunk, his wrinkled skin sagging and even more wrinkled. "Kithzina is here and would like to talk with you."

Cormun twisted his head to look at Torgil. "Tell him that a prisoner has no say in the matter. If she wants to talk to me, that's her choice."

Torgil turned back to Skeeter. "Cormun said–"

"I heard him." Skeeter shook his head and stepped aside as Kithzina glided past him to stand a few paces away from where Cormun sat on a hard wooden dining room chair, the seat and back cushions removed.

"I understand you refuse to eat what has been provided for you." She frowned at him, wondering what he had done with the seat cushions.

"A prisoner is normally given bread and water. I am merely eating what any other prisoner eats."

Kithzina's lips pursed. "I will tell you again. You are *not* a prisoner."

Cormun tilted his head to gaze up at her. "Is my ship repaired so that I can go back home?" When she didn't answer, he shrugged. "I am a prisoner."

With a frustrated huff, Kithzina twirled around and marched out.

"Why are you doing this?" Skeeter demanded.

"Tell him," Cormun said to Torgil, "that I only share my thoughts with other gnomes, gnomes I can trust."

"Cormun said –"

"I heard him." Inhaling a deep breath, Skeeter said, "Let me see what I can do."

A knock on the front door interrupted him. Jerbo opened it to a grim-faced Pemstoke.

"Lady Kithzina wishes to speak with Cormun at her home," he said.

Cormun heard him and replied, "A prisoner goes where he is ordered to go."

Pemstoke opened his mouth to rebut the absurd prisoner idea but decided it was a waste of time arguing with the cantankerous old gnome. Leaning in through the doorway, he said, "You all are invited to attend."

Fifteen minutes later, the five gnomes stood in Kithzina's large living room. She sat on an overstuffed chair near the fireplace. The small box containing the magairite originally given to the gnomes sat on a side table next to her chair. In addition to Pemstoke who stood behind Kithzina's chair, five halfling soldiers had strategically positioned themselves to guard against any surprise move by the gnomes.

Assuming a royal air, she loftily said, "You claim that you brought back our magairite to redeem your friend. Is that true?"

"Yes," Cormun answered.

"Then you are liars."

Pemstoke dramatically opened the box to reveal it was empty.

Unfazed, Cormun shook his head. "The magairite was there when we arrived. Apparently, halflings aren't as honest as they claim to be."

Instead of anger at the accusation, Kithzina chuckled. "It is you who are dishonest. Yes, we did find the magairite. However, not all of it was there. You attempted to swindle us to rescue your friend."

Cormun shook his head, uttering a slow sigh. "You call us liars and show us an empty box. When we claim that there was magairite in the box, you say, 'Yes, we know there was magairite in the box,' which means you took it out while accusing *us* of being liars. We are not halflings who treat others with contempt and make false accusations. We knew it was not all there and we would have explained why, but you never gave us the chance to explain. The first thing you did was imprison us."

Kithzina's lips tightened. "How many times do we have to tell you that you are not prisoners?"

"Like I asked before, is my ship repaired so we can go back home?"

"Why is some of the magairite missing," Pemstoke interrupted.

"Ah, now we come back to the matter at hand," Cormun said with a paternal nod. "Some of the magairite you gave us was placed in a display case in the mineral warehouse." He went on to describe their escapade stealing the magairite.

"The display case was locked," Jerbo added. "I'd have to break the glass to get it. I figured if I left it alone, no one would notice the rest of the magairite missing until after we were long gone. With a little luck, they might not have noticed it was missing until we got back."

"We've jeopardized our own lives," Torgil said, "trying to rescue our friend while keeping your secret safe. All we wanted to do was go to Ynys Malfor, give back the magairite and bring Skeeter home."

"And now, in addition to calling us liars, you want to imprison us here," Cormun said.

"For the last time," Pembroke fumed, "you are not prisoners."

"Is my ship repaired so we can leave?"

"Yes," Kithzina quietly replied.

"Pardon?"

"Your ship is repaired for your return. It's been ready since yesterday."

A thick silence filled the room until Cormun seethed, "Why didn't you tell us yesterday?"

Kithzina turned her head to give Skeeter a look of brave sadness. "There were other things to consider." Her gaze lingered a moment before returning her attention to Cormun. "You are free to leave anytime you wish. However, there are restrictions to your departure."

"We can't tell anyone about you," Torgil said. "We know that and will always abide by that."

"And you can never come back here or to Ynys Malfor," Pemstoke said, "ever… all of you."

Cormun was about to agree when he saw an overwhelming sadness on Skeeter's face gazing at Kithzina, and realized they loved each other. It took him another few moments to work through a gnome and a halfling wanting to be together. Nothing like this had ever happened before that he knew of. Would this happen again if gnomes and halflings had daily dealings with each other?

He frowned in thought, chastising himself at the same time. So intent on being an aggravating pain in the butt trying to be as obnoxious as possible, he had allowed his own anger to block the obvious. While he refused to budge from the house, the other gnomes were out enjoying life, coming back and telling him how nice and kind the halflings were. Would gnomes be as accepting?

The other gnomes likewise saw Skeeter's look of despair and shared a quick nod of understanding.

"We can always say that we didn't find him," Warvyn lamely said.

"Then you really *would* be liars," Kithzina replied, still gazing at Skeeter.

"We already *are* liars," Torgil pointed out, "when we said that he was probably dead, knowing he wasn't. We lied to protect you."

"What's one more little fib?" Jerbo agreed, wishing they were already home and done with all this business so he could devote his attentions to Ella Waywocket. They'd been gone for too long as it was, and who knows what other young gnomes were vying for her attention.

"What is it about gnomes that terrifies you?" Cormun asked.

"It's not gnomes," Pemstoke said, pointing out the obvious. "It's our way of life. Once word gets out that we are here, all that will change. We were safe and happy, living our lives unaffected by others. When you showed up, we knew our safe and secure little world would never be the same. That's why we left."

"But not all of you," Nimble countered. "Some chose to stay where they were, accepting what might happen."

"They are fools," Pemstoke fiercely said.

"Isn't that rather harsh?" Cormun said. "Instead of running away, they chose to adapt and overcome if necessary. I think you've forgotten a very important point. Gnomes and halflings share the same aversion for the bigger folks. We've managed to avoid them for hundreds of years because our islands are far enough away to be of any interest to them. Instead of hiding away from each other, we ought to be looking out for our collective interests. I think gnomes and halflings could benefit from each other."

"There are many who feel the same way," Kithzina replied. "Some strongly enough that they chose to stay behind."

"And others who knew better," Pemstoke tersely said.

"I take it you prefer that gnomes and halflings never see each other ever again," Cormun said.

"Yes," he quickly affirmed before remembering who was present.

"And not everyone agrees with you, Pemstoke," Kithzina snapped.

"Most do," he stubbornly answered. "That's why we're here."

"They were never given the chance to decide," she countered. "The Council made the decision on its own."

"It was a majority vote," he self-righteously said.

"Exactly my point," she retorted. "We uprooted an entire island without thinking this through."

"Yet here you are," he shot back.

"Yes," she coldly replied. "Here I am because you managed to sway the Council."

"They made their own choices based upon sound reasoning," he countered.

"I hate to barge in on this fascinating discussion," Cormun interrupted, "but this gets us nowhere. You're here and that's what matters, regardless of what transpired to get you here. And we're here now. According to you," he peered intently at Pemstoke, "we have two options; either all gnomes leave, including Skeeter, never to return or we remain here, never to return home."

"That is correct," Pemstoke airily replied.

"Is that the Council's decision?"

"Of course."

Cormun nodded. "Just like you gave us no choice when you imprisoned us, you again give us no choice to make our case." He twisted his head to look at Kithzina. "Is this the halfling way, to dictate what happens to friends and strangers by a small group of individuals who claim they know what's best for everyone?"

Pemstoke stiffened to full height. "How dare you imply that–"

"I'm not *implying* anything," Cormun continued. "I'm merely stating a fact. Why not let us make our case to the people? What are you afraid of?"

"This is preposterous," Pemstoke fumed. "I will not allow

this."

"So you're now king of the halflings?" Cormun taunted.

"Of course not," he replied, a little too quickly.

"Though you'd like to be king."

"No," he said, though not with as much conviction as one would expect. "We have no king."

"Then why are you making the decision? Allow us to talk to the Council."

"He has a point," Kithzina quietly said. "Everyone has the right to petition the Council. It's in our laws."

"Halfling laws," Pemstoke countered. "And you're just going along with what he says because you're infatuated with this gnome." He hooked a thumb at Skeeter.

"And you're arguing because you really do want to be king," she retorted. She curved a hand at Cormun. "This wise gnome here has noticed in the short time he's been with us what most halflings deal with every day – your aspirations to place yourself above the rest of us."

"That's not true," he huffed.

Ignoring him, Kithzina turned to Cormun and the other gnomes. "I will ask the Council to hear your petition. I will let you know if I am successful. Otherwise, your choices are as Pemstoke has stated."

*

Back at the guest house, the gnomes, Skeeter included, gathered in the dining room. To their surprise, the ale kegs had been replaced with several kegs of a dark sweet stout, along with fresh bread and several varieties of cheese.

Sipping the ale, Nimble licked his lips and sighed with contentment. "I could get used to this."

"What are you going to say to the Council," Skeeter asked

Cormun, "or are you still not talking to me?"

Cormun cocked an eyebrow at him. "Imagine a gnome falling in love with a halfling… what would they say back home? What would his parents say?"

"They think I'm dead, remember?" He walked over to grab a tankard and filled it with ale. "It's funny, isn't it. When I volunteered to stay here, you all thought it was the noblest thing a gnome could do. Then you get back and learn it was all for nothing, but to keep their secret safe, you tell everyone I'm dead. Now you're here wanting to fix everything and it's not working out like you planned. And somehow, it's my fault."

He turned to fix Cormun with a sharp eye. "I never asked you to come here. I was content with my decision. Believing the rest of my life would be spent here, I chose to immerse myself in what it meant to be a halfling, though never forgetting I was a gnome. The halflings welcomed me, gave me every kindness. I even found a love interest. Life was good."

"Then we showed up," Torgil said with an understanding nod.

"Exactly. You should have left well enough alone."

"How were we to know?" Warvyn complained. "We thought we were on a noble quest to rescue you."

"What you've done is complicate things. If you stay here, you lose everything back home. If I go with you, I lose the one woman I truly love."

"Unless I can convince them otherwise," Cormun said.

A loud thump on the door startled them. Jerbo strode over and opened the door to a young halfling a head shorter than him.

"Lady Kithzina says the Council is ready for you."

"Now?" Cormun blinked in surprise. "That was fast."

The halfling shrugged and curled an arm at them. "Follow me."

Ten minutes later, they were deposited at a central hall buzzing with activity. Halfling scribes, copyists, clerks, accountants, and archivists scurried across polished granite floors, up and down wide sets of stairs, in and out of offices, all with the utmost aura of efficiency.

The young halfling led them through the crowds to a second-floor chamber where five halflings sat in high-back chairs perched on a raised platform. Cormun recognized Kithzina who sat in the middle, Pemstoke to her right.

"Welcome friends,' Kithzina said with a smile.

Cormun noted she was the only one who smiled, which did not bode well.

"You already know myself and Pemstoke," she pleasantly said. She leaned forward to glance at the older halfling with greying hair and thick busy eyebrows, who sat next to Pemstoke. "To his right is Erryl, our oldest and wisest Council member.

Erryl grunted in begrudging recognition with a slight tick of his head.

"To my immediate left is Mylo and to his left is our youngest but equally wise member, Gyllian."

Cormun did a quick study of the Council. Both Erryl and Mylo were older, with faces that said they were irritated that they were called away from whatever they were doing to sit here and listen to a gnome. Gyllian, however, was a pretty halfling with curly auburn hair and bright eyes. She looked to be a little younger than Kithzina.

"I've asked the Council to listen to your petition," Kithzina said to Cormun.

Cormun dipped his head in respect. "Thank you, Lady Kithzina, King Pemstoke, and Council members."

"I'm not a king," Pemstoke snapped.

Cormun frowned in pretend confusion, while watching the reactions of the other Council members. It was as he suspected; not everyone was a fan of Pemstoke.

"My mistake," Cormun apologized. "You'll have to forgive an old gnome. When one gets past 400 years old, one tends to confuse things now and again."

Gyllian sat up in her chair. "You're 400 years old?" she marveled.

"That I am, young lady," he said with a warm smile. "I'd venture to say that I'm more than ten times older than you, yet here you are, a member of the Council. You must be very gifted indeed to be chosen to sit with the selected leadership of the halflings."

"Get to the point," Pemstoke sourly complained. "Your false flattery gets you nowhere."

"Where you see flattery," Cormun calmly replied, "I see a compliment. And in all my 400 years, I've never known a compliment to be wrong."

"Well spoken," Kithzina said with a nod.

"Yet I do not wish to waste the valuable time of the Council, so in accord with King Pemstoke's wishes–"

"I said I'm not the king," Pemstoke growled.

"But wasn't it you who said that you wouldn't allow the Council to meet, that you wouldn't allow me to talk to these fine halflings?" Cormun slowly arced a hand at the other Council members.

"That… that's not what I meant," he stiffly replied.

Mylo leaned forward and twisted his head to look at Pemstoke. "Then what *did* you mean?"

"He's taking it out of context," Pemstoke lamely answered.

"Actually," Kithzina sweetly said, "he's not taking it out of context. What you said was, and I quote, 'This is preposterous. I will not allow it.' That certainly sounds like someone speaking as though he had the final say."

"But that's not what I meant," he stubbornly stated, "and you know it."

"How about we let our guest continue," Erryl interrupted, his voice a warm baritone, "instead of listening to us squabble?"

"Thank you, Master Erryl," Cormun said with a short bow. "I believe you all know the reason we are here, so I will not belabor the point. However, I feel the options offered are in neither of our best interests, both halfling and gnome. To say that we must either stay here forever or all go home and never return is short-sighted, for it dictates that the two races most suited to each other must be forcibly kept apart. It's like I told King Pemstoke–"

"For the last time," Pemstoke loudly snarled, "I am *not* a king!"

Ignoring him, Cormun continued. "I said to him that I thought he had forgotten an important point, a very important point. Gnomes and halflings share the same nervous concern when it comes to the bigger folks, and even dwarves and elves. We prefer not to have to deal with them, and we've managed to avoid them for hundreds of years because our islands are far enough away to be of any interest to them. Instead of halflings and gnomes hiding away from each other, we ought to be looking out for our collective interests. I think gnomes and halflings could benefit from each other, sharing and trading knowledge and resources."

"What makes you think halflings and gnomes would get along?" Erryl asked.

"Because we are very similar in nature. Like you, we have no king," he slid a grin at Pemstoke. "Instead, like you, we rely on the wisdom of our elders. Like you, we prefer peace to war and will do our utmost to avoid conflict. However, like you, we will not back down when confronted with dire situations. Again, like you, we want to prosper in life, enjoy a good ale, a fine cheese and fresh warm bread, hot from the oven, with melted butter for dipping." He chuckled. "My goodness, my mouth is watering. I'm thinking of your fine stout that would find a very receptive audience back home."

That got Mylo's attention. "You like my stout?"

"That exceptional ale is your making?" Cormun said, impressed. Mylo bobbed his head. "Master Mylo, I believe you would have great difficulty keeping sufficient supply once gnomedom discovered it." He inwardly grinned, watching the halfling's face as he calculated barrels and profits.

"Words coated with honey," Pemstoke sourly complained. "He's trying to bribe you, pure and simple."

Cormun cocked an eyebrow at him. "You would deny Master Mylo earning a profit?"

"Of course not," Pemstoke retorted, "but–"

"Then quit interrupting," Mylo said, giving him a stern frown before turning back to Cormun. "Please continue."

"I'm not sure there's much more that I can say," Cormun replied, "other than halflings with special talents, like Master Milo here, will be more than welcome by gnomes. Instead of mutually excluding each other, we ought to be enjoying the benefits that halflings and gnomes have to offer."

"And what do you have to offer in return?" Pemstoke sneered.

"Machines that make life easier," Torgil called out, "and, uh… weaving."

"And music," Skeeter added. "With the halfling talent for telling stories and legends, and the gnome talent for music and instruments, just think of the songs we could create."

"And many other things," Cormun said then narrowed his gaze directly at Pemstoke. "What is it exactly that you hate about gnomes?"

"I don't hate gnomes," Pemstoke answered with an air of superiority.

"You must. Otherwise you wouldn't have packed up everything you owned and leaped onto a passing island to get away."

"He has a point," Gyllian sweetly said then leaned forward to look to the side, past Mylo and Kithzina, leveling an intense stare at Pemstoke. "No sooner had the gnomes left Ynys Malfor that fear spread like a wildfire. But fires usually burn out unless someone continues to feed them… someone like… you."

Pemstoke stiffened and his face hardened. "I resent your

implication. I had nothing to do with the urge to move. Halflings know a threat when they see it."

"So now we're a threat?" Cormun said, raising an eyebrow. Before he could continue, Gyllian spoke.

"I believed we were too hasty all along. We allowed ourselves to get caught up in the hysteria of being discovered."

"Then why didn't you say anything?" Pemstoke demanded.

"I did," she evenly replied. "Have you forgotten?"

"Then why didn't you stay with the others who remained behind?" he scoffed.

"Because, just like you, I am a member of the Council. How would it look if the Council were divided? Though Kithzina and I voted against leaving, you three voted to leave. We had no other choice."

"You are right," Mylo said, nodding. "Instead of providing wise counsel, we allowed ourselves to get caught up in the fear." Shaking his head, he exhaled a sigh and sat back. "And now it will be another five years before we can get back to our island."

"While this is home for now," Gyllian pointed out, "it can never be where we once lived, our true home on Ynys Malfor."

"You would go back if you could?" Cormun ventured.

"Yes," Gyllian asserted then shook her head in frustration. "Yet I fear it will be like Mylo said. We are stuck on this island for another five years."

Cormun solemnly nodded. "Perhaps not."

The Council and other gnomes turned their attention to him.

"What do you mean, 'perhaps not'?" Mylo said.

"Remember how we got here?" Cormun explained. "We gnomes have all kinds of airships, especially ones used to transport cargo… things like custom furniture or large barrels of ale." He gave Mylo a half-smile.

"This is madness," Pemstoke spouted. "You expect us to trust you? How do we know you're not bringing back some army to invade our island?"

Cormun slowly shook his head. "Other than magairite, which gnomes no longer need, what is there that Halflings have that would make gnomes go to war? And why would we even *want* to go to war? Gnomes avoid conflict unless it is pressed upon them, just like halflings. So the very thought of gnomes massing an attack against halflings is absurd from the start." Turning to the other Council members, he spread his hands. "You see an old gnome before you. Until I discovered that Halflings lived on Ynys Malfor, I was quite content to spend the rest of my days in the comforts of my own home. Yet circumstances caused me and the other gnomes here to go beyond the comforts of our daily lives."

He slid a glance at Skeeter. "It is obvious that our young friend here has grown quite fond of halflings and would rather stay here than go back home." He shifted his gaze to stare intently at Pemstoke. "You've already seen how gnomes and halflings get along. Why should it be any different if we daily interacted?"

"Do you really have enough airships to move us back to Ynys Malfor?" Gyllian said, her eyes bright with possibilities.

"Yes."

"I think we've heard enough," Erryl interrupted. "We thank you for your time and will consider your proposals."

Recognizing they had been dismissed, Cormun dipped his head and led the others out of the chamber. They were quiet as they followed the young halfling back to their house, each with his own thoughts. Halfway back to the house another messenger came racing up.

"The Council wants you back," he breathlessly said.

"That didn't take long," Cormun chuckled.

Standing again before the Council, Cormun noted Pemstoke's sour face.

"We accept your offer," Erryl solemnly said. "It's about time we stopped pretending no one else lives in this world."

"Then we need to get going," Cormun urged. He gave Kithzina a knowing smile. "I believe our mutual friend prefers to remain here."

"How long will it take to get your airships here?" Gyllian interrupted, determined to get off this floating island.

"A month or two at the least," Torgil responded. "It'll take us two weeks to get back."

"And this island gets farther away each day," Nimble added, "which means we need to leave as soon as possible."

"How will you know where to find us?" Gyllian asked.

"We'll find you," Jerbo confidently said.

"That's not what I asked," she said, though not unkindly.

"I've been keeping a record of the island's position since our arrival," Cormun said with a sly smile. "I also assume your scientists know the trajectory of the island. Between us, I'm sure we can come up with an accurate location."

"Then you better get going," Kithzina announced with a broad smile.

*

Their jubilation evaporated when they emerged around the last street corner to stare at their ship resting on pillars in the middle of the field.

"Where's the envelope?" Nimble sputtered.

"The envelope's gone," Warvyn repeated, stating the obvious.

Torgil immediately cast an accusing eye at the Council members before noting that Pemstoke was missing.

"We're not going anywhere," Jerbo glumly said, his hopes of reuniting with Ella Waywocket suddenly dashed.

"Is this some sort of cruel joke?" Cormun demanded.

Instead of answering, Kithzina turned to one of the six

halflings guarding the ship. "Where is the envelope?"

He shrugged in reply. "It wasn't here when I started my duty."

"And you didn't think to ask?" Cormun snapped.

"I was told to guard the ship," he indignantly replied, "and that's what I'm doing, so don't tell me how to do my job."

"Where's Pemstoke?" Skeeter interrupted, asking the obvious.

"Go find Pemstoke," Kithzina ordered two of the guards.

Before they had a chance to obey, the halfling in question sauntered up.

"Where's the envelope?"

"As if you didn't know," Warvyn sneered.

Pemstoke splayed his hands. "Why should I know where it is? This is *your* ship. We did *you* the favor of guarding it."

"That means one or some of the guards is responsible for its theft," Cormun said, turning to Kithzina. "What is the halfling penalty for stealing."

Kithzina shook her head. "Halflings are like a very large family. A halfling who steals from another halfling is unworthy of being called a halfling because he is robbing his own family. The punishment is exile… never to return to the family he betrayed. I will begin an immediate investigation." She gazed intently at Pemstoke. "We will find whoever is guilty and he will be punished to the fullest extent of the law. Isn't that so, Councilman Pemstoke?" If she hoped he might be intimidated to implicate himself, she was quickly disappointed.

"Of course," he readily agreed. "In fact, I'll lead the investigation."

"The fox guarding the henhouse," Nimble quietly intoned to Cormun.

"That's all well and good," Cormun groused, "but we're wasting time. The longer we remain here, the longer it will take until we come to a point in time where it's no longer viable to even try."

"What do you mean?" Gyllian fretted.

"What I mean is that unless we can find the envelope, we'll have to make one."

"And that could take some time," Skeeter acknowledged. "The longer it takes, the farther away we travel."

"What do you need to make a new envelope?" Kithzina asked.

"Finely woven cotton, sealed in and out with varnish," Cormun answered, "and large enough to lift the airship. We'll also need enough coal to create the gas needed to fill the envelope."

"Then, like you said," Kithzina affirmed, "we don't have time to waste." She turned to the other Council members. "I propose we immediately divert all our efforts in crafting an envelope."

The others quickly agreed, except Pemstoke who shook his head. "By the time we got anywhere near where we needed to be, we'll be heading back to Ynys Malfor. I say why not wait until we get back there?"

"You've out-voted," Gyllian retorted. She twisted her head to gaze at Cormun. "We will need your expertise."

"Willingly granted," he said with a nod. "May I ask that you provide guards for the ship in the meanwhile? If someone can make off with the envelope, who knows what mischief they might do to the ship."

"It will be done," Erryl sagely nodded.

*

The gnomes were more than impressed by the collective energy and effort of the halflings. While the call went out for bolts and lengths of finely woven cotton fabric, a rotating guard assumed security for the ship. At the same time, a call went out for provisions. Once the reason for the demands was explained, there was no shortage of volunteers or supplies.

Watching the scurrying and frenetic activity, Cormun chuckled, observing that there were quite a number of halflings who apparently had never wanted to leave Ynys Malfor.

But not everyone shared that same excitement. Though Pemstoke had been soundly outvoted, it did little to stop him and his small group of loyal followers from making snide remarks and acting a hindrance whenever they could. Supplies designated for the gnomes mysteriously disappeared or ended up on the other side of the island.

And then the original envelope was discovered.

Halfling children playing near a dried-up quarry noticed an odd colored shape beneath the debris of leaves and limbs and rotting tree trunks. The discovery might have gone unnoticed except for the child who decided to tear a piece of the fabric and make a pirate's headscarf just like the one in his picture book at home. When his mother saw the strange outfit and learned the location of his find, she immediately notified the Council.

Soon enough, the gnomes, the Council, and a number of other curious halflings had assembled at the edge of the quarry, staring down at the few bits of envelope peeking through the tangled debris. Skeeter and Nimble were the first ones down.

Lifting a sliced piece of envelope, Skeeter shook his head then craned it back to look up at Cormun. "It's all like this, all sliced to shreds. Someone obviously didn't want us to leave."

"All of it?" Cormun moaned.

Nimble crawled over to another spot and pulled out a larger piece. Too numb and angry to say anything, he merely shook his head and held it up for Cormun to see.

Kithzina saw the despair on his face. "We are so sorry."

"We will find out who did this," Gyllian vowed, "and they will be punished to the utmost of halfling law."

"What does it matter anymore," Cormun grimly said. "What's done is done." He cast an evil look at Pemstoke who stood off to the side, gazing down at the two gnomes, a puzzled frown creasing his forehead.

Exhaling a resigned sigh, Cormun turned to the Council. "We still have a long way to go before we're ready."

"We're working around the clock," Kithzina reminded him.

"I know, I know," he replied. "I'm just ready to get going."

"I understand," she tenderly said, placing a gentle hand on his arm. "It will happen... soon enough."

*

The halflings were true to their word and gnome hopes rose as the size of the envelope continued to grow. Cormun examined the product along the way, inspecting seams and joints. Nodding with anticipation, he figured another two weeks and they would be ready for a test inflation. Add another week of checking for leaks or weaknesses and then another week of sailing tests, they had perhaps a month left here.

He had been carefully logging in the trajectory data every day, cross checking his findings with the halfling astrologers and scientists. If they left a month from now, depending on wind and weather, it would probably take them three weeks or more to get back to Ynys Malfor and then another week to get back home. All told, they had at least a month of sailing above a vast sea, providing this envelope held together. If the envelope failed, they were all doomed... lost forever. Pushing aside these dreadful thoughts, he turned to see Kithzina approach. She seemed perturbed.

"I need you to come with me."

"What's wrong?"

"You'll see."

She silently led the way back to the central hall and up to the second-floor Council Chamber where the other gnomes had already assembled. Leaving Cormun in the middle of the room with the gnomes, she ascended to sit in the middle chair.

The mood was grim as Cormun nodded at the other gnomes while noting that four of the five Council chairs were occupied. Pemstoke stood to the side, facing both the Council and the gnomes, surrounded by three halfling guards. Cormun also noted the room was filled with a goodly number of respected citizens.

Kithzina gazed intently at the gnomes then at Pemstoke then back to the gnomes and surrounding crowd. "I've called you all here to expose a traitor in our midst, a halfling who does not understand what it means to be a halfling, what it means when a halfling gives his… or her word of honor." She nodded in acknowledgement to the ladies in the audience. "We come here today to reveal the guilty halfling who destroyed the gnome airship."

"I had nothing to do with that," Pemstoke snarled.

"Be quiet or I will have you gagged," Kithzina threatened.

"You have no right," he shot back. "I am a Council member just like the rest of you."

"One more outburst and you will be gagged," she warned.

"I always knew it was you," Gyllian dismissively said. "You hated the gnomes and did everything you could to stop them."

"Patience, Gyllian," Kithzina soothed. "All will be revealed." She turned back to Pemstoke. "Do you deny that you hate the gnomes?"

"I don't hate them," he protested. "I just don't see the need to change hundreds of years of safety for an uncertain future."

"Oh puh-lease," Gyllian mocked. "It had nothing to do with an uncertain future. It had everything to do with a certain gnome who stole the heart of the woman you wanted. I've seen the look on your face whenever Kithzina and Skeeter are together. Don't deny it."

"Then your logic is faulty, which is to be expected of one so young," he sniffed in disdain. "If I wanted to keep them apart, why would I destroy the one means of getting rid of him?"

"He has a point," Erryl observed, leaning forward to look at

Gyllian.

'He's jealous, I tell you," she stubbornly replied.

"That may be," Erryl said, "but it does not explain the destruction of the ship's envelope."

"Perhaps this might help," Kithzina interrupted. She nodded to a guard by the main doors.

Opening the door, the guard beckoned a middle-aged halfling into the room. He marched boldly forward to stand before the Council.

Kithzina smiled kindly at him. "I believe everyone here knows Bricker Thistletop here. He's one of our finest bakers."

The halfling preened at the compliment.

"He's been assisting us in the search for the airship's envelope. Tell us all what you've found."

"I found this," he replied, pulling out a finely made jackknife, "at the quarry where the envelope was found." He held it up for all to see.

An awkward silence settled before Erryl cleared his throat and frowned. "Um… what does that have to do with anything?"

"Patience, my friend," Kithzina answered then nodded at the guard by the door.

Once again, the door opened and a young halfling in his mid-20s entered. He looked around at the group and grinned in dimwitted amusement. There was a ripple of giggles in return for they knew this young man, usually described as 'a sandwich short of a picnic.'

"Welcome Merric Shortbridge," Kithzina warmly said.

"That's not all that's short," a voice snorted.

"None of that here," Erryl sharply retorted.

"Merric," Kithzina continued. "Do you recognize the knife in Bricker's hand?"

When Bricker displayed the knife to him, Merric's eyes

widened in joy. "My knife, my knife." He reached for it and frowned when Bricker wouldn't let him have it. His jaw jutted out and he scowled. "It's mine. Give it to me."

"When did you lose your knife, Merric?" Kithzina asked.

"Lost it when we were cuttin' up that balloon thing," he answered, still staring at his knife.

"How did you lose it?"

"Larko asked to see it and I said OK and him and Eldon start tossin' it around and I yell at him to give it back, but he throws it over my head and Eldon missed catchin' it and I can't find it because it's dark and when I went back the next day, I still couldn't find it," he bitterly replied.

"Why were you in the quarry?"

He frowned at her. "Like I said, we were cuttin' up that balloon thing."

"Why were you cutting up that balloon thing?" Kithzina asked, smiling at him.

Merric shrugged. "Larko said he'd give me half his honey butter sandwich if I helped him."

"Did he say why he was cutting up the envelope," Erryl asked, "I mean, balloon thing?"

Merric shrugged again. "Said she wanted it cut up real good so no one could use it ever again."

"She?" Erryl sputtered, eyes wide in shock.

"Yeah."

"Kithzina?"

"No," he huffed then pointed to Gyllian. "Her."

A stunned silence engulfed the room before Gyllian indignantly said, "This is absurd. Are we to trust the words of this imbecile halfling?"

"Yes," Kithzina said, "we do trust his words, for he tells the truth. But, as is halfling law, we won't condemn on the words of one witness. Therefore, I call upon Larko Gardner and Eldon Coopersmith to present themselves for evidence."

The doors opened and the two named halflings cautiously entered, fully aware of their culpability.

"This has gone too far," Gyllian snapped. "These halflings can't be trusted. They'll say anything to save themselves. Besides, why would I want to have the airship destroyed? I gain nothing from it."

Kithzina twisted her head to peer intently at her. "But you do."

"What?" Gyllian sniffed in disdain. "You think I'm jealous of you because of him?" She thrust a finger at Skeeter.

"He has nothing to do with it," Kithzina replied then dipped her head at Pemstoke. "He does. You wanted him out of the way so that your friend, Carissa Meadowfield, could assume his place. Knowing Pemstoke was opposed to the gnomes being here, you saw an opportunity to get rid of him. You almost succeeded."

"This… this is absurd," she bristled. "I am a Councilwoman of the Halflings. I will not be insulted or falsely accused like this." She stood up as though intending to leave.

"Sit down," Erryl snared. "Neither you nor any other halfling is above the law. If you are innocent, it will be proven. If not…"

Gyllian wavered a moment in indecision before plopping down in her chair.

"Tell us, Larko," Kithzina said with a firm voice. "Are you responsible for the destruction of the gnomes' airship? In other words, are you the one who made the decision that the envelope to the airship was to be destroyed?"

"Think before you answer," Erryl said. "Are you willing to suffer the consequences of another's choices?"

Larko swallowed hard, his eyes flitting between Gyllian and the rest of the Council. Yet, he was no fool. "I was only following orders. She is a Councilwoman and I assumed she spoke for the Council."

"Liar," Gyllian spouted.

"I am not," he indignantly replied. "You came to me and told me the Council wanted to make sure the gnomes never left this island, that you needed my help, that it had to be done in secret to make it look like Pemstoke was responsible because he had lost the trust of the rest of the Council."

Unable to think of a reply, Gyllian stared daggers at the halfling.

Kithzina turned her attention to Pemstoke. "Would you please resume your rightful place on the Council."

Both relieved and angry, he marched up onto the platform and deliberately sat down.

Kithzina looked to her left and right at the Council members. "I propose a vote of no confidence in Councilwoman Gyllian. I also call for a full investigation into her crimes. Further, that she be removed from all Council business until such time as a replacement has been elected."

"I second the proposal," Erryl immediately declared.

"All those in favor?" Kithzina said.

Four 'ayes' answered.

"Opposed?"

"Of course I oppose," Gyllian sourly said.

"By a vote of four to one," Kithzina said, "Councilwoman Gyllian is hereby removed from Council business until further notice." She turned a disapproving eye on her compatriot. "I'd say 'don't leave this island,' but you have nowhere else to go."

Doing her best to retain some semblance of dignity, Gyllian stood and calmly walked out of the Council chambers.

"Apologies all around," Kithzina said, "but especially to Pemstoke and our gnome friends." She turned her attention back to Larko and Eldon. "You two are to remain available for further questioning. You are to have no contact with Gyllian from now on. Is that understood?"

"Yes, Kithzina," they replied.

"Then you may go." Waiting until they pushed through the doors, Kithzina then addressed Cormun. "How soon can you be ready?"

"It all depends on how soon we can get a new envelope," he answered. "Then we'll need time to inflate it and test for leaks, a trial run and then if everything is satisfactory, we'll head home. So, to answer your question, if the envelope can be finished in two weeks, we can leave two weeks after that."

"Until then, we are all at your disposal."

*

Some say anticipation makes time slow down. Others say it's a matter of perspective. For Cormun and Jerbo and the others, time seemed to drag. For Skeeter, despite the bold statements of his returning, he couldn't shake the feeling that once gone, he would never see Kithzina again.

There were too many variables to consider. This island was continually moving away from Ynys Malfor. It would take them at least a month to get home and during that time, this island would be a month farther away. And for each day they delayed back home was a day added on to his separation from Kithzina. And then there was that nagging thought that when they did head back to this island, no matter how long it took, the island would always be ahead of them.

"You're not thinking straight," Cormun harrumphed. "Our ship travels faster than this island does. Otherwise, how'd we manage to get here in the first place?"

Skeeter shook his head. He knew Cormun was right, but it didn't matter. If he left with them, Kithzina was lost to him. "Why do I have to go? You all are coming back anyway."

Cormun placed a hand on his shoulder and gazed kindly at him. "If she truly loves you, it won't matter how long you're gone."

"Easy for you to say," he griped.

"What are you worried about?"

Skeeter stared at him, surprised he couldn't see the obvious. But then, Cormun was an old gnome and romance was probably a long-forgotten part of his life. "I'm a gnome and she's a halfling," he explained. "That right there is cause for problems. Then you add in that she's the most powerful and influential halfling on this island, even though she's part of the Council. You notice she sits in the center? There are plenty of halflings who would like her as his wife."

"She loves you?"

"I believe she does," Skeeter answered.

"Has she said so?" When Skeeter hesitated, Cormun shook his head. "You're setting yourself up for a fall, lad. If she really does love you, you'll know it when we return."

"But that could take months," Skeeter complained.

"Love doesn't have a time limit," Cormun softly said. "If she loves you, truly loves you, she will be waiting for you." Watching the anguish on the young gnome's face, he said, "Remember when we first arrived at Ynys Malfor?"

"Yes."

"Was she involved with another halfling then?"

"No."

"If she wasn't attached to anyone when she didn't even know you existed, why would she suddenly change now that she knows you are here?"

Skeeter blinked at the revelation and suddenly felt a weight evaporating off his shoulders. Why didn't he think of that? Cormun was right. Yes, he would leave with them. After all, he needed to ease his parents' pain. At the worst, it would be a couple of months before they returned.

"You know how to get back?"

"Of course," Cormun huffed, the answer obvious. "I was doing this airship thing long before you were born. Besides, I made a promise to Kithzina. We're going to return with enough ships to help them move back to Ynys Malfor."

"That's right," Skeeter brightened. "We *have* to come back."

*

When the day came to depart, it seemed that all of halflingdom had come out to bid them safe voyage. Kithzina conducted a brief ceremony, offering words of encouragement and reminding them of their promise to return. She shook each of the gnome's hands, saving Skeeter for last. Instead of a handshake, she gave him a hug and a tender kiss on the lips, much to Pemstoke's annoyance.

"I'll be waiting for you," she whispered. "Hurry back."

His heart churning with emotion, he wanted to tell her how he felt, but the words wouldn't form. Instead, he exhaled a deep breath. "When I come back, I won't ever leave again."

"I'm counting on it," she smiled. "Now go so you can come back all the sooner."

"C'mon Skeeter," Torgil called down from the ship's railing. "We're burning daylight."

Giving Kithzina one last look of longing, Skeeter spun around and clambered up the rope ladder. Once aboard, he gave her a wave as they released the mooring lines.

Kithzina heard the engines sputter and catch and the propellors began spinning. Slowly, the ship turned, rose into the sky and headed towards Ynys Malfor.

"Think they'll come back?" Pemstoke questioned.

"Why wouldn't they?" she replied, still watching the ship float away. "Cormun promised to come back to help us move."

Pemstoke cocked an eyebrow at her. "Do you really want to see a fleet of gnome ships invading our way of life?"

"Our way of life changed the day they came to Ynys Malfor," she said. "There's no going back now."

"There are other islands," he pointed out, "just beyond the farthest limit of this island."

"I know about them, Pemstoke," she reminded him, then ticked her head at the gnome ship growing smaller in the distance. "We'll still need their technology to get to them. And if it's all the same to you, I'd like as few folks as possible to know about those islands."

Her response surprised him. "You're not as keen as you make out to be about these gnomes."

"I like to keep my options open," she said, still staring at the gnome ship.

"What about this Skeeter fellow?" he pressed.

"Skeeter's different," she answered. "He's not like the other gnomes. Had you spent more time with him and them, you'd see the difference."

"I was too busy being accused of destroying their ship," he sourly replied.

She nodded in understanding. "Sorry about that, but I had to let it play out to unmask Gyllian."

He folded his arms and twisted his head to gaze at her. "Speaking of Gyllian, she needs to be exiled, but it's not like we have a lot of options." He turned back to stare at the diminishing airship. "Should have sent her with the gnomes," he said, half in jest.

"I did," she grinned.

*

Cormun and crew were several hours out when Nimble discovered the castaway down below in the hold, bound and gagged and soundly asleep. Told about the wayward halfling, Cormun went below to see. Upon recognizing their passenger, he burst out laughing.

"Get rid of all your problems at the same time." He nodded

with admiration.

"What do we do with her?" Nimble asked.

"We drop her off on Ynys Malfor then head for home." He turned to Skeeter. "We've all been gone for some time. We're going to cause a quite a stir when we suddenly show up, you especially, because everyone thinks you're dead."

"Think they'll accept the reason you didn't tell them the truth?" Part of him wished they had never showed up. He had been happy living with the halflings. Another part said it was bound to happen eventually.

"While your parents will be mad, I expect most others will understand." He scanned the sky, thankful for the warmth from the sun then up at the makeshift envelope, offering a nervous prayer that it would hold until they arrived safely at home.

"You know I have to go back," Skeeter firmly said.

Cormun chuckled and nodded. "I never thought otherwise." He placed a hand on his young friend's shoulder. "When we get back home, you'll need to take charge. Assert yourself. You know the halflings better than any gnome. If our two communities are going to work and grow together, it's going to take leadership. That's why I'm going to push for you to be elected to the Council."

"Me?" he sputtered, eyes blinking wide.

"Yes, you." He rested his arms on the railing and gazed out over the endless ocean. "You are the future of gnomes and halflings." He turned around to see the other gnomes lost in their own thoughts as they busied themselves with taking care of the ship. Torgil, an expert now at piloting, saw them looking at him and gave them a wave.

Cormun smiled and waved back at him, suddenly wishing he was years younger so that he could see what the world would be like with gnomes and halflings living together. Still, he wasn't dead yet, and how many gnomes could say they'd traveled across the ocean in search of a friend living amongst the halflings?

Turning to Skeeter, he said, "The world as we knew it changed the moment we left Ynys Denligh in our search for magairite. We ended up leaving a friend behind for what we thought was a greater good. Little did we know that the greater good was the uniting of halfling and gnome communities."

He inhaled a deep breath, savoring the bouquet of the ocean. By the gods, he so loved being out over the water, sailing his airship, away from the chatter and hubbub of daily life. When his time finally came, this is where he wanted to be, watching his last sunset before his eyes shut forever. Until then, he had work to do for these young gnomes needed all the help they could get, and he was the one to help them.

"C'mon," he grinned at Skeeter. "Let's go see what our passenger has to say for herself."

THE END

Esin of Vaelkesh
A.G. Porter

Chapter 1

The sky above them darkened as the sun lowered behind the mountains. Rain pelted their heads and cloaks as they made their way through the road that was more like a massive mud puddle, slowing their progress from the Ash Mountains with muck pulling at their feet. They had been traveling nonstop for days and the rain wasn't letting up.

"Esin," Cielle called to her from up ahead.

Her sister came riding toward her, blonde hair drenched even through her cloak. She was beautiful, but her eyes were tired. They were pushing themselves too hard. But, in their current situation, Esin did not feel as if they had any other choice.

Keres was dead as we're her parents, and Zanna had killed them both. That was only two years ago. It felt like ages had passed since she had been on the run, hiding in dirty tavern rooms and makeshift shelters. Running from her own sister.

Esin had awoken to the sounds of screams and the castle shaking as if the ground itself would swallow them whole.

She had made her way, avoiding falling debris, to her parents. She knew they would be in their sitting room. When she reached her destination, she saw a large figure standing before them, covered in armor so dark it made her think of the night's sky.

She heard her father try to explain something and she soon realized that the figure was her sister, Zanna. What had she done to herself?

"You are not my father," Zanna was saying. "You killed him."

"What are you talking about, Zanna," her father questioned.

These accusations were flung at her father a few more times. Esin was thoroughly confused. She knew Zanna was her adopted sister. It was no secret. In fact, her human lineage made her famous. It was known her human father had died in a raid. Right? What was she getting at?

Suddenly, Zanna slung her mother and the next moment she was impaled with pieces from Zanna's armor. Esin felt her world tilt. Blackness pricked at the edge of her vision.

Surely, she didn't see this. Surely this was a bad dream. Her mother was sleeping in her bed and would be up shortly, waking them and getting them ready for the academy. When realization hit and a scream was about to tear its way up her throat, just as her father's head hit the ground, Cielle had clamped a hand over her mouth. Her sister pulled her through the castle and out of a secret entrance.

They were both being lead through tunnels full of rats and dirty water. She looked up to see Kerym, her father's most trusted guard, pulling them by the hand. He had always been there, in the background, guiding her family.

She looked over at him, he had always been stoic and strong. He looked even more grim with the rain pelting down on him. They had found nothing at the Ash Mountains. If they didn't take shelter and rest, they would be no help to her people or Vaelkesh. They had to stop.

"Kerym," she called and the silent elf came to her side. "Please find us a place to set for the night. Alynx will help you."

Alynx nodded and rode forward with Kerym. The younger elf admired Kerym and Esin knew it. She was sure Kerym did as well, but he treated Alynx with indifference, the same way he treated everyone else.

They both hurried off and it wasn't long before they found a somewhat dry piece of land up ahead. They quickly set up the tents and huddled in, wrapping themselves in warm, dry blankets. Kerym passed around tough but tasty meat that Esin gratefully ate.

She had never liked the stuff before, but after eating what she could find, she would willingly eat anything that filled her belly. Merith, the other in their party, took a seat next to her. It was a wonder that any of them had escaped. Truly she was thankful he was alive, but she couldn't help but feel tense around him and not because of his station. After all, he was the crowned prince of Vaelkesh. A prince she believed to be spoiled and out of his league. Still, he had shown he could survive, that she would give him.

"Sire, here," Alynx handed Merith a flask.

"Please, Alynx, just Merith," the young prince said to the guard.

"Yes, sire," he said and then caught himself, his face reddening. "Yes, Merith."

Esin tried her best not to roll her eyes. Alynx was doing his best to cater to Merith in every way he could. It was his job, but Esin just wanted to hit them both over the head with her sword.

When Zanna took over the kingdom, Merith lost his parents and his crown. The elves of Vaelkesh were scattered. Zanna was the queen now and she ruled with fear and pain. Kerym had somehow saved her life, Cielle's, Alynx's, and the prince, Merith's. The five of them left and had been on the run since.

She looked for Javaid, her sisters closest companion and the last person to see either of her sisters, but had only heard whispers of his whereabouts. What she knew of why Zanna had done what she had, was only told in hushed tones in the back of taverns. Through all of the stories and rumors, one thing remained the same, she had killed Keres, her sister, and took the Armor of Dusan.

She also knew it took place at the Ash Mountains. That is why they explored the mountains many times though were not able to stay for very long because Zanna was looking for her. Her, Cielle, and Merith. Keres was killed by Zanna and so was her other sister, Siofra.

She and Siofra had been close in age. To Esin, Siofra was her best friend. The night that Zanna had entered their home, Siofra was not as lucky as she. She was taken by dragon fire. It was quick and cruel. It was just her and Cielle now.

Last month, they had received word that Javaid may have been near the Ash Mountains again. Unfortunately, he was not. Esin knew in her heart they would find each other. Perhaps a part of her was longing for some semblance of the family she once knew. Javaid was a big part of that.

"What are we do to now?" Cielle asked her as they used each other for warmth.

All eyes went to her. She felt heat move up her neck and settle in her cheeks. She didn't understand why they turned to her. She was only 12-years-old. Cielle was 16. Alynx was a few years older than Cielle, and Kerym was old, even for an elf. Why did they look to her?

"Javaid was last seen near the mountains," Esin told them, trying her best not to squirm under their stares. "We must find him."

"It's been over two years, milady," Merith said, his young face full of worry. "Are we sure this is still the best course of action?"

"I believe it is," she said to him even though inside she felt so lost. "He was the one with Zanna when … all of this happened. He might know something we can use."

"Don't you think he would have done so by now? Or found us?" Cielle asked.

It was a reasonable question. No one knew where Javaid was. They also didn't know why he hadn't found them if he knew how to save her sister. That was the end goal, at least to Esin. Find Javaid and save Zanna from the armor.

"I don't know, Cielle!" Esin snapped and her sister flinched; she instantly felt guilty. Standing up and taking a deep breath, she looked around at the party, "We're heading for the Floating Isles tomorrow. Come or don't. No one will fault you for your decision."

Chapter 2

The next morning, rain still pummeling their heads, the entire party was up and headed toward the Floating Isles. Merith was right beside her, his horse black and sleek. It was a palace horse, the one he managed to take with him when he fled for his life.

Esin didn't know much of how he was able to get out, but he ran into their party on the way out of the city and had been with them since. Esin and Merith grew up together. He was only two years older than her and they attended a lot of the same programs and classes at the Library of Vaelkesh. He was older, but she was smart and was put into upper-level classes.

Merith had always been kind to her, but he was royal and she had little patience for them. While she respected the king and his family, she thought his father was haughty and frivolous, that thinking extended to his family. It may not have been fair, but she felt it was justified.

She kept those thoughts to herself as they moved through the mud and muck. Like her, Merith had lost his entire family. At least she still had Cielle. There was also Zanna, and Esin could not help but wonder how far gone her sister truly was.

Esin and Zanna had been extremely close. Of all of her sisters, Zanna was who she confided in and leaned on. She believed in her sister. She was caring and wise. And Zanna had always believed in her. Zanna protected her, always had, and she knew that her sister loved her.

She wanted to believe Zanna was a victim. She couldn't reconcile the sister she knew with the monster saw that night.

In just two years, Zanna and her witch had laid waste to a majority of Vaelkesh and was expanding to other territories. Those who had survived the siege, were now under her rule, at her mercy and she gave little of that, if any. Out in the Ash Mountains they were as far from her influence as they possibly could be and even still felt her presence.

What she had done was on the lips of everyone. They were afraid. Even though many did not admit it, what happened in the palace of Vaelkesk affected the entire realm.

For days they skimmed the base of the Ash Mountains. At night they would make camp, huddled together for warmth, and then start all over again. Finally, they reached a small city. They were stopped at the gate to state their purpose and Kerym played his part as widower with 4 children to take care of. As always, they were shown pity and allowed into the city.

After finding lodging, they stopped for the night, thankful for a dry place to sleep. Esin and Cielle met Merith in the tavern, eager for a warm meal, but also listening to the chatter.

As long as they kept dirty faces and their pointed ears covered, they could pass for humans. Even though they were children, if they were found out to be elves then the townsfolk would be wary of them and hurry them out.

The three of them sat at a table, ordered their cheapest but heartiest soup and listened to what was being said around them. Kerym and Alynx were surely on the rooftops of the city officials, battling the weather, listening as well.

Esin began to think that news of Zanna had not reached this place or it didn't affect them enough to care, but then she heard two city guards talking in the corner.

"The governor is nervous," one burly guard was saying to his younger counterpart. "Vaelkesh may be far away, but their reach extends beyond our town and further. Already the new queen is demanding an increase of taxes."

"I heard that came from the witch who whispers in her ear," the skinny man said. He sipped his soup through a broken toothed mouth, his blue eyes wild and searching.

"It doesn't matter where it comes from," the older guard said. "That's less coins in our pockets and less food in our bellies. With the fever killing nearly a third of our population, we're already struggling. Meals like this will be far and few."

"And what are we to do?" the skinny human asked. "It's not like we can fight a half-blood queen with magic armor and a witch by her side."

"No," the older man agreed, taking a bite of bread. "But the male elf, Javaid, it is said he knows how to stop her. Last I heard, when he was travelling through here, he was on a mission to the Floating Isles. Why, I don't know, but he took a few of our men with him."

Esin tried not to jump up from her seat. Like Merith and Cielle they pretended not to know what was being said in the corner of the seedy tavern. They finished their meal quickly, but not enough to draw suspicion and hurried to their room.

"We have news," Kerym said as he slipping throw the window with Alynx, shaking off the rain and cold.

"As do we," Esin told him.

They each shared their information. Esin told them what she had overheard and Kerym confirmed it when he said that the governor of this city was discussing that very same thing within his chambers.

"Do we move tonight then?" Cielle asked.

"I think we should rest and let the storm pass," Kerym offered. "We will not get much further in this, and at least we will be well rested."

"I agree," Esin nodded. "We move in the morning. First light."

*

Esin could not sleep. The storm raged outside, Cielle kept throwing her arm across her in their shared bed, and despite the fact that it was cool outside, the room felt smothering. Sighing, she got up, washed her face in the water basin, and freshened up as well as she could. She missed the hot baths she could spend hours in at home. Her light blonde hair always smelled of flowers, and her skin was soft from the many oils and lotions that were available to her.

Now, she smelled like her horse and her hair was matted with dirt and mud. Her face was smudged and her body was tired. She had been spoiled and privileged, there was no denying that. Esin never felt as if she didn't deserve the life of a high elf, she cared for those who were less fortunate. However, she also knew she could do better.

She quickly got dressed and made her way down rickety stairs to the tavern below. There weren't many people in there at this early hour.

"You're up early," Merith greeted from a dark corner.

She nearly jumped not seeing him at first. Her sight was keen, but elves knew how to not be seen if they didn't want to be.

"As are you." She walked over to his table where he drank a hot up of tea.

"Can I get you anything, Miss?" the inn keeper asked, wiping his hands on his apron, a habit she was sure he formed long ago.

"Just some tea, please." Esin gave him one brass coin and the man bowed before leaving them. She turned to Merith. "What are you doing here?"

"Storms always keep me awake," he shrugged, his silvery hair shimmering in the candle light. "And you?"

"Anxious, I suppose." She sat down as he gestured toward a chair.

She felt odd sitting so close to him, so intimate. He was the crowned prince and going from treating him as an intangible object to a commoner was jarring. It didn't seem to faze him, but to her, it felt wrong. To be fair, everything had felt wrong since Zanna's attack.

"Are we making the right decision?" he asked her suddenly, worry creasing his youthful brow.

"I hope so," she said honestly. "If Javaid doesn't have a starting point, then I don't know what else to do."

"I never spoke to Zanna … before all of this," he admitted, looking almost shameful. "I never really spoke to anyone, though. Was she always like this? Did you see this in her?"

"No," Esin shook her head. "Zanna is good. She is always kind to me. She protects me from the others. You know how siblings are." Esin laughed, noticing how she talked of Zanna in the present. "They always go after the youngest. But, Zanna, she stood up for me. She is … my sister."

"So was Keres," Merith reminded her gently.

"This has to be the answer." She looked up at him and knew he saw the desperation in her eyes. "It has to be."

He nodded and then laid his hand on top of hers. It was warm, such a contrast to the cold, drafty tavern.

"It has to be," he agreed with her.

They locked eyes and for the first time, and Esin saw him as more than a spoiled royal who didn't know what it was like to be anything else. They didn't come from much different worlds. And, if she could change, so could he.

"Here you are, young one," the inn keeper came up and Esin pulled her hand away.

"Thank you," she said to him with a nod.

"Your accent is not one we hear out here much," the inn keeper said to her. Esin immediately tensed. "Your entire party sounds different."

"We're not from around here." She told him the cover story they had concocted. "Just a few towns over. It's just us and my father. We are heading to his family's farm now that my mother … it's just us now."

"Was it the fever?" the innkeeper asked.

She was used to questions when they entered these small towns. It was always the fever. After Zanna took power, a strange plague had overtaken the land. Many believed it was a spell cast by her witch and Esin didn't doubt the rumor's validity.

Once she told them her mother had died, they assumed it was the fever and not many people kept conversing with her. It was usually because people felt uncomfortable talking about death. Apparently, this innkeeper didn't mind.

"Yes," Esin looked down at her hands. While the story was fake, the loss of her mother was true and fresh.

"It is going to get us all in the end," the innkeeper said, hanging his head. He looked back up as if the sentiment was nothing more than words. "Where did you say you were from?"

"They didn't," Kerym said to him as he suddenly appeared at the innkeeper's side, causing him to jump. "Children, we're leaving."

"Yes, father," they said together and stood up.

They quickly left the inn and headed for the stables to gather their horses. Kerym did not like staying in one place for too long and Esin agreed. Especially when there was an innkeeper who asked too many questions. Too many questions got you killed.

Chapter 3

With the morning came the rain and some fog. The weather would make it harder to see, but it would make it harder for anyone pursing them to see them as well. It was a gamble for sure and it felt silly to her, but she didn't complain. Esin was a gambler by nature. She wasn't very good at it, but she always tried. She didn't understand why some people ran from a bet in a card game when they had nothing to lose. Even if they would lose, they still had the chance to win.

That's how she felt about it all at the moment. There were no promises that they would find Javaid. This could be a wild chase where the fox turned out to be just the wind. Javaid might not know how to save her sister. Still, this was her only hand and she was going to play it.

"Esin," Kerym came up to her, his steed breathing hard.

He had strayed behind in case they were being followed.

"What is it?" she felt her heart drop.

"There is someone following us. Three from what I could see," he announced. "I don't know who they are working for; their cloaks are indistinguishable. But they are indeed following us."

"What do you suggest we do?" Merith asked, riding up beside them.

Esin looked at her sister and Cielle's face was tight and pale. She was frightened. So was Esin. While they had been taught to fight by their father from a young age, neither one of them had seen battle.

"Was it the innkeeper?" Cielle wondered. "He was asking so many questions."

"It probably was him," Esin agreed.

"You should ride ahead," Kerym said to them. "Alynx and I will lay in wait for them. The three of you must keep heading to the Floating Isles."

"What if you need our help?" Merith asked, concern etching his brow. "I can fight."

"So can I," said Esin though she felt her skills were lacking. "Five against three is better odds."

"You are the crowned prince," Kerym said to Merith. "You must stay safe. You must also keep these maidens safe as they are just as much our future as you are."

Merith nodded and grabbed Kerym's shoulder. He looked at him and then at Alynx. "Be blessed."

"And you, sire," he bowed. "Now, we must all ride hard. When we reach those cliffs," he pointed behind them, "keep going. Alynx and I will catch up to you. I will give you a signal so you know it is us."

Esin gave Kerym a look of sorrow and squared her shoulders. This was her duty to her kingdom. Kerym was a seasoned warrior and Alynx, while young, still had battle experience. She told herself they would be fine.

"Let's go," she said to the group and urged her horse forward. She had to trust Kerym. He would keep Alynx and himself safe. The rest was up to her. Kerym had given Merith the duty of getting them to safety, but she felt it was her responsibility instead. This was her fight.

The journey to the cliff's edge was quiet as they pushed their horses hard through the rain. There was a weight that hung over them, the unknown of what was coming next. If she could just see passed these mountains, maybe her path would become clearer. Instead, all she saw was mud and dark clouds.

When they reached the base of the mountains, Kerym and Alynx veered off and they continued on the path. Esin's heart ached in her chest. She didn't want to leave them behind, but she also knew that Merith had to be kept safe. He was the future king. They had to hold this together for as long as it took to put him back on the throne.

They traveled until nightfall and took shelter in a nearby cave. It was late by the time they heard someone approaching.

"Wait here," Merith whispered.

"Not a chance," Esin drew her sword. "You're not going alone."

"My job is to keep you safe," he said, irritation in his voice.

"No, your job is to survive," she told him and walked toward the entrance. "We do this together."

"Alright, alright," he sighed.

Esin looked back at Cielle who had fallen asleep on her mat. She looked frail. This life wasn't for her, but Esin knew she was doing her best. Turning back around, they headed out into the darkness.

There was tiny pinprick of stars in the night's sky. The rain had slacked off, but large gray clouds still hid most of the night sky.

Both of them hid behind a large boulder. Peering over the edge they saw two figures in the distance, their horses moving fast.

"Could it be them?" Merith asked.

"There is only one way to find out," Esin said to him.

Esin called out a bird's song. It was piecing, bouncing all over the mountain, and Merith had to cover his ears. She watched as the riders stopped.

There was a brief pause and one of the cupped their hands over their mouth and the sing-song sound was returned to her. It was Kerym. This was something he had taught her long ago and instructed her to use it if they were ever separated.

Esin found herself smiling and moved her way down the rocks. Merith followed her and soon they met up with Kerym and Alynx.

"He's hurt," was the first thing Alynx said to them and moved from his horse.

"It is not that bad," Kerym tried to sound reassuring, but Esin could see the sweat across his brow.

"Come, let us get into the cave," Esin said to him. "We can take a look."

Merith showed Alynx were to hide the horses as Esin lead Kerym into the cave. Their entrance stirred Cielle from her sleep. She noticed right away that Kerym was hurt.

Cielle had been so much like their mother. They were natural caretakers and had an infinity for herbs and remedies. She helped Kerym sit down and removed his cloak.

He indeed had a nasty wound on his shoulder. Esin could see the blood through his tunic. They removed the blood drenched cloth and Cielle got to work.

While Cielle worked, they talked. It turned out that Kerym and Alynx had fought off their pursuers. It had been a close call and Kerym had injured his arm, stabbed by one of the attackers.

There didn't seem to be anything broken, but the wound was deep enough he wouldn't be able to use it for some time.

"How bad is it?" Esin asked Cielle.

"I can make it," Kerym interjected, cutting Cielle off.

She frowned at him and then looked at Esin. "The herbs will help speed up the healing process. He can ride, but hopefully we don't run into any more trouble."

They were all relieved that they hadn't been followed into the mountains. This meant that whoever was after them knew they were heading to the Floating Isles. They had gotten their message through.

"Who was it?" Esin wondered.

"It was Zanna," Alynx said as they entered.

"How do you know?" Cielle asked.

"The assassins wore her sign," Kerym said, grimacing as he moved. "And one of them said as much."

"They spoke to you?" Merith was surprised.

"It was a message," Kerym continued. "It was from Zanna. She knows you two are still alive," he pointed to the sisters, "and she knows about the prince."

The three of them didn't move. It was as if they were frozen in place as they listened to Kerym.

"She wants you to return to Vaelkesh," he continued. "She said if you did, she would pardon you. You could be in her court."

"And if we don't?" Esin asked. She finally sat down next to the fire, needing its warmth.

"Then she will come for you," he told them. A chill ran up Esin's spine.

Chapter 4

No one slept that night except for Kerym, and that was only because of the tea that Cielle had made and forced him to drink. Esin wished she could have some of her special tea. Maybe if she slept through this then all of her problems would be fixed by the time she awoke. Knowing that wasn't going to happen, she rose from her sleeping mat and began rolling it up. There was no sense in searching for rest when it would not at least meet her halfway.

Merith raised up when he saw her move. She said nothing to him as he began rolling up his own mat and then stoked the fire. They had refilled their food supply at the town, but were trying their best to ration it. It was several more days' journey to the Floating Isles, and they would need as much strength as they could muster, especially Kerym.

Merith cooked up a hearty breakfast and Esin assisted. They worked in silence as if knowing exactly what the other one was thinking or what the other was needing. Merith gave her a small smile and Esin felt her chest tighten. There was still so much longer to go for both of them and she had held so many preconceived notations about him.

She ignored all the emotions welling up inside her and focused on the task at hand. After they cooked up the eggs, potatoes, and sausage, Esin rolled it inside a thin soft bread and packed one in everyone's satchel. After that, they woke the others up and told them they had to get moving if they wanted to reach the next stop by nightfall. She waited to stir Kerym, giving him extra time to sleep off the fight from the night before.

She knew they could wait no more once she saw dawn approaching. Merith and Alynx went to tend to the horses while Esin made her way over to the other side of the fire. Kerym was still sleeping. He looked peaceful, but the truth was he was in a great deal of pain. They had given him some herbs to help with that, but they couldn't keep giving them to him. She knew Kerym well enough to know he wouldn't ask for any.

Cielle came over and sat down beside her. "How are you feeling?" she asked her, setting her kit down by Kerym's feet.

"I'm fine," she lied. "How about you?"

"I miss my home," she confessed. "I miss my mother and sister."

"I know," Esin agreed.

"What are we going to do now?" she asked. "Are we ever going to go back?"

"We can't." Esin's heart broke. "Zanna is lost to us right now. If her words are true then we would be standing on the side of a monster. No, we must keep moving forward. We must find a way to save her or..."

"Or what?" Cielle asked, but Esin could tell by the look on her face that she knew the answer.

"Or stop her," Esin said at last. A tear ran down Cielle's cheek.

Cielle reached out and took Esin's hand in her own. They sat there for a moment, just holding each other. Esin didn't cry even though she felt like she wanted to, that she needed to. Cielle let the tears flow freely and Esin found herself envious of her tender-hearted sister. She wanted to know what it was like to live your life expressing exactly how you felt at all times. How freeing.

Soon, Kerym began to stir. Cielle cleaned her face and went to him. She inspected his wound and cleaned it, dabbing it with more salve, and re-bandaged it. Elves didn't take as long to heal as most, but it still took time.

Kerym proved that as he grunted while putting his shirt back on. Esin tried not to smile as she watched Cielle's face turn red and then hurried to get her supplies together, moving away from them.

It was true that Kerym was handsome, even more so amongst his peers. He was far too old for her sister, but Esin could see why Cielle found him attractive. He was brave, strong, and had risked so much for them. She would be forever in debt to him.

They left soon after day break. The terrain slowly changed from a wet muddy surface to hard, dry patches and the sun began to peak out of the clouds. By midday, they were removing their cloaks because of the heat and their horses needed frequent water breaks. It was hot and the sun was not being kind to their fair skin.

Despite the heat, Esin draped her cloak back over her head, to save herself from the unforgiving sun. Soon the hard cracked soil faded into rough sand. She could feel the sun through the cloak and knew they couldn't make it much more.

Looking over at Kerym, she saw his face was waxen and sweat dripped from his brow. Cielle looked as though she might fall from her horse and the beasts didn't look much better themselves.

"We need to set up a tent," Merith said to her and she agreed.

She, Merith, and Alynx worked quickly. They put up one tent for all of them and did their best to cover the horses. After they entered the tent, they passed around the water and drank their fill. They were cramped, but the heat had taken so much out of them.

Cielle checked on Kerym's bandage and after that she was fast asleep. Kerym was asleep himself and Esin could feel her eyes growing heavy. This didn't seem right. Something was wrong.

"Merith," she said and her words came out garbled. "Something…it's not…"

She looked over at him and began to slump against Alynx, the elf guard's eyes closing. They were in big trouble.

*

Her eyes slowly opened. The first thing she noticed was it was dark and cold. She rolled over on her side and then sat up. Grabbing her head, she looked around, noticing her friends were nearby. They were inside a cave.

"You're awake," a voice said and Esin whipped around.

She clumsily stood and reached for her blade. It wasn't there. She glared up at the figure that slowly came into the light of a burning fire. It was a woman with long, gray braided hair. Her skin was dark and her eyes were brown. They reminded her of Zanna's.

"I'm not here to harm you, child," the woman said in a calm voice. "We saved you from the sun."

"Who are you?" she asked as more people began peeking around the fire at them.

"My name is Olenore," she said to them. "These are my people."

She gestured around at everyone. There were twenty of them, then thirty, and then more than she could count. Some were close to her age while others looked very young and they all looked strong. Tired, but strong.

"You do not need to be afraid," she said to her. "I know who you are."

"How?" she wondered, surprised.

"We don't get many elves around here," she smiled warmly. "We especially do not get elves with Vaelkesh steel. You are running, sisters of Zanna. And he is the crowned prince, I presume."

"We are looking for the elf Javaid," Esin said hopefully. "Have you seen him?"

"Yes," she said, and Esin's heart soared. "In fact, he told us to give you a message once you passed our way. Firstly, he asked us to not let you die in the sands."

Esin felt her ears burn with shame. After all they had been through, they were nearly stopped by the desert sun. It made her feel inadequate. Who did she think she was trying to save Zanna?

"Did … did he say anything else?" she asked cautiously, trying to hide the wariness in her voice.

"Yes," Olenore said with a smile. "He told us to give you this."

The woman reached into a pocket of her robe and slid a dagger to Esin. It was beautiful. A dark purple blade with golden writing and a dark shading on the hilt.

It had belonged to Zanna. In fact, she had one just like it. Their father had given it to them during Winter Solstice. He had one made for all the sisters.

"Why did he leave this for me?" she asked.

"He said you would find out," Olenore told her. "To use it when you felt all hope was lost."

Esin felt annoyed. She didn't want Javaid leaving her clues. She just wanted to know what she had to do. She wanted to know if this was all an empty pursuit and if she should just give up.

Deep inside, she knew that just couldn't be true. She was on this quest for a reason. Javaid had left the dagger behind for a reason other than a sign that she was on the wrong path. Esin had to keep her faith intact because at this moment, it was all she had.

Olenore guided her toward the fire burning at the center of what looked like a town courtyard. She looked up to see a small hole at the roof of the cave that allowed the smoke to leave. All around her the people began going about their business. Some went back into their homes that were dug into the side of the cave and others were working on things.

The people had a water system, vegetation that was growing, and many of the small children sat and listened to an older man tell stories. Lamps that seemed to be connected in some way were aligned down many different paths, allowing them to see their way through. This truly was a small civilization, deep inside a cave.

Soon, the others began to stir. They were disoriented at first, just like her, but when Esin assured them they were not in danger, they relaxed. Olenore took a look at Kerym's wound and gave him more salve and herbs to drink. She and Cielle discussed his treatment and she gave her sister more supplies.

Olenore invited them into her home. Surprisingly, it was warm, cozy, and not all what she imagined. It was lit in the same way as the streets.

The home was tiny, so the party squeezed in, but it wasn't as uncomfortable as the tent they shared. She served them a hearty stew she had cooking on some sort of steel stove. It intrigued her.

She had never seen anything like it before. In fact, the village was filled with wonders. Their lighting system was genius.

They eagerly ate their fill and the old woman also packed them cheese, dried meat, and bread.

"How long have you lived in these caves?" Esin asked as they sat at the table.

"For as long as I remember," Olenore told them. Memories seemed to cloud her eyes. "My ancestors called this land home long before our recorded history, yes, even before the elves. There used to be lush fields and vast lakes. There was a shift of power in the land, and the elves came, and with their arrival, our waters dried and our crops vanished. We are a resilient people. Our king brought us to the caves and here we thrived. We venture out in the day at times, but only when it is necessary and to save the untrained traveler from time to time." She finished with a smile.

"We do not have record of you in our books," Kerym told her.

"No, you would not." She smiled at him. "The elves wanted to forget us, so they did."

"Even when you were suffering?" Esin asked.

"The elven king did not care about us," Olenore told her. "He only cared about his people. The reasons our lands dried out was because the neighboring elf clans wanted our water, so they took it, diverting it where they wanted. In the end, we all lost it. That is why they moved to the green fields of Vaelkesh."

"I am sorry for that," Merith said.

Olenore offered him a gentle nod, an acceptance to his apology, but still holding on to past grievances. Esin did not blame her. Her people had suffered because of greed and cruelty while the elves had flourished.

Esin looked over at Merith. She could see that sins of his forefathers weighed heavy on his heart. Kings of all nations could be cruel. They could be unjust. When one tries to save their own people at the expense of others, it doesn't make them a hero. It makes them cruel.

"It is not something that was your fault, young prince," Olenore patted his hand. "We must learn from the faults of our fathers and do better."

Merith nodded his head in agreement. Esin could see the determination in his eyes, in his posture. She knew in that moment that if Merith were to make it back on the throne, he would be a good king. He would do whatever was right, for all people.

Chapter 5

Olenore had convinced them to stay the night. Kerym was worse for wear after the ordeal with the sun. The kind woman told them he should be better for it in the morning. She offered up her house for them to sleep somewhere for the night. They weren't sure how many nights of rest they would get out of the elements, so they agreed.

Esin nearly felt guilty for letting sleep claim her. Rest and sleep seemed like a luxury that she could not afford, not while her mission was incomplete.

Her words to Cielle came back to her. *Save her or stop her.* This what it had come down to. Zanna wanted them back home. Esin did not believe for one moment that Zanna meant them no harm. She was there when her parents were killed, murdered by her own sister.

No, Zanna would finish her job of wiping out their entire line. Esin knew she had to protect herself and Cielle. She had to protect the future of Vaelkesh.

"Mind if I join you?" Merith asked.

She looked up at the young prince. His color was back after the night of rest. Esin hated admitting to herself that she had worried for him. And it was for more than just him being the crown prince.

She nodded her head and he sat beside her at the fire. Esin was packing up the supplies that Olenore and the others had given them. Merith looked at the dagger and she quickly stuck it in her bag. This wasn't something she wanted to share with anyone.

"This place is wondrous," he told her, running his hand over mushrooms that shriveled and hid away at his touch. "It pains me that my people treated them so unjustly."

"Our people," Esin said, tying her bag up.

"What?" he looked at her.

"It was our people," she told him, looking him in the eye. "It was our ancestors who took more than they gave. We are in this together. We have to be."

"You make it sound like an obligation you do not want." He almost sounded irritated.

"It is an obligation," she said to him. "We can be better than the people before us. I have to be."

"We," he told her, standing up and holding out his hand to her.

"What?" She looked up at him.

"We," he said again, his hand still outstretched. "We are in this together. Together we can make a better future."

Esin slowly reached up and took his hand. He pulled her to her feet and they looked at each other for a moment. When did this boy become so mature? It was only last year he teased her and caused a ruckus with his friends.

"Together," she agreed. "But first, I have to figure out how to stop my sister."

*

The group moved through the dark tunnels, each of them with their own torch. Their horses were left with Olenore and her people. They couldn't travel this way. It was dark, cold, and wet, not to mention cramped. Thankfully, they could stand fully erect, but the walls were close. Esin was sure Kerym could reach out and touch each side with no issue.

Kerym led them, his torch illuminating the way. His steps were sure and steady, and his eyes never left the path ahead. If there was anyone that Esin wanted with her during this time, it was him.

Esin followed closely behind, her heart pounding in her chest. She couldn't shake the feeling that something was watching them from the shadows. She was telling herself it was all in her mind, that being surrounded by darkness on an unknown path would put anyone on edge.

As they made their way deeper into the tunnels, the air grew thicker, and a strange smell filled their nostrils. Esin felt a chill run down her spine, and she shivered despite the warmth of her cloak.

They entered a chamber with a high ceiling. There were three different directions they could venture. Olenore told them to use the center tunnel. They began making their way across the wide cavern when Kerym suddenly halted, holding up a hand to signal the others to stop. He turned to face them, his eyes narrowing in the torch light.

"I sense something," he whispered. "Be on your guard."

Esin drew her sword, as did the others, holding it at the ready. Olenore told her that sometimes bandits would use the tunnels to move through the desert, but it was only during the height of summer. She did, however, warn them that there were other things to be wary of in the darkness.

She could hear the faint sound of footsteps echoing through the tunnels, growing louder with each passing moment. Her heart raced as she waited for whatever was coming.

And then, nothing. The sound died and they were left in silence other than the flicker of flames and their bated breath. Just when Esin was sure she imagined the noise, a roar broke through the silence.

"Trolls!" Kerym yelled.

That was all he could say before an onslaught came out of the left side tunnel. Esin's heart seized and it was as if time slowed down. She threw her torch, hitting one charging troll in its broad chest. Its white, tangled hair went up in flames and while it was flailing around, Esin ran it through with her sword.

Dark liquid spurted out, drenching its chest and covering her face. She didn't have time to think about what it was as another troll was on her in seconds. She could hear the others around her fighting as well. Out of the corner of her eyes, she saw Cielle use her sword to cut down a troll.

She was inwardly rejoicing that her sister wasn't cowering in a moment like this. Fear colored her features, but she was fighting.

They all had to. Nearly thirty trolls surrounded them. They were outnumbered, and Esin didn't have time to worry if everyone could hold their own.

Her sword, already slick with blood and gore, sliced through another troll's neck. She felt a sharp pain and looked down at her foot. A fallen troll had stabbed her through her leather boot. She kicked it in the face with her free foot and reached down, pulling the dagger free, then removed the troll's head from its shoulders.

On they battled, cutting down as many trolls as they could. Esin wasn't sure how long they had been fighting. Only survival instincts kept her going. The pain in her foot was starting to spread up her legs and she could feel herself limping.

"Esin!" she heard someone shout.

A pain in the back of her head let her know that someone had hit her hard. She fell forward on her hands and knees, her sword scattering across the chamber floor. Quickly she rolled onto her back and within seconds a troll was on her, trying its best to wrap its grimy hands around her throat.

She held it back with all her power, but it was so strong. The thing had snow white hair, but it was matted with dirt and blood. She turned to see if anyone could help her, but they were all fighting. No, not everyone. She noticed that Kerym was on his knees, holding his side.

Fear swept through her. She had to get to him, but this troll was relentless and she had no weapon. That was when she felt something hot against her side. It was in her pocket. She reached down, still holding off the troll and pulled out the dagger that Javaid had left for her. Hadn't she put it in her bag?

Without having time to react to the thought, she brought the dagger up and stabbed the troll in the throat, over and over. Warm blood poured all over her. This was another thing she didn't have time to acknowledge.

Shoving the dead troll off her, she ran, scooping up her sword and making her way to Kerym. As she arrived, she cut down two trolls who were on top of him. When she pulled them away, she saw that Kerym was alive, still holding his side. He didn't look well.

A scream broke out and Esin snapped her head in the direction of the sound. Alynx fell to the ground with a sword through his stomach. Cielle's voice filled the cavern with a sound that pierced her soul. She watched as her sister ran to his side. Merith jumped in front of a troll that tried to take advantage of the chaos.

Looking around, she felt lost. What was she going to do to help everyone? They were going to die. She felt the dagger in her hand and not just because it was heavy, but because it was hot. She glanced down and saw that the purple blade was glowing.

It was magic. It had to be. Her father had always found a way to protect them. He was still doing so beyond the veil. And Javaid said to use it when she needed to.

Esin was filled with knowing and hope. She raised the dagger above her head and reached out, allowing the magic to take her over.

Fire, hot as the sun, shot out of the blade. For a moment, she thought it was going to consume them all. She could feel the heat on her skin nearly to the point of pain. Instead, the flames were sentient. They knew where to go and who to consume.

She watched as they made their way to each of her enemies, taking them into their fiery embrace. The trolls who were somewhat smart noticed the magical flames working their way through their ranks and began to run down the tunnels. Unfortunately for them, the fire was also intelligent. It blocked their path and ate them alive. Their screams filled the rocky cavern until they were silenced forever.

When all the trolls were vanquished, the flames disappeared and they were shrouded in darkness. Esin could feel the magic had taken its toll. She slumped to her knees and clutched her chest. Her breath came out in small, shallow gasps.

Merith ran to her side and took her face in his hands. She could make out his concerned features in the dim light. His eyes searched her face. He was scared, but intrigued.

"What was that?" he asked. "What was that magic?"

"Esin!" Cielle cried. "Esin, please! He's bleeding. I can't stop it."

Merith and Esin ran to her call. Esin stumbled, her body still weighed heavy after the magic had nearly depleted her strength, but with Merith's help she made her way to her sister's side.

"I can't help him," Cielle cried, looking to her. "I can't."

"Hush now, sweet Cielle," Alynx breathed, but coughed. "I'll be fine."

Esin moved his hand away from his gut. It was hard to see the wound with all the blood. She quickly pushed his hand back down, trying to stop the flow. Kerym wobbled over to them, his own wounds flowing freely, but at least he was standing.

"Alynx," Esin said to him.

"I know." He grunted and smiled up at them. "I know. And I know that you are going to save us all, Esin. You are going to restore our kingdom. You are…"

Alynx stopped talking. His breaths came in short gasps. He looked up at the tiny pin prick of light and smiled. Then he was gone. Cielle burst into tears and flung herself on him. Esin could feel her own emotions take over and her eyes burned. She bowed her head, her heart shattering.

Esin didn't know what to do. She wanted to comfort Cielle, but her own emotions were too raw. She turned away from the scene and walked toward the entrance of one of the tunnels.

Wind moved through the small passage and whipped her hair around her face, but she hardly noticed. All she could focus on was the loss of Alynx. He had been her friend for as long as she could remember. They had grown up together in Vaelkesh, and she had always admired his bravery and his ability to make anyone laugh.

But now he was gone, and she didn't know what that meant for the rest of their journey. The weight of his absence felt like the entire mountain pressing down on her chest.

Suddenly, she felt a hand on her shoulder. She turned to see Merith standing next to her, unshed tears in his bright blue eyes.

"We have to keep going," Merith said softly. "For him. He wouldn't want us to give up."

Esin nodded. They had a long way to go. They couldn't give up now. She had to keep moving forward. For her kingdom, and for Alynx. For everyone who had been lost.

Chapter 6

The air was heavy in the deep, dark tunnels of the mountains. No words were passed between them and the silence was loud. The loss of Alynx had turned the tide for all of them. The hope they had felt at being close to their goal was all but gone. Esin truly believe that finding Javaid would somehow be the answer to everything, to saving her sister.

Now, it seemed foolish and far-fetched. He had given her the dagger for a reason. Maybe he knew what it could do. Or, maybe he just knew it belonged to her family and now that most of them were dead it should be with her. Did he know its abilities? She hoped it was a sign that she was on the right path.

They traveled through the tunnels for several more days. Olenore had told them that the end of the tunnels would bring them as close to the Floating Isles as the city of Murthan. Until Olenore had told her about the city she didn't even know it existed.

Some of her people who didn't want to live in the tunnels had founded the city years ago. It was a port city with a thriving shipping economy according to her new friend. They stuck to themselves and were wary of outsiders, especially elves, Olenore warned. Esin felt uneasy about it so they decided to camp outside the city and enter under the cloak of night.

It was less conspicuous and she hoped she could find passage on one of the many vessels. As they made their way towards the outskirts of the city, the group stayed low and moved quickly with their hoods pulled over their heads. Esin could feel the rough stone of the dagger pressing against her thigh, reassuring her of its presence. She knew, or rather she hoped, that it was a valuable asset, one that could potentially save her sister's life.

The group stopped at the edge of the city, ducking behind a stack of crates. They could hear the sounds of merchants haggling and sailors shouting as they loaded and unloaded cargo onto the various ships in the harbor. Esin scanned the area for any ships that looked like they were headed towards the Floating Isles.

There were a few that caught her eye, but none of them looked like they would be willing to take on passengers. They were all heavily guarded and had crews that looked more like they would cut throats than set sail. Esin's heart sank as she realized that their journey would not be as easy as she had hoped.

She turned to Merith, who was peering out from behind the crates with a look of concern on his face. "What do we do now?" Esin asked, feeling defeated.

Merith furrowed his brow in thought. "We could try to find a smaller ship, one that's not as heavily guarded. It might be a risk, but it's our best chance."

Esin nodded, grateful for Merith's quick thinking and that she wasn't having to make all of the decisions for once. They began to make their way through the docks, sticking to the shadows and trying to avoid anyone they saw. It wasn't long before they came across a small dock hidden away in a secluded corner of the harbor. There was only one ship there, a small wooden vessel that looked like it had seen better days. Esin could see the captain on deck, a grizzled old man who was smoking a pipe and keeping a watchful eye on his ship.

"Let me do the talking," Kerym said and he limped forward.

"I don't think that is a good idea," Cielle grabbed his arm. "You look one wrong step away from death."

"I'll go," Esin said at last. "If it looks like things are going south then…"

She trailed off and began heading toward the captain. He saw her approach, but only because she wanted him to. Taking her in from head to foot, he stopped when he saw her pointed ears. Instinctively, he placed his hand on the hilt of his sword.

Esin was young, with soft features so her presence was still welcoming to most humans. Not that she had many runs with them living in Vaelkesh, but when she visited the cities with her sisters, they were trusting of her. That didn't seem to be serving her tonight as the captain's expression went straight to narrowed eyes and a hard stance.

"Evening, good sir," Esin began.

"Elves are not welcome here," he spat on the ground. "Even if they are young ones."

"I got that impression upon our arrival," Esin nodded her head.

"Our?" he looked over her head.

She hadn't meant to say that. If he sent anyone out to find the rest of her crew, they were in no shape to fight them at the moment. Kerym was already dangerously close to collapsing and everyone else, including her, was tired to the bones.

"My family and I," she decided to stick to their story even if she changed it a little. "My father and siblings are trying to find passage to the Floating Isles. We have relatives there. My mother has gone on to the After."

"I didn't think there were elves that far out?" He eyed her, but she was hopeful as he didn't automatically say no.

"Very distant relatives, but yes, they have lived there for a while," she tried her best to explain. "We don't know them well, but after my mother's passing, my father needs the help. After the fall of…"

"Yes," he nodded, rubbing his beard. "I have heard of the dragon armored queen and what she's done to your lands. The elves are getting a taste of what they have done to the rest of us."

Esin tried not to take offense to that. She wanted to shout at him. While she didn't deny that the royal family had done some terrible things, it didn't take away from the fact that Zanna was killing innocent elves and their families. Hers included.

"It's no wonder you're fleeing," he said, assuming he knew all he needed to. "How many of you are there?"

"Five," she said and then her heart seized. "F-four, sir. We lost … we lost a brother traveling through the tunnels."

"Damn trolls," he spat on the ground once more. "I'm sorry for your loss. Those monsters are worse than e…"

"Elves?" she finished for him and he gave her a soft smile.

"I don't like many elves." He looked at her with beady black eyes. "But I like you. What can you pay?"

They settled on a silver piece for each member of the group. Half when they left and half when they got there. Luckily, they were departing that next morning. All they needed to do was find lodging for the night and the captain, Baylth, had given them some suggestions.

Esin crashed into the bed of a very small room that they all shared. Cielle tended to all their wounds and then climbed into the bed with her. As she let sleep claim her, she heard Cielle crying.

Chapter 7

They met Baylth the next morning at the dock. Even in the early morning hours, the birds were singing and flying around, looking for food. A strong wind blew in from the ocean, the smell a mixture of salt and fish.

He gave Kerym a once over as they approached. The elf did look better after some herb enforced sleep, but his face was still ashen and sweaty.

"You're not going to die on my ship are you, elf?" the captain asked him as Esin gave him half the payment.

"Not if I can help it," Kerym said, which caused Baylth to give a gruff laugh.

"I can put you in two rooms." He led them onto the ship. "Females, even if you are elves, and I believe you know how to take care of yourselves, it would be best if you stayed below deck."

"Why?" Cielle asked him.

"I don't condone any violence," Baylth looked her at seriously. "But I sail with a rough crew who don't like elves and they like females even less. It's for your own safety."

Cielle nodded and Esin bristled at his words. Especially the way he said "female" as if that was the only way to describe them. She had heard of how some humans treated their women. Elves respected their mothers and wives. They were able to learn, fight, and live how they wanted. She believed they still had a long way to go. For example, not letting Keres in the King's Guard. However, for the most part, they were an advanced people who showed equality to all of Vaelkesh.

But only in Vaelkesh, a voice in her head told her.

That had to change. She looked over at Merith and knew in her heart that it would. He was good and would grow into a just king. That thought alone pushed her forward even though she felt like she could stop right there and sleep for a thousand years.

As they set sail, Esin retreated to the small cabin she shared with Cielle. The room was cramped and smelled of salt and mildew. She couldn't help but feel uneasy about the journey ahead. The thought of traveling with a crew that didn't respect her or her gender made her skin crawl. She knew that she would have to be on her guard at all times.

Cielle, who had already found a small corner to rest in, looked up at her with concern. "Are you all right?" she asked.

Esin forced a smile. "I'm fine. Just tired."

Cielle nodded and closed her eyes again, settling into the small space. Esin watched her for a moment before turning to the small porthole window. The ocean was vast and endless, the waves crashing against the side of the ship with a relentless force. It was both calming and terrifying all at once.

She couldn't help but wonder what was waiting for them at the Floating Isles.

Esin stared out at the endless horizon, lost in thought. She knew that Javaid was their only hope to save her sister, but what if they couldn't find him? What if he was already dead, like so many of her family members? The weight of the task ahead of them was suffocating.

As she sat there, lost in thought, she felt a strange sensation in her pocket. It was the dagger, the one Javaid had given her. It seemed to be calling out to her, pulsing with an otherworldly energy.

She slowly retrieved it from her pocket, gazing at it in awe. The hilt was made of a dark, almost black metal, etched with intricate designs that glittered in the dim light. The blade itself was razor-sharp, almost alive in her hands.

She grasped the hilt tightly and closed her eyes. She prayed that the dagger would give her some sort of answer. Javaid had left the dagger for her for a reason. It wasn't just a family heirloom. It couldn't be.

She heard a knock on the door and turned to see Merith standing in the doorway, his expression serious. "We need to talk," he said.

Esin nodded and followed him outside. They made their way to a corner of the ship where it was quiet and dark. Merith turned to her with a look of concern. "I don't know if Kerym is going to make it." Esin's heart dropped.

"He is strong," she said, more to convince herself. "He will pull through."

"Esin," he continued. "We need to prepare for the worst."

"Why are you telling me this?" She could feel anger rise in her chest.

"You know why," Merith said, catching her eye. "If he makes it through this voyage and we get the Floating Isles … a terrible decision might have to be made."

"What?" She was hot and her shirt was clinging to her skin in an uncomfortable way.

"Kerym may have to be left behind," he said. She realized where the conversation was going.

"So we just abandon him?" Esin nearly yelled. "Is that what we have come to? Just leaving family to die?"

"No, that's not what I'm saying." He shook his head.

"Oh, I know exactly what you're saying, *prince*." She said it like an insult. "That's what we are known for, right? Using someone up until they are no use to us anymore and then discarding them."

"You are not listening to me, Esin." He sounded tired.

"I hear you loud and clear." She spat and then made to leave.

He grabbed her shoulders and she instinctively grabbed the dagger and held it at this throat. She knew there was murder in her eyes and Merith flinched at her expression. They stared at each other for a long moment.

The blue of his eyes glistened in the low light. His face was pure and perfect in the way youth often is. Flawless skin, despite the hard travel and trials they had endured. That made her even more angry. What gave him the right to look so beautiful with such cruel words leaving his mouth?

Slowly he released her and she lowered the dagger. They stood there for a moment longer. His eyes searched her face and she felt exposed even though they were shrouded in darkness.

"What I should have led with was Kerym himself sent me to you," Merith continued. "He doesn't feel like he has much longer and he told me that if it comes to it, we have to leave him behind to continue our mission."

Esin felt shock course through her body followed closely by guilt. She had assumed the worst in Merith and she could see the hurt etched across his face. Instantly she felt remorse and wanted to erase the accusations from his mind.

"Merith," she started, but he held up his hand.

"It's alright, Esin," he gave her a small smile. "Just do me a favor and stick to your room. I don't trust this crew. Their views are barbaric, but unfortunately, we are at their mercy."

"Of course," she nodded.

With that Merith lead her back to her room and bid her a goodnight. Cielle wanted to know what they had discussed, but she wasn't in the spirits to talk about it.

Kerym couldn't give up. Not now. She knew that he would fight with everything he had, but she wasn't sure how much longer he could. The thought broke something inside of her. Losing Alynx had taken so much out of them, but if she lost Kerym, she wasn't sure if she would survive.

Chapter 8

For days they sailed the open seas. It was smooth at first, but then the waters turned choppy and the sky faded from bright blue to gray. Dark clouds hung low overhead, and Esin could feel the pressure from a storm bearing down on her spine.

Sleeping was nearly impossible, and she felt she was going insane being cooped up in the small room with Cielle. She knew her sister was feeling the same way. And as much she loved her sister, if they didn't reach the Floating Isles soon, she was going to lose her mind. Cielle wasn't doing anything. It wasn't just her own thoughts.

It was everything they had faced and would face in the future. It was this ship and its crew. It was how Merith had to bring them food because they weren't allowed anywhere on the ship.

"Esin," Cielle said softly. "I haven't…I didn't want to bring it up…after Alynx…"

"Speak, Cielle," Esin pinched the bridge of her nose, feeling a pain behind her eyes.

"The dagger," she looked up from the bed she sat on. "What was that? Father gave us all a dagger, but I didn't know it could do that. Why didn't he tell us? Why did Javaid give it to you? Did he know?"

"I don't know," she answered honestly. "I don't know anything. I have my suspicions, but I don't know."

"What are you thinking?" Cielle wondered. "Please, tell me, because I am lost."

Esin took a deep breath and looked out the small window, watching as the waves crashed against the ship's hull. "I think father knew more than he let on," she said after a moment of silence. "And I think Javaid must have figured something out. That's why he left it for me."

Cielle's eyes widened with hope. "Do you think he has a plan?"

"I don't know," Esin admitted and sat down. "But I suppose we have to tr..."

The ship suddenly lurched to one side, throwing Esin and Cielle off the bed and onto the floor. There was a loud crack as something snapped, and the ship began to tilt dangerously to one side.

"Get up!" Esin yelled, grabbing her sister's hand and pulling her toward the door. "We need to get to upper deck!"

The two sisters stumbled out of the room and into the hall. They met Merith and Kerym as they ran out of their own room. Kerym had looked better, but he was on his feet. His face was gray and haggard and his shine was dull. It hurt Esin's heart, but there were more pressing matters.

They rushed up the creaking staircase and came out on the deck. The sailors were busy pulling ropes and the captain was in a wrestling match with the wheel. Giant swells were rocking the boat back and forth. People were having trouble staying on their feet.

If the group of elves weren't graced with a stronger equilibrium, they would have more trouble themselves. Even so, it was hard to stand on their feet. The waves crashed over the bow of the ship as they sailed through each swell, drenching them with cold, salty water.

Esin could only stand there. She wasn't a sailor. She had no magic to save them and bring them to shore. It was possible this could be it. Their journey may end here in the vast depths of the sea.

There was a feeling of dread in the pit of her stomach that suddenly overcame her. Something that told her that there was more out there than the storm.

"Merith..." her voice was barely a whisper, and her words were cut off by the sound of a song.

It was loud and rose above the crashing of the waves. Esin immediately covered Merith's ears. Cielle turned and covered Kerym's. Merith looked at her with concern and fear. He was clearly confused.

"Cover your ears!" Esin cried out. "Don't listen! Sirens!"

It was already too late for some of the crew. They stopped their work and stood stock still in place. The men rocked back and forth with the ship, falling over and getting back on their feet, the same distant look on their faces.

"It's the song!" Esin screamed over the loud waves.

"Cover your own ears!" Merith tried pulling from her, but she held tight.

"It won't affect me," she shook her head. "Sirens only go after men."

She heard the song louder, a chorus of voices signing a beautiful, but sorrowful song:

"And when the sun shines no more;

will you still be there on the darkened shore,

and wait for me,

your love to be,

we can be together forevermore."

She had heard of this before, but she had never thought she would have to face it. The sirens' song was known to lure men to their deaths, but not just any men, men who were weak-willed, and easily tempted. She had to get control of the crew before it was too late.

She let go of Merith's ears, hoping he could withstand the temptation, and went to the main deck to take charge. The song was louder now, and she could see the crew members slowly losing their minds to the mesmerizing melody as they began making their way to the ship's edge. They were swaying to the beat of the song, and their eyes were glazed over with a faraway look.

Esin grabbed the halyard and swung herself up to the mainmast. From there, she had a vantage point of the entire deck. She looked out into the ocean and saw figures in the high waves. One stood out amongst the group.

She raised herself out of the water enough for Esin to see her dark hair and grayish purple skin. Her voice carried over all the noise from the sea and sky. She felt the hair on the back of her neck stand up, as the haunting melody filled her ears. Men began jumping from the ship. No, it wasn't jumping; it was falling. They simply walked to the edge and just kept going.

As each man fell, one of the figures would dive underwater and not return. Esin tried not to imagine what they were doing, but she knew.

Without warning, a figure appeared on the deck. It was a woman, with long dark hair and piercing dark eyes, the same ones she had seen just moments ago.

"We do not harm our sisters," she said to Esin. "But we will take all the men."

"What if I can't let you do that?" Esin asked her.

"You do not have a choice," the woman told her. "What man here is worthy of saving."

"I know of two," Esin said.

"Lies," the siren nearly sang. "No man is worth saving."

"I'm sure you have reason to believe that," Esin reasoned with her. "But I beg you to spare just two. I will be indebted to you."

"Why do you care for these men?" She gestured toward her group. "He is too old for you, so is it the boy you love? Love is fickle."

"I love them both," Esin said, feeling her heart flutter. "They are my family. The only ones I have left."

"What will you give in exchange?" she asked, her wispy eyebrow raised.

"What do you want?" Esin asked.

"A strand of your white hair."

"Why?" She was wary.

"It is what I ask for," the siren said. "Do you accept? For the men you claim are good?"

She looked at her group and Merith was shaking his head no with his ears still covered. Cielle still held on to Kerym, her mentor was barely on his feet. She took a deep breath and reached up, pulling a strand of her hair out of her head. It didn't hurt, but she felt she was doing something irreversible.

"I will take the others," she said with a smile and took the strand of hair. "All of them."

The siren smelled the hair and closed her eyes as if she were savoring the scent. Esin didn't know what she could smell with one strand of hair, but she didn't know much about sirens other than their tendency to sing men off of ships.

"What will you do with the hair?" Esin asked.

"Elves were made with magic," she said, placing the hair in a small satchel at her waist. "There is powerful magic coursing through those veins. Elves could be stronger, but they forgot how to use that magic long ago. Sirens have not. With this one strand, you have saved my people even if you don't understand how. For that, I thank you. You are a friend to the sirens."

"Thank you for not eating my friends." Esin tried to smile.

The siren gave her a stern look and then dove off the ship. Esin turned and watched the sailors as they splashed into the ocean. Part of her felt sorry for them, even guilty, but they were bad men. Merith and Kerym were ten times the men they were. She would trade them all for her friends.

Chapter 9

After all the sailors had fallen to the song of the sirens, they were left alone on the ship. The storm seemed to build, pounding the ship with powerful waves and strong winds. Esin felt lost. She knew nothing about sailing. None of them did. They were in trouble.

"What do we do?" Cielle asked, fear in her voice.

"I don't know," Esin admitted. "I don't know."

"Watch out!" Merith yelled as a huge wave crashed onto the deck.

Esin was nearly washed off the ship. She saved herself by stabbing the dagger into the wood of the deck and holding on. She went to stand, but another wave pushed her down once more. Soon, waves were coming in quick succession.

The ship was titling dangerously and there was nothing she could do. They were at the mercy of the ocean gods and the gods were angry. Another wave, high and strong, crashed down on top of them. Esin felt herself being pulled and heard the cracking of wood. The last thing she remembered was hitting the cold ocean water below.

*

Sunlight burned her eyes and she shielded them with her arm. Esin's mind was garbled with panic and incoherent thoughts. There was a long period of time where she couldn't think and was confused about what was happening.

When her vision cleared, she found herself on a rocky shore. It was a beach covered with small, black pebbles. The sky was dark and water lapped at her. She sat up, trying her best to clear her head. She reached up and touched a painful spot on her head and her fingers came away with bright, red blood.

"Esin!" Merith called to her.

She turned to see him running down the beach toward her. He had a gash across his cheek that was bleeding heavily, but other than that he seemed to be in good shape after being in a shipwreck.

A shipwreck. That's right. Her memories were coming back to her. The sirens. The storm. She was lucky to be alive. Looking around she noticed she didn't see her sister or Kerym. Wobbly, she stood up and began calling for them.

"Cielle! Kerym!" She moved down the shore.

Merith finally reached her and took her in his arms. He hugged her close as if he was afraid to let go.

"Where are they?" she felt tears sting her eyes.

"Kerym is just over there," Merith said. "He's in bad shape."

"And Cielle?" she wondered.

"I can't find her," he said, and Esin felt her world tilt.

Not Cielle, too. Please, to all the gods I pray for her safety. Please!

"Esin!" She turned around so fast she nearly fell. "Esin!"

Cielle was limping toward her. She held her side as if she was in terrible pain. Esin ran to her, feeling dizzy. Grabbing her sister, she hugged her tightly.

"Ow! Ow!" Cielle yelped. "I think I have some broken ribs."

"Cielle, I'm … are you ok?" Esin was overcome with emotions.

"As much as I can be." She nodded. "Your head is bleeding."

"I'll be ok," Esin said to her, scared to take her eyes off her beautiful sister.

"Where is Kerym?" Cielle asked.

Merith lead them back to the old guard. Kerym was propped against a large black rock, his skin ashen and his shoulder bleeding. Cielle began rendering aid to him. Esin knelt beside him and pressed her forehead to his.

"You turned out all right, little one," Kerym said, and Esin felt her heart break.

"Please," she whispered. "Don't leave me."

"It's only for a time," Kerym told her. "We will meet again. And I will always, always be with you."

"I can't do this without you." She finally looked at him.

"You can do anything, Esin," Kerym told her. "You got us to the Floating Isles."

"But…" she looked around. "I don't see them."

"Look harder," Kerym said to her. "Just through the mists."

Esin looked out at the water and scanned it. She didn't see anything until, just there, the outlines of land masses came into view. They were large, the size surprising even her.

"We did it Kerym!" She smiled. "We made it."

When she turned to look at him Kerym was already gone. A sob tried to escape her throat, but she held it back. Instead, she laid her head against his chest, hugging him close for a very long time. It was long enough that Merith had to coax her to let go.

She didn't want to, but she knew she had to. Kerym had believed in her. Looking at her sister and Merith, she knew they believed in her, too. She had to believe in herself. Now, how did they get on the floating islands?

*

She surveyed her surroundings, taking in the vast ocean and the massive floating islands in the distance. The sun was setting, casting a hazy glow through the mists that made the islands seem almost magical.

Merith spoke up, breaking her out of her reverie. "We'll need to find a way to get to the islands," he said, his shoulders tense, but his voice was determined.

They moved further down the beach, all the while her heart in pieces inside her chest, rattling with each step. She wasn't sure if she would ever feel safe again, if she would ever feel anything.

"There!" Cielle suddenly shouted.

They gazed in the direction she indicated. As the fog dissipated, they noticed how the stones on the shoreline gradually moved upwards, and saw that someone had created steps into the solid rock.

"Looks like we have to go up," Esin said, taking in a deep breath.

Without further discussion, they began climbing. There wasn't much to talk about. This had been their destination and they were nearly there.

She took one step after another, the stairs slick from the ocean spray. Even though the sun was hidden behind a thick mist, the climb made her sweat profusely. But she didn't stop. She had to get to the top.

As she climbed, she noticed that the stairs were becoming narrower and more treacherous. She had to take extra care not to slip and fall. Her heart was racing, but she kept going, hoping the others were doing ok. She was afraid to take her eyes off the path ahead, lest she fall.

As she approached the top, she noticed that the staircase ended in a small platform. She took a deep breath and stepped onto the platform.

There was nothing.

It was an empty, barren land, cold and desolate. For as far as her elf eyes could see, she saw a void. She felt her heart deflate. They had come so far, lost so much, and for what.

"Look!" Cielle pointed. "The other isles."

Esin looked through fog and could see the rest of the Floating Isles in the far distance. It looked vast and covered in greenery. Faintliy, she could even see buildings, a city, and other dwellings.

"That's the gnome cities," Merith stated, looking with her.

"Do we keep going?" Cielle asked, exhaustion in her voice.

Esin didn't answer because she didn't know. For the first time in this long journey, she felt unsure. Of course, there were so many questions and doubts she had, but she still knew what her goal was. Get to Javaid. Save Zanna.

Javaid was here, somewhere. Perhaps he was even with the gnomes. Maybe she could convince them for their aid in getting her home back. It all felt so far away, even though they were right here.

There was a noise that caught all of their attention. It sounded like fabric flapping in the wind, like one of the flags that adorned the Vaelkesh castle. They turned, following the sound as it moved.

The group moved closer together, drawing their swords. Something was moving above them.

As they looked up, they saw a figure gliding towards them, its wings flapping in the darkened sky. The creature was like nothing they had ever seen before - a bat like creature, but the size of a small horse, with razor-sharp teeth and claws. It swooped down towards them, its eyes glowing with a fierce hunger.

Instinctively, the group moved back, their swords raised. But the creature was too fast, too agile. It landed on the ground in front of them and let out a deafening screech. They could feel the wind from its wings as it towered over them, ready to attack.

For a moment, they hesitated, unsure of how to approach this new threat. Esin stepped forward, her sword dirty from troll blood, but knowing it was still sharp and true. She was ready to charge this beast, to protect her friends and all of Vaelkesh.

She took off, running at the beast full speed. Cielle and Merith on her heels. They too knew they had to keep fighting. As she reached the creature, two more flew down and joined its companion.

Esin wasn't sure if they would make it out of this alive, but she had to try. When she reached the creature, she leapt into the air, bring her sword down hard and fast. She connected with the creature's neck and slid down, bringing her blade along with her. Warm blood and a wild roar came out of the monster.

It tried to move, but staggered and fell at her feet. She wasted no time to go help her sister and together they brought the beast down, just as Merith slayed his own.

They grouped back together, breathing hard. Merith took his sleeve and wiped the blood from her forehead.

"Your wound is still bleeding." He looked concerned. "Let me take a look."

She wanted to argue, but didn't have the energy. She sat on a nearby rock and let Merith and Cielle tend to her. Just as Cielle was dabbing at the wound, another roar sounded in the distance. They immediately stood, sword at the ready.

When the mists cleared, Esin's heart sank. There were at least twenty of the creatures flying in their direction. She had no doubt that they could take down at least half on a good day, but they were hurt and tired.

She looked over at her companions and saw the look of fear on their faces but also determination.

"Hey," she said to Merith. "If we don't make it out of this, you're not as bad as I thought you were."

"You're not too bad yourself," he half smiled at her.

"Will you two stop your love lost goodbyes!" Cielle screamed. "Esin, use the dagger!"

Esin had been so fearful that this was the last time she would see her friends and had forgotten she had another weapon. She hurriedly retrieved the dagger for her side and brought it out in front of her.

Holding it up to the sky, she called on the same power that had come to her aid before. Nothing happened. She stood there, her arm in the air, the creatures still flying at them. Esin brought down the dagger and looked at it as if that would tell her what was wrong.

"Esin!" Cielle screamed. "If you're going to do it, do it now!"

"It's not working!" she screamed back in irritation.

She held the dagger up again but it still didn't work. Maybe it was a one-time deal and she had already used all the magic. The creatures were so close now and she didn't know what else to do.

Suddenly there was a loud roar overhead, different from the screams of the bat-like creatures. They looked up and saw a dragon, scales the color of crimson blood. Behind it, another that was gold, its armored body seemed to glisten even in the misty sky.

The dragons flew around the creatures, circling them in. The red dragon let out a loud roar and blew fire from its open mouth. At least seven or eight of the monsters caught ablaze and began plummeting to the ground. The gold dragon barreled at another one, opening its wide mouth and clamping down on the neck of the nearest beast.

Fire was filling the sky and the monsters began to retreat. After a moment, the remaining creatures who escaped flew into the mists. The dragons flew back and forth as if the make sure they were gone and then landed in front of the group.

Esin and the others backed up, swords still drawn. She didn't know if the dragons had saved them from the creatures or saved them for themselves.

The dragons were massive and fierce looking. While they were the most beautiful thing she had ever seen and wanted to touch their leathery wings, she still knew they could fry them to a crisp.

Then she saw a figure move on the dragon's back. They were covered in armor and easily slid to the dragon's wing and onto the ground. As they approached, Esin instinctively backed away, knowing who stood in front of her.

"Zanna," she said in a whispered breath.

"Hello, little sister," Zanna said.

Chapter 10

The armor she wore covered her from head to foot in black dragon scales. It was the Armor of Dusan. Esin had seen her sister that night her parents were killed. She was the one who had done it. Zanna was magically fused with the armor, melded with it. Bound to it.

The armor had taken over who she was and twisted it. This wasn't Zanna, this wasn't her sister. This was a monster who had claimed her sister's body and soul. How could she ever think Zanna could be saved?

"Cielle," she said to her other sibling. "You two have been quite troublesome. You've interfered with all of my plans, but at least it wasn't for nothing. You did bring me the child king."

The golden dragon landed behind them and another rider stepped off in very much the same fashion Zanna had. Esin recognized her as the witch who was with Zanna when she killed her parents. Rage filled her and she wanted to enact her revenge, but knew if she did, they would all be in trouble. She had to remain calm and see if she could get them out of this, even though that seemed impossible.

The witch walked gracefully over to Merith, her tall frame draped with a flowy dress. It was impractical for fighting or riding dragons. She wore no armor, either. It was her way of showing strength. She had enough power; she didn't need a shield.

When stories of witches were told, she had always imagined them gaunt and ugly. This witch was beautiful with dark hair and a youthful appearance. She circled Merith with a twisted smile on her beautiful face.

"Can I have him?" she asked. "Young would-be kings are my favorite."

"We have to put on a show," Zanna commanded. "He remains alive and untouched. For now."

The witch pouted and ran a long finger down Merith's face. He pulled back, and there was fear in his eyes.

"Don't touch him!" Esin snarled.

"Oh, are we in love, little elf?" the witch teased. "I promise I won't hurt him too badly, when the time comes."

"Zanna, please," Esin turned to her sister. "This is not you. Stop this. All of this and we can start over."

"Sweet, little sister, there is no going back," Zanna moved forward a step and her large dragon shuffled behind her, snorting a plume of smoke out of its nose.

"Zanna, if only…" Cielle began.

Zanna cut her off with a sneering laugh. "If only what, Cielle? If only I hadn't killed our parents? If only I hadn't taken over the kingdom? If only I hadn't become the most powerful being in all the land?" She shook her head. "No, there is no 'if only.' This is who I am now. And you two can either join me or die."

Esin and Cielle exchanged a look of desperation. They knew there was no reasoning with Zanna, not anymore. She was lost to them, consumed by the power of the armor.

"We can't do that, Zanna," Cielle said to her, tears in her eyes.

"You know, I never liked you," Zanna said and she raised her hand.

As she did, pieces of her armor seemed to melt and pool at her feet. It was a black, inky puddle that vibrated with power. Zanna raised her hand again and the liquid became solid, forming into a black blade. She took hold of the pommel and raised it in a fighting stance.

With a sudden burst of speed, Zanna lunged towards Esin, her sword fierce and sharp. Esin barely had time to raise her own sword in defense before Zanna's blade met hers with a loud clash.

Esin felt the impact reverberate through her arm as she struggled to keep her footing against Zanna's overwhelming strength. Cielle rushed to her side, her own weapon at the ready.

Merith made a move to help, but the witch waved a hand in front of his face and he fell to the ground.

She picked up his unconscious body and began walking back to the golden dragon. They were going to take him. They were going to take him and execute him in front of everyone in Vaelkesh. She knew it in her heart that's what Zanna had meant by making an example of him.

Esin wanted to help him, but the three siblings were locked in a vicious battle, each one swinging their swords with deadly accuracy. Zanna's dragon took off and circled overhead, adding to the chaos with jets of flame.

This had to end. Merith couldn't be taken. She had to get to him, but she didn't see how that was going to happen. Zanna was making it hard for them to even deflect a simple blow. Esin had a feeling she was only toying with them. If she wanted them dead, she would have done it by now. She was enjoying this.

For what seemed like an eternity, the battle raged on. Esin and Cielle fought with all their might against their once-beloved sister, hoping to break through the armor's hold on her. In truth, it had only been a moment. The witch was just securing Merith to the harness on the dragon.

"Stop!" Esin yelled at her. "Stop! You can't have him."

She wished the dagger at her side would work once more. She could save them all. Instead, she grabbed it and threw it at the witch with all of her strength. The move was so sudden that even Zanna stopped her assault, watching the dagger sail through the air.

The small, sharp blade found its target. The witch stopped what she was doing and looked down at her chest. A ring of red seeped around the blade, staining her white dress. She looked up at Esin with a look of hatred so pure that the young elf felt it in her soul.

The witch fell, rolling off the dragon and onto the cold, wet soil of the floating isle. Esin had been decent with the dagger, but never that good. The dagger must have an accuracy spell on it for it to hit the witch the way it did.

"You've killed my witch," Zanna said to her. "That was my job when her usefulness expired. I guess I must take something from you. It's only fair."

Zanna charged once more with inhuman speed and plunged her blade through Cielle's middle. Esin's entire world stopped. Everything was moving in slow motion and images of her parent's murder flashed into her mind's eye. Bile rose in her throat, but what came out was a horrified scream full of anger and pain.

Cielle turned and looked at her. She gave Esin a small and hopeless smile. Her eyes were full of tears and seemed to convey to Esin her own hopelessness. Zanna pulled the sword out and Cielle dropped to the ground.

Esin slide to her knees and crawled over to Cielle. She laid her head on her sister's chest, not hearing a single beat of her heart. She closed her eyes, unable to take anymore. This loss was too great. If Zanna wanted to kill her, Esin would not fight her. She had no more fight left.

"I have always loved you, Esin," Zanna kneeled in front her. "I would make room for you in my kingdom. Join me. We can be a family again."

Esin cried, holding tight to Cielle. After all they had been through, this was it. Every single person in her family was lost. Zanna to the armor and the rest of them to the After.

Esin took a deep breath and lifted her head. She stared at Zanna, her mind racing with conflicting emotions. She had loved her sister, once upon a time, but now she couldn't bring herself to trust her. Not after everything that had happened. Not after Cielle was gone.

"Your kingdom?" Esin spat out the words. "You mean the kingdom you destroyed? The one where you killed our parents and destroyed everything we held dear?"

Zanna didn't even seem to flinch at the accusation, her eyes narrowing. "I did what I had to do to enact my revenge. Your parents, my grandparents, lied to me my entire life. They wanted me to believe I was fully human, indebted to them for sparing me from bandit parents. Instead, your father killed his own son and my mother. All because she was human and he was an elf and created me, a half-blood. Should I be grateful my life was spared? No. The elves have taken too much from all of Vaelkesh. They deserved worse than I gave them. They owed me."

Esin laughed bitterly. "And you think by doing what you have you are any better? No. You're worse."

"I did what I had to do," Zanna repeated, her voice growing colder. "And I'm offering you a chance to join me. Together, we can rule this land."

Esin shook her head. "I'll never join you. I'd rather die and join my family. The family that truly loved me. The family that would have done anything to protect me. Like you once did."

"That can be arranged," Zanna told her. "Any last wishes."

"I want to see your face," Esin said. "Take off that helmet and look me in the eyes. That is the least you can do."

Zanna said nothing for a moment. Esin thought maybe her wish wouldn't be granted. Slowly, the helmet melted away from Zanna's face. She was just as Esin remembered. Beautiful dark eyes and sun-kissed skin. Her flaming red hair was a mass of curls, framing her head like a crown of fire.

"You are not that much changed, sister," Esin said to her. "Your eyes are colder, but I can still see the stars."

Zanna's expression betrayed her for just a moment. Her hard mask of hatred slipped and Esin's sister came through.

"Esin!" Merith yelled.

He was awake. When she had killed the witch, her magic over him had ended. She looked up just as he was throwing the dagger in her direction. Esin and Zanna reacted at the same time. Zanna tried pushing her sister out of the way, but Esin was small and quick.

She dodged Zanna, rolling, and as she rose to her knees, she caught the dagger. Turning a split second later, with Zanna right in front of her, Esin shot to her feet and plunged the dagger forward, calling on all the gods and the power that was once given to her.

The short blade hit its target, sinking into Zanna's left eye. She cried out in pain and as she did so, Esin felt the power surge through her. Flames ignited through the dagger and exploded outward, sending Esin flying backward.

She landed hard near Merith, who helped her to her feet. They both looked at Zanna, her face ablaze and thrashing, trying to put the flames out. Her dragon roared overhead and the golden dragon shot up to the sky to join its companion. The beasts almost seemed to be crying, their roars like a sorrowful song.

Esin felt sick to her stomach. This wasn't the outcome she had hoped for. She wanted to believe that Zanna could be saved. Maybe, with enough time, she could have been. That was one thing they didn't have. Time.

Zanna's dragon circled around, hovering over her burning sister. For a moment, Esin thought the dragon might make a move to save her, but it didn't. It shot up into the sky once again and disappeared into the mists.

The golden dragon followed after its companion, leaving the scene behind them. Esin turned away and looked at Merith, who was holding Cielle tightly in his arms. A hollow feeling filled her stomach. Something had died inside her. She had lost two sisters in one blow. The pain she felt was going to eat her alive if she didn't move.

There was still work to be done. While the threat of her sister's reign was over, they still needed to let the people know that Merith was alive and reinstate him as king. Vaelkesh was undoubtedly in chaos and if there was no ruler, she was afraid of what might happen to it.

There was a flutter of wings overhead and she and Merith stood, certain Zanna's dragon had returned for its revenge. Instead, a dragon of the brightest blue bursts from the mists, followed closely by several more.

Dragons had been scarce for thousands of years. Seeing two was unthinkable. Now, she saw an entire fleet. Under different circumstances, it might fill her with wonder and joy, but truthfully it only reminded her how drastic things had changed in the past two years.

Esin and Merith didn't know what else to do but move forward. After they lit a pyre for Cielle and Esin blessed her spirit into the After, they continued walking.

The floating isle was vast, and became even more barren the further they walked. There was a small shrub here and there, and a small tree clinging to life, but much didn't grow. Esin assumed it was because the mists hid the sun.

There was movement in the distance. Her eyesight was keen, but even for her it was hard to see in this heavy fog. It didn't help she was weary from the fight and everything else. Her heart felt heavy and she just wanted a nice place to sleep. With a figure moving toward them in the distance, she didn't see that happening any time soon.

She and Merith stopped, preparing for whatever lay ahead. By Merith's face and stance, he was just as exhausted as her. Whatever the witch had done to him had taken much. His eyes looked hard and he had jumped at any little sound. Now, he just looked angry.

"Javaid?" she whispered as the figure emerged from the shadows. "Javaid!"

She ran to him and nearly tackled him with a hug. He held her tight. It wasn't the most comfortable hug considering the armor he wore, but she didn't care. Javaid was her family. The only one she had left.

"I didn't think we would ever find you." Esin felt tears fall from her eyes.

She cried, thankful he was alive. While she knew this fight was far from over, this seemed to be a victory for her, for all of them.

"I am here," he told her, pressing a kiss to the top of her head as more people came out of the dark mists.

Men and women, from all parts of Vaelkesh it looked like, stood behind him. Some faces she recognized, but many she didn't. These were survivors. Those who had fled for their lives and left their homes because of Zanna's reign of terror. They looked at her and Merith with wonder and hope.

And, to her surprise, there were many gnomes with them. A part of her knew that Javaid would make friends with the native peoples of the Floating Isles. She bowed to one of the gnomes and he bowed in return.

"They have offered their assistance," Javaid explained. "Myself and many people from Vaelkesh owe them our lives."

"Thank you for what you have done for my people," Merith said to the strong gnome and to Javaid.

"Your majesty." He bowed to Merith who nodded to him in return. "You both look weary, but I must admit how good it is to see you."

"Javaid," Esin's voice trembled. "Zanna…she…I…"

"She is gone," Javaid nodded. "I saw her dragon. We came to help you, but it seems you did not need it."

"You left me the dagger," Esin said to him. "Did you know?"

"I had my suspicions," he nodded. "It was left on … Keres. I kept it because … because it was hers and I knew your father had given it to her. When we sent Keres on to the After, this dagger took in the fire and stored it. I knew then it had magical properties. I tried using it, thinking it might be a weapon, but it would not work for me."

"It had to be used by someone from Esin's line," Merith offered.

"Yes," Javaid said. "I believed so. I left it with Olenore and told her you would be coming to find me and to make sure she gave it to you."

"That explains the fire," Merith observed. "If it stores power, like the fire, then it must expel it on command."

"It makes sense," Esin agreed, knowing that if not for the dagger, she and Merith may not be alive. She also knew that this could be very dangerous in the wrong hands.

Esin looked down at the dagger in her hand, feeling the weight of it. Zanna had taken everything from her, but this dagger was a reminder of the woman who had given her hope and strength. Keres. Her sister. All of her sisters.

"Thank you," she said to Javaid, her voice still thick with emotion. "For coming back for us. For bringing everyone here."

Javaid gave her a small smile. "You are my family, Esin. These people are my family. We take care of our own."

Merith stepped forward, looking at the group gathered around them. "We have won a great victory today," he said, his voice steady and strong. "But our fight is not over. Zanna may be gone, but her legacy remains. We must work together to rebuild and create a better Vaelkesh for all of us."

There were nods of agreement from the group, and Esin felt a surge of pride for her people. They had much left to do, but together they could rebuild and do better for all people.

THE END

A Dark Quest
Selah J Tay-Song

Rivenielen kept his hood deep when he entered the inn. All eyes turned to him. Elves were rarely seen near the Ash Mountains, and an elf traveling alone rarer still. His shimmering white silk cloak and delicate silver armor set him apart from the miners in rough spun clothes drinking at *The Dancing Ram*, the last human foothold before the hills turned to craggy peaks and the land grew too grim and bleak for life.

The innkeeper, who might have been the dancing ram himself with a mop of curly gray hair and a thick white beard, gave him a hard look that made Riven want to tug his hood down even further. The glare faded when Riven set a handful of silver coins on the scarred oak counter.

"Your best room for the night, a bath, and a private dining room."

"As you say, M'Lord. We haven't a private dining room, though. You'll have to eat in here with my other patrons."

"I'll skip dinner." Riven still had some dried fish and berries in his rucksack, and the sight of the glowing red mountains in the distance this afternoon had chased away his appetite.

"Suit yourself," the innkeeper muttered, counting off a few coins and sliding them back over the counter.

A beefy, red-faced man at the end of the bar hollered, "Wa, his Lordship'd rather starve than eat w' the likes of us?"

To which another man slurred, "Probably heard you belch when he walked in, Connor! You can't blame him not wanting to eat with the likes of you!" And the inn erupted in laughter.

Riven did not join in. He stared down the chuckling innkeeper until the man's grin evaporated and he called for a serving girl to show Riven to his room. It was small and drafty and the mattress was as hard as Riven had suspected it would be, but blessedly the steaming tub was in the room, not in a shared bathing room, and the blankets were thick enough to keep out the chill sweeping down off the mountains and over the plains.

Riven waited until he no longer heard the serving girl's footsteps in the hall, then barred the door and moved a heavy chest of drawers against it. He pushed back his hood, shed his cloak and armor, and slowly stripped away his fine linen clothes, revealing himself to the standing mirror before the tub.

His silver hair was greasy and dusty from his long journey, and now flecked with ash from the so-named mountains of his destination. His brow was heavy, his eyes pools of blackness. And his skin, no matter the angle of the light, was always dark, like the blue-green water of a deep forest pool.

Riven stared at his dark reflection, hating it, as always, and as always, wishing the mirror lied.

*

The day Sindranielle found the baby was like any other spring day in the forests south of Laewaes. She was frolicking in a bend in the stream, letting the frothy rapids push her down to a deeper pool where she startled serene fish. An otter family discovered her, and after some curious hesitation, the pups joined her play while the adults hunted in the shadowy banks. After a while, a few of Sindra's elven friends came to join her. Their splashing and laughter, some of the more stoic elves later said, could be heard all the way to the halls of the royal palace.

In the midst of a splash battle between the young otters and the elves, Sindra looked up the river and saw a dark object about the size of a loaf of bread teetering at the edge of the little waterfall above the rapids. She swam swiftly in hopes of catching it. But the thing fell over the falls and broke apart, and when it came through the rapids, she saw that it was two things; a small basket woven from black spider silk, and a tiny, wriggling creature.

She reached the bottom of the rapids at the same time as the wriggling thing, and plucked it gingerly from the water. The basket floated on past, and was soon out of sight around the next bend. Otters and elves alike crowded around to see what she had found.

It was a tiny elven baby, with perfect little toes and fingers. It was wailing and tears streamed from its eyes, which were squeezed shut with the effort of crying. It was flawless in every way, except that its skin was a dark greenish blue. At first, she thought it was a trick of the light on the water of the stream, but the sun came full out of a cloud and she saw that the color was in the baby's skin.

Sindra had never seen an elf like this, of any age. She cradled it to her breast and rocked it in the water, trying to comfort it. She had no babies of her own, and had little hope to, for love had come and gone too many times, and her heart was in pieces. Holding this strange, tiny babe seemed to stitch the pieces back together.

After a while the babe stilled, but Sindra kept holding it, enjoying the warmth of its skin against hers. One of the otter pups crept close and gave its heel a sniff. The pup snarled and splashed backward through the water, away from the babe. The other pups scattered, and regrouped to look on from a distance. The other elves drew in closer.

"I believe you've found a little dark elf whelp," one of them said. "What an ugly, evil creature."

"How would you know?" Sindra felt suddenly defensive. "No one of our generation has ever seen a dark elf. You can't know that he is one of them."

"I've seen paintings of them in Laewaes," the elf said.

"He's right," said another. "You should let it go on downstream, Sin. This evil little creature will cause nothing but trouble."

"Better yet, bash its head against a rock and drown it," said the first elf.

Sindra grasped the little creature closer. "I'll do no such thing! He's mine, I found him, and I'm keeping him. He's only a little river elf, after all."

To this, all the elves began to speak at once.

"A river elf! Then where are his webbed fingers and toes?"

"Do you not see the peaked forehead and thin lips? Classic dark elf features."

"And his fingers, tapered almost to a point."

"Mark me, this will be a vessel of evil in our midst."

"It should be put out of the forest at once."

"It should be exterminated!"

But Sindra had already slipped away and swam to the shallows, keeping a tight grip on the little elf babe. Her playmates did not follow, and she soon heard the sounds of merriment resume in her wake. Stepping out of the stream, she dried the babe and wrapped him in her shirt.

"You are mine," she affirmed again. "I shall call you Rivenielen."

*

Riven woke to the sound of hammering at a nearby blacksmith anvil, and shouts of someone selling sheep in the street below. He had slept, and he was cleaner than he had been in days, but he felt tired and sore. The air here was choked with ash and smoke from the mountains, and his lungs hurt. He missed the clear air of the forest, the sparkling stream, the enchanting lanterns that graced the boughs of his mother's dell.

He rose from the warmth of the bed to the drafty room and quickly pulled on his clothes. Cold didn't touch an elf the way it troubled humans, but this particular coldness reminded Riven of where he was and why.

When he tossed his cloak over his shoulders, Riven paused with his fingers on the silken hood. After a long moment, he left his hood down. Last night he had been too weary to bear the stares and trouble it would invite to leave his face uncovered, but today was another matter. He couldn't skulk around this town in broad daylight with his hood up. Clinging to the edge of the Ash

Mountains, this little settlement was wary of strangers, with good reason. Better to reveal himself now, than risk misunderstandings later.

Riven did not look at himself as he passed the mirror standing before the tub.

When he entered the common room, every eye settled on him. Fortunately, it wasn't as busy as it had been last night. The innkeeper, a barmaid, and a few patrons picking at a greasy breakfast stared at Riven as he approached the bar.

Fear tightened the lines around the innkeeper's eyes. Riven regretted his decision to reveal his dark face. Now he would have to be extra polite.

"A better room I have never stayed in," he said in the soft, lilting tone of the forest elves. "I thank you kindly for your hospitality. The bath was hot, the bed free of pests. I will recommend your establishment heartily."

Riven watched a familiar cascade of confusion, then suspicion, then acceptance roll across the man's face. "That's a relief, then," the man said. "For a moment I thought you were one of them bully dark elves what plagues the miners along with the trolls and goblins. How does a regular elf like yourself come to be so dark of skin, if you don't mind my asking?"

"I fell in a tar pit when I was a wee elf," Riven said blandly. "Am I too late for breakfast?"

The innkeeper turned a dark red himself and muttered that Riven could have a seat, and breakfast would be forthcoming. Riven soon faced a steaming bowl of porridge swimming in a pool of sheep fat. The maid who brought it could not take her eyes off him.

When he had finished eating, he asked the innkeeper if there was a horse trader in town. The smithy, he was told, often brokered such trades.

"Thank you for your hospitality," Riven said. He walked out the door and across the street, drawing stares and double takes the whole way and leaving silence in his wake. The sheep auctioneer went quiet for a full minute, then resumed his trade in stuttering tones.

Once the blacksmith calmed down enough to bargain, selling his horse went smoothly. Levaril was of finest elven stock, an unprecedented find in these parts, and the smith was pleased to get her for a steal. Riven cared little for the coin, but he was relieved to see that the smithy's horses were kept in clean stalls and well-fed. Parting with Levaril was another matter. For the first time since he rode away from Laewaes, Riven suffered a moment of doubt in his quest. Levaril had been his, and he had been hers, for nearly as long as he could remember. He stroked her mane and kissed her nose and fed her his last apple.

He wanted to promise he would come back for her, but it would be a lie. He had no idea if he would survive his quest. Most likely, he would not.

When he stepped back outside, the sheep auction was winding down. The sheepherder was loading a few unsold sheep into the back of his wagon. He was blunter than the innkeeper when Riven approached him.

"What's a dark elf doing with a forest elf's cloak and armor?" he asked. Everything about him was rough, his hands, his voice, his clothes. It made Riven feel itchy. "You steal them?"

"I am a forest elf," Riven explained wearily. "Born and raised. I know I look like the dark elves, though. It's a common mistake."

The sheepherder narrowed his eyes. "One of you lot came through my farm once. Spat right up out of the ground near the well. Killed a bunch of my stock for the fun of it, gave me the fright of my life, then laughed and went on down the road with a merry tune. Should I be grateful?"

Riven sighed. "Perhaps you should. Dark elves are said to be impulsive and quick to anger. He might have killed you on a whim. I wouldn't know. I'm a forest elf. I have coin, and I need a ride up to the mines."

He jiggled his purse to emphasize the request. The sheepherder stared suspiciously, then finally shrugged. "Well. If you were one of them, you wouldn't be paying, would you? You'd just kill me and take my wagon. Hop up there. You'll ride with the sheep."

As he put up the stock ramp, the sheepherder paused and said, "Then again, maybe your coin is a ruse, and you're going to murder me once we're out of town with no witnesses."

Riven paused with one foot on the wagon bed. He looked the sheepherder evenly in the eye. "If I were a dark elf, I would have no need to kill in secret. They glory in the killing. If I were one of them, I would enjoy killing you in front of the whole town."

The sheepherder made no more protest. Riven sat down amongst the sheep. He was shaking. He told himself it was with distaste, for having to discuss the habits of dark elves, whom he found repulsive.

But deep down, he knew he was unsettled by a different feeling. For a moment, as he spoke of how he would kill the sheepherder if he were a dark elf, something unbidden had leapt up inside him. For a moment, he felt not horror and disgust, but glory and bloodlust. For a moment, he *wanted* to kill the sheepherder with the whole town watching.

The sheep eyed him placidly as the wagon began to roll and jolt down the rutted road. They were wondering if he was dangerous, too. "I am a forest elf," Riven told them, and then he repeated it several times, as if saying it could erase the memory of the dark feelings he had just experienced.

*

Sindranielle tried to keep her foundling from prying eyes as she nursed him on the milk of a kindly, discrete badger who lost her kits to a stoat, but the forest holds few secrets. By midsummer, it was in the song of every bird and on the lips of every elf south of Laewaes that a tiny dark elf lived in the fern dell just past the daisy meadow.

Soon, Sindra found herself summoned to bring Riven before the Royal Family in Laewaes. She considered fleeing the elfin lands instead of answering the summons, but decided against it, for where would she go that Riven would be welcome? She wanted to raise him in company, not living as a hermit in some distant reaches. The isolation caused by the scorn of the other forest elves was already distressing to her.

So she made the trip into the city and at sunset, she mounted a winding stair in the palace, clutching Riven close to her breast. His dark little face peeked out from the silk wrap she had swaddled him in. He was sleeping peacefully, lulled like a weary traveler by the soft, magical lights and low, haunting music at the heart of the forest elves' city.

The palace was made of stone, but carved so that the columns looked like great trees, their spreading branches supporting the levels, and the staircase Sindra was directed to take seemed to wind around a great trunk. At its top, the flat roof of a small, high tower looked out over the forest surrounding Laewaes. The wood was growing dark, only twinkling with faint glimmers of lamp lights, and the night sky spread out above, thick with achingly bright stars. If she hadn't been determined that Riven should sleep through this indignity, Sindra would have woken him to see the sight.

The rooftop itself was lit by only starlight. At the end opposite the landing of the stairs, a tall figure clad in silver silk, wearing a delicate silver crown upon her brow, sat upon a throne made of fiddleheads and moths wings. Her beauty was so great it made Sindra's throat catch. Beside her, a wide, shallow bowl sat atop a pedestal, its dark waters gathering starlight.

"Be welcome, child of the forest." The elf's voice was like moon shadows, soft and deep. "I am Princess Arafrenielle Moonling, the Royal Scryer. It has been given to me to pass judgment upon your foundling."

Sindra held Riven closer and said nothing.

"Rumors abound of a darkness in the babe. I wish to put them to an end. I would see the truth for myself." Princess Ara stood and stepped down from the dais upon which her throne sat. She lit a lamp and hung it from a chain that ran over the roof, then took a few steps toward Sindra. Sindra was not short for an elf, but the princess seemed to tower over her.

Sindra took a step back. "He's a river elf," she said nervously. "I found him in the river, and if he's a little darker than most it's because he's a river elf."

"Show me," Princess Ara said in a voice that could not be denied.

Sindra could not disobey a member of the Royal Family. She lifted Riven from her breast and slowly pushed back his wrap to reveal his dark face to the lamp light.

"Bring him to me," Princess Ara said.

Sindra stood frozen, and the princess stepped forward and plucked Riven nimbly from her arms, cradling him to her own chest. Sindra shivered, waiting for something awful to happen.

Riven opened his eyes then. He looked up and saw Princess Ara's broad, gleaming face framed in starlight. His mouth split into a grin and he giggled and grabbed his own toes.

The princess smiled back at the babe, but then her expression stilled, and her next words made Sindra cold all over.

"The rumors are true. He is a dark elf. How has a dark elf come to the heart of our kingdom without triggering any of the wards?"

Sindra resisted the urge to snatch her baby right out of the princess's arms. "He isn't evil," she insisted. "The wards only sense evil, right? There's your proof. He's just a dark little river elf."

Princess Ara stared long and hard at the foundling, then as swiftly as she had taken him, she set Riven back in Sindra's arms, careful, like he was a glass bauble. Hope rose in Sindra's chest, but the princess merely said, "Hold him for me a moment."

For a long time, the princess stood entranced before the glimmering scrying bowl. Sindra considered taking the opportunity to flee, but she had no doubt that there would be guards waiting for her on the stairs. She considered creeping forward to see if she could catch a glimpse of the future for herself, but the glamor of Princess Ara's command held her still. So she used the time to cradle Riven against her body, to smell his hair and savor the weight of him in her arms, in case it should be the last time she held him.

After what seemed an eternity, Princess Ara stepped away from the scrying bowl and returned to her seat. She gazed down at Sindra with a very serious expression.

Finally she said, "Here is my judgment in this matter: you will keep little Riven and raise him as your own. The Royal Court will issue a proclamation that Riven is a citizen of Laewaes, due the same rights and safekeeping as the rest of the citizenry. Any who seek to harm your foundling will face the wrath of the Royal Family."

Sindra felt she might faint with relief. Yet the princess continued, "But you must know this: a day will come when I will call on Riven to fulfill a quest for the kingdom. When that day comes, you will relinquish him fully to my service."

Sindra cared not for some distant future, only that Riven be allowed to stay with her today. "Of course he will serve his people, once he is of age to be of service," Sindra said. "May we go home now?"

"Allow an hour for my scribes to write up the proclamation," Princess Ara said. "I will summon them now. Come. You may await the papers in the feast hall below." She rose, and stroked Riven's cheek in passing. The gesture was warm, but Sindra could not help but shiver. The princess left the platform, and for a moment, before following her, Sindra held Riven alone in the darkness, contemplating the star speckled scrying bowl.

*

The sheepherder left Riven at the end of a rocky road, in front of the dark mouth of a gash cut into a desolate grassy hillside.

"Are you certain this is it?" Riven asked as he hopped out of the back of the wagon and passed the sheepherder to stand by the horses, peering into the blackness of the cave. "Where are all the miners?"

"Not much left to mine up here these days. And the higher mountains are too dangerous. Work becomes scarce. Seasonal, like."

Riven mistrusted him, but he didn't argue. Even if this were not the mines, it was surely a hole in the earth, which would do just as well for his purposes. He thanked the sheepherder, but the man was already turning his horses in a circle in the wide level space abutting the cave. The sheep stared warily out the back of the wagon at Riven as they jostled down the road, as if they expected him to give chase.

Riven stood for a while on the gravel of spent ore. The sun did not shine this close to the Ash Mountains, the sky being blanketed in smoke and ash. The air was not fresh. But it was the last daylight Riven would see for a long time, perhaps forever. A hole in the earth in this place meant he was near certain to encounter goblins, trolls, and the very thing he had come to find: dark elves. After taking a deep breath and gathering his scattered courage, Riven squared his shoulders and stepped into the shadow of the cave's mouth.

The air within was stale and metallic. It was pitch dark, and Riven's glowing pendant revealed only the merest highlights, barely keeping him from tripping over twisted wrecks of ancient mining carts. It was quickly apparent that he had been betrayed; this was indeed a mining shaft, but one that had not been used in decades, perhaps a century. He wondered what the sheepherder meant by leaving him out here, but he did not wonder long. Barely had Riven passed under the dark lip of the cave than he was set upon.

There were five of them, shadowy, graceful figures with long, slender limbs like spider legs. When Riven saw their dark, blue-green faces gleaming by his light, just before they cut him down, he understood why humans feared him, why so many among the forest elves shunned him.

For a moment, before the whack on his head turned out all the lights, Riven was looking at himself in five dark mirrors.

He came to in utter blackness. Someone had taken his armor, his cloak, his glowing pendant, and all his weapons. The floor under him was rough and cold. Somewhere behind him, water was dripping.

His head rang and he was bruised all over, scraped and bleeding in places, but nothing vital seemed broken. He was able to sit up, then stand, but neither action clarified his predicament. He heard only his own breathing and the *drip, drip, drip* of water. He walked cautiously toward the sound, just to have something to walk toward. He reached out and felt the drops fall in his palm. He tasted the water gingerly. It tasted faintly metallic, but not putrid. He drank a little and leaned against the wall, resting, thinking.

A crawly sensation passed over his knuckles. Riven lifted his hand and shook it vigorously, but the tiny legs did not let go. Another thing crawled over him, and another, and suddenly Riven was swimming in spiders as if he had stepped into a giant nest. He ran blindly, batting them off himself, until like a fool he ran straight into a wall and fell to the ground. He was not unconscious, but for a moment he was stunned, lying helpless while hundreds of little spiders crawled over him.

Somehow in the heart of his panic, he had the presence of mind to realize that they were crawling in a single, unified direction. He forced himself to stay still and lay under the stream of spiders. They weren't biting him. In fact, they didn't seem concerned with him at all. They were moving as a single mass away from the drips at the back of the cave. After a moment Riven stood, careful not to crush any of the spiders, removed his boots, and tiptoed among them, using the direction of their crawling over his feet to guide him forward.

He walked like this for what seemed like hours, in total darkness, following the spider migration to its ultimate source. Many times, he nearly turned back, terrified of what the spiders might be going toward. He had no weapons, no way to protect himself or fulfill his mission, even if he did find what he suspected lay at the end of the spiders' journey. But he kept going. He was closer than he had yet been to fulfilling his quest; he could not turn back now.

After he had walked so long that his bare feet ached, a blue glow appeared in the distance. It grew, and soon Riven saw patches of glowing fungus growing on the walls. Now he could see the spiders, spindly little black motes, who alone would not have been anything to be afraid of, but in aggregate were terrifying. He stood to the side and put his shoes back on, letting the bulk of the torrent of spiders pass until he was walking among the rearguard.

The fungus grew thicker as they went, until it lined the walls entirely, its brightness hurting Riven's eyes, which had been so long in the dark.

Blinded as he was now, he almost walked into the dark elf before he saw it. As soon as he realized it was there, he threw up his hands and knelt.

"Please, I only want to talk," Riven said.

The elf took a step back, looking down at him suspiciously. As Riven's vision continued to adjust, he realized it was a female he was looking at, with a mane of luscious silver hair ending in wavy tips. He had always thought of his skin as ugly, but the greenish blue hue looked beautiful on her. It was darker than his own, dark as starless midnight. Her eyes were pools of darkness even deeper than her skin. She carried a basket woven of spider silk, and he had apparently interrupted her work, for she held a small knife in one hand, and a chunk of the glowing fungus in the other. She stared down at him in perplexity.

Riven did not entirely understand the feeling coursing through him, but he knew it was not hatred, or fear, or disgust.

*

Twenty years after the day Sindra scooped Riven out of the water in the otter pool, she woke in the dappled sunlight of her forest glade with a sensation of cold terror shriveling her chest. She sat up in alarm and looked for Riven. He was still sleeping on his bed of cedar leaves and moss, a few feet away from hers. She relaxed, but could not shake the sense of premonition that this day would take him away from her, even as the morning progressed as normal, picking spring lilies and looking for skylark nests in the meadows.

Then, just as the setting sun was streaking the western sky violet and orange, the summons came. And as she had feared, it came for Riven alone.

Sindra delayed as long as she could, seeing that he dressed in his finest clothes, draping her heirloom silver pendant on his dark brow. She warned him again of the courtesy due to Princess Ara, reminded him of the ritual bowing and deference he must show. She held him at arm's length and looked proudly upon his slender figure. Though his dark skin made him a target for mockery from the other young elves, and had caused him to grow up in an isolation that pained and angered Sindra, to her it was a thing of beauty, like the evening sky in summer, or Roselake from a hawk's vantage.

Finally, she could delay him no longer, so she hugged him tightly and told him again to be good and respect the Royal Scryer. She watched him ride off toward Laewaes with mist in her eyes and a fear that she would never see him again.

*

Riven knew his mother was afraid for him, but he had not been able to tease the reason why from her. He had grown up with tales of how wondrous and just the Royal Family were, so why should he fear an audience with one of them? If anything, he was excited to finally see Princess Ara face to face, rather than the great distance from which he had seen her at yearly festivals in the city. His heart thudded in his chest as he mounted the long spiral staircase to the top of her tower, but it was not fear, it was the sense of possibilities, that he might finally have a chance to be someone among the forest elves. Someone other than an outcast.

The sun had set by the time he reached the roof, and the stars were coming on one by one in the evening sky. The forest was a misty gray mass stretching out for miles on all sides. The roof was lit by magical lanterns that glowed a soft orange against the sky. A tall, regal woman sat on a throne of bleeding heart and dragonfly wings, the folds in the silver silk of her dress made warm by the orange glow of the lamps.

"Be welcome, Riven." Her voice was deep, like the bottomless pool under the tall waterfall where Sindra took him to bathe as a child.

Riven knelt and said the proper courtesies, but Princess Ara interrupted him. "Rise," she said, and she rose too, and together they walked to the edge of the roof where a large scrying bowl sat. "What has your mother told you of your origins?"

"Not much," Riven said, suddenly wary. The other elven children had plenty to say about the matter; Riven's father was an orc, Sindra had had relations with a black goat who lived in the hills, she had found him under a rock, he was an enchanted beetle. But when asked, Sindra would only say, "You're my son, and you're perfect."

"The time has come for you to know. Riven, you are a dark elf, cast out as a babe by the underworld kingdom, for what reason we know not. Sindra found you in the otter pool, floating in a basket. She took you in and defended you against those who said you would one day exhibit your evil nature."

He thought she would say more, but she was silent, her graceful form outlined in the darkening sky, waiting. As he began to catch up to the meaning of her words, not just the sounds of them, Riven felt dizzy. It was not just the height of the tower that made him lightheaded. The story the princess had so casually told twisted and turned in his mind. On one hand, he could not believe it possible. Sindra was his mother, and if he was darker than the forest elves, well, any number of explanations could be given for that. On the other hand, her words made perfect sense. They allowed Riven, for the first time, to slip into a story about himself that seemed to fit him like a garment.

"That's impossible," he said. "I am a forest elf."

"I'm afraid it is true. I have seen the dark elves, even battled them long ago when the lands of Mirstone were young. You have their look."

"Sindra is my mother," Riven protested. "I'll never believe otherwise."

"Sindra loves you as a mother," Ara said gently. "In her eyes, and mine, you are one of us. But you must be aware that not everyone in our kingdom feels the same. Even some of the other members of the Royal Family fear you will be a gateway for evil and corruption to enter Laewaes."

Riven was silent. If he were a dark elf, the wide berth given by the other elves made sense. Riven had heard tales of dark elves, of their evil exploits, their quickness to anger, their pleasure in hurting and killing. Like orcs, trolls and goblins, they belonged to the evil races of Mirstone. If the other elves of the forest thought Riven was one of this brutal race, of course they would scorn his company. Especially the elders, who, like Princess Ara, had lost loved ones in the ancient battles.

"What can I do?" Riven asked finally. He turned half away from the princess, so his plea seemed almost addressed to the forest herself. "I have tried to fit in. I live by the principles of loyalty, honor, compassion, and respect that Sindra taught me. I cannot help how I look, nor my parentage, if what you say is true. How can I truly be a forest elf?"

Princess Ara took his thick fingers in her slender ones and led him to the scrying bowl. The gleaming surface made Riven shiver.

"My duty within the Royal Family is to keep an eye to the future. That is why my tower is so tall, taller even than that of the High King and Queen. The scrying bowl gathers the light of the stars, concentrates it, and reveals to me all these stars have seen and all they ever will see."

Riven peered closer into the bowl, wondering if it would reveal the future to him, but all he saw was the liquid fire of the lanterns and the fading sunset.

"I have seen two futures for this kingdom," Princess Ara said, and even though Riven was still reeling from her revelation that he was a dark elf, he felt the import of her words, and awe that she would confide her visions.

"In one future, the dark elves come to our lands and take us by surprise. They burn the forests, pollute the river, and sell our people as slaves to the goblins. This kingdom ceases to exist and will be forgotten.

"In the other future, a young elf accepts a quest to infiltrate the kingdom of the dark elves. He defeats their fearsome queen and brings her head back to Laewaes, where he presents it to me on this very roof. There is a great celebration, and he gains the favor of the Royal Family."

"Who is the elf?" Riven wanted it to be him, but he did not dare to hope.

"I cannot see his face in the scrying. But I think you, of all elves in this kingdom, would stand the best chance of completing such a quest. I ask you to go to the realm of the dark elves, and bring me back the head of their queen."

Of course. It made all too much sense. With the appearance of a dark elf, Riven could sneak among them, perhaps even gain an audience with their queen. A forest elf, he supposed, would be killed on sight.

"It is a bitter thing," Riven said finally into the nighttime hush settling over the forest as the birds ceased their songs. "That I should be the one for this quest, not because I am brave and well-loved, but because I am outcast and flawed. But I will do it. I will prove that I am truly a forest elf, and not one of them."

"I will not send you unprotected," Princess Ara said. She sounded unsurprised, as if she had never doubted Riven would accept her quest. "You will have the finest enchanted armor we can make, and weapons spelled never to miss their mark. Spells of protection against their dark magics will be woven into your cloak. You will have every enchantment we can offer. With this, and your heritage, and your good forest elf nature, you cannot fail."

*

Standing in his small clothes in the tunnel of glowing fungus, Riven stood slowly, keeping his hands visible, keeping his eyes on the beautiful dark elf maiden. He was painfully aware of his vulnerability, without his enchanted armor, cloak or weapons. He wondered if Princess Ara had considered the possibility that he would be set upon by dark elf thugs who would use no magic, only fists to defeat him. It seemed a blindness, a thing she should have been able to see in her scrying bowl.

"What a strange spiderling you are," the lovely dark elf said, and Riven's heart fluttered all the harder. "Her Majesty will be much perplexed to see you arrive."

"I'm not a spider," Riven said. "I'm a dark elf, like you. I was lost as a baby, raised in far distant lands. I come to these caves seeking the home of my parents."

"Drow," she said slowly.

"Pardon?" Riven said.

"We call ourselves Drow."

"Pardon," Riven said again, feeling sheepish. "My sincere apologies. Let me begin again. I am Riven, stolen from the Drow as a babe, and I am here to discover my parentage. What is your name?"

"I am Arandra," she said. Riven wondered if it was a sign, that the first Drow he should meet would share a name so similar to the princess's name.

"Arandra," he said. "I'm pleased to meet you. Might I help with your gathering?"

She clutched the knife tighter. Riven felt a moment of sorrow for this gorgeous creature, that she had to live her life among the dangerous Drow in constant fear and distrust. Perhaps there would be some way to bring her back to the safety of Laewaes, once his quest was complete.

"Queen Kaleith is mother to us all, so if you are truly a Drow, she is where you will find your parentage—like the other spiderlings."

Riven looked down and realized the stream of spiders had passed out of sight around a bend. He could hurry after them, if they were heading to the dark elf queen, but he did not yet wish to leave Arandra's presence.

"I'm afraid I've lost my way," he said, only half feigning his embarrassment. "Could I impose upon you to show me the way to this Queen Kaleith?"

Arandra frowned at him for a long moment, her knife shaking a little in her hand, as if wondering if she could trust him. Riven did his best to look a little helpless, and it wasn't difficult; he did not feel very grand, in little more than his small clothes. Finally, she tucked the knife away and set the piece of fungus in her basket.

"I will take you to the city," she said. "But I cannot promise you an audience with Kaleith. It is said that she will see anyone, but she does not give Drow favor over spiders. And there are a lot of spiders seeking audience with her. You may have to wait a very long time, traveler."

Riven followed her like a lamb through twisting, glowing tunnels. As they walked, the passages widened and branched into a twisting maze that Riven surely would have been lost in if he was traveling alone. They set a fast pace, and eventually overtook the river of spiders. Arandra stepped delicately through it, carefully not to crush a single one. Riven did his best to imitate her graceful steps, with less success. He could not track the passage of time by the sun or stars down here, but it seemed to him that hours had gone by before Arandra drew to a halt and he nearly walked into her back.

"We have arrived at Cinlu," she said.

Riven experienced a moment of vertigo when he stepped out onto the stone ledge above the subterranean city, for looking down on the sparkling blue lights of the Drow realm was almost identical to standing at the top of Princess Ara's tower, looking out over glittering Laewaes and the surrounding forests. The ceiling of this huge cavern even glinted with patches of blue fungus approximating starlight. Riven wrestled with a rising sensation in his chest, a swelling of nostalgia and memory, a twisting of memories of this place and of the forest where he had been raised. He struggled with all his might to discard the sensation that he had come home.

The city was more brightly lit than the tunnels, and this allowed Riven to see the spiders more clearly. They were pouring in from all the other tunnels that opened onto this great cavern, all headed toward a towering palace in the center of the city.

"What's with the spiders?" he asked.

"Queen Kaleith lays her eggs in the distant tunnels," Arandra said. "When they hatch, they are drawn to her."

"Queen Kaleith is a spider?" Princess Ara had neglected to mention this point. Riven wasn't sure if that would make his task of taking her head easier, or harder.

Arandra looked at him oddly. "You really aren't from this realm, are you? You look so much like one of us, but you're like a baby Drow. You know nothing."

"You are right," Riven said. "I know less than nothing, for before today I thought all dark elves were ugly and evil, but I find you are beautiful and wonderful."

Arandra grew a deeper shade of blue, and her voice softened. "You poor creature. You've believed everything the surface dwellers say about us, haven't you? You truly don't know your own kind."

"Show me," Riven said. "Tell me. What does it mean to be a Drow?"

And though he told himself he was only gathering information before he made his strike, Riven could not stop the feeling welling inside of himself, a deep yearning that he had never been able to name, a desire to know who and what he was.

Arandra met his eyes, and for a moment they held each other in regard, and Riven thought something wonderful that he could not even imagine was going to happen, but the moment passed and Arandra looked away.

"You look like you haven't had a decent meal in days," she

said. "Whether you enter the palace today or tomorrow will make little difference. Come."

Riven found himself accompanying the maiden down a quiet side street of the city. Other Drow passed them, and at the sight of each one Riven tensed, but like Arandra, they seemed to be busy with some task, carrying baskets somewhere, repairing masonry, tending little fungal patches on the walls of the houses. Some eyed Riven with curiosity, but none offered any threat, and many did not even seem to notice him. He supposed that Cinlu was large enough for anyone who looked like a Drow to remain anonymous here.

Arandra pushed open the door to a humble little house of stone. Glowing fungus lit the interior with a blue light that Riven was beginning to find comforting. She bade him take a seat on a stone bench while she went into one of the back rooms.

She came out presently with a set of wool and leather trousers and a woolen hat and jacket, which she handed to Riven. "You can use the room back there to change," she said. "This will keep you warmer than that thin stuff you're wearing."

Riven suddenly thought he had perhaps misjudged this situation entirely. Arandra appeared not any older than himself, certainly not old enough to be married yet, but now he imagined an aggressive Drow husband coming home from a day working— perhaps as a guard. Riven imagined him wearing a sword—to find a young upstart in his clothes. He was about to refuse her kindness when she added, "They belonged to my father. He has no need of them anymore. A gang of goblins attacked his company in the outer mines. They might fit awkwardly, but better than being cold."

Riven hoped his relief did not show on his face, but he suspected it did, because Arandra wore a gentle smile as she began to light a fire in the hearth.

The clothes fit well enough, if only a little tight, and Riven returned to the front room to be served a hearty bowl of mushroom stew. He ate with a better appetite than he'd had in months, really since Princess Ara had sent him on this quest. Something about being in Arandra's presence made eating pleasurable.

"What courtesies does your queen command?" Riven asked. "Please, tell me what to do so I don't make a fool of myself in front of her."

"You must hide nothing from her," Arandra said. "Kaleith sees all with her many eyes, knows all. If she thinks you are hiding something, she will be angry."

Riven hoped the dark elf maiden was exaggerating her queen's powers. If she knew why he was there, Kaleith would be very angry, indeed.

"But you need not face her yet. You may rest awhile here," she said as he scraped the bottom of the bowl with his spoon. "You must be weary from your travels. Tomorrow, you can get in line with the other spiders. You will likely wait days for an audience; one night will make no difference."

"Why are you being so kind?" Riven asked Arandra bluntly. Lovely as she was, he still could not set aside a suspicion of the dark elves, that somehow her kindness was part of an elaborate ruse.

Arandra set down her bowl and moved the kettle off the fire for the soup to cool. "You remind me of my father," she said. "Most of us have grown accustomed to living in these dark caves, and for myself I have known nothing else, but my father was one of the older Drow. He remembered the days we lived under the sun. These caves fit him worse than his clothes fit you. He had the same kind of restlessness you harbor. Mother said it was why he joined the warriors again, after centuries of retirement."

Her answer was so plainspoken and earnest that it scattered all of Riven's mistrust again. "You have not always lived in these caves?" he asked.

Arandra laughed. "Of course not! Why should anyone choose to live in a cave? Once, the Drow covered the whole of the lands you call Mirstone. We were a people of the dark; worshiped the moon, and kept counsel at night, but we lived under the stars, not under earth. Then the day elves grew jealous of our lands. They wanted them for themselves. We went to war, many, many hundreds of years ago. We were beaten back to the plains of the Ash Mountains. For a long time, we lived there in peace, for the day elves would not go near the blasted lands. Then the goblins and the trolls and the orcs came. We fought them to a standoff, and then we sent to the day elves for help, but no help came. We were beaten back into the caves. Only a few of us survived, rallied around Queen Kaleith. She allied with the king of the spiders down here, and raised an army of spiders to keep them out of the tunnels, buying us enough time to build Cinlu. Eventually we gained a reputation, and the orcs and goblins and trolls now rarely risk our tunnels."

She glanced down with the last sentence, and Riven realized that must have been how her father died.

"I'm sorry for your loss," he said awkwardly. He wasn't sure if he meant her father or the whole thing, the place of the Drow on the surface world. He was reeling from her version of the history he had grown up with, that the Drow had started the elf war, that they had come out of the underworld with their spider queen and tried to conquer the surface. He wasn't entirely sure he believed Arandra's version, but he was certain she believed it—just as surely as the forest elves believed their version.

Riven teetered in that moment, no longer a forest elf, but not truly a Drow either. He recalled his quest. He had assumed he would have to pretend to fit in with a bunch of aggressive, dangerous warriors in order to get into the dark elf city, to get close to the queen. Not that he would be discussing history over mushroom stew with a beautiful maiden.

He set his bowl down. "I thank you kindly for your hospitality," he said. "But I must see the queen immediately."

"I can show you—"

"I will find it on my own." Riven regretted his curt tone when she lowered her eyes again, but he did not apologize. He needed to be gone before she made him abandon his quest.

He backed out of the dwelling, rambling his thanks for the clothes, the food, her presence, her tale. Outside, the lights of the city were dimmer, an artificial evening. The city still brought him awe, but he missed the stars.

The palace was even grander up close than it had been from a distance. It towered above the rest of the city like a series of massive obsidian stalagmites. Fungus of every color coated the stone columns, making it blaze like a gem, but even the color it threw off was dim, as if the very fungus was corrupted by the evil that lay within. Spiders streamed into every orifice of the building. There were no guards, and somehow that seemed more ominous to Riven than if he faced an entire dark elf army at the wide portcullis.

At first, he wondered how he was to find Kaleith in the web-like inner passages of shiny black stone, but soon it became apparent that he had only to follow the spiders. *The other spiders.* He tried not to think of it that way, but the thought impressed itself on him nonetheless. He joined the river of arachnids, trying not to step on what he could not help but think of as his siblings, trying to maintain his stoic forest elf courage as their legs and mandibles brushed his bare skin.

Somewhere near the heart of that massive web-shaped building, the forward motion of the spider swarm stopped altogether. Riven found himself at the back of a massive crowd of spiders, his view forward blocked by the spiders standing on the shoulders of others, and spiders dangling on their threads from the ceiling. Behind him, more spiders continued to crowd in, and soon he was completely surrounded.

Riven urged himself to patience, using calming tricks Sindra had taught him long ago. But his skin crawled and he squirmed with impatience as minutes ticked past with no change. After what seemed a very long time, the spider crowd inched forward minutely, carrying Riven with it. It continued to move forward at intervals, slower than molasses.

After the fifth or sixth such inching forward, Riven lost his patience. He took off the hat Arandra had given him and used it to gently sweep aside the spiders in his path. The creed of the forest elves forbade indiscriminately killing the creatures of the forest, and Riven supposed that must apply even to these horrid things. Some of the spiders scrambled to flee the hat, but others held firm to their place in line, refusing to give way. Riven stepped nimbly around the remaining ones, but it grew more difficult the further he traveled toward the middle of the web, for the spiders concentrated into a mass so thick that he could not nudge them aside without risking crushing some against the bodies of others.

After some hesitation, Riven pressed forward, crushing a few spiders under his feet. He felt a sense of rightness in the action, that to approach the dark elf queen was to prove that he was strong and ruthless. Surely only the heartless won audience here.

The web of passages opened into a large chamber where a broad set of steps led to a high dais. The steps were swarming with spiders, but the dais was clear except for a grand throne of gleaming obsidian. Rather than the spider Riven had expected, a beautiful Drow lady sat on the throne, gazing down at him with cold, dark eyes. She was tall and slender as Princess Ara, draped in gray silks and shiny topaz jewels that looked like the glossy orbs of spider eyes.

As Riven ruthlessly mounted the steps, he saw a spider scramble ahead of him onto the dais. It approached Kaleith and huddled at her feet. She turned her eyes from Riven and examined it. After a long moment, she pointed a slender finger, and it grew before Riven's eyes, shivered and morphed and expanded upward and out. Suddenly a nude Drow boy stood before the throne where the spider had been.

"Be welcome," Kaleith said. Her voice was rich with time. "You are home. Go into that room behind the throne, and my attendants will dress you and show you to your chambers."

Riven had paused to watch this spectacle, and while he stood frozen another spider approached the throne. Kaleith stared at it for a long moment, then pointed to another door, to the other side of the throne.

"Be welcome," she said again. "You are home. You will find nourishment behind that door. My attendants will induct you into the spider army."

Riven did not want to take the step that would put him within range of that finger, did not want to face her judgment. He had imagined stealing a weapon off a guard and facing down a monstrous spider queen, lopping her head off and fleeing the city. He had never dreamed there would be no guards, and that the queen would be nearly as enchanting as Arandra.

But he had come here to face her, and face her he must. He stepped onto the dais.

Kaleith's eyes finally settled on him. She examined him for a long moment. He wondered if she would turn him into a spider.

After several moments of silence had passed, she snapped her fingers. Five Drow came through the door the Drow boy had disappeared into. One of them carried a bundle, and he set it at the Queen's feet. It fell open, and Riven was astonished to see his cloak and weapons scattered on the floor. But he was even more astonished when the five Drow came forward and knelt before him.

"We apologize for assaulting you in the mines," one of them said sheepishly. The rest muttered something that sounded like apologies under their breath.

"It is their duty to patrol the mines looking for goblin or human incursions that could threaten Cinlu," Queen Kaleith said. "They will be more circumspect henceforth. You may be dismissed."

For a moment Riven thought she meant him, but the five Drow trooped away, leaving him alone on the dais with her.

"Come forward and reclaim your belongings, young wanderer," Kaleith said. "Do not be afraid. The spells on them are unmolested."

Riven was deeply afraid. Not that Kaleith might strike him down, or order her hordes of spiders to attack him. If she wanted him dead, he understood he would be dead by now.

No, what Riven feared was how deeply he wanted to obey that rich, husky voice. He understood how it would work with her. Not a straightforward quest, as Princess Ara had asked. Kaleith would give him small commands at first, nurture his loyalty until he was eating out of her hand. Then it would be something larger, like killing a rival, until finally he would be commanding her armies when she attacked the forest realm full force.

For this reason, he stopped himself from mindless obedience and remained still in front of her. "If you want to break me, you will have to use force," he said.

Sadness flitted across her ebony eyes, but Riven remained firm, guessing this was part of her ploy. "Very well."

She snapped her fingers and Riven braced himself for the worst as the dais filled with spiders. They swarmed with single purpose to his belongings, picked them up and ran with them as one toward Riven. Soon he felt them tickling his whole body as thousands of spiders pulled off the clothes Arandra had lent and redressed him in his armor and cloak. He shuddered, but would not give Kaleith the satisfaction of watching him run away screaming.

The spiders struggled under the weight of his sword, but eventually they brought that too, and Riven stood before Kaleith as he had intended to arrive, clothed fine as a forest elf prince and decked with enchanted weapons. He felt the protective arms of Princess Ara's spells enfolding him. Kaleith had spoken true; the spells were intact.

As the last spider exited the armhole of his shirt and skittered away, Riven realized that he need not wait any longer. Kaleith stood before him as if waiting for him to strike. His hand was on his hilt. He had only to draw the weapon.

"Why do you hesitate?" Kaleith asked. "You did not hesitate to stomp on my spiderlings down there. What is the difference between them and me?"

Riven hung his head, ashamed. Then he raised it again. Surely this was part of her ploy, too, to get under his skin. Surely the dark elf queen did not value the life of every little spider under her command. So instead of the apology that was on his lips, he tried an awkward piece of the truth: "I did not expect you."

The sadness flickered in Kaleith's eyes again. "We have become a hard people, trying to hold onto what remains of us. The surface dwellers think us evil, but like them we can be both beautiful and terrible."

"What of the sheepherder?" Riven asked, drawn into the argument against his better judgment. "Is slaughtering a man's livelihood for the fun of it part of protecting your kingdom?"

"As I said, we can be both beautiful and terrible. The Drow who patrol our borders with the surface get carried away sometimes. The sheepherder had been warned not to try to enter the old mines looking for gems. He continued to do it, so we sent a stronger message. When he dropped you off there, he meant for you to die, I believe. And you might have, were you not so hardy."

"There are kinder ways to protect borders," Riven insisted.

"Is that so? And how would your royalty handle an intruder into the forest?"

"He would be captured, not beaten and left for dead. Brought before the court. Warned, if his intentions were ill, never to return to the forest. We might give him a little fright with wolves and bears on his way out. But he would leave unharmed. And we'd never go to his lands and slaughter his livelihood in retribution. We don't go looking for vengeance, or trouble."

"And yet, here you are. Looking for trouble. Slaughtering my children."

Riven's cheeks warmed. "Well, I'm not really a forest elf, am I? I'm one of you at heart."

She laughed but there was little mirth in the sound. "And yet you hesitate."

"I suspect you've enchanted my sword in some way I cannot sense. When I strike, the blow will rebound and kill me."

She bared her teeth in something that was definitely not a smile. "Try again, youngling."

Riven recalled Arandra's words about Kaleith getting angry if he hid himself. He steered as close to the truth as he dared.

"The Drow maiden who guided me to Cinlu was kind."

"And for that you spare my life?"

Riven shivered. He was on the verge of lifting his sword. She bore no visible weapons, and no spells she cast would penetrate the enchantment of his cloak. Her neck was bare. It would not take much strength to cut through her flesh.

But Riven found it would take more strength than he had. Princess Ara had told him he would find Kaleith monstrously evil. He wanted to believe that, but he found he could not see this creature as evil, any more than he could see Arandra as evil. Perhaps she had done evil things. But he was beginning to suspect that in the ancient wars, both sides had committed acts of evil.

"Speak, youngling." Kaleith's eyes were canted with rage. The ebony glitter of her jewelry seemed alive. Something was moving under her dress.

Riven remained silent, not wanting to voice the words that were ricocheting through his mind. If he voiced it, he would have to face the truth of it.

Kaleith roared, an inhuman sound: "Tell me why you hesitate, if you value your life!"

Riven took his hand off his hilt. He backed away from Kaleith, staggered to the steps, tripped over his cloak and fell face down on the incline. Spiders scrambled and skittered away from him.

He did not see her transform, but he felt her meaty breath on the back of his neck. A huge spider leg pinned him where he lay. A giant mandible brushed his jugular.

"Tell me," she clicked in his ear. "Strike my head off, or tell me why you won't. Or I will bite your head off!"

"No," Riven said in a small voice. "You won't."

"Won't I?"

"You won't," Riven said more firmly. "You are terrible in your anger, but in your heart you are as good as Arandra. Or even Princess Ara. This is why I won't strike you down. There is no justice in it."

The horrible breath at the back of his neck abated and the leg and mandible withdrew. Her voice grew soft and rich again. "At last, you speak the truth. You have a good heart, too."

"No," Riven said. He did not lift his head. "I killed your spiders without remorse. And I wanted to kill the sheepherder. I imagined killing him, and it brought me joy. If the Drow aren't evil, where did that come from?"

"You mistake the bloodlust of anger for moral impurity, youngling. I could have killed you just now, you made me so angry with your evasions, with your hypocrisy for killing my babes and sparing me. Yet you do not find me evil, so why should your anger at the sheepherder's treatment of you make you evil?"

Riven's head spun as he tried to sort out her logic. He was still making sense of the idea that the Drow—and the forest elves—and himself—were not evil, but something vastly more complicated than good and evil. Kaleith offered her hand to help him regain the dais. He took it, but kept his eyes cast down.

He had crushed yet another spider in his tumble, and it limped onto the dais with a broken leg. Kaleith picked it up with the same grace with which she had helped him up. She held the limping spider in her hand until it glowed and shimmered and shook. Then in a flash of glitter, it was whole again, and she set it down. It scurried off to join the spider army.

"I'm sorry I crushed your spiderlings," Riven said earnestly. "I didn't know—"

"I'll accept your apology, if you accept my men's apologies for beating you and leaving you for dead in the old mines." Kaleith returned to her throne as she spoke. Another spider walked forward, and she turned it into a little Drow girl and sent it through the proper door.

Riven stood awkwardly at the edge of the dais, unsure of what to do next, feeling lost and disoriented. He wished his life could be as simple as being pointed through a door, on the other side of which was a place where he belonged.

"Why so sad?" Kaleith asked before her next spider

approached. "Did you hope the world could be divided so neatly into good and evil?"

"No, I'm glad to find the Drow are not what we thought they were. It's just, I failed my quest. I was to bring the head of evil Queen Kaleith of the dark elves and lay it before Princess Ara. But there is no evil Queen Kaleith to slay. I must return home empty-handed, and I will never win acceptance from the forest elves."

"Perhaps there is another way for you to fulfill this quest of yours," Kaleith mused.

*

The soft orange lanterns brought mist to Riven's eyes as he rode Levaril into Laewaes, followed by a hooded figure on another mount, wearing his cloak. It felt good to be under the towering giants of the forest again, to feel the breath of the wind against his skin, to hear the birds singing themselves to sleep and the lower, harmonizing tones of elves singing back to the birds in the distance. But Riven's world was vastly larger and more complicated than it had been when he left. Coming home here was no less coming home than standing and looking out upon the city of Cinlu with its stalactite spires and glowing fungus. He wondered if he would ever fit fully into either world.

This evening would either be a step toward acceptance into the world of the forest elves, or complete banishment from it. After leaving their horses with the palace groom, Riven squared his shoulders, hefted the spider silk sack, gave a reassuring smile to the person wearing his cloak, and mounted the spiral staircase of Princess Ara's tower.

Princess Ara sat waiting upon her throne, scrying bowl glimmering in the evening starlight beside her. This was no surprise; word would have been spread by every little creature the moment Riven passed the edge of the forest. And with the hooded figure accompanying him, it was also no surprise that the finest warriors of the forest elves were arrayed between Riven and his guest and the council.

Princess Ara stood and stepped forward, standing breast to breast with the warriors. She did not look afraid or angry. Disappointed, perhaps? Riven couldn't read her expression.

"Well?" she asked. "What has become of your quest, Riven? Have you brought me the head of the dark elf queen?" She ignored the hooded figure, though the eyes of all the warriors were focused there.

Riven unshouldered the heavy bag and set it on the ground in front of Princess Ara with a *thunk.*

"My quest took a turn from your vision, Majesty," he said. "I have brought something from the realm of the Drow, but it is not what you requested. A head of sorts, but not her head."

He opened the top of the bag and pulled down the sides, revealing a large crock of tarnished silver in the shape of a giant spider's head. Topaz eyes reflected starlight up to Princess Ara, who stared at it in amazement. Riven lifted off the lid, and where the spider's brains would be, he pulled a handful of delicate Drow jewelry, made of precious metals and decorated with opals, topaz, sapphires and emeralds.

Princess Ara took a step back, and the warriors surged forward. "You should not have brought these things here, Riven," she said. "They could be enchanted with dark elf magics."

Riven had been steeling himself for this moment. "With all due respect, Majesty, there is nothing to fear in this gift. It is a sign of good faith from the Drow queen."

For a long moment, no one on the rooftop moved. Then the hooded figure stepped forward, and slowly lowered the cowl of her borrowed cloak, revealing herself as Arandra. Her lovely silver hair gleamed in the lanterns. Her blue-green skin made her face appear as a shadow. A single spider, a gift from Kaleith for the dangerous mission she had agreed to, dangled at her neck like a pendant.

Arandra stepped forward and knelt on one knee beside the gleaming treasures. "Princess of the Forest Elves, I speak before you on behalf of my mistress, Queen Kaleith of the Drow. She wishes to pursue peace between her people and yours. This gift is a token of the trade that is possible between our people."

Ara's expression remained serene, but several of the warriors gasped at the sight of an ancient enemy in the heart of Laewaes. A tense silence, underscored by the eerie song of elves singing faraway in the city, thickened on the rooftop.

Riven waited, every muscle in his body tense. He had tried to dissuade Arandra from this, once Kaleith told him of her plan. Arandra, it turned out, was minor Drow royalty herself. Her father was of Kaleith's generation, one of the leaders of the Drow before they were pressed underground.

As the silence dragged on, the warriors appeared more and more agitated, and Riven feared someone would loose an arrow in haste. He itched to put his body between her and the warriors. Then Princess Ara stepped forward, out of the line of warriors, and put a hand out to Arandra.

"Rise," she said so softly that Riven didn't think anyone else on the roof could hear. "Rise, and be welcome to Laewaes. You need have no fear of harm during your stay. I will bring you before the Royal Family, and we will compose a message of peace to Kaleith."

Princess Ara drew Arandra to her feet and Riven felt so relieved he thought he might faint. His quest, though altered, was complete.

There was more to it than that, of course. There was a great argument, resulting in political rifts among the Royal Family, about whether to trust the Drow visitor. The High King and Queen settled these in Princess Ara's favor, but resentments simmered in silence. The gift from Kaleith was checked and triple-checked for dark spells, and at last decreed safe, and incorporated into the Royal treasury. A matching gift was selected from the treasury and packaged to be returned with Arandra, along with a message of peace and the wish for mutually beneficial trade. Once all this was completed, on the night before Arandra was to depart for Cinlu, this time with an honor escort of ten warriors, one of them a minor member of the Royal Family, a great celebration was held in

Laewaes.

Princess Ara's rooftop was one of many feast sites, covered with tables laden with roasted peacock, fresh bread, fine cheese, and all the fruits of the forest. After hours of eating, drinking and dancing, Riven found himself beside the scrying bowl in the twilight of morning. Most of the forest creatures and elves had drifted off to sleep the day away. His head was pleasantly bubbly with thimbleberry wine. Sindra had her head pressed to Arandra's, sharing memories of Riven as a child. Princess Ara, leaning off an arm of her throne to talk to a couple of elf princes who were still making merry, saw Riven was alone and came to stand beside him at the scrying bowl.

"I do not understand, Majesty," Riven said. "You said that either we would go to war with the Drow, or Kaleith's head would be brought to you, but though we brought a mock of a head, in truth neither has come to pass. Did you not scry this possibility?"

"The scrying bowl shows myriad possible futures," Princess Ara said. "I did not consider peace would be one of them. And I never dreamed Kaleith would even make the first overture of peace. Sometimes it takes fresh eyes, eyes untainted by the wars of the past, to see the truth of the future. Do you wish to look?"

Riven was astonished at the offer. The use of the scrying bowl was a great honor and a great responsibility, usually available only to the royal elves. He had never considered that he might one day have the opportunity to look into the future.

He looked out over the dusky forest, toward the eastern mountains where a crack of light was beginning to let the dawn through. Then he looked toward the throne, where Sindra and Arandra stood with their heads close together. He was struck again by Arandra's beauty and courage, in coming all the way here without knowing what she would find. Princess Ara had given him leave to accompany her entourage, to serve as an informal ambassador to the Drow. He had not yet made up his mind. He did not want to leave home so soon after his return. But suddenly, watching Arandra toss back her silver hair into the first rays of sunlight, he knew where he belonged.

He turned to Princess Ara and said, "Thank you, but I do not wish to look. I can already see the future I will create."

THE END

The Lost Dagger of Mirstone
Craig A. Price Jr.

Lyra's straight brown hair blew gently in the breeze as she walked through the winding streets of the crowded elven city. She pulled her cloak tighter around her pointed ears, trying to go unnoticed by her peers, while taking in the scents and sights of the bustling market. The sweet smell of fresh bread mingled with the sharp tang of spices, and the vibrant colors of the merchants' wares caught her eye. She shivered as she glanced around. Lyra sensed something was off. The usual vibrant and joyous atmosphere of the elven city felt tense and somber. She heard whispers of a theft and a missing artifact as she passed by groups of elves huddled in conversation.

Was this why she was being summoned? She had not heard of any thefts recently, or had it been something the council had kept secret until now? Obviously, the deer was out of the woods at this point.

She neared the council chambers, and her heart raced. She knew something important was happening, and a part of her hoped she would be called upon to assist in any way she could.

Lyra took a deep breath before entering the council chambers. She saw the solemn expressions of the council members and felt a knot forming in her stomach. She knew that whatever they were about to ask of her must be dire.

"Lyra," the eldest of the council, a wise and respected elf, spoke. "We called upon you for a matter of great importance."

Lyra listened intently, knowing that anything the council would ask of her must be urgent and crucial to the welfare of the kingdom. She had a track record for finding objects, a trait she obtained as a young girl. Her mother had first noticed it when she discovered a key to a hidden dwarf alcove during the conflict. It only progressed from there. As a young girl, many of her friends would ask for her aid to find their lost trinkets. Lyra always found what she was looking for. She didn't know how to explain it. It was like an additional sense. She focused on something—what she wanted to find, and she could zone in on it. Lyra would feel an impression within her where she needed to go—what she needed to do.

"We learned that a precious artifact of our kingdom had been stolen and was now located in the human kingdom," the elder continued. "This artifact is vital to our way of life, and its loss will bring great harm to our people."

Lyra nodded, understanding the gravity of the situation. She licked her lips, her curiosity getting the better of her. "What is the artifact?"

The elder wrinkled his nose. "The First Dagger of Moonling, enchanted by House of Maumer. Wielded by none other than Naelmir over a thousand years ago when he united the elven houses who had scattered across the land."

Lyra's knees buckled. Naelmir was a legend in the elven society. Without him, they would still be living in chaos. No wonder she hadn't heard about this before now. If anyone knew this dagger was missing, it might lead to civil war. The elves had lived together in peace for a thousand years.

"How long has it been missing?"

The elder attempted to look away from her, seeming to not want to admit to the truth. Finally, another council member cleared his throat. "Two hundred years."

"How?"

"Do not be concerned with the specifics. We have only recently learned of its location." He turned back to the elder.

"We prepared a map of the human castle where the artifact is believed to be hidden," the elder said, handing over a piece of parchment to Lyra. "It is a dangerous mission, and you will face great peril, but we trust in your abilities, given the past."

Lyra looked at the map, studying it carefully, but not accepting it. She knew the human kingdom had not been a friendly place for elves in the past, and the thought of going there alone was daunting. But she also realized the importance of the mission could not be understated. People on the streets knew an artifact was missing, but they didn't realize what the artifact was. If they had, the elven cities would already be spiraling into chaos. She had to do this fast, efficient, and before anyone knew the wiser.

"I accept the mission," Lyra said, bowing to the council.

"Very well." The elder's tense shoulders relaxed. "Be careful, and remember the importance of this artifact to our kingdom. Do not utter a word of this conversation to anyone. We are counting on you."

The elder passed her the map and she studied it further, committing every detail to memory. She knew that she had to be meticulous in her planning and execution, and she hoped that her training as a skilled archer and tracker would aid her in her mission.

When the elder had spoken of the missing dagger and the importance it held for their kingdom, Lyra's mind had raced. She knew she had to do everything in her power to retrieve it, but the thought of facing the dangers of the human kingdom filled her with trepidation. Lyra had never even met a human. For the most part, elves only associated with other elves, except recently with the dwarven conflict they had overcome.

She left the council chambers, her heart pounding with the weight of the task ahead. She knew that the success of her mission could mean the difference between life and death for her people, and she was determined to see it through to the end.

Lyra walked through the narrow cobblestone streets of the elven city, her mind continuing to race as she contemplated the task ahead. She had known that she had to prepare meticulously for her mission to retrieve the stolen artifact from the human kingdom, and she had already begun to plan her next steps.

Lyra walked into her home, a cozy cottage nestled in a grove of oak trees. She took off her cloak and sat at her wooden table, pulling out the map of the human castle from her satchel and laying it across her table.

She studied the map carefully, her keen elven eyes taking in every detail. She noted the location of the castle's entrances and exits, the positions of the guards, and the layout of the interior. She took a deep breath, mentally preparing herself for the daunting task ahead. This wasn't something she could just rush in. She had to be careful. Especially with humans. They were savages, or so she had been told. The things they did to elven prisoners…she shuddered even thinking about it.

Lyra rose from her seat and moved to the wall where her bow and quiver of arrows were kept. She selected a sturdy bow made of the finest elven wood and examined each arrow, ensuring they were sharp and straight.

She felt the smooth wood of the bow in her hands and took a deep breath, feeling a sense of calm wash over her. It was her father's bow long ago. Lyra hadn't picked it up since the funeral. She ran her fingers across its engravings, a love song to her mother. Lyra missed the two of them dearly. She remembered her father teaching her how to use it, and her mother teaching her how to make the arrows. A tear threatened to escape to her cheek as her eyes welled up, but she quickly brushed them away, pushing the memory of her mother and father out of her mind. Lyra was alone now, and nothing she could do would change what had happened.

She had known her skill with the bow had been unmatched among the elves thanks to her father's training, and she took comfort in the fact that her bow would be her greatest weapon on this mission. A part of her believed her father would be with her as long as she carried the bow with her.

Lyra moved to the center of her cottage, where a small table had been set up with various tools and supplies. She pulled out a roll of thin wire and a set of lock picks, knowing she would need them to bypass the castle's locks and traps. She then took a small leather pouch from the table and emptied its contents onto the surface. A variety of herbs and powders spilled out, each carefully selected for their specific uses in elven medicine and magic. Lyra selected a few that she believed would be useful in her mission, tucking them into her satchel.

She moved around her cottage, gathering the supplies she would need, taking in the familiar scents of her home. The sweet fragrance of honeysuckle and lavender mingled with the warm aroma of freshly baked bread, and she felt a sense of comfort and familiarity wash over her. It reminded her so much of her mother.

Lyra packed her satchel and took one last look around at everything, knowing that she might not return for some time. She took a deep breath and walked out the door, determined to see her mission through to the end.

When she stepped out of her cottage, she felt the cool breeze of the forest caress her face. The scent of pine and earth filled her nostrils as she made her way toward the edge of the trees.

As she emerged from the cover of the trees, Lyra was met with a stunning vista. Rolling hills and verdant valleys stretched out before her, their lush greenery swaying gently in the breeze. The sky above was a vibrant shade of blue, dotted with fluffy white clouds that seemed to dance in the sunlight. Tingles formed along her spine as she took a moment to appreciate the beauty of the world around her, knowing that this might be the last time she would see it. She took a deep breath and continued on her journey, her heart heavy with the knowledge of the dangers that lay ahead.

Lyra felt the earth beneath her feet as she walked for the next week, the soft grass tickling her toes through her sandals. Birds chirped in the distance and the rustling of leaves in the wind combined for a melodic tune. She took in every sight and sound, knowing that each one could hold a clue or a warning that she couldn't afford to miss.

The sun began to set, casting a warm glow across the landscape. Lyra continued on, her steps light and graceful as she moved through the terrain. She knew she had to cover as much ground as possible before nightfall, as she was nearing her destination, and she pushed herself to keep moving.

As the darkness of night began to set in, Lyra reached a small clearing. She pulled out her map and examined it carefully, looking for the next landmark on her journey. She noticed a small river that she had to cross, and she set off toward it.

When she approached the river, Lyra was met with the sound of rushing water. She heard the gentle lapping of waves against the shore and the distant chirping of crickets. She approached the riverbank and took a deep breath, knowing that the next leg of her journey would be even more treacherous than the last.

Lyra waded into the cool water, feeling the gentle current tug at her legs. She kept her eyes fixed on the opposite shore, her heart pounding with the knowledge that the human kingdom was just beyond. Lyra knew she was not alone on this journey and that the eyes of the human guards might be watching her every move. She needed to be cautious.

Everyone told her humans weren't as keen and intelligent as elves, but she had nothing to compare them to. She moved ever watchful, expecting a platoon of humans to surround her at any moment. Lyra was swift and silent, a trait most elves had, though she was even more so. A game Lyra liked to play when she was young: hide and seek. Elves were silent, but she honed herself even more. Soft on her feet, she could sneak around anyone, but she usually knew where everyone was when she did. The humans were an unknown to her. She didn't know where their sentry was. Lyra didn't know their patrol patterns. All she had was hearsay, and it wasn't much because elves kept away from the savage humans.

With a deep breath, Lyra continued on her journey, determined to retrieve the stolen dagger and return it to her people. She pushed through the brush and into the vast opening. Green grass as far as her eyes could see, and in the far distance, a small castle. Thunder rolled overhead. It was still a long journey, and she hesitated for only a moment before gathering herself and continuing on. She intended to reach the castle before morning.

She walked all night until she stood at the edge of the human kingdom, staring up at the towering walls of the city looming above her. The sky was dark and foreboding, the only light coming from the faint glow of torches flickering along the city walls. She could feel the weight of her mission bearing down on her as she began to make her way toward the city gates.

Lyra moved with all the stealth and grace of her elven heritage, her footsteps barely making a sound as she moved across the cobbled streets. She kept to the shadows, her eyes scanning the area for any sign of danger. The scent of sweat and oil filled her nostrils, mingling with the musty smell of old stone.

As she approached the city gates, Lyra could feel her heart pounding in her chest. She knew the guards would be on high alert, and any mistake could mean certain death. She took a deep breath and stepped forward, her eyes fixed on the guards stationed at the gate.

She could feel their eyes upon her as she approached, their swords glinting menacingly in the torchlight. Lyra could feel her nerves beginning to fray, but she forced herself to remain calm and collected. She knew that she couldn't afford to let her guard down for even an instant.

When she reached the gate, one of the guards stepped forward, his hand resting on the hilt of his sword. "What is a pretty little thing like you doing out so late?"

"Yeah," another guard chimed in. "Shouldn't you be keeping someone's bed warm?"

"If not, then you can keep mine warm." The first guard chuckled, elbowing the man next to him.

Lyra met his gaze without flinching, her own eyes steely and determined. "I am quite all right, thank you. I simply lost track of time."

The guard studied her for a moment, sizing her up before nodding his head and stepping aside. "Suit yourself, but keep my offer in mind."

Lyra took a deep breath trying to not roll her eyes, thankful for her cloak hiding her elven ears, and stepped inside the city gates, the sound of her footsteps echoing off the stone walls. She could feel the weight of the city's history pressing down on her, its walls and corridors steeped in centuries of blood and war.

She moved silently through the city, her senses on high alert. The sound of her breathing was the only sound that broke the silence, the only indication of her presence in the shadows. She moved quickly but cautiously, her eyes scanning the area for any sign of the dagger she had come to retrieve.

As she moved through the crowded streets, she could feel the press of bodies against her, the heat of the sun beating down on her back. She heard the distant hum of conversation, the clatter of dishes from nearby taverns, and the occasional laughter of children playing in the alleyways.

Lyra's elven eyes darted from side to side, taking in the vibrant colors and bustling activity around her. She noticed the intricate carvings on the buildings, the ornate fountains adorned with statues, and the colorful banners fluttering in the breeze. The city was a stark contrast to the serene forests of her homeland, but she remained focused on her mission.

The hairs on the back of Lyra's neck stood on end as she moved deeper into the city. Lyra could sense she was not alone. Eyes watched her every move. She knew the guards would be closing in on her soon, and that she had to act quickly if she hoped to escape with the dagger.

Lyra approached the castle, and the air seemed to grow heavier, filled with a sense of foreboding. The stone walls rose high above her, casting long shadows across the courtyard. Lyra could feel the weight of its history in the very stones beneath her feet, knowing that she was stepping into a place steeped in power and intrigue.

She moved cautiously, her ears attuned to the faintest of sounds. The echoes of her footsteps reverberated through the empty corridors, the sound muffled by the tapestries and velvet drapes that lined the walls. The scent of age and musk hung in the air, a testament to the castle's long history.

Lyra's fingers brushed against the rough surface of the stone walls as she navigated the labyrinthine passages. She could feel the coolness of the stone against her skin, the texture telling tales of the many hands that had touched it over the centuries. The occasional gust of wind whispered through the corridors, carrying with it the distant sound of voices and the faint scent of candle wax.

As she drew closer to her goal, Lyra's heart quickened. The anticipation mingled with a tinge of fear, knowing that she was about to confront the guards and face the consequences of her actions. Her breath came in shallow gasps, the taste of adrenaline on her tongue, as she steeled herself for the final confrontation.

With each step, Lyra's senses heightened, her awareness of the world around her sharpened. The air felt charged with energy, as if the castle itself held its breath in anticipation of what was to come. She could hear the faint rustle of armor, the creak of leather, and the hushed whispers of the guards preparing for her arrival.

Lyra knew that the odds were against her, but she couldn't let fear consume her. She focused on the task at hand, drawing upon her elven grace and agility. Every movement was deliberate, every sense finely tuned, as she prepared to face the challenges that lay ahead.

The doors were locked, and she immediately withdrew her lock picks, glancing around her to ensure no one neared. Licking her lips, shivers traveling down her spine, she began working on the door. No one was around. She was sure of that. Lyra had been studying their movements, and she had a few minutes before the next patrol. However, she needed to act fast. The door clicked, and Lyra paused, steadying her breath.

With a final surge of determination, Lyra pushed open the heavy doors leading to the chamber where the artifact awaited. The room was bathed in a soft, golden light, casting a warm glow on the intricate tapestries and gilded furniture. The guards inside turned their attention towards her, their eyes wide with surprise and alarm.

She had hoped the room was empty. Unfortunately, she was not that lucky.

Lyra's heart pounded in her chest as she prepared to confront her enemies, her senses heightened and her spirit aflame. She knew that the fate of her people and the destiny of the artifact rested on her shoulders, and she would not falter. Everyone had told her humans were slow. She hoped they were right.

Lyra spotted a glimmer of light in the distance. She moved toward it swiftly and cautiously, her heart racing with excitement as she realized she had found the artifact. It was a small golden-hilt dagger, intricately carved and inlaid with precious gems balanced on a small display pillar. She could feel the power radiating from it, the very air around it seeming to shimmer with magic.

She was fast, faster than the human guards could keep up with. Perhaps she would get away before they could react.

Lyra reached out to grab the dagger, but as her fingers closed around it, she heard footsteps approaching. She froze, her heart pounding in her chest as she turned to face the source of the sound.

It was the group of guards, their swords drawn and their eyes fixed on Lyra. They had her surrounded—at least a dozen, their expressions grim and determined. How had they surrounded her so fast?

Lyra knew she could not hope to fight her way out of this. She took a deep breath and tried to calm her nerves, knowing that she had to think quickly if she hoped to escape with the precious artifact.

She held up her hands in a gesture of surrender, her eyes fixed on the guards. "I don't want any trouble," she said calmly. "I am just here for the dagger."

The guards exchanged a glance, their expressions unreadable. After a tense moment, one of them stepped forward and nodded towards the dagger in Lyra's hand. "That belongs to us," he said firmly. "Hand it over."

Reluctantly, she held out the dagger toward the guard. "Very well," she said quietly. "Take it. But know this—it is a powerful artifact, and it should be wielded with caution."

The guard took the dagger from her hand and studied it closely. His eyes narrowed in suspicion. After a moment, he nodded towards his companions. "Take her to the dungeons," he ordered. "We'll question her there."

Lyra turned around and saw a gap in their defenses. Their overconfidence would be their undoing. She knew she had to act fast. The guard closest to her left had sheathed his sword, hand outstretched for her elbow, as was the guard on her right. The others had started to put their swords in their scabbards, or relax their hands on their hilts. She didn't hesitate.

While everyone's eyes were away from her feet, she slammed her right heel hard onto the foot of the guard on her left, leaning forward and pulling his broadsword out of his scabbard. Lyra slammed the hilt of the sword into his temple, then spun to the other guard, slashing the sword against his platemail.

Lyra didn't want to hurt these humans. She didn't want to kill. But she needed to get out of here, and she would do what she must. The other guards scrambled to get to her, but they weren't fast enough. Lyra wasn't the most skilled with a sword, but her mother had taught her the basics—including the seven forms: Swat the Bee, Catching Butterflies, Raging Hummingbird, Balancing the Water Lilies, Chasing the Squirrel, Raging Deer, and Whispering Fireflies.

With all the humans closing in around her, she needed a chaotic form and chose Swat the Bee to start. Lyra didn't give anyone a chance to react, as she pushed forward, her blade flashing in the torchlight as she swept from one opponent to the next, disarming them as efficiently as she could. She quickly transformed into Raging Hummingbird to move from attacking one opponent to the next in quick succession. Lyra focused her attacks high, low, high. She aimed for shoulders and kneecaps. Lyra didn't want to kill them if she could help it.

A dozen opponents, and in less than a minute, she had disarmed them all. Perhaps these humans were as weak as some of the others elves had claimed.

Her victory was short-lived. Suddenly, the room filled with the sound of alarms and the clamor of soldiers. Lyra knew her presence had been discovered. She needed to escape the castle at all costs.

Lyra stepped forward to the jaw-dropped captain, and snatched the dagger from his hand. He blinked, but didn't bother trying to stop her as she turned around and ran.

With the dagger in hand, Lyra pushed her way through the disarmed and injured guards. She moved to the exit of the room, stepped outside the door, closed it, then pulled out her lock pick again. This time, she was planning on jamming the door. It only took a few moments, but once satisfied, she smirked, then rushed off into the darkness.

Her arm throbbed, and as she turned a corner, she decided to inspect it. A tingling sensation moved from her arm up her neck as she noticed the open cut and blood spots on the ground. Perhaps the humans weren't as inept as she thought. Ripping off a piece of her shirt, she knelt on one knee and began applying herbs to her wound before tying her arm to prevent blood flow and contamination.

Lyra had delayed too long. She noticed a squad of soldiers rush past her hiding spot toward the jammed door. They hollered as they attempted to yank it open. She looked both ways down the hall before sprinting back to action. Lyra moved faster than she had before, and hoped no more humans would find her. She was so busy looking around her that she failed to look right in front as she collided with a young man.

The man fell backwards, as did she, onto the ground. Her hood fell off of her head, exposing her tall ears to the surprised man.

"You're—you're an elf." His eyes widened.

Lyra's scrambled to her feet and clutched the dagger tighter.

"Please don't kill me," he begged.

She took a step forward, her composure faltering. "Who are you?"

"I am a mere servant, like my father before me." He bowed his head.

Lyra brushed off the dirt from her clothes as she glanced over her shoulder.

"Take me with you?"

Lyra spun back around, eyebrows raised as she looked down at the man. He got to his feet, not bothering to wipe his own dirt off of himself, though to be fair, he was covered in grime. Perhaps human servants didn't care for themselves as much as nobles and soldiers. For a human, though, he was attractive. A clean-cut face with medium length straight brown hair falling into his eyes. Deep green eyes that Lyra almost got lost in for a moment before shaking herself out of it. He was a human.

"I don't have time for this," she whispered.

Lyra turned the corner for one last glance before she stepped past the man toward the exit.

He shook his head. "I wouldn't go that way."

She turned around, raising an eyebrow.

He glanced down the hall past her. "They will be watching the main exit."

Lyra chewed her lip. "There is more than one."

He smirked. "There are a lot of hidden exits."

"Take me." Her nose wrinkled; her jaw tightened.

"Will you take me with you?" He placed his hands on his hips.

Lyra stepped close to him, abruptly edging her dagger close to his neck. "Now."

He gulped. "Yes, ma'am."

The man turned around and led her down a hall. She cautiously followed, hoping the human wasn't bringing her into a trap. He went into a dead-end corridor, and Lyra began to get skeptical until he entered a room. She followed him, still holding onto the dagger with a tight grip. The room was small, with nothing but a chair and bookshelf. He casually strolled over to the bookshelf and lifted a black leather-bound from its shelf. The entire bookshelf popped open slightly. He reached around it and pulled it out, revealing a dimly lit passageway.

"What is this?" she asked as she stepped inside.

He pulled the bookshelf closed, blocking anyone from seeing where they went. His lips formed into a smile and he held his hand out. "Name's Tyrone. Nice to meet you."

Lyra accepted his hand, eyebrows furrowed, still suspicious of the man. "Lyra."

"I've never met an elf before, but I have heard a lot about you. Is it true you can loose an arrow a league away and strike true?"

Lyra ignored the question. "How did you know about this place?"

"My family has been servants to the nobles of this castle for generations. We've paid attention and learned a lot. More than most of the nobles know about this castle. A lot of them have forgotten over the generations, but we have not."

Lyra marveled at the intricate red carpets and scenic pictures adorning the walls as she followed him down the hallway. "Why do you want out of this place?"

Tyrone dipped his head. "Truly? I've never been out of the castle. My father escaped, but he was the only one. My brother," he gulped. "My brother tried to escape. He tried to leave."

"What happened?" Lyra loosened the grip on the dagger.

"They hung him." His eyes met the floor.

Lyra's mouth dropped open.

"We're not free here. Nobles can do as they want. Merchants and mercenaries come and go. Servants? We stay. It's all we can do." Tyrone shrugged.

"That's awful." Lyra tilted her head to the side.

He inclined his head. "So, why did you come here?"

Lyra glanced at the dagger briefly, then met his eyes. "An artifact was stolen from us. I came to retrieve it."

"That dagger?" He scratched his chin. "That has been in the castle a little over a hundred and fifty years."

"Correct." Lyra was impressed by his knowledge of it.

"Why now?"

"Excuse me?" She placed her hands on her hips.

"Why wait until now to take it back?"

Lyra looked down at the dagger. "As far as I can tell, it wasn't until recently that it was discovered where its location was."

"Funny." He paused, glancing over his shoulder at her.

"What's that?"

He rolled his shoulders, then continued walking forward. "The story I've been told was the dagger was gifted to us by the elves."

Lyra furrowed her brow. That couldn't be correct, could it? Surely the elves wouldn't have given such an artifact to the humans. She shook her head, not wanting to believe it.

The next hour was silent as they traversed through the hidden passages inside of the castle. Lyra followed him cautiously. She didn't tuck away the dagger. Honestly, she didn't want to let it out of her sight. She felt sorry for the human she was following. If he told the truth about the life of a servant. She heard humans lied more than other races. Elves didn't lie. They had no need. However, it was true they didn't always reveal the entire truth. But it was seldom needed.

They finally reached the end of a passageway where Tyrone stopped. He slowly turned around, the dim torchlight he carried casting shadows across his grim face. His posture was straight, and sorrow filled his eyes.

"There is where we part, milady." He pushed open the wall, revealing a dark alley in the middle of the city. "I trust you'll be able to find your way back home."

Lyra's eyes twinkled as she stepped out of the hidden castle and into the musky air of the city. It obviously wasn't a nice alley she'd stepped out onto. Though, to be fair, nice alleys may be a little too noticeable for people sneaking around. She spun around, almost forgetting the human who'd helped her. "Thank—"

The door was closing behind her. "Wait... Tyrone."

He cracked open the door slightly, his puffy eyes meeting hers.

"Come."

"You mean it?"

"I do. I am in your debt."

Tyrone licked his lips. "Will I be welcome there?"

Lyra shrugged. "There's only one way to find out. As for I, I will vouch for you."

Tyrone stepped out of the castle and into the alley, closing the hidden door behind him. For the first time, Lyra saw a smile on his face.

She led the way out of the city. There were still a lot of questions on her mind. What really happened to the dagger originally? How had humans come to possess it? And Tyrone... perhaps humans weren't as bad as she originally thought. Her quest was over... but her investigation was just beginning.

THE END

The Ashlight Dolmen
Keith Robinson

1

Helden paused for a swig of water.

After three days of climbing, the view just got better and better. Even if her quest came to naught, at least she'd experienced all that the Ash Mountains offered. Of course, most dwarves had no reason to travel this far, let alone up a treacherous trail that clung to the cliffs.

This evening's sunset was even more spectacular than ever, in part because each day took her that much higher up the mountainside. But with the increasing beauty came the hardship of thinner air and cooler temperatures. She'd need *all* the blankets tonight.

She stashed her water bottle and continued up the path, eager to find a safe place to hole up for the night. She'd reach her destination tomorrow. In fact, tomorrow should be an altogether easier day because, according to the map, the path leveled off for the last leg of the journey.

It amazed her that a path existed in such a remote setting. She kept her gaze on her sturdy boots, one foot after another, using her thick walking stick for support as she followed the narrow and often crumbling trail. A step to the left would send her toppling down the mountainside, whereas a step to the right would put her up against a sheer wall of towering rock. There had been wider sections along the way, a few caves here and there, but for the last three days she'd been acutely aware of exactly two routes of travel: up or down.

Her short sword hung off her waist at one side, her battleaxe off the other. Both had chafed her thighs. She couldn't remember ever wearing her helmet and spaulders nonstop for so long, and she wanted to tear them loose and throw them off the mountain. Her wool shirt and leather bodice stank, not to mention her pants. The straps of the heavy backpack continued to dig into her shoulders.

Visions of a hot bath filled her mind occasionally.

But she felt good, despite minor discomforts. If nothing else, she'd bulked up some extra muscle in her already handsomely stocky legs.

One thing that had bothered Helden the entire way was the short look-ahead. The path continually zigzagged, hugging the cliff, giving no indication of potential dangers lurking around the next corner. For all she knew, a troll waited just out of sight.

The path widened slightly. Helden paused again, looking with interest at a cave-like opening to her right. It didn't go deep, and she doubted it would even protect her from a hard, lashing rain. But it was something.

There might be a much better place to sleep just ahead, or it might take another hour or two for the path to widen again. Suddenly weary, she knew this was it. This little alcove would do for her third night on the mountain.

Shrugging off her load, she groaned and flexed her arms, then put her back to the rock face and lowered herself down. Her muscles screamed in protest. She wouldn't be getting up again until dawn. One good thing about a long hike and rationing her water was that she didn't need to piss very often.

She pulled out all four blankets and arranged them around her. The strips of dry-cured pork still smelled fine, so she chewed on one. Tomorrow, when she reached level ground and the path widened onto a plateau, she'd set a trap for a rabbit. Or maybe take down a goat, if she chanced across any.

A scuffling sound down the path caused her to freeze mid-chew. She held her breath, listening hard as she slowly leaned forward to look.

Nothing.

That didn't mean there was no danger, just that she couldn't see around the bend. Her hand grasped the hilt of her sword, and she waited.

In theory, travelers occasionally passed each other going up and down this path. In practice, she imagined it would be quite difficult when loaded up with huge backpacks and weapons. While one could press themselves against the wall, the other would have to skirt the edge and risk slipping off—or, with unscrupulous strangers, being pushed! She imagined the safest method would be for one party to lie down flat so the other could step over them. Not exactly dignified, but safer all round.

If she had a traveler so close on her tail, then he or she had been following her for three days, or was fast enough to catch up. She doubted either was the case. It had to be a goat, or a large bird, or some other critter.

Or a troll.

No, not a troll. They were good climbers, but she doubted one would bother staying out of sight. It would simply attack. Anyway, the sun was still up, and everyone knew daylight burned their skin.

Helden relaxed. If not a troll or fellow traveler, then it couldn't be anything to be concerned with. In fact, she crossed her fingers that a mountain goat would stroll into view. It would make a nice change from chewy, dry-cured pork.

It didn't take long to get sleepy. Keeping her helmet on for warmth, and wrapped in the blankets, she watched the sunset and listened to the absolute silence. She quickly dozed off.

2

She woke up with a cold nose.

Though tightly bundled in four blankets and huddled in the alcove, with her helmet jammed on her head and thick braids covering her ears and face, her nose seemed to have chilled to the point of frostbite. She'd have to change her family name from Frostback to Frostnose.

Dawn had arrived, though none of the sun's rays fell on her west-facing alcove. She grunted and began to move, fighting through the usual aches and pains as her muscles began to warm.

Now she needed to piss, and urgently. Still grumbling, she extricated herself from the blankets, rolled onto her knees, and struggled to stand. "I feel old," she muttered.

Shivering, she quickly pushed her pants down and squatted downslope from her gear. The release felt good, and her trickle of urine steamed its way off the mountainside.

Damn, I stink.

She'd heard talk of waterfalls and springs on the top of the mountain, close to where she was headed. The idea had stuck with her until it became an expectation of reality, but she hadn't considered how much cooler it would be at such an altitude. Some enjoyed ice-cold bathing. She did not.

Helden packed up and got on her way again, chewing once more on a strip of pork and swigging from her water bottle. Today was the day. In the next few hours, she'd reach her destination.

Partway into her hike, enjoying the landscape as she so often did, she caught something in her periphery. By the time she looked again, there was nothing out of the ordinary to see. Still, it bothered her, so she repeated the casual sideways glance time and time again, taking in the grassy moors, rolling hills, rocky slopes, and craggy peaks—and beyond, the glittering sea to the far west.

There it was again—that movement behind her.

She tried not to let on that she *knew*. It had to be a person. No creature would be so stealthy and secretive. And a troll wouldn't need to be. Someone was following her.

The path finally leveled out, and the steep rock face to her right dropped away until she could see over the top of it. The trail wound inland, away from the dangerous edge. Grass sprang up. Windswept trees came into view. And her look-ahead lengthened. Though the path still zigzagged, the hairpins became much less severe.

Helden caught her breath and faltered. There it was! Forgetting her pursuer for the moment, she stared with awe and excitement at the monument ahead—a very simple but impressive arrangement of two giant stone slabs standing upright, and an even bigger, flatter capstone perched on top.

The Ashlight Dolmen.

So-named after the moonlight shining on the Ash Mountains, the dolmen had stood for many centuries, or perhaps thousands of years as some claimed. Nobody knew for sure.

Helden picked up her pace, then glanced over her shoulder once more—and stopped dead.

She *was* being followed. And whoever it was had come out into the open.

Her full attention on the stranger, she stood her ground with her hand on her hilt, making it clear she was not intimidated by her secretive follower. As the figure approached, she made out the details with increasing ire.

An elf. Tall and thin, wearing nondescript and somewhat shabby grey robes, carrying a staff that stood taller than he, and with the stride of someone who no longer felt a need to hide and wanted to close the distance as quickly as possible.

"Hello there!" he called.

Helden ground her teeth and half drew her sword.

The elf's wrinkled, weathered face suggested he was an elder, yet he moved with grace and strength. His long, white hair was tucked behind his pointed ears and hung down his back, except when a breeze caught it.

"I mean you no harm, young lady," the elf said as he came strolling up.

"*You*? Harm *me*?" she spat. "Why are you following me?"

His eyebrows went up. "Following you? What makes you think I'm following you?"

"Come on, old-timer. You've been following me for days. Admit it!"

He offered a smile and looked out to the west. "Is there perhaps another route to this spot that I'm unaware of?"

"This is the only path, and you know it."

"Indeed I do, my dear. Therefore, with two people on the same path for days on end, it's inevitable that one might *appear* to be following the other." He grinned, showing even teeth for someone so old. "I did, however, try to keep my distance to avoid an awkward entanglement within the confines of the narrow footing."

Helden slowly slid her sword back into its sheath and relaxed her grip. "So you're going to the same place I am."

"Is that a question?"

She frowned. "Well, are you?"

"That depends, dear lady."

"On what?"

"On where you're going."

Helden clenched her fists. "Where do you *think* I'm going, you old fool?"

"Ah, well, in that case, I might ask you the same question in the same unfriendly tone."

The conversation paused there. Helden decided in that moment that the elf was no threat to her. But she also decided he was an irksome meddler that might just end up tossed from the cliff if he didn't wipe that smug smile from his ugly face.

3

Helden tried at first to ignore him. She simply shrugged and continued on her way. It quickly became clear that he had no intention of leaving her side. Being at least two feet taller than her, even his most casual pace easily matched hers. To shake him off, she'd have to start running—or knock him down with a swift blow to the head.

"It's rather splendid, isn't it?" he exclaimed.

"What is?" she growled.

"The Ashlight Dolmen. I've always wanted to see it, you know. What about you? My name's Vespyl, by the way. Vespyl Tramorin, at your service."

She said nothing. Exchanging names would alter the dynamic of their tenuous relationship, making it more difficult to remain hostile. She had no desire to accompany this elf for the rest of their time on top of the mountain.

"I'm from House Maumer," the elf added, breaking the silence.

Against her better judgment, this news piqued Helden's interest. "So you're a wizard."

"You could say that, yes. And what's your name, my dear?"

She ground her teeth, then sighed. "Helden Frostback."

"From which clan, Helden? No, wait, let me guess . . ." He scrutinized her. "I'm going to guess you're of Stormguard."

"Is that a question?"

"Am I right?"

Somewhat reluctantly, she nodded. "I'm a wizard, too."

"Splendid! Ah, but of *course* we're wizards. Who else would come here to see the dolmen? Tell me, Helden—do you plan to sleep under it?"

"Obviously."

Vespyl nodded. "Indeed, indeed."

Something occurred to her then. Something a little more specific than the simple fact that she had an unwelcome companion. "Are *you* intending to sleep under it? Because I doubt there's room for two, and I was here first."

The old elf chuckled. "Calm yourself, young Helden. I wouldn't dare encroach on your place of slumber. First, it wouldn't be proper. Second, what makes you think I *want* to sleep under it?"

Surprised, she almost faltered in her step. "Why wouldn't you? Are you telling me you came all this way up a mountain to view the dolmen . . . and *not* sleep under it?"

"Your quest and mine vary, Helden. Perhaps we have the same goal, but our method differs."

She huffed through her nose. "Why are elves always so high and mighty?"

"Why are dwarves always so short-tempered?"

"Are you making fun of my height?" she demanded.

"Are you making fun of mine?"

Shaking with anger, Helden reached for her sword and struggled to restrain herself. As much as this old duffer angered her with his smart-mouthed comments, slicing his throat open wasn't the answer. Not only would that moment of uncontrolled fury haunt her forever, it would likely get her into very hot water indeed.

Being short-tempered wasn't her fault. All dwarves were. Her own fuse happened to be shorter than most, and already lit. Elves annoyed her just by virtue of their ridiculous height, and their silver tongue didn't help. She'd always maintained that an elf with no legs and a taped mouth was the minimal requirement if any kind of friendship were to be forged.

"I fear I've upset you," Vespyl said after a while. "My apologies. You must ignore the ramblings of an ancient wizard like me."

"Then stop talking," she growled.

He laughed, sounding almost melodic. "May I ask, dear Helden, exactly what you understand about the dolmen? What is the word on the street in dwarven territory?"

Helden considered that for a moment, trying to think of a single reason she shouldn't tell the elf what she knew. Failing, she sighed and gave a shrug. "It's what all dwarves know. The Ashlight Dolmen has been here for centuries, perhaps millennia. It's said that if you sleep under the dolmen on a moonlit, starry night, the gods will bestow you with the gift of healing."

"Ah, yes. And is that interpretation precise? About sleeping under the dolmen on a moonlit, starry night?"

"Well . . ."

"As opposed to, say, a cloudy, rainy night? Or a hot day?"

"The moonlight and stars are necessary," she said a little more haughtily than she intended. "They say the moon must be visible, and the stars should twinkle. That suggests a clear evening."

"And sleeping? Why *sleep* under the dolmen? How about a doze? Why shut your eyes at all?"

Helden threw up her hands in disgust. "How should I know? It is what it is."

The elf nodded, his lips pursed. "Then let me ask you this, if I may?"

She sighed, wishing this journey would end already. "Go ahead."

"After so many hundreds of years, perhaps millennia, how many dwarves—or elves, or humans, or gnomes—how many people have come away from the Ashlight Dolmen blessed with the power of healing? Hmm? How many, do you think? A hundred? Fifty? Ten? Hmm? Maybe five?" He gently gripped her arm. "One? Do you know of even *one*?"

"The story wouldn't have been passed down through

generations if there was no truth to it," she grumbled.

"True, true. And *that* is why I'm here. It is that delicate straw to which I so resolutely clutch. Without it, there is no reason to believe this dolmen isn't simply a collection of pointless rocks."

Helden's frustration with the elf faded. To her surprise, she found him . . . interesting.

"And what's *your* belief?" she asked. "The elves, I mean. What's their understanding of the dolmen?"

"Much the same as yours, my dear. Except . . ." Vespyl paused and looked off into the distance.

"Except?"

"Well, the thing is, Helden, I possess a parchment that tells a slightly different tale. I admit the alteration is miniscule, but it's an alteration all the same, and one that might offer you and I a more interesting outcome tonight."

She ground to a halt and turned to squint up at the ridiculously tall elf. "What *kind* of alteration?"

Vespyl smiled and looked down at her. "This is the part where you're going to get very annoyed with me."

4

"Tell me," Helden demanded, her hand automatically reaching for her sword again.

Vespyl didn't appear to notice. "Look, we're nearly at our destination. It's fascinating, isn't it?"

"Quit stalling."

He was right, though. They'd arrived at the Ashlight Dolmen. It was both smaller and larger than Helden had expected—smaller in that it stood only just tall enough for an elf to walk under, but larger because the stones, by any standards, were *huge*. How could anyone stand the two megaliths upright? And how could anyone lift the capstone up on top? It was impressive.

As she understood it, elves believed 'dolmen' to be a misspelling of 'tolmen,' meaning 'stone with hole.' Dwarves mocked this, certain the word 'dolmen' simply meant 'stone table.' In any case, everyone knew what a dolmen was—which was ironic, because nobody knew what a dolmen was *for*.

Though the midmorning sun was already strong in the clear sky, the space within the standing stones was extremely dark. The grass didn't grow there. Instead, a depression in the dirt suggested many, many people had lain there—perhaps up to three at a time, if they were friendly.

"You mentioned an altered telling of the story?" Helden asked, distracted.

Vespyl slid his backpack off his shoulders. It was much slimmer than hers. He traveled light, despite the chill in the air. "Ah, well, if I tell you about that alteration, then we might not see the desired results."

"What does *that* mean?"

"It means, dear new friend, that I cannot tell you—yet. The parchment I mentioned is a prophecy. And I fear that speaking this prophecy aloud will prevent it from happening."

Helden's frustration grew. "Prevent *what* from happening?"

"Therein lies the problem. Simply telling you what will be prevented from happening may be the very thing that prevents it from happening."

She let out a cry of exasperation and turned away. The old fool had better shut his mouth for the next few minutes lest she cut out his tongue and feed it to him. Grinding her teeth, she threw off her backpack and started to pace.

"Do you carry this parchment?" she growled.

"I do."

"Is it in Elven?"

"Indeed it is."

Helden ground her teeth some more. Stealing it from him wouldn't work unless she suddenly developed the ability to read their ridiculously convoluted native language. Even their names were hard to decipher. "You, sir, are the most frustrating creature I've ever met."

She ignored his chuckle and started poking around the dolmen. Circling the monument with a critical eye, she found nothing noteworthy, nothing that might warrant closer scrutiny. Just solid stone blocks, cold to touch, a little moss here and there. Overhead, the capstone provided a superb shelter against the heaviest of downpours, though it looked like the depression underneath had flooded again and again despite attempts to dig gulleys around it.

Sleep under the dolmen on a moonlit, starry night.

This didn't dictate that one had to sleep in the muddy depression at its heart. It could simply mean sheltering against a megalith, sitting upright beneath the overhang. That would still be sleeping *under the dolmen.*

A moonlit, starry night seemed clear enough too, though any time from dusk till dawn would fit the description—as long as the moon was out and stars were present.

The gods will bestow you with the gift of healing.

That line was fairly straightforward in one sense, but also a little vague. What, exactly, was the gift of healing? A magical, divine power? Or simply knowledge? She smiled to herself. If she dozed against one of the standing stones after dark, and a traveling scholar happened to stroll by and drop a tome stuffed full of long-hidden witch-doctor cures, that would technically fulfill the prophecy. It just wouldn't be very exciting.

As she squatted at the edge of the depression, hidden in shadows, she peered out at the elf. He stood calmly, looking toward the west, the breeze tugging at his hair and robe. This parchment he'd mentioned, with its *altered telling* of the story . . . She had to learn of it. Clearly, something about the wording had intrigued the old wizard enough to venture all this way.

"I'll sleep under the dolmen," she growled under her breath, "but, come morning, if I'm not bestowed with the power of healing, then you and I will have serious words."

Her fingers curled around the hilt of her sword.

5

Dusk was a long way off, and Helden grew impatient. To make matters worse, the elf wouldn't shut up.

". . . You see, I believe the power of healing could be a weapon in the wrong hands," he said as they sat together in the sunshine.

Helden frowned. Without taking her eyes off the distant mountain peaks in the clear blue sky, she took his bait and said, "Why?"

"Well, I don't know you very well, young Helden, but suppose you were a very selfish dwarf with a penchant for recognizing a fast way to make a lot of coin. Suppose you were the sort of dwarf who would use the power of healing for financial gain. Once your clans understood the extent of your healing ability, they would be desperate enough to pay whatever you charged in order to save their lives from a terminal illness."

Helden ground her teeth. "I would never *charge* for such a thing."

"Ah, but are you sure? Imagine it—day in, day out, saving lives as well as healing minor ailments. Where does it end? What if others from across the land heard of your ability and came to you? For instance, I'm a mere elf, yet I have several ailments."

He took a moment to push his sleeve up. Helden was shocked to find some terrible scarring on his forearm. It looked like he'd been burned fairly recently, and it had to hurt constantly.

Vespyl saw her discomfort and nodded. "I also have an affliction in my lungs that is sure to condemn me to an early death. If you, a dwarf, had the power to heal, would you agree to help an old elf like me?"

Doubtful, Helden thought, growing weary of his nonstop tongue.

"Therein lies the problem," Vespyl went on. "Where do you

draw the line? When do you get to rest? What's in it for you? Suppose you grew weary of people lined up outside your door?"

"The only thing I'm weary of, Vespyl, is your constant nattering."

The elf chuckled and absently scratched at his chin. "I'm simply saying that even the most virtuous character must eventually tire of their good deeds and seek recompense—small at first, perhaps free lodging at an inn while they heal its guests, a complimentary meal and some ale on the house—that sort of thing."

"Rightly so," Helden muttered.

"Quite. But perhaps you wish to take time off, and yet the sick and dying continue to pester you, and rather than deny them, you demand a nominal payment designed to filter out those with a sniffle or cough, and—"

"Do not trivialize this!" Helden exploded. "If, tonight, I were bestowed with the power of healing, I would *never* turn away the sick. But my people would not seek to bother me with petty ailments! I think you speak of the elves, Vespyl. You are not as hardy as us dwarves."

Annoyingly, the elf chuckled again. "I'm certain you're right, my dear." It seemed he might have finally run out of steam . . . until he added, "Still, you may be underestimating the weight such a powerful gift would place upon your shoulders. While your intentions may be righteous, those in authority might seek to—"

"*Enough*, old man!"

Helden got up and stomped away. She could read him like a book. He was attempting to dissuade her from sleeping under the dolmen and obtaining the power for himself. Well, it wouldn't work. She personally knew three dwarves whose lives would drastically improve if their longstanding ailments were cured—two of them cousins, and one a close friend. She did not intend to fail them.

It was only after her anger faded, and her pacing slowed, that she noticed a prickly sensation on the back of her neck. Her fingers touched the hilt of her sword, and she stood still, holding her breath. That feeling of being watched . . .

She scoured the craggy rocks that rose from the grassy slopes, looking for signs of a visitor. They could be anywhere. Though the dolmen stood on an expansive plateau, this was by no means the peak of the mountain. Cliff faces loomed a short walk away. There were trees and bushes, too. An army of orcs could be watching, and she might not know it.

Or trolls.

The notion gave her a chill. Then again, trolls wouldn't venture into the daylight. She was safe—for now.

Tonight would be another story.

Helden began searching for possible hiding places. If a troll were to show up, she wasn't fool enough to believe she could defeat it with a short sword and a battleaxe. Perhaps a couple of basic defensive spells would work, but a small hidey-hole would be safer, somewhere deep and narrow enough that a giant couldn't reach her. There was no shame in cowering when the odds were stacked so unfavorably.

She hacked at bushes, peered behind boulders, squeezed into gaps, and found nothing that a troll couldn't reach into with ease. Hanging off the side of the mountain wasn't an option, as trolls were adept at climbing. And even if ascending a tree would help, none of them was tall enough.

There were no visible caves, either. It seemed the entire mountain favored the trolls. If one wanted to pick off a traveler, it would do so with ease. How had previous visitors survived the night? In fact—

She shivered. What if they hadn't? How many visitors to the dolmen had perished at the ghastly hands of a troll? Maybe the dolmen was a form of sacrificial altar, and nobody lived long enough to warn others.

"We need to find a secure place to hide," she called to the elf. "In case of trolls tonight."

Still sitting on the grass at the edge of the cliff, Vespyl twisted around to study her. "I rather thought we'd pool our magical resources and conjure a spell or two."

Helden sniffed. "That's all very well, old man, but I see no sense in relying solely on our wizardry skills when solid rock will do the job so well. We just have to find a fissure. I'm going to search that craggy line of boulders over there. Perhaps you could make yourself useful?"

The old elf grinned at her and nodded. "So be it, my young friend." He started to climb to his feet, relying heavily on his walking stick as he straightened up.

Helden gave a nod, pleased that he hadn't resisted her request. When it came down to it, at least he understood—

At that moment, the ground collapsed under her feet. It was just a small, crumbling section at first, but she sank to her knees before she had a chance to react. And even as she spread her hands out to the side to catch her descent, the sinkhole simply opened up all around and swallowed her.

She fell into the darkness.

6

Helden groaned.

The moment consciousness returned, a splitting headache pounded her with a terrible vengeance. Wincing, she gently touched the side of her head and was appalled at the lump she found there. Annoyingly, her helmet had done nothing to protect her, because it had fallen off during her tumble.

Her tumble . . .

It came back to her in a flash. She'd sunk into the ground, into darkness. The loose soil and rock had gone with her, sliding down a narrow shaft of rock, and then she'd dropped into freefall, in absolute darkness. Seconds later, she'd hit the ground. Her ankles had twisted, she'd banged her knee, rolled, tumbled down a hard slope, slammed into more rock, then slipped some more. She remembered the metallic dinging of her helmet bouncing away, and then—then pain as her head struck a hard surface.

Gingerly, she opened her eyes. The blackness scared her for a moment; it was so complete that she feared her eyesight had failed. Then, gradually, she made out a smudge of grey in one direction. It was so faint that it only revealed itself if she squinted and looked off to the side.

With a throbbing head, she carefully sat up and checked for other injuries. One ankle hurt, but she didn't expect it to cause much more than a limp. Otherwise, she counted herself lucky to have avoided broken bones.

How far had she fallen? By rights, she should see a shaft of daylight above. Nothing of the sort presented itself no matter how hard she scoured the darkness.

Earlier, Vespyl had mentioned pooling their resources and using their combined magic to ward off trolls. She'd resisted the idea because, secretly, her sorcery skills were limited. Wizarding wasn't easy. Not all dwarves of Stormguard could conjure powerful spells. Helden certainly couldn't.

She could manage a dab of light, though. Placing her palms together, she focused on channeling body heat down her arms to her fingers. That surplus heat emerged from her skin, charged with energy that crackled and flashed until a steady glow appeared.

With the small ball of light pulsing in her hands, she worked on it a little more, imagining herself blowing gently on newly lit kindling. The glow intensified until her surroundings began to brighten.

A cave. Well, no real surprise there. The ceiling had to be five times her height, full of nooks and crannies, probably home to numerous bats. She'd landed on piles of boulders and slid to the bottom. Even if she climbed to the highest point, the ceiling was far out of reach.

She still saw no sign of the shaft she'd fallen into. There were a few dark spots on the ceiling, but she expected *daylight*.

"Vespyl!" she croaked. She swallowed, cleared her throat, and tried again. "VESPYL!"

No answer.

"Where in hell's name is he?" she growled. After a pause, she added, "For that matter, where in hell's name am *I*?"

Holding her ball of light one-handed, she steadied herself on the smooth, sloping rocks at her side and picked her way across the chamber, squinting to make out the details of the far walls. It took a few minutes of limping to figure out she'd fallen into the end of a long, wide passage. With the ceiling so high, she had no choice but to explore deeper and hopefully find a way back to the surface.

The passage—some fifteen feet across—curved around to the right. Once around that bend, she caught the faintest of breezes, a chill in the air that gave her hope. Somewhere in this godforsaken place was an exit. She just had to keep moving, carefully, so as not to—

Her foot twisted, and she cried out. Her ankle was already weakened by the fall, and now she'd worsened the sprain. She cursed herself and ground her teeth. Then, breathing new life into her fading ball of light, Helden pressed onward, gingerly testing her footing before shifting her weight.

A little farther on, she stopped dead and stared in wonder.

A small opening in the wall revealed a view of the distant, moonlit sea. The breeze she'd felt earlier came from here. It was stronger now, whistling gently, cool but welcome. It certainly chased away any stale air! But . . . was this the way out? Because it didn't strike her as a viable exit. Quite the opposite, in fact.

She clambered over the rocks to get to it. The light glowing from her palm flickered like a candle in the breeze, but it held fast, illuminating her path. Ferns grew near the opening, sprouting from around the base of the rocks in hidden pockets of soil. A network of thick root systems sprawled across the ceiling. With myriad plants and great swaths of moss, it was clear the cave saw plenty of sunlight and driving rain.

When she reached the opening and pushed aside the vegetation, her fears were confirmed. If she leaned out far enough, she could look down on the sheer cliff below—and the deadly drop it represented.

A hole in the mountainside. What am I supposed to do with this?

Panic began to set in. Her light revealed no further exits. This seemed to be in an isolated cavern within the mountain, with one way in and out—or two, if you counted the sinkhole she'd dropped through.

This is for the birds! she thought, her mind beginning to spin. *Or a slender wyvern's nest!*

Of course, it could just as easily be the lair of a troll. Such a creature could easily scale the cliff to get in and out of this place.

Suddenly fearful, she snapped her fingers into a fist and extinguished the light, then ducked down and held her breath. If a troll were already here, perhaps it was sleeping. Perhaps she'd been lucky so far. Another five minutes of clambering and she might have walked right into it.

But no. The opening was too small. Trolls were broad. She doubted one would fit through the gap.

Helden squeezed herself into a crevice between boulders, trying to decide what to do. That it was night began to percolate in her brain. She'd fallen into the sinkhole and knocked herself unconscious, meaning she'd been lying in a heap *all day*? If that were the case, Vespyl might have given up looking for her and set off on his journey home.

Or *he* might be asleep. With Helden's disappearance, he could be laid out under the dolmen right now, stealing her claim to the power of healing!

Anger stirred inside her.

But then a thought crossed her mind and gave her a thrill of excitement. The rocky tunnel she'd ended up in stretched under the grassy plateau above. Under the path she and Vespyl had used, and under the cliff edge they'd sat near to gaze out at the sea.

And . . . under the dolmen.

7

"A moonlit, starry sky," Helden murmured, gazing out into the night.

Could it be that simple? For hundreds of years, visitors had slept directly under the dolmen, sprawled in that sorry depression in the dirt. All the while, this chamber existed *beneath the ground*. Nobody knew of it because there was no way in or out—at least no *obvious* way. She'd literally fallen into it by accident.

She began to laugh. The irony of it! She might very well be the first to sleep under the dolmen on a moonlit, starry night, and the gods might even bestow upon her the gift of healing! And then . . .

And then what? She was stuck here for eternity!

"Get a grip," she growled. Cupping her hands to her mouth, she yelled, "VESPYL! ARE YOU THERE?"

The old fool refused to answer. Perhaps he was deliberately ignoring her for reasons she couldn't fathom.

Go to sleep. Lie down right here on these smooth boulders, in the moonlight, and rest. My head hurts, and my ankle hurts. Perhaps I'll be given the power to heal, and by the time morning arrives, I'll be fit as a fiddle and ready to attempt a dangerous climb.

A careful scout in the light of her magic revealed a small, still pool of water among the rocks. She examined it, thinking it had to be tainted or stagnant. To her surprise, it looked perfectly clear. When she cautiously tasted it, she found it crisp, almost sweet.

Her hopes rose tenfold. But she puzzled over it, too. How could there be a pool with no trickling stream to feed it? The only way she could think of—

Glancing up, she raised her palm to study the ceiling. Her ball of light picked out a single, thick stalactite directly over the pool. It was dry, but she would wager her favorite battleaxe that the hanging column dripped steadily during a downpour. Somewhere on the surface above, rainwater collected in a depression and trickled through the soil and rock . . .

Her mouth dropped open. The depression under the dolmen! Could it be that she'd pinpointed the *exact location* of the monument? The rainwater would start out muddy, but by the time it filtered through the rock and dripped from cracks in the ceiling, it would end up crystal clear.

Helden settled herself on a flat boulder to the side of the pool. She could reach into the water if she so desired. A shaft of moonlight stretched into the chamber and played over her other hand. And the dolmen stood some thirty feet above her head.

This is it. This night is mine. I'm ready. Bestow me!

Less than a minute passed before movement caught her eye. She raised her palm toward it, squinting as her faithful ball of light struggled to chase away the shadows. There! An indiscernible creature, almost completely silent, easing toward her . . .

Its head appeared, and she stifled a gasp. Drawing her sword, she avoided any sudden movements and slowly raised her weapon, preparing to strike as soon as her foe was in range. Snakes weren't her biggest fear. Still, this one had to be big, judging by the size of its blunt head.

The serpent slithered gracefully over the boulders. As it came into the light, the bronze coloring became apparent. Helden relaxed a little. This was a constrictor—dangerous, but hardly in the same league as a venomous biter. It was an Aesculapian, known for—

Her mouth dropped open again as a revelation struck her. "What does this mean?" she muttered.

The snake reacted to the sound of her voice. It paused and stuck its tongue out, where it quivered for a moment.

"I don't think you're going to hurt me," Helden said in a soft tone as she hefted her sword, "but if you try to wrap your coils around me, understand that I will cleave you in two."

Apparently unconcerned, the snake moved closer until its blunt nose nudged up against her ankle. At around six feet long, it climbed her leg, circling as it went, and she was very much afraid she'd have to kill it after all. She tensed, trying to decide how to dispatch the serpent. Chop its head off? Stab it through the brain?

It wrapped once around her thigh before continuing up her belly and chest. The black eyes gave nothing away, but she couldn't help feeling it meant no harm. Still, she aimed her sword, thinking that a simple thrust would penetrate the skull.

The snake paused. Clinging to her leg for support, it leaned outward from her torso to peer at her eye to eye. The creature was heavy. She could easily imagine how powerless one might be if caught in its constrictions.

She relaxed. "You're just a friendly old soul, aren't you?" she murmured. "Curious about me, checking me out."

Sheathing her sword, she tentatively stroked the snake's head. It barely flinched, though it stared unblinking while flicking its tongue back and forth.

"An Aesculapian," she said. "Known in legend as healing snakes. I don't know if I should be enthralled or disappointed. Can it be that the myth of the dolmen stems from sightings of Aesculapian snakes? Or is there more to it than that?"

The snake, of course, didn't answer. But it began to move again, keeping its head still while slithering more of its body up hers. It tightened around her thigh, and she frowned.

"I'll allow this as long as you're not wrapped around my chest or neck. I know how constrictors operate. Every time I breathe out, you'll tighten a little more."

Despite her confidence that she could escape this relatively docile threat, unease worked its way into her gut. The hackles on her neck stood on end. She felt . . . *something*. A sense that she might be underestimating this creature.

Her hand curled around the hilt of her sword once more.

Movement at her feet surprised her. She glanced down to find a second snake weaving its way around her ankles. And a third easing into view from behind.

"Gods!" she cursed.

Her ball of flame extinguished as she drew her sword and started to struggle free of the Aesculapian's grip on her thigh. It tightened, but the other two quickly encircled her other leg, and though she tried to lift her foot and swing it free, they moved fast to ensnare her.

In a panic, Helden flailed and thrashed and swung her sword, but her encumbered feet took away her balance, and she ended up pitching forward. Her elbow crashed against a boulder, and she cried out. Trying to roll, she quickly realized the three snakes were already hampering her every move.

Any reluctance she might have had about killing such beautiful creatures evaporated in an instant. The first snake seemed to hover overhead, almost ethereal in the faint moonlight from the opening in the rock wall. She thrust her sword into the serpent's neck, and it recoiled and hissed, its entire body going into a muscular spasm. Blood spilled from the wound as she yanked the blade out again. That blood spattered her face, and she blinked and gasped as some of it touched her lips.

When she opened her eyes again, she was appalled to find at least half a dozen bronze-colored heads looming over her—and half a dozen serpent bodies quickly tightening their grips on her limbs. So tight were the constrictions on her arms that her fingers lost their strength, and the sword dropped with a clang onto the rocks.

She tried to sit up, to roll, anything at all, but a scaly body had wrapped around her neck and was busy squeezing . . . squeezing . .
.

Helden felt for her dagger, or her battleaxe, but all she could think about was her inability to free her limbs and her struggle to keep breathing.

So this is it.

This is how my life ends.

Strangled by snakes.

Right before she blacked out, stars pricked her vision. Stars! She would have laughed at the irony if she weren't so busy dying.

8

"Helden, wake up."

She groaned.

Vespyl loomed over her, a shadowy figure whose long hair hung in her face. "I found you at last. Or rather, I found a way into this secret cavern without breaking my neck in the process."

Helden rubbed her throat and looked around. Shafts of daylight from the wall opening revealed at least a dozen Aesculapian snakes slithering between boulders and dangling from the thick, branch-like vines nestled in the ceiling. One dead snake lay close by, a trail of blood down the side of the rock it lay across.

"They didn't kill me," she croaked.

"It would appear not."

The snakes ignored her. She couldn't imagine why they'd tried so hard to squeeze the life out of her and then shown mercy, especially as she'd dispatched one of their own in the process.

Despite the bewildering event, she felt . . . all right. Her ankle should have been swollen and painful, but it was not. The lump on her head had vanished. In fact, she sensed no bruising or aches at all.

She sighed. "Well, I'm done with this nonsense. Vespyl, the power of healing is all yours—if you can find it. It could be these snakes healed me as I lay here all night. They're Aesculapians. The myth may have derived from their presence in this cavern. Perhaps healing was all they intended for me when they . . ."

Regret struck her as she gazed at the dead snake. Had she mistaken its motivation?

"As far as I'm concerned," she said, "the myth of being bestowed with the gift of healing is exactly that—a myth."

Vespyl said nothing as he helped her up. Taking both her

hands, he tugged and ended up grunting under her weight. He still seemed shaken long after she was standing. It amused her that this skinny, gangly elf would have such trouble despite the annoying height of his kind. They might be tall, but they were weak.

"Now, let's get you out of here," he said in a trembling voice. "There's a passage over yonder—but it's very narrow, and I fear you may not squeeze through."

Helden retrieved her sword and sheathed it. "Are you saying I'm fat, old one?"

He laughed. "Not fat. Sturdy. As all dwarves are."

Leaving the writhing snakes behind, Vespyl led them into the utter blackness she hadn't yet explored. Sharing the same thought, they both conjured small balls of fire in their palms, and after sharing nods of approval, they concentrated on picking their way over the rocks without twisting an ankle.

It was indeed a tight squeeze. Vespyl went first, grunting as he turned sideways and leaned into the maneuver. It meant his back was arched, and all he could do was shuffle inch by inch until he'd passed between the protruding walls.

Helden knew straight away she'd never fit. She was, as he'd feared, too sturdy. Rather than attempt it and make a fool of herself, she stood in contemplative silence, watching as he turned around and held his light high.

"Helden?"

She sighed and shook her head. "This passage was not meant for my kind. I'll have to backtrack. Perhaps you can find the shaft I fell in through and pass down a rope?"

After a moment, he nodded. "I could do that. However . . ."

Something in his tone got her back up. Here it was. Here was the elf she'd distrusted from the start. "State your demands," she growled.

Vespyl chuckled. "My, you're astute. All right, I'll cut to the chase."

He paused, gathering his thoughts. Helden let her own light fade so that only his face was illuminated while he fished in a capacious pocket and withdrew a rolled parchment. He pinched the bottom between the last two fingers of his fireball hand while unrolling it with the other. The glowing light lit up the ancient Elvish wording.

"This parchment," he said in a faraway tone, "tells of the dolmen in the Ash Mountains, and how the gift of healing will be given to he or she who sleeps under it. This is much the same as any other version of the prophecy. However, and I quote: *'The gift bestowed shall never leave.'* So you see, dear Helden, I fear you may be stuck here."

He quietly rolled up the parchment and slipped it back into his pocket while Helden stewed on his words.

"That's it?" she grumbled after a while. "That was your big secret? Why couldn't you simply tell me that from the start?"

"Because I feared it would influence your decision to search for the secret. If you knew you could obtain the gift but never leave here with it, then why bother searching?"

She balled her fists. Half a dozen counterarguments sprang to mind, but she voiced none of them. Instead, she let out a slow breath and tried reasoning. "The so-called wise words of your parchment may well be wrong, Vespyl. If you let down a rope as I suggested, I can escape this prison, with or without the gift of healing. Besides, it's clear to me I *don't* have the gift of healing. I was not bestowed with the honor. I'm not the person of that prophecy. I'm just a dwarf who failed like so many others. There's no reason for you to walk away and leave me here."

"I beg to differ, young Helden." The elf's flame flickered softly as he gazed at her—or gazed in her direction at least, where Helden still stood in the shadows. "When I helped you up back there, I *felt* it in you. The power courses through your veins, and that power immediately helped me. As I stand here now, my body heals. See?"

He lifted his sleeve. The terrible scarring wasn't nearly as bad now. His skin pulsed and glowed softly as the tissue continued to mend.

Helden tried to hide her amazement, but it came through in her gasp. "This . . . this isn't possible!"

"Oh, but it is, Helden. My lungs, too, feel . . . lighter? The affliction is gone. Your gift is swift and miraculous. And such a gift cannot be wasted."

"But . . ."

Her mind whirled. The Aesculapian snake she'd stabbed . . . Its blood had spattered her face and dribbled into her mouth. Could that be it? An act of self-defense had bestowed her with the gift?

So nothing to do with stars, or a moonlit night, or even sleeping under the dolmen. Just a lot of nonsense dressed up to make a myth sound more exotic. Did it matter that Aesculapian snakes were common across the land?

The elf seemed to believe these particular snakes were special, if the specifics of his parchment were anything to go by.

"I felt sure you would obtain the gift," he said, "and the prophecy suggests that your gift shall not be permitted to leave. So here you are—a dwarf with the power to heal. And we cannot risk you leaving this place and losing your ability, so I shall make sure you are well fed and cared for . . . during your long stay here."

She laughed with derision. "You can't be serious! Do you really think I won't escape this place?"

"Then escape, young Helden. By all means, try. Squeeze your ample frame through this passage. Levitate out of the shaft through which you arrived. Or perhaps exit through the opening on the cliff and scale the mountain wall as if you were a troll. Do your best, Helden." He smiled. "But just in case, I will leave you with whatever spare food I have, and I will hasten to return with a legion of elves—mainly the sick and dying. My terms will be simple. Heal us, and we will keep you alive."

And there it was. Her blood boiled, and she wanted to reach through the tight passage and strangle him. But even if she managed that, it would likely seal her own fate.

The words he spoke were truer than Helden liked. Escape from this place seemed unlikely for someone of her stature, although perhaps she might manage it after fasting for several weeks . . . and if her sturdy, dwarven bone structure didn't thwart the only plan she had.

"You will suffer for this, Vespyl," she growled. "Your body may be healed, but your heart blackens by the minute. I believe the underworld will claim your soul before long. And that's if I don't rip out your throat first."

Vespyl dipped his head. "I hear you, Helden. But I do this for my people, as you would for yours. It wasn't by chance that you and I met here at the Ashlight Dolmen. I watched, and I listened, and I knew you'd be here." He paused, then gave a nod. "I will return. Until then . . ."

He said no more as he turned and faded into the darkness. Seconds later, he was gone.

And Helden was alone.

Bestowed with the gift of healing.

ABOUT THE AUTHORS

Alison Reeger Cook (A.R. Cook) is the author of THE
SCHOLAR AND THE SPHINX young adult fantasy novels, THE
SCALE SEEKERS high fantasy series, and short stories found in
CHRONICLES OF MIRSTONE (Dragonfire Press), WOMEN OF
THE WOODS (Fabled Collective), WILLOW WEEP NO MORE
and SHADOWS OF THE OAK (Tenebris Books), and THE
KRESS PROJECT (Georgia Museum of Art).

Her theater plays have been performed and work-shopped at the
University of Iowa in Iowa City; Western Springs, Illinois; and
Atlanta, Georgia. She has placed as a finalist in various
screenwriting competitions, including the Austin Film Festival,
Screencraft, The Script Lab, and The Launch Pad. She resides near
Chicago, IL, with her husband Dave and their furry diva, Daisy
May.

Visit her at www.scholarandsphinx.wix.com/arcook, or visit her on
Facebook (www.facebook.com/ARCookAuthor) and Twitter
(@arcookauthor).

—

Richard Fierce is the author of over 30 fantasy and sci-fi books,
including his bestselling series Dragon Riders of Osnen. A
recovering retail worker, he now works in the tech industry when
he's not busy writing.

He's married with 3 stepdaughters (pray for him!), 3 grandchildren
(he's young!), 3 dogs (huskies!), and 2 ferrets. Basically, he has a
zoo.

His love affair with fantasy was born in high school when a
friend's mother gave him a copy of *Dragons of Spring Dawning* by

Margaret Weis and Tracy Hickman.

You can check out all of his books at www.richardfierce.com

Follow him on Facebook, Twitter, or Bookbub.

—

Jeremy Hicks is an archaeologist, author, and the co-founder of Broke Guys Productions. Alongside long-time friend Barry Hayes, he co-authored *Finders Keepers* and *Sands of Sorrow*, the initial installments of the *Cycle of Ages Saga*, first as screenplays and then novelizations. *Delve Deep*, the third installment, is Jeremy's first novel as a solo author. He has published a number of short stories in various anthologies, including the Amazon #1 best-seller *The C.A.M. Charity Anthology – Horror & Science Fiction*.

You can visit Jeremy's website at https://jjeremyhicks.com/

—

David Alan Jones is a veteran of the United States Air Force where he served as an Arabic linguist. A 2016 Writers of the Future silver honorable mention recipient, David's writing spans the science fiction, military sci-fi, fantasy, and urban fantasy genres. He is an author, a husband, and a father of three. David's day job involves programming computers for Uncle Sam.

You can find out more about David's writing, including his current projects, at his website: davidalanjones.net

—

pdmac spent a career in the US Army before transitioning to education as a university Academic Dean. He transitioned again and now writes fulltime. He has a MA in Creative Writing and a Ph.D. in Theology. He is a member of the Blue Ridge Writers Guild, the Steampunk Writers and Artists Guild, and the Georgia Writers Association. A diverse author, writer, and editor, he has also edited a Literature anthology, served as managing editor of an archaeology magazine, ghost-written an autobiography, and has had poems, short stories, articles, and editorials published in various literary journals, magazines and newspapers. His most recent short stories appear in the *Short Story America* anthologies III and IV, *Poets in Hell*, *The Mulberry Fork Review*, and the Fantasy Anthology *Chronicles of Mirstone*. He has also sung back-up for Broadway plays, provided voice for radio plays, and acted and directed theater stage productions. In his off time, he and his wife enjoy cycling, kayaking, and occasionally backpacking sections of the Appalachian Trail. Additionally, he and his wife love to travel, their favorite place so far being Crete, Greece.

You can visit pd's website at
http://www.pdmac-author.com/

—

A.G. Porter is the author of The Darkness Trilogy, a YA Paranormal Thriller, and two poetry collections, Pieces of My Heart and Pieces of My Soul. She is currently writing a spin-off of her The Darkness Trilogy characters, as well as a new YA Paranormal series, The Sacrifice of Ava Black, and her next poetry book. When she isn't writing, she's either busy being the coolest mom on the planet, crafting, or reading. Mrs. Porter lives in Alabama with her husband, Billy, and her amazing boys, Brenton, William, and Garrett.

You can check out her website here:
https://agporterbooks.wixsite.com/author/n

—

Selah J Tay-Song is living proof that if you persevere, you'll catch your dreams. She decided to be an author at the age of six. Today she is the author of the Dreams of QaiMaj series, an epic fantasy series described as magical, poetic and engrossing. When she's not writing, she's stalking the urban river otters that live less than a mile from her home in the Pacific Northwest.

You can check out her website here: www.selahjtaysong.com

—

Craig A. Price Jr. is a USA Today bestselling author of Claymore of Calthoria Trilogy, Dragon's Call Trilogy, Dragonia Empire Series, Space Gh0st Adventures Series, and several other titles available in alternate realities. He loves to read, write, cast spells, and spend time with his beautiful wife and three children. He dreams to one day become a full-time wizard, but until then, he'll settle for being an author. With more than a dozen novels under his belt now, it's only a matter of time before he settles for world domination, but until then, you can follow his author journey as he takes over one reader's soul at a time.

Visit him at https://www.craigaprice.com/

—

Keith Robinson is the author of 30+ fantasy, sci-fi, and spooky supernatural books primarily for middle-grade readers but suitable for all ages. Though best known for the Island of Fog fantasy books, he's also the author of the Sleep Writer sci-fi adventures and, more recently, the Darkhill Scary Stories. He wrote the dark fantasy *Quincy's Curse*, and co-wrote the two-book *Fractured* tale with Brian Clopper. He typically writes three books a year while drinking hot tea.

Visit him at https://www.unearthlytales.com/

As always, thank you for supporting the writing community!

9 781958 354438